HAV3N

HAVEN

A NOVEL

BY Tom Deady

GREYMORE PUBLISHING

Boston, Massachusetts

❖ 2016 ❖

Greymore Publishing
PO Box 6834
Holliston MA 01746
www.greymorepublishing.com

The characters and events in this book are fictitious.
Any similarity to real persons, living or dead,
is coincidental and not intended by the author.

Trade Paperback Edition

ISBN: 978-0-9906327-2-6

Cover Artwork and Design © 2016 by Gail Cross
Interior Design © 2016 by Desert Isle Design, LLC

For Shannon and Alyssa...

THE GATES of Braxton State Prison slammed shut behind Paul Greymore and for the first time in almost seventeen years he was outside of them. He looked around, mildly unnerved by the unfamiliar openness of his surroundings, and lit a cigarette. He took a deep breath and began walking toward the parking lot, constantly turning his head back and forth, up and down, taking in all the sights he once thought he would never see again without the obstruction of a twelve-foot wall. He half expected a heavy hand to fall on his shoulder, turn him around, tell him there was a mistake. But not once did he look back. He had been looking at the inside of those goddamn walls for too long and had no interest in seeing them again from either side.

He reached the parking lot and immediately spotted Father Neil McCarthy waiting for him. The old priest looked like a mirage with the heat coming off the asphalt in waves making him seem ghostlike. In Paul's sensory overloaded mind he feared the man might disappear if he blinked his eyes. He shook his head at this bizarre thought and jogged over smiling. He stepped on his cigarette and extended a hand to the old priest, thought better of it, and hugged him. The old man patted Paul's back lightly, then took his shoulders and held him at arm's length. Neither man knew what to say, so they remained silent. The moment stretched and finally McCarthy broke the awkward quiet. "Let's get going," was the best he could do.

When they were in the car and heading out of the parking lot Paul finally spoke. "I'm really out," he said in a shaky voice. His eyes were filled as he looked at the priest. "You saved my life, Father. If it weren't for you I'd be dead, or a lifer." The priest drove on, concentrating on the road.

Finally McCarthy spoke. "We've been preparing for this day for a very long time, Paul. Now is the time to move ahead, start over. From now on we will not discuss the past. It's a dead end road."

Paul fell silent, lost in thought. He flipped down the visor to shade his eyes from the sun and frowned when his own reflection stared back at him from the vanity mirror. His fingers inadvertently traced the deep grooves in his face as his mind slipped down a familiar path. A path he often traveled, wondering what his life might have been like if not for the accident that left him so scarred.

When Paul was a toddler he had reached up and grabbed the handle of a pot on the stove. His mother was just steps away, but it was far enough. The pot contained water, in a raging boil, and she was helpless to prevent Paul from pulling it down on himself. The water scorched his face, miraculously missing his eyes. When the doctors finished doing what they could, his face looked like a melted candle. Angry white valleys of scars surrounded by raised berms of too-red skin made him an outcast. It wouldn't be until years later that Paul would see a likeness of himself in a movie called *A Nightmare on Elm Street*.

Memories, another dead end, a path that led nowhere. He flipped the visor back up angrily, preferring the blinding sun to his own reflection and the memories it brought, ignoring the knowing glance from Father McCarthy. He was jarred from his thoughts as he saw the sign that marked the on-ramp to Route 95 South. The sign read: *Haven 70 Miles*.

I'm going home, he thought. For the next hour the two men drove and talked, the conversation becoming more relaxed as the miles slipped past. When McCarthy exited the highway and headed east, Paul squirmed in his seat. *Maybe this is a mistake*.

Father McCarthy seemed to sense his nervousness, "It's going to be alright Paul."

"I'm going back to the town where a lot of the people believe I killed their children. I'm not so sure this is a good idea."

"We've talked about this, Paul. Haven is your home. You have friends there."

The words did nothing to squelch the growing fear that he was heading into a bad situation as the *Entering Haven* sign blurred past. "Father...I just wish I could remember what happened that day..."

"Maybe being home will help you with that. Let's get some gas, and then I'll take you around and show you how much things have changed and how much things have stayed the same." Father McCarthy nosed the car up next to the pump. "I'll go pay if you don't mind pumping," the priest said as he got out of the car.

"Sure, not at all."

A blanket of heat surrounded Paul when he opened his door. He had forgotten how hot it was after being in the air conditioned car. He stood beside the car, stretching his limbs. The AC had also stiffened him up during the ride and it felt good to get the blood flowing again. Sixteen-plus years of time on his hands had packed pounds of muscle onto his lean body. He wondered how he would find the discipline to continue those grueling workouts now.

Paul watched the gaunt figure of the priest shuffle past a group of teenagers who were hanging around a Coke machine. The priest nodded a greeting and one of the youths said something in return which sparked laughter from the other two. The priest stiffened, then shook his head and continued inside to pay the cashier. *Punks*, Paul thought as he went to the other side of the car and read the directions on the side of the pump. Ignoring the *No Smoking* signs, he lit a cigarette as he put the nozzle in and turned on the pump. *This will be my last*, he thought, remembering the promise he made to quit if he ever got out. As he watched the numbers clicking away on the gas pump, a shadow passed by. He half-turned expecting to see Father McCarthy returning from inside the station. Instead he was looking at five inches of steel.

The punks had come up behind him and spread out, surrounding him. As soon as they got a closer look at Paul their expressions changed. He was used to this reaction but these kids made no attempt to conceal their revulsion as they stared in horror at Paul's disfigured face. The apparent leader with the knife regained his composure, leaned casually against the car, and spoke first. "If you're traveling with the Father, does that make you a mother?" he asked, his voice attempting to sound genuinely curious.

It's no different on the outside than it was on the inside, Paul thought. The other two punks cackled at their master's wit. Paul continued to stare at the one with the knife, holding his gaze. He was just a boy, probably no more than fifteen or sixteen. The punk's mocking smile slipped into an ominous stare as Paul continued to eye him.

"You didn't think that was funny, huh Mama?" Again the expected snickers from the other two.

"What's the meaning of this?" came the priest's voice from behind the knife-wielding punk. "Put down that knife before someone gets hurt!"

The one standing next to the leader turned to face the priest. He was a big kid and he knew it; he was no stranger to using his size to intimidate. He took a threatening step forward and Father McCarthy stumbled backwards, bumping into the gas pump. The expression on his face was more of surprise than fear. "Shut the hell up. Who the hell do you think you're talkin' to, your freak friend, huh, *Father*?" The last word he literally spit out, spraying the priest with drops of saliva. This seemed to shock the old priest more than the physical threat the kid posed and his hand now shook as he reached to wipe his face.

The sight of his friend being harassed and hearing that word infected Paul with a deadly rage. He shivered in spite of the suffocating heat as his entire world was reduced to this kid. Before any further humiliation or hurt could be inflicted, Paul acted. In one motion he grabbed the wrist of the one holding the knife and twisted, sending the blade skidding to the ground. With his other hand he swept the gas nozzle into the side of the kid's face, splitting his cheek wide open and spraying gas in his eyes. The kid fell back clumsily against the car. Blood flowed freely from his open cheek and it was already beginning to swell, the cheekbone cracked as neatly as the skin was.

With his free hand the punk was clawing at his own eyes, trying to wipe the gas out of them. Paul dropped the nozzle, which clattered to the ground next to the knife. He plucked the cigarette out of his mouth and held it close to the punk's face. As the smoke drifted under the kid's nose, he suddenly stopped struggling. "No, please, man, no," was all he could mutter.

Paul didn't hear him. *Freak.* The word echoed through his head, reverberating across every nerve. He inched the glowing tip of the cigarette closer to the punk's gas-soaked face. A part of him knew that gas fumes are more flammable than the liquid itself but that part of him was submerged beneath a red ocean of rage. The one who had bullied Father McCarthy glanced at the knife then quickly back at Paul. Paul just shook his head and the boy suddenly became fascinated with his own Timberlands.

"Start walking," Paul said calmly. When neither of the punks moved, he shouted, "Now!"

They both turned and began walking toward the road. Paul faced the fallen leader. He had managed to open his eyes, but they no longer showed the defiance and boldness of moments ago, only fear. Paul's thin grasp on his anger faltered as he saw this. Now he was in control of the situation, but instead of relief he was being consumed with fury.

"You want to know what it feels like to look like this?"

His hand began to shake and move closer to the boy's face. *I've been out for less than two hours and I'm on my way back in.* Paul glanced at the priest, his face shimmering through the gas fumes, and knew immediately what the man was thinking.

Father McCarthy had made the seventy mile trip to Braxton once a month for almost seventeen years, never doubting that Paul was innocent—until now. It was the look of doubt in the old man's eyes that made Paul squeeze the cigarette out between his fingers. The punk slumped down lower against the car.

"If I hear of any trouble to my friend or the church, I'll come looking for *you*. You pass that along to your girlfriends."

The boy nodded anxiously, sending droplets of blood through the gas-soaked air.

"Get lost." The punk staggered to his feet then stumbled toward an old Mustang parked by the Coke machine, one hand still clutching his bleeding cheek. Paul could see the attendant taking it all in from inside the station's small office.

"Are you alright, Father?" Paul asked as he picked up the gas nozzle and the knife. He closed the blade and slipped it into his pocket.

The priest nodded.

"I guess that's what you meant by the way things stay the same."

"I don't mean to make this any worse for you but I think the one you hit was Dale Crawford."

Paul eyed the priest for a moment. "I suppose I don't need to ask if he's any relation to my good friend Officer Crawford."

"Only son. And it's Chief Crawford now."

"I don't know why I would have expected today to play out any differently."

"Welcome home," the priest said with a smile. Paul couldn't help but smile back in spite of the gnawing feeling of dread that had overtaken him.

(2)

SPRING HAD arrived in Haven, Massachusetts, and it promised to be a season in hell. The calendar claimed it was the first of May but the thermometer argued mid-August. For the third day in a row, the temperature broke ninety degrees, officially making it a heat wave according to the giddy local weathermen. Just two weeks ago, dirty mounds of snow were still scattered about the town from the infamous Blizzard of '78 but that seemed as distant a memory as last year's World Series. As distant and as forgettable as far as Dennis O'Brien was concerned. He hated winter, and to have it extended into spring was as painful as the Yankees winning it all. Denny looked up from his seventh grade history book as the old yellow school bus rattled from the pavement onto the dirt road that led to his house. Denny usually took advantage of being the last passenger by getting a head start on his homework, but the stale heat in the bus made it difficult to concentrate. *Or maybe it's the headache from Dale Crawford's sucker punch,* he thought. He absently rubbed the side of his head, thinking of the Charles Atlas ad he had seen in a comic book. He was tired of being the kid who gets sand kicked in his face.

The gears shrieked in protest as the bus crept up the steep hill, burping a cloud of blue smoke in its wake. The shimmering heat lent sharp contrast to the just-budding trees lining the road. Denny gathered his books as the weathered cape-style house came into view. He hurried off the bus, absently saying good-bye to the red faced driver known only as Stubby. Stubby nodded and mumbled unintelligibly through his cigar as he reached over to pull the lever to close the door. Denny made his way across the road as the bus turned around on the shoulder and headed back to town. As soon as the bus had passed, Denny was nearly knocked over by the greeting he received from his 6-year old black lab/retriever mix, Bear. The daily ritual never failed to make Denny smile, no matter how bad his day had been. Since he had started taking the bus, Bear would always be there waiting for his return from school to greet him with slobbering kisses.

Once in the house, Denny threw his books on the table in the hallway, glancing involuntarily at the spot above the table where the wallpaper was less faded than the rest. The spot was in the distinct shape of a cross. He entered the kitchen where Janice O'Brien stood at the counter peeling potatoes, surrendering not so much as a glance as her son entered the room. She was a tall woman and the weight she'd lost over the past couple of years had cut sharp angles to her figure and sharper lines on her once youthful face. Death had a way of doing that to people.

"Mom, I'm going to Billy's for a while, and I'm taking Bear." She looked at him as if she had never seen him before. The blank look always frightened Denny. *What if she doesn't know me? What if she never remembers me?*

Then her eyes cleared and she answered, "Okay, be home in time for dinner." She went back to peeling, satisfied the subject was closed.

Denny quickly changed into shorts and a t-shirt before heading out. By the time he walked the quarter-mile to the Cummings' house, Billy would be getting home from baseball practice. He and Billy had been best friends for as long as Denny could remember. They made a good team: Denny the smarter, funnier of the two, Billy tougher and more confident. They had become inseparable. He ambled down the steep road with Bear, stopping occasionally to let Bear sniff around. Halfway down the hill, Denny called Bear over to his side and kept a close eye on him. Mrs. Lovell's house was just up ahead.

Doris Lovell loved cats. She fed any stray that passed her way and of course they never left. The kids called her "Cat-woman." Nobody really knew how many cats she had but Denny figured there to be close to a hundred. She kept no other pets and lived alone since her husband's death. Denny didn't like cats to begin with, but the number of them that Mrs. Lovell kept flat-out gave him the creeps. Even Bear seemed to sense something not-quite-right about so many cats together and tended to leave them alone. Sure enough, there were several of them roaming around the yard, sprawled in the driveway, sunning themselves on the fence—basically they were everywhere. Bear's tail went down and he let out a low growl but he stayed right by Denny's legs. As they passed the house, Denny could hear Mrs. Lovell's voice but couldn't make out what she was saying. He knew she was talking to the cats, though: he could tell by the sing-song tone, like she was talking to a child. The next house they passed was the old Greymore place, empty for years, but creepy nonetheless. The house crouched in the overgrown yard, hiding from the world behind washed-out shutters. The peeling paint was now some unrecognizable color and a gutter dangled from the edge of the roof, one strong gust away from impaling the tangle of shrubs below. Denny quickened his pace.

He arrived at Billy's to find his driveway empty. *Shit, he's not home yet*. He walked up the steps and was about to knock anyway when the door flew open, almost knocking him off the porch.

"Oh, Denny! You scared the crap out of me."

"Hi, Julie," was the best response he could muster, feeling the heat rise in his cheeks. Julie Cummings was three years older than Denny but that didn't stop him from having a full-blown, knee-weakening crush on her. He found her attractive in a way he couldn't describe. It wasn't that long ago that she would hang out with Denny and Billy, goofing around or playing flashlight tag or hide-and-go-seek. This school year she'd started hanging with a different crowd. It was inevitable, Denny guessed, but he missed seeing her on a regular basis. Since she had "matured" Denny found himself tongue-tied whenever she was around.

"Billy's not home. My mom was picking him up after practice and taking him for a haircut and stuff." Just as she finished, a car whipped into the driveway leaving a cloud of dust as it slid to a stop.

Denny's stomach went into an immediate knot when he saw Dale Crawford hop out of the Mustang's driver seat and head toward them. "What the fuck are you doing talking to my girl, O'Brien?" He loomed over Denny scowling, fists clenched at his sides. Dale was a big kid, tall and bulky. Still a year away from getting a driver's license, that didn't stop Dale from terrorizing Haven from behind the wheel of the Mustang. Having the Chief of Police as your dad had its privileges. Dale's build would have made most kids his age turn to sports, but Dale chose bullying as his favorite sport. He wore a black Harley t-shirt with the sleeves cut off. His thickly muscled arms were covered with home-made tattoos. But it was the bloodstained bandage on Dale's face that riveted Denny's gaze. It was big and it was fresh. He certainly didn't have it when he gave Denny the love-tap to the skull at school. He consciously made an effort to pull his eyes away, knowing it would only piss Dale off to catch him staring. He heard Bear's guttural snarl and finally looked away to make sure Bear wasn't going to do anything more than make noise. The dog's ears were pinned back and his teeth were bared but he was making no move toward Dale. Denny was both relieved and disappointed.

"Leave him alone, Dale, he's just looking for Billy. Did you get in another fight?" Julie sounded disgusted.

"Shut up, Julie, it's none of your business."

Denny wished he was older, bigger, stronger, and tougher. Then he'd show Dale a thing or two about how to talk to people, especially nice girls like Julie. But he was none of those. "Tell Billy I stopped by," he squeaked as he backed away. Julie smiled and nodded before turning away. As Denny started back up the hill, he could hear the heated argument between the two and his own anger and humiliation burned inside of him.

(3)

FATHER MCCARTHY waited patiently for the teapot to whistle, glancing hopefully at the closed guestroom door. After the incident at the gas station, Paul had lapsed into a morose silence. Instead of taking Paul around town and risking any more negativity, McCarthy took Paul to the Liberty Tree Mall in Danvers to get him clothes and toiletries for life on the outside. He'd hoped that the spectacle of the state-of-the-art mall would boost Paul's spirit but it seemed to have the opposite effect, driving him into a deeper mood, perhaps reminding him of how much he'd missed. They'd returned to McCarthy's for a mostly-silent dinner, and Paul had soon after retired to the guest room.

McCarthy felt himself being pulled down into the abyss of Paul's despair. This was a day they had both hoped for, waited for, and it had been ruined almost as soon as they crossed the Haven town line. Doubt gnawed at him; perhaps returning to Haven *was* a mistake. Maybe Paul would be better off starting fresh, a new life where nobody knew his past. McCarthy made his tea and took it out on the small deck off the kitchen. There always seemed to be a breeze, a *heavenly* breeze, one might say, on the deck, no matter how hot and stagnant the air was.

McCarthy recalled his first meeting with Greymore, almost seventeen years earlier. It was through a program designed to offer one-on-one religious counseling to inmates. Braxton worked with churches of all denominations in surrounding towns to facilitate "spiritual growth" among those convicted of violent crimes. At the time, McCarthy was assigned to a small parish in Peabody and had time on his hands. He felt inexplicably drawn to the program with a force almost as powerful as the one that led him to him the priesthood. For a time, he didn't understand what had driven him; the work was thankless, a bunch of bad people feigning contrition to make their chances of parole better. Or for the older ones, to make their chances of staying out of Hell better.

Then a new inmate joined the program, and McCarthy found his answer. The man, just a boy really, was so lost, so vulnerable… and as McCarthy got to know him, became friends with him, so clearly innocent. McCarthy began to look forward to the weekly visits, and as the other inmates drifted away and eventually the program lost funding, McCarthy continued the visits on his own time. The friendship grew over the years, and McCarthy spent time researching the case, becoming all the more convinced of Greymore's innocence. When the tragedy occurred in Haven with Father Krieger and the parish needed someone, McCarthy pulled in every favor he could to get the assignment. Not long after, as it became evident that Greymore was not far from release, McCarthy planted the seed of returning to Haven.

Greymore had been outwardly appalled at the first mention of it, but McCarthy thought (*hoped?*) he saw desire in Paul's eyes. A longing to go home. He hadn't pushed, but had coerced in his own way, mentioning the goings-on in Haven and how beautiful the lake was and how faithful the townspeople were. Slowly, Paul warmed to the idea. Eventually, Haven became all he spoke of. McCarthy had been careful not to mention Crawford's rise to Police Chief, and Greymore had never asked. It was a lie of omission that McCarthy thought was for the best. Until now.

After seeing what happened at the gas station first-hand, McCarthy finally understood people's reaction to Greymore's appearance. It was a form of prejudice, no different than racism or anti-Semitism. It was based in fear and ignorance and McCarthy found it offensive. But that made it no less real, and as he had witnessed today, no less dangerous. Had his own naïveté put Greymore in danger? Surely his release would have been well-publicized, and his face so easily recognized...how had he not thought this through? All he wanted was for Greymore to come home to the town he loved and have a good life. And he had played on Greymore's own desire for the same thing to lure him back. As bad as McCarthy now felt, he also understood the agony that Paul must be in.

He finished his tea and sat holding the empty cup, a mixture of emotions startling him. The feelings of guilt and shame he understood: he had not been completely honest with Paul and misled him. He knew how to fix that, knew he *would* fix it. But there was something else, something that felt somehow worse. Off in the distance a dog barked, somewhere else a car horn honked. On McCarthy's deck, the breeze he came out looking for finally kicked up, gently setting in motion a set of wind chimes that hung off the deck's railing. The sound usually calmed McCarthy but tonight it put him on edge, and he realized what he was feeling.

The chimes sounded to McCarthy like a telephone ringing. He immediately thought of a night long ago, when he was just a boy. The same sound had awoken him in the darkest part of the night; it seemed to go on and on. His father was a sound sleeper and his mom, a nurse, was working the night shift at the hospital. Young McCarthy stumbled out of bed, suddenly afraid. The ringing continued as he made his way toward his parents' room, his heart beating faster, and suddenly he wanted to cry. Finally he heard his father pick up the phone. He stopped in the hallway, paralyzed with fear, and heard a sound he had never heard before: his father crying.

McCarthy's mother had been killed in a freak accident. A faulty piece of medical equipment had short-circuited, electrocuting her. She was surrounded by people whose job it was to save lives, in a building full of medicine and machines to do the same, but she died anyway. Somehow, he had sensed it even before he heard his father crying. Most would say that everyone knew a phone call in the middle of the night was bad news, but McCarthy thought it was something more. He had felt it in his heart, and it was a terrible, powerful feeling.

The chimes did indeed sound like the ringing of a phone and McCarthy knew what had been hiding behind the guilt and shame. It was just as powerful as it had been when he was a boy, just as terrible, and again he felt it in his heart: dread. The gentle breeze jingled the chimes again and McCarthy shivered, his heart beating too fast in his chest. What was going to happen? The breeze was no longer a welcome friend; it carried a message that McCarthy did not want. He stood and went shakily into the house, knowing that sleep would not come but choosing the stuffy heat over the ill wind that was blowing on the deck.

(4)

THE NEXT day at school was uneventful for Denny. Even the teachers seemed lethargic from another day of unrelenting heat and restless children. The big talk was Dale Crawford's face and Paul Greymore's return to Haven. Rumors were flying that Greymore was the one responsible for messing up Crawford. Dale was telling everyone that Greymore attacked him at McCauley's Gas Station, "catching him off-guard." The story got pretty vague after that when Dale was asked why his father, the Chief of Police, didn't have Greymore arrested.

Paul Greymore was known to most Haven residents as "The Butcher." He had gone berserk years ago, before Denny was even born, and killed a bunch of kids. He'd been in prison ever since. The Butcher had become Haven's boogeyman. Stories were abundant and a common warning from parents to children was "be home on time or the Butcher will get you." Which made little sense since the Butcher was locked safely away in Braxton. Or he was, until now. Denny didn't believe most of the stories; they had taken on the sound of tall tales over the years. Although he knew the ones about Greymore's looks were true. Greymore had been disfigured as a child and most people had been afraid of him *before* he started killing kids.

On the bus ride home, Denny stared out the window at Greymore's house. It looked as creepy as it did every day, but to his relief, it looked as empty too. A frown crossed his face as the bus crawled to a stop in front of his house. The front walkway was empty. Denny and

Stubby exchanged their mumbled goodbyes and a feeling of dread settled in the pit of Denny's stomach as he hurried off the bus.

"Where's Bear?" Denny asked, barging into the house.

His mother was just coming down the stairs with a basket of laundry, "He's been in and out all day, trying to find a cool place to lie, I guess."

"Is he in or out now?" Denny asked, but her eyes had already started to cloud over and Denny knew her mind was far away, thinking of a different little boy. Denny went to the backyard and as the screen door banged closed behind him, his uneasiness grew. After searching the yard, Denny went back inside and after changing out of his school clothes looked around the house, starting upstairs and working his way down. By the time he got back to the kitchen, he was getting very anxious. His mother was now starting dinner and looked like she was back to reality for the moment.

"I had to get some things off the cellar shelf earlier," she said. "Maybe he scooted down the stairs while the door was open. It's the only cool spot in the house."

Denny headed for the hallway leading to the cellar stairs. He opened the door, flipped on the light, and stopped. He hated going down into the cellar. Nothing had ever happened to promote his fear, but it was there nonetheless. A single bare bulb glared from far end of the cellar and barely illuminated the bottom of the stairs. The dim light that did reach was full of odd-shaped shadows and pockets of darkness.

"Bear, come on up Bear," he called. He held his breath, waiting, hoping, for the jingle of the dog's collar, but only silence. He exhaled slowly and began his descent. After only a couple of steps, the air changed dramatically. The rank smell came first, then the coolness, almost to the point of being cold. *Like a grave,* Denny thought, as he continued down the creaky stairs. He jerked his hand back suddenly when it touched a silky substance and he frantically wiped the tattered web on his pants, picturing a gigantic hairy spider on the other end of it. He silently cursed every horror movie he had ever watched.

When he reached the bottom step, Denny glanced around for possible places for a dog to hide. There seemed only three likely spots. First he checked under the workbench. Nothing there but more spiders. For no reason other than to quell his growing fear, he grabbed a rusty hammer from the assortment of unused tools littering the workbench and slowly made his way to the back of the cellar to look on the other side of the furnace. Nothing there but some old boxes. *You know what's in those boxes, Denny.* He shook his head to clear that thought and paused. Only one other place to check.

In the back corner of the cellar a doorway led into what appeared to have been some sort of washroom in some long-forgotten time. Denny had only been inside it once and that had been enough for him. The sink was barely recognizable because of the thick coat of mold that covered it. What appeared to be a tub was nothing more than a two-foot high wall of cement in the far corner, half-filled with a scum-coated pool of water. The thoughts of what might be living in that was what kept Denny away, but he had to check. He reached the doorway and leaned inside. Shafts of dirty light from the window at the top of the wall glistened off the wet floor and walls. The dripping and gurgling sounds that came from the rotted pipes echoed loudly in the small room. The rafters above were festooned with webs and one engorged spider dangled threateningly above him.

A sudden rattle and hiss from the pipes made Denny jump and his eyes widened as he watched the stagnant pool of water begin to churn and bubble. He backed up slowly, dropped the hammer, then turned and ran back to the stairs. Picturing some reptilian beast rising from the slimy water, he stumbled madly up the stairs. At the top, he burst through the door, slammed it behind him and put the small hook-and-latch type lock in place. He leaned against the door for a moment straining to hear slippery footsteps on the stairs. His heart was jackhammering in his chest and his whole body trembled. When he finally caught his breath, convinced nothing was following up the stairs, he walked into the kitchen and immediately felt foolish. His mother was standing in front of the sink with the water running. When she turned it off he could hear the pipes rattling as he had a thousand times before. Turning the water on must force air in the pipes to make the water churn in the tub down in the cellar.

Grinning sheepishly to himself he went out the back door to continue searching for his dog. The picture in his mind of a ferocious monster being held at bay by the old hook-and-latch lock made him giggle.

Denny stepped onto the back porch and started for the woods beyond his backyard. There was an old picket fence separating his yard from the woods. The fence, once a glistening white, was now faded and chipped, missing several pickets. A feeling of sorrow momentarily replaced his anxiety when he remembered his father joking about calling the fence dentist to fix the broken "teeth." So corny, but that was part of what made him such a great dad. His dad had fixed a few of the broken pickets that day and had let Denny bang in a few of the nails. Denny shook off the memory and slipped his thin frame through one of the gaps and stepped onto a trail that led through the thick, newly-budding bushes.

Beyond the trail the woods became dense and went on for miles. Denny had spent quite a bit of time out here and knew his way around. Today the woods seemed a bit darker and thicker than usual. He began walking, blaming his jitters on the fact that Bear was not by his side. "Bear, come on Bear!" he called occasionally. But even the sound of his own voice sounded eerie in the humid air. Narrow fingers of sunlight reached through the trees, creating shadows that shifted when a rare breeze whispered through. The normal sounds of the woods began to sound somehow threatening to Denny. "Bear, come on out now," he called softer this time, afraid he was attracting unwanted attention.

A rustling noise up ahead stopped him in his tracks. The entire forest seemed to go silent. Denny was about to turn and run when a chipmunk darted across the trail. He suddenly realized he was holding his breath and exhaled a long sigh of relief. What was wrong with him, he wondered. First the cellar and now the woods. He decided to head home and ask the neighbors about his dog. As he made his way back he couldn't shake the uneasy feeling that had come over him since he saw the vacant walkway from his seat on the bus.

(5)

DENNY YELLED in to his mother and waited a moment for a reply. When none came he shook his head and started down the street. It seemed his mother was becoming more and more distant and he feared someday she would be gone, trapped in the world that she occasionally disappeared to. A world where his father and brother still lived.

The air remained hot and heavy even though the sun had begun to move lower in the sky. The trees, filling daily with more leaves, and greening lawns added to his feeling of loneliness without Bear by his side. It felt more like a late Indian summer day than it did early spring, the kind that made Denny ache with their beauty but sad in knowing it might be the last before winter. Something stirred in the bushes to his right and made him jump. It was just a cat, a sure sign that he was approaching Mrs. Lovell's house. A few steps further Denny saw a couple more cats chasing each other across the street. By the time he reached the fence that lined Mrs. Lovell's property, he could easily spot a dozen of them. Denny started up her walkway and began to feel uneasy. So many cats.

The Cat-woman was often the subject of lunchroom conversations and the stories ranged from weird and creepy to outright absurdity. Like stories about the Butcher, it was difficult to separate fact from fiction. The most common Cat-woman story was that she had killed her husband, or more specifically, had ordered her cats to kill him.

It sounded so ridiculous most of the time, but now surrounded by them...*if they wanted to, they could tear me apart,* he thought.

Mrs. Lovell's voice floated out the open door, "No, no it's not time for dinner yet," in that same voice he had heard yesterday, like she was talking to her grandchildren. Denny waited to make sure there would be no answer and then knocked on the door. *Of course there is no answer; she was talking to one of the cats.* She appeared at the door and smiled, "Look everyone; it's Danny from up the hill." Then the smile turned to a frown. "You don't have that nasty beast with you, do you?"

"No ma'am, and it's Denny." The smell of cats drifting from the house was putrid, a pungent mixture of urine and cat food.

Now that her cats were in no danger, the smile returned. "Yes, Denny-the-dog and his master Danny, how lovely. What can we do for you Danny, is your mother well?"

Denny held back his grin. *She can remember the names of a hundred cats and their birthdays but when it comes to people...*

"She's fine, Mrs. Lovell. The reason I'm here is I was wondering if you had seen Bea...my dog today?"

"No, but if I had you can bet I would have chased him off." Then she moved quickly and *(catlike)* gracefully out onto the porch and added in a conspirator's whisper, "He frightens the children you know."

With the door open and Cat-woman closer to him, the smell of souring milk and dirty litter boxes was overpowering. Denny began to feel nauseous and light-headed. "Yes ma'am, he doesn't mean to, he's just being a dog."

Three cats, one Siamese and two mangy looking gray and white ones were taking turns wrapping themselves around her legs. Others lined the porch railing and window sills. They all seemed to be staring at Denny.

"Would you like to come in and have some milk? I always keep plenty of milk around." She smiled, but Denny thought even though her mouth was smiling, her eyes weren't. Those eyes seemed to say, "Sure, I killed my husband, and I'll kill you too if you give me a chance."

Now some of the cats were beginning to rub against his legs. Denny felt like he was trapped in a dream. He pictured himself in that house surrounded by cats, drinking his milk *(from a bowl)* when Mrs. Lovell shouts, "He's the one with that mean dog, children!" and all the cats jump on him, clawing and biting. He shivered in the hot afternoon air. "No thank you, ma'am. I think I'll just keep looking for my dog. Goodbye."

"Goodbye Danny, good luck." She glided silently back into the house. As he walked back to the road he heard her voice, again with that song-like cadence, "Would you like to play for a while before dinner?"

As he paused at the end of the walkway, just for a moment he thought he heard several of the cats meow in reply. He glanced up the hill, then down, then at the position of the sun. He decided to walk down to Billy's house and ask about Bear, and if he was lucky Julie would be home. He couldn't figure out why she wasted her time with a loser like Dale Crawford. Julie was always so nice and Dale had been a raging asshole for as long as Denny had known him. As he made his way down the dusty road, that uneasy feeling began to creep up on him again. *At least I have a reason to be nervous this time,* he thought.

The reason, of course, was the old Greymore Place. Any solace in getting past Cat-woman's house immediately jumped ship. Denny would have to walk past the boarded up house to get to Billy's. Yesterday, it hadn't been a big deal. It was just an old, creepy house with a scary history. But now, knowing Greymore was out of prison, maybe even back in Haven, made it a different story. *Maybe he's actually come home*, Denny thought with a chill. *The Butcher, that's what they called him.* Even though it all happened years before he was born, Denny knew about The Butcher, as did everyone else in Haven. Back in '61 there was a series of murders in Haven, mostly children. Late that summer Chief Crawford himself (*Officer* Crawford back then) caught Paul Greymore red-handed with his latest victim still warm in his arms. Right behind the very house Denny was now approaching. The house had been closed up ever since but it still gave

Denny the creeps just to walk past it so he quickened his pace as he neared it. The tall hedges surrounding the lawn were out of control. Although the grass was still brown from the winter, Denny could tell it hadn't been cared for in years. As he passed the driveway, the house itself came into clear view. The faded paint, the sagging boards covering the windows, the rickety front porch: it all looked more menacing today. Denny noticed that even the graffiti that covered the house was faded and unreadable, and that the entire front of the house was covered with stains from the countless eggs thrown every Halloween. He speed-walked until he was safely past the house, never taking his eyes off it, as if it might grow legs and chase him.

When Denny reached the Cummings' house, Billy was in the driveway throwing a tennis ball off the roof and catching it. "Hey Billy."

"What's up, Denny?"

"Not much, I'm looking for Bear. Thought he might have wandered down here." Denny glanced around not expecting to find Bear but hoping to see Julie.

"Nope, haven't seen him, and she's not home, either," he added with a wink. He threw the ball up and took a couple unsteady steps back and caught it again. "Want me help you look for him?"

"I don't know where else to look. Maybe I'll just wait and see if he comes home on his own. We still camping out this weekend?"

"Sure, why not. My dad said we could use his tent and lanterns if we're careful."

Denny liked the idea of having the tent instead of sleeping out in the open. "Sounds great. We can start out right after school Friday."

"I'll bring the tent and stuff up Thursday after school and catch the bus with you on Friday. We can hike until it starts getting dark, and then set up camp. My dad says there's some caves a couple miles in." He threw the ball again and waited for it to bounce down. When it did, Denny leaped up next to him and deftly caught it one-handed. Denny threw it back up and they fought each other to catch it, immediately caught up in a game of "off the roof." When the dark blue car drove slowly up the hill, both boys paused to stare. Both assumed it was someone visiting Cat-woman and resumed the game.

THE CAR bumped off the smooth pavement onto dirt, a moment later turning into the driveway of Paul Greymore's house. Paul sat staring at the house, unable to believe where he was. He knew most people sent to prison for the length of time he was would have made arrangements to sell their house, but he couldn't bear to part with it. He felt he would have been giving away the last part of himself that existed before going to prison. For the entire time he was locked up, he had secretly hoped that someday he would return and now here he was. The angle of the sun as it began to dip behind the trees created odd shadows, giving the old house a surrealistic look.

Sensing Paul's fragile mood, McCarthy spoke. "I still owe you a grand tour of Haven but I thought we should take a look around up here before it gets dark. I wish I could have had the place cleaned up for you before you got here."

After the incident at the gas station the day before, Greymore had spent a restless evening waiting for a visit from Chief Crawford, but it never came. Today, he and McCarthy had gotten Paul's bank account in order, visited the DMV to find out what Paul needed to get a new driver's license...normal person things...before coming back out to check on the house.

"Please, Father, you've done more than enough as it is. Let's have a look."

The two men got out of the car and went up to the front door, carefully avoiding the rotten planks of the steps and porch.

"Hope the key still works," Paul said pulling it from his pocket. He licked his lips nervously and put the key in the lock, trying to hide the shake in his hands. The old lock resisted, frozen in place by time and the elements. Paul pushed the door and the wood holding the lock crumbled. He pushed again, and with a screech of protest, the door opened and Paul stepped inside his childhood home. The closed-up smell of the house hit him immediately, as did a deep sense of nostalgia, engulfing him as he stood looking at the living room.

The old priest put his hand on Paul's shoulder, "Let's look around, you'll have plenty of time to think later."

Paul nodded and began making his way through the house, every step bringing back more memories. His father teaching him how to tie his own flies, his mother baking cookies while he stood on a chair helping her with the batter, the three of them playing rummy, the laughter and the love.

Even in the fading light he moved familiarly through each room, assessing what would have to be done. Surprisingly, the damage was minimal. Mostly broken windows from vandals and some wood rot, but structurally the old house seemed sound and mostly needed cosmetic work and lots of fresh air. The reputation of the Butcher had kept the worst of the vandals away throughout the years. As they appraised the bedrooms upstairs, Paul jumped as a scratching sound came from above.

BILLY AND Denny played off-the-roof tirelessly, neither paying any attention to the time of day. Sometime later, Billy was winning by two points when he threw the ball up. Both boys pushed and shoved. Denny, tall and wiry, against Billy's slightly shorter, yet bulkier frame. They jockeyed for position but the ball never came down. "Did it go over?"

Billy shook his head, "Nah, it's stuck in the gutter."

Denny stared up at the gutter, wondering how many balls they had lost up there over the years. When he looked down, he was surprised to see how long the shadows had grown. The sun was beginning to dip below the tree line. "I gotta get home, anyway."

Billy looked around, also surprised by how quickly it was getting dark. The heat made them forget that it was only May and the days were still shorter than the summer days it felt like. "Want my dad to drive you up the hill?"

Denny hesitated, it would be nice not to have to walk by the Greymore place but he didn't want to sound chicken. "No, I'll walk. Only takes a few minutes." *Especially if I run.*

"Okay, see you tomorrow."

"See you later." They slapped palms and went their different ways; Billy to the comfort of his house and Denny to a darkening walk up the hill.

Once the sun began to go down, the temperature went down with it. Denny was covered with sweat from the game but was beginning to get chilled as he headed up the hill. The sun was fully behind the trees now, leaving the street bathed in an eerie orange-yellow light. The shadows cast by the mostly-bare trees looked like prison bars on the ground around him. As he approached the Greymore house he began to get nervous. All the stories about the Butcher floated through his mind. Once while getting his hair cut he overheard some of the older men talking. They said some of the bodies were found completely skinned, others with various parts missing; most were never found at all.

As he reached the overgrown hedge at the start of the Greymore property he suddenly stopped. His heart was now racing. *Did I just hear voices?* He told himself he was being silly and continued walking. The sunlight squeezing through the bare trees was growing dimmer as the sun set, now casting a reddish glow over everything. The darkness would soon close in on Denny. He reached the opening in the hedges at the start of the driveway and this time it was what he saw that made him stop. There was a car parked in the driveway! Denny stood frozen for a moment staring at the car. Time seemed to stand still as his mind reeled to understand what this meant. His paralysis was broken by the sound of rusty hinges groaning in protest after years of immobility. It was this sound that sent him running up the hill for home not once looking back to see who...*or what*... came out the front door of the Greymore house.

(8)

"I GUESS we might need an exterminator." Paul commented as another creature scampered across the attic above them.

"Probably mice or squirrels," the priest offered as they made their way back down the stairs.

Paul nodded, "You're sure it's no trouble for me to stay with you until I get this place in shape? It may take a while."

"Not a problem Paul, take all the time you need." They both stopped at the front door when they noticed the figure of a boy silhouetted in the dimming light at the bottom of the driveway. Father McCarthy squinted, trying to get a clearer look at the boy's features. He pushed open the screen door to step out on the porch when suddenly the boy turned and ran up the hill. The old priest stood on the porch looking in the direction that the boy had gone.

"Do you know him?" Paul asked, stepping out on the porch,

"I think so but I can't place from where," the priest replied. Paul could see the old man's wheels turning, trying to remember. "I'll be right back, Paul. I need to see who that was." There was a sense of urgency in the man's voice that Paul was unaccustomed to. McCarthy headed to his car quickly and backed out of the driveway, leaving Paul to face his thoughts alone.

Paul sat down on the top step of the porch, pulled a wrinkled pack of cigarettes from the pocket of his jeans, and unconsciously lit a cigarette. He was about to take the first drag when he remembered his promise. He looked at the butt for a moment, and then crushed it under his foot. He stood up and walked around to the backyard. Mother Nature had completely taken over the property in back. He slowly walked to the edge of the lake that bordered his property. The last bit of daylight slipped away as he reached the sandy shore.

Across to his left he could make out lights in the Barrows' house. *It's not the Barrows' house anymore,* he thought. *They're all dead.* He pushed that thought out of his mind and looked straight out across the blackness of the lake. No houses bordered it as far as he could see, only his, Barrows' *or whoever lives there*, and the Lovells' on the other side. Who knew if they were still there? Paul had grown up here, spending summers fishing, swimming and canoeing, and winters skating. He had a childhood full of happy memories from this place but the one that came to him now was not one of those. The vision of his past was so sudden and intense that it paralyzed him.

The rain was coming down in steady streams and the wind was unseasonably cold, pelting raindrops into Paul's face like bullets. The canoe was dangerously close to sinking. Paul rowed furiously toward the shore, the rain rolling down his face mixing with tears. The girl on his lap remained motionless. Please let me be in time, *he thought and increased his pace. Suddenly waves of dizziness overtook him, threatening unconsciousness. Paul closed his eyes for a moment and it passed. The wounds on his legs were bad. The water at the bottom of the canoe was a sickening weak-tea color from all the blood he had lost. Finally the shoreline came into sight. He expended all his reserve energy covering the last few yards to shore. But he had to go on. He picked the girl up from his lap.* When I get her straightened out, I have to go back and make sure I killed it. *He carefully stepped out of the canoe, knee deep in the lake. Panic overtook him when he thought of the possibility that it* wasn't *dead and he frantically stumbled to the shore. His head was spinning now and the house seemed to be moving further away as he walked toward it. He realized the hit he took on his head may just be worse than his legs.* I've got to be in time, *he thought again. This was his last thought before collapsing to the ground.*

HAVƎN

A loud splash from across the lake pulled him back from the memory. *Just a bullfrog,* he thought, but suddenly began to feel fear creeping up on him. That was the first time he was able to remember anything about that day. *But how did I end up with the girl, and both of us hurt so badly? And what did I think I killed that night?* Suddenly Paul was not sure he wanted to remember. What he did know was that the girl died from her wounds and Officer Crawford found them both, arresting Paul for her murder. *But I didn't kill her, I tried to save her. I don't remember but I know it's true, and I think Crawford knew it too.* He shook his head and started walking back toward the house to wait for the priest.

(9)

DENNY WAS just approaching Cat-woman's house when he saw the flicker of headlights behind him. For a moment he paused, debating whether or not to stop at her house for help. *Some help*, he thought and kept running. Sweat poured out of him and his breath came in desperate gasps. He was just fifty feet from his house when the dark car pulled beside him. "Slow down son, I just want to talk to you."

Denny turned quickly and was surprised to see a priest's collar on the driver of the car, although the driver's face was hidden in shadows. "It's Father McCarthy, son, slow down a moment."

Denny looked again to his right as he reached the edge of his front yard. It *was* Father McCarthy! Denny stopped, suddenly feeling foolish for taking off like he did. He bent over and put his hands on his knees, trying to catch his breath.

"Do you remember me from church, son?" the old priest asked. Denny nodded still unable to speak.

"I remember you but I haven't seen you in a while and can't place your name."

"Denny...Dennis...O'Brien," he managed between gasps.

Denny saw the look of confusion on the old man's face clear when the name finally clicked. "How is your mother doing, Dennis?"

Denny had finally caught his breath. "She's doing fine, Father."

"We miss you at mass, Dennis, both of you."

"Yes, sir."

"Perhaps you'd like to come on Sunday?"

Denny was getting uncomfortable with the way this was going. He began to fidget, digging his sneakers into the dusty road. "You'd have to speak to my mother about that, Father."

"That would be fine son. Is she home now?"

Oh no, Denny thought, *this is going to be bad.* "She was when I left after school, I'm sure she's waiting for me with dinner."

"It will only take a minute and then I'll leave you folks to your dinner. Does that sound okay?"

"Sure, you can pull into the driveway."

The priest maneuvered the car into the driveway and turned off the ignition. Denny waited as the old man got out of the car. As he shut the door behind him, the porch light blinked on and Denny's mother looked out the front door. "Denny, did Billy's dad drop you off?"

The old priest stepped into the circle of light thrown by the bare bulb above the screen door. Denny watched as his mother's face registered surprise, and then quickly turned to something worse. She threw the screen door open and stepped onto the front step screaming, "What are you doing at my house? I want you out of here! Stay away from me and my son!" Her face had turned crimson when she first recognized the priest and now it was bordering on purple.

"Mrs. O'Brien, if you'll just give me a minute..."

"I'll give you nothing! Haven't you taken enough?"

Denny was shocked at this outburst. He knew his mother had no use for religion since the accident, but he couldn't believe she would talk this way to a priest. Father McCarthy's face had paled, his expression unreadable. "Mom, he just..."

"No!" She took a step closer to McCarthy. "You people took my husband and son and now you come back for more?"

The old priest opened his mouth to say something, and then thought better of it. He backed slowly to his car as if he were afraid to turn his back to the woman. When he bumped into the fender he turned and got in. "Goodnight, folks. Sorry to have troubled you," he mumbled as he backed out of the driveway. Denny stood for a moment, unsure of what would happen next. Suddenly his mother burst into tears. She put her face in her hands as her body was wracked by violent sobs. Denny ran to her and put his arms around her. "Mom..." Then he was crying too.

His mother bent down and hugged him fiercely. "Oh, Denny, I miss them."

"Me too," whispered Denny, forgetting all about Father McCarthy being parked in the driveway of Paul Greymore's house.

>> <<

Father McCarthy drove slowly down the hill, shocked by what had just happened. McCarthy had filled in for Father Krieger frequently before being permanently assigned to Haven. He remembered the O'Brien family well and the tragedy that had befallen them. He was aware that Janice O'Brien had given up her faith since the accident, but the sheer hatred she had displayed had affected him deeply. The priest pulled the car into the driveway of the Greymore house and left the engine running as he stepped out. Paul got up from the front steps and walked toward him. "Are you alright, Father? You look upset."

"Fine, fine," the priest answered. "Let's get going, shall we?"

They drove in silence until they reached the small cottage that served as the rectory where McCarthy lived. They stepped inside and Paul took in more details of the house than he could the night before. They stood in a large living area furnished with only a couch, a recliner and a reading lamp. The walls all around the room were lined with bookshelves, crammed with volumes of all sizes. The priest's bedroom was off to the left, a small kitchen and bath were in the back of the house, and the guest room where Paul slept was off to the right. Paul had gone straight to his room last night, and this morning they had left the house right after breakfast. For the first time, Paul glanced at some of the titles on the closest bookshelf and was surprised to see titles ranging from the expected religious works to mystery and suspense novels. One entire shelf was filled with books on such diverse subjects as Bigfoot and the Loch Ness Monster to works on voodoo and witchcraft.

"Quite a collection, Father."

"Reading is my hobby. I'm afraid I have a weakness for mysteries of all sorts. I often think if I didn't become a priest I would have either been a detective or off searching the Himalayas for the Abominable Snowman."

Paul smiled at the old man, "I can't thank you enough..." The old man waved his hands to silence him.

"I won't hear it again, Paul. I wish I could offer more comfortable lodgings..." This time it was Paul stopping the old man in mid-sentence.

"Don't forget, Father, my previous host." He said with a grin. The old man hinted a smile but his face remained somber.

"What happened with that boy, Father? It's really bothering you."

The priest shook his head slowly; he seemed to have aged years in just the last few hours. "His name is Dennis O'Brien. He and his mother live just up the hill from your house."

Paul thought about the Hillview Street he knew, from *before*. "The only houses up there were the Lovells' and the Blaakman's, I thought."

"That's right, Paul, Dennis' mother Janice is Moses' daughter. O'Brien is her married name. Up until three years ago, the O'Brien family were very active members of the church. James O'Brien, Denny's father, worked at the Converse factory in Malden. Denny's older brother, James Jr., was a gifted student and a great athlete. He played varsity football as a freshman, filling in for the injured quarterback late in the year. James Sr. had gotten him on at the factory for the summer, plans of college and tuition already on his mind. He was to train Jimmy on the machinery on weekends before Jimmy could start full-time." The old man paused, running his hands through his generous head of white hair.

"On one of those Sundays, the two left the house. They stopped at Teddy's for coffee and donuts, and then headed for the factory. At the next intersection they were broad-sided by a speeding car that ran the stop sign. O'Brien's car skidded off the road and rolled down a steep embankment. James Jr. was killed instantly, his neck broken.

James Sr. sustained severe head injuries and died three days later, never regaining consciousness.

"The driver of the other car was thrown from his vehicle and ended up with some cuts and bruises and a broken arm. That driver was Father Jason Krieger. He was running late for Mass, copying Bible verses while he was driving to use in his sermon that morning. He had also been sampling the stock of the wine closet all night with another priest. He was convicted of reckless driving and manslaughter, given a suspended sentence, and was never seen by the people of Haven again. Not long after, he committed suicide in the confessional of a New Hampshire church." The old priest sighed deeply, obviously pained by the story.

"Ironically, that's how I ended up here, to replace Father Krieger. Dennis' mother never really got over the accident. She chose to vent her grief by rejecting the Lord and blaming anyone involved with the church for the deaths."

Paul watched the man as he spoke, wishing he had the right words to say to the priest. Instead he remained silent.

"I'm going to read for a while before turning in. We can take in the rest of Haven tomorrow. Goodnight, Paul. I'm glad you're here."

"Goodnight, Father." Paul watched the man move slowly into his bedroom, wanting to stop him and tell him about the memory he had at the lake. But the old man was so deeply troubled by the boy and his mother that Paul didn't want to burden him. He went into his own bedroom and flopped onto the small bed. He inadvertently ran his fingers across the grooved scars that mapped his face while he considered his chilling recollection earlier in the evening. *What did I think I killed? Was it some kind of animal?* Seconds later he was sound asleep, while the old priest read well into the night.

(10)

DENNY SAT next to his mother on the couch, his eyes on the television but his mind far away. He couldn't concentrate on the mindless sit-com with its canned laughter and meaningless conversation. His mother had settled down quickly during dinner, saying nothing more about the accident or Father McCarthy, not saying anything at all: they had eaten in silence. Denny wanted to talk to his mother, talk about how *he* felt about the church, which was not at all how she felt. Denny missed the weekly Mass he had grown up with. He was unlike most kids his age who were forced to attend church every Sunday: he had actually enjoyed it. Church always had a strange calming effect on Denny and he deeply missed that. Several times he had tried to spark conversation but he was beginning to think he missed an opportunity to really open it up in the driveway after Father McCarthy drove away. He mustered up his nerve and tried again.

"Mom, do you remember that time in church when me and Jimmy were fighting over a candy bar?" He watched his mother's eyes for a sign. Her face seemed to soften at the memory. "It was a Hershey bar. I tried to grab it from him and knocked it out of his hand onto the seat in front of us. Before we could grab it, Mrs. Benson sat down right on it. It was so hot in there that day. When she stood up..." he suddenly started giggling at the memory, hoping it would be contagious. His mother remained motionless, staring at the television. "When she stood up the chocolate was melted all over the back of her dress just like she…" his laughter was out of control and he struggled to finish. "She…she looked like she had…had an accident…" he was doubled over now but his eyes never left his mother. Her face lit up and a smile cracked the corners of her mouth, then it was gone.

Denny stopped laughing, "Mom, you remember that, don't you?" For a moment Denny didn't think she was even going to answer.

"Of course I remember, Denny." And that was all she said.

"Mom, I really used to love Sundays. Dad would get up early and cook us all pancakes or French toast, and then we'd all go to church together." His mother remained silent. Denny waited as the seconds stretched into minutes and knew this time she wasn't going to answer. He decided to go for it. "Don't you miss those times, Mom? Because you and I could go…" Denny felt sick to his stomach, felt tears welling in his eyes. She was gone. "Mom, I miss them but I miss you, too. The way you were before…" She remained silent. Giant tears rolled down his face. "…when you were my mother," he choked out.

A single teardrop spilled from his mother's eye but she would not turn to him. Denny was racked with sobs, pent up despair flowing out of him, but no second tear came from his mother. Denny had never before felt so alone. He ran upstairs and flung himself on his bed, shaking with emotion. He was anguishing over the deaths of his father and brother. He was somehow enraged and tormented with grief at the same time at his mother. He had avoided this day ever since his mother had begun slipping further and further away. Secretly he had hoped it would end with his mother coming out of her mourning as she hugged him tightly to her. He had desperately prayed for that ending, yet he had put off the confrontation. Tonight was the reason he had put it off for so long. Out of fear that this would be the real ending, with him all alone and his mother trapped in a world that he was no longer a part of. The part of Janice O'Brien that was his mother had died in that accident, too.

No, he told himself, *his father and brother were dead but he was not, and neither was his mother!* She was there somewhere, buried beneath so much anger and grief that she couldn't find her way out.

Denny sat up and wiped his face. He could not, *would* not let himself fall into that trap. He just had to figure out a way to break through to her. It had happened tonight in the driveway with Father McCarthy. That was it! The old priest had gotten through to her by just showing up, maybe that was the key. The hopelessness he had felt only moments before was turning into a dangerous optimism.

Denny knew better than to shatter his new-found hope by going downstairs and talking any more to his mother. He knew he would have to take it slow. He roamed about his room, picking up a football and tossing it up in the air as he paced. A fan hummed away in one of the windows, cutting a helpless, hot breeze through the humid room. He plopped down at his desk and examined the football, unable to make out the faded autograph. It reminded Denny of better times, of Jimmy. He placed it on the floor and sent it rolling slowly across the room, not wanting to think about those times, not now.

Instead, he opened his top drawer and took out his journal. He always felt refreshed by putting his thoughts on paper. The very act of writing things down, seeing them in black and white, helped him to really think about them. Sometimes that was a scary prospect, when it came to the things that hurt, like his dad and Jimmy. Like his mom. But most times it helped him figure things out. So he wrote it all down. He paused when he got to the part about Bear, pen poised over the paper, a hollow feeling in his chest. His dog should be curled up under Denny's feet, like he was every night when Denny sat at his desk. Denny would absently reach down and pat him or scratch his head. He swallowed hard and kept writing. It didn't get any easier when he began writing about Father McCarthy and the confrontation with his mom. But it raised a question: what was Father McCarthy doing at the Butcher's house? Denny figured he must have gone to the wrong house; he could picture McCarthy driving out to talk to his mom but pulling into the wrong driveway.

When Denny was working out something in his mind, he did it in the form of a conversation. He would throw an idea out there, and the other voice in his head, The Voice of Reason or The Great Oz, whatever it was, would reply. Denny didn't always like the answer, but it forced him to work through the tough spots. Tonight, the answer he got frightened him. *But wasn't he coming* out *of the house, Denny? Yes, I think he was. And we know what that means, don't we?* He stopped the conversation cold. He knew exactly what that meant. He went back to the journal, finishing up with his idea of asking Father McCarthy for help. Now this was a better conversation to have with his mental advisor. He began planning what he would say, and that's when the long day finally caught up with him. He put his head down on his folded arms, *just for a minute,* he told himself, and was asleep immediately.

He woke groggily, stiff from sleeping hunched over his desk. It had become somewhat routine for him to fall asleep while writing in his journal. When he didn't write them down, his thoughts seemed to swim around in his head, making sleep difficult. He placed the journal back in the drawer and switched off his desk lamp, his eyes slowly adjusting to the darkness. From here, he could see all the way down the hill. Everything. Cat-woman's house, the Butcher's, Billy's, and of course, the lake. The surface shimmered under the quarter-moon's glow, only an occasional ripple disturbing the glass-like appearance in the stagnant air. Denny often sat looking at the lake; the serenity of the view usually had a calming effect. Not so tonight. The tranquility seemed like a facade. Like there was some-thing else hiding, lurking, just out of sight. His gaze shifted beyond the lake to the silhouette of the old hospital. He never realized how it seemed to loom over the lake. Even though that place had its share of disturbing stories, it never seemed so menacing before. He shook his head, thinking about how lately everything spooked him. The cellar, the woods, now the old boarded-up hospital and the lake. As he watched the smooth water, a stray cloud extinguished the moonlight, turning the lake black. Denny found his way to bed and dreamed of nothing.

(11)

PAUL GREYMORE removed another handful of dead leaves and branches from the gutters of his house and glanced up toward the sky for a moment. The sun was hidden behind a thick haze yet the heat was stifling. *Too hot for this time of year*, he thought as he threw the debris to the ground. He reached his gloved hands into the gutter and this time what he pulled out sent him down a forgotten path to his childhood. It was an old "pinky" ball, barely recognizable from the years spent in the gutter. Paul remembered spending hours during the summer with his best friend Joe Cummings, playing "off the roof." It seemed so long ago and so much had happened to him that he wondered if the memory was even real. He felt such a deep sadness that he decided to take a break and began climbing down the ladder.

Paul had been shocked to find out from Father McCarthy that Joe and his family had moved into the Barrows' old house right down the street, and now an idea was forming. As quickly as it came, the sadness began to dissipate as he considered the prospect of visiting his old friend. *What if he thinks I did kill all those people? Why else wouldn't I have heard anything in seventeen years?* He pulled the gloves off his hands and wiped the sweat from his face with the sleeve of his sweatshirt. With any luck he would have the house livable in a few weeks. *Then what?*

The sound of an approaching car caught his attention and his heart skipped a beat when the police cruiser pulled into the driveway.

Despite the sweltering heat, Paul felt a chill course through him when he saw Cody Crawford step out of the car. The big man ambled slowly across the yard, and Paul moved forward to meet him. Paul was surprised he recognized the man so quickly because the years had not been kind to him. When he testified against Paul at the trial, Crawford looked like he had been cut from granite sitting up on the stand. He had been tall and broad shouldered but now his muscles were buried beneath layers of fat and he carried an enormous gut in front of him. When Crawford got closer, Paul noticed the deep lines on his face and the blood vessels that looked like fireworks exploding on his nose. His eyes were hidden behind mirrored sunglasses.

"So you really are back," Crawford said, "I didn't think you'd ever get out."

Red flashes of anger threatened to take control of Paul but he held back. "Fine thanks, how are you Officer Crawford? I've been expecting you."

Blood began to rise in Crawford's face. "It's Chief Crawford now."

"Congratulations. The news hadn't reached me," he lied.

The Chief leaned back on the front fender of the cruiser and pulled a cigar from his pocket. He placed it between his yellow teeth and scratched a match against his belt to light it. His movements were slow and deliberate. He was obviously trying to work on Paul's nerves. Finally he took a big puff on the cigar. "A little warm for a sweatshirt, isn't it Greymore? But I bet you've been in hotter places over the years, eh?"

Paul's agitation was growing but he refused to fall into the man's game. He inadvertently reached to his pockets for cigarettes that weren't there. When he did, Crawford jumped up, his hand moving to his holster. The car bounced on its shocks from the sudden release of weight. Paul put his hand back down to his side. Sensing control of the situation, he said, "You look a little nervous Crawford, something bothering you?"

Crawford whipped off his sunglasses and pulled the cigar from his mouth. Getting right in Paul's face he yelled, "Damn straight something's bothering me, you freak. The shit I thought I cleaned from this town came oozing back, and I don't intend on waitin' for more kids to get killed before I clean it up again! I don't want you in my town and neither does anybody else, except that bleedin' heart preacher friend of yours!" Crawford's breath stank of cigar smoke and stale whiskey and his face was a deep scarlet, veins pulsing in his forehead.

Freak. That was the word that fueled Paul's anger. He leaned closer to Crawford, locking his eyes. "I didn't kill those kids. You knew that seventeen years ago but you pinned it on me anyway. Maybe over the years you even talked yourself into believing it, but I didn't kill them." *Freak*. The word echoed in his head. He stepped back and pulled off his sweatshirt. The thick cords of muscles in his arms and chest rippled under his sweat-soaked skin. The skin itself was a hideous roadmap of scars, mirroring the ones on his face. "This is all I have to hide, Crawford. See this one," he pointed to a long scar running across his left shoulder, "that's for not giving my last cigarette to one of the yard bosses. And that one across my stomach is for not giving a blow job to one of the queers. And this beauty on my chest is from one of the guards because I didn't call him sir! But my arms, Crawford, they're my scarlet letter. Look at them, you bastard!"

The scars on Paul's arms were not the random doing of a carelessly slashed knife, they were carvings. On the worst night of Paul's life, a night that had driven him to consider if his life was even worth living, the other prisoners had marked him. Etched sloppily down one arm was the word "pervert." The ugly scars on his other arm formed the word "freak."

"I spent seventeen years in Hell, all thanks to you. These are my secrets, my past. What about you, Crawford? What scars do you hide behind your badge and gun? What do you relive on the dark nights when sleep won't come and save you from your thoughts? Do you think about taking away my *life*?" Paul pulled the sweatshirt back on. "I endured things in there that I will never forget, no matter how hard I try. But now I'm home. Don't you dare call this your town Crawford, it brings Haven down."

Crawford swallowed hard and took a puff on his cigar. Unable to meet Paul's stare, he folded up his sunglasses and hung them on his front pocket. "My son told me what..."

"Your son's a shit, Crawford, just like you." He reached into his pocket and pulled out the knife that the younger Crawford had wielded. "I told you I've been expecting you."

Crawford again went for his holster and this time he drew the weapon. He held the gun aimed at Paul's chest. "Are you threatening me, Greymore? We can end this here and now."

Paul smiled coldly, "You'd love that wouldn't you Crawford? You could say I pulled a knife on you and you shot me in self-defense. What's another lie considering what you've already learned to live with?" For a few seconds, Paul thought the man was actually going to shoot him. Crawford held the gun on him for another long moment and finally slid it back into his holster. Then he grabbed the knife and slid it into his pocket.

"When you give that back to your kid, you can pass along a message to him. If he ever puts that thing near my face again, I'll feed it to him."

Crawford squinted and his face turned a shade redder. He put his sunglasses back on and perched the cigar between his teeth. "I'll be watching you Greymore."

"You can watch all you want, Crawford, but not from my property. Now get the fuck off my land, and don't come back without a warrant."

Crawford stared at him for a moment from behind his sunglasses, and then he spit on the ground and turned toward his car.

Paul watched him back out and drive away. He walked slowly toward his backyard and out to the lake. He always came out here to think when he was growing up. He sat down on a rock near the water's edge and looked out over the lake. Out on the water, a couple of kids were fishing from an old rowboat. The sound of their laughter carried across the water, surprising Paul with a memory of him and his only real friend fishing on the lake a million years ago. Or so it seemed. Everything that had happened in the past and since his return to Haven was spinning in his head. So much had been taken away and now Crawford wanted to keep taking. Greymore would not let it happen. He wanted his life back. He decided he would pay a visit to Joe Cummings.

(12)

THE CANOE drifted lazily around the middle of the lake while Tony DeMarcy drifted in and out of sleep. The lake itself was motionless, as still as the humid air above it. A day too nice to waste sitting in class, especially on a Friday, Tony had decided earlier. Above him the sky was a hazy whitish-blue, the sun a shimmering fireball behind the haze. Tony pulled his Red Sox cap down over his eyes and started to doze again.

Tony's family had moved from Haven to the more desirable town of Bristol last year. Tony had fought the move with everything he had: how he would miss his friends, how damaging it might be to change schools, not that his grades could get much worse, but still he had tried, and lost. So when he woke up this spring morning he decided he would cut school and go look up some of his friends in Haven, God knows they won't be in class today. It took longer than he expected to hitch a ride, and he arrived in Haven after the last school bell rang. He looked for Dale Crawford and the rest of the guys at Teddy's Spa, but they were gone. Tony figured those guys had already burned through all of their allowed absences and couldn't miss another day of school or they'd be stuck going to Summer School. Tony had one more day to kill and that was today. No great loss, he thought, the two joints in his cigarette pack wouldn't have to be shared. That's how Tony ended up spending his final day on Earth floating around on the lake with two stogies worth of pot working their magic. The thought that he might just stay here on this canoe forever was beginning to seem very reasonable.

The last time Tony could remember being on the lake was a few summers ago. He and his dad had been fishing from their old row-boat. He smiled as the memory tuned in, becoming clearer in his mind. He and his dad used to do things together all the time, before Tony had started hanging around with the "wrong crowd." Tony had started reeling in, when his line went tight. At first he figured he was stuck on an old tree branch, but when he pulled his line up he discovered he had hooked a rusty old side-view mirror. "How could this get out in the middle of the lake, Dad?" he had asked with all the innocence and curiosity reserved for nine-year-old boys.

His father had smiled and told him that it probably got there attached to the rest of the car. When Tony frowned, his father had explained. "People take out insurance policies on cars, just like they do on houses or on themselves and their families. That way if they smash up the car or it gets stolen, the insurance company pays them for their losses. Some folks take advantage of the insurance company. When they need money or they don't need their car, they simply call the insurance company and say the car was stolen."

Tony had sat turning the old mirror over in his hands when the realization hit him. "Then they dump the car into the lake."

"That's right. They take them over to Hospital Hill and just roll them off the cliff." At this he pointed across the lake to where a sheer thirty foot face of rock stood above the lake, beyond which stood the old insane asylum.

It suddenly occurred to Tony that his father knew an awful lot about the subject. More than someone just picks up in passing. He thought of the old Ford wagon that had been stolen a few years back.

"Under the lake is just like a mountain that got covered with water. It's almost all rock. That's why you hardly ever see any weeds when you're fishing or swimming. Other than some rocky ledges, the lake is pretty much bottomless."

A sudden ripple broke the mirror-like surface, then another. Something bumped the canoe stirring Tony into semi-wakefulness

56

from his memory. He pulled his Red Sox cap off his face and looked around. Swirls of current were forming in the lake all around the canoe. Tony sat up, only to be knocked back down when the canoe began rocking violently. He sat up again, now fully awake, and his eyes widened when he saw the whirlpools that surrounded the small canoe. He quickly grabbed the life jacket that had been serving as a pillow and strapped it on. Another blow to the bottom of the canoe threatened to overturn it, but it remained afloat. Then all the turbulence stopped. The whirlpools dissipated to small ripples just as quickly as they had come, and soon the lake was glass-smooth again.

Tony shook his head, wondering if he had been hallucinating. He moved into the middle seat and grabbed the oars. Dream or no dream he was heading for the shore. He began rowing, immediately breaking a sweat in the blistering heat. He reached for the cap to keep the sun off his head when the rear of the canoe was suddenly thrown upwards. Tony was sent flying through the air as the canoe slapped back to the water, miraculously landing right-side up. Tony hit a second later, six feet in front of the canoe. The life jacket kept him above water and he quickly looked around to see where the canoe was, gasping from the shock of the cold water. He looked back and forth from the canoe to the shore, unsure of which way to go. The shore was still a good thirty yards away, but the canoe offered little safety even if he got back in it. *What the hell bounced it out of the water like that?* He scanned the shoreline for someone to yell to for help, but it was deserted. Not surprising since the rest of the world was either in school or at work.

After being unable to find his old gang, he had walked through the woods to get to the lake. When he came across the canoe just sitting there tied to a mooring he couldn't resist. Now he would give anything to be sitting in class listening to Mrs. Fryman drone on about the Civil War. He decided to head for the shore but when he started to swim toward it, he discovered his foot was tangled in some weeds. The harder he pulled to try and free it, the tighter the weeds seemed to close around his ankle. He looked down to try to see what was wrapped around his leg, but the reflection off the surface wouldn't allow it. He tried to push himself under to see but the buoyancy of the vest was too great. He reached one hand down and tried to pull his leg up enough to free himself, but whatever was tangling him up had him too tight and his leg wouldn't raise enough to meet his hand. He stopped struggling for a minute, listening to the water lapping around the canoe and thought of his father's words.

The lake is pretty much bottomless...that's why you hardly ever see any weeds.

The words pounded in his head. He began breathing harder now, shivering in the cold water. He held his breath for a moment and put his face in the water. The lake was pretty clear and he could see down to his knees before it began to get really murky. He could make out his sneakers only because they were so white. Whatever was around his ankle blended in too well with his jeans and the darkening water to make it out. He pulled his face out of the water and wiped his eyes. Then he felt a sharp prick on his ankle, not unlike that of a bee sting. Immediately his whole leg began to go numb. It felt a lot like the numbness in his face when the dentist shot him up with Novocain to pull a bad tooth. Panic seized him and he began to struggle madly to get toward the canoe. He felt like he was in a dream, trying to run with legs that only move in slow motion. The numbness was spreading rapidly and soon all movements stopped, and strangely he felt calm. As he floated motionlessly, he noticed his impressions of his surroundings were suddenly intensified. All the colors seemed brighter and clearer. He could smell crocuses in the stifling air, and freshly cut grass. He couldn't remember why he had been struggling to escape such a wonderful, serene feeling. Then something began to pull him under. With a sudden jerk, he went completely under, orange vest and all. As his lungs filled with water, his father's words echoed in his head. *The lake is pretty much bottomless...that's why you hardly ever see any weeds.*

The empty canoe drifted lazily around the calm lake, a Red Sox cap sinking slowly next to it.

{13}

"LET'S STOP and take a break." Denny said, sweat dripping down his face.

"Okay, but just for a minute. I really want to find those caves my dad told me about," Billy replied, swatting at some gnats that were buzzing around his face.

Denny sat down on a fallen tree trunk and opened his canteen. He drank greedily, and then poured some water over his head. The weather continued to be unseasonably hot. The day had dragged on endlessly at school and Denny was relieved to finally be out in the woods. The whole week had been one ordeal after the next and for a while it looked like the trip might be cancelled. First there was Bear's disappearance, then the Cat-woman called Denny's house raving about his dog eating some of her cats. When Denny had tried to explain again that Bear was still missing, she would not hear it. She claimed seven or eight of her cats were gone and it must have been that awful dog that took them. On top of all that was the return of the Butcher. Denny had seen him from the bus for the last couple of days working on his house. Rumors were flying all over school about Paul Greymore and how he had attacked Dale Crawford. Dale was saying that his father was going to put the Butcher right back in jail first chance he got.

"How much further until we get to those caves?" he asked Billy.

"My dad said if we went straight in from the back of your house for about two miles the woods should start sloping downward. There are some burned-out foundations there from the old military storage plant that blew up during World War Two. On the other side of the buildings we'll start going uphill again and the caves are in the far side of that hill somewhere."

"Let's go before it gets too dark to find anything."

They shouldered their backpacks and headed deeper into the woods. An occasional squirrel or chipmunk darted out in their path but other than that they were on their own. Denny wished for the millionth time that Bear was with them. There had been no sign of his dog all week and Denny was beginning to fear the worst. Every day he got off the bus without Bear's greeting was another lesson in sadness. The nights in his room were lonely, empty. Occasionally Bear would stay out overnight and Denny knew the dog would wander through the woods to the lake following whatever it is a dog follows. But this time he was gone too long.

The shadows had started to grow longer when the boys noticed the change in the woods. They had been hiking through a thick forest of mature pines, oaks, maples and birches and the usual ferns and brambles that grew between. Now the trees were smaller and the ground was much more open with the bushes and vines not as congested. Denny stopped and sniffed the air. Bear would have picked this up a while ago, he thought, and his eyes welled. It was the smell of long dead ashes, like finding a campfire in the spring that hadn't seen a flame since the previous summer. It was rather unpleasant, the smell of bad history.

When he noticed Billy eyeing him with an expression that clearly thought Denny had lost his marbles, he simply said "We're close," and started walking. Mixed among the new growth Denny saw the crumbled, blackened trunks of the trees that had fallen victim to the fire. A few were still standing, held in place by roots that were just as dead as the visible trunks, but most were in ruin on the ground. In several places they had toppled over on top of one another and again Denny thought of old, dead campfires, these ones built for giants.

Finally, the first of the crumbled buildings came into view. They ran over to it and climbed over the rubble. It was really nothing more than a cement shell. The entire wooden structure had burned completely, the ashes scattered by decades of wind and rain.

Denny tried to recall what he knew of this place. He remembered his mother telling him stories about it because his grandfather had been killed in the explosion. The buildings had belonged to the military and served as an ammunition storage facility. Just before the end of the war, a massive explosion had devastated the entire complex, killing everyone on the base. Denny's mother said she remembered thinking the Germans had bombed them, the explosion had been so loud. Air raid sirens had sent everyone into their cellars. She sat down in the dark cellar praying with her mother, expecting another explosion to rip through the night. A few hours later a neighbor told them what had happened and she knew her father was gone.

As Denny jumped over the crumbling wall he noticed how strangely untouched the ruins looked. There was no trash or empty beer cans that would usually accumulate at a spot like this over the years. Then he thought of the hike they made and figured it was hardly worth coming this far in the woods to drink. All of the old access roads were long ago grown over, and now that he thought about it, not too many people ever mentioned knowing the place existed. Like it was one of Haven's dirty secrets.

Denny and Billy rummaged around the building for a while and decided to move on before it got too dark. They came across several other building shells, all in the same state of ruin and abandonment. They were on the perimeter of the last set of buildings when they realized how dark it was getting.

"Looks like we won't find the caves tonight." Billy sighed.

"That's alright. We'll camp here and start fresh first thing in the morning."

They worked quickly setting up the small tent, but had to light the lanterns in order to finish the job. Denny pulled a small transistor radio from his pack and tried to tune in the Red Sox game. All he got was static and he turned it off in frustration. After getting the tent up, they immediately built a fire outside the entrance as the night was cooling off rapidly. An owl kept them company, *whooing* loudly as they cooked hot dogs and beans over the fire. After they ate their meal, the two boys talked into the night.

The usual subjects of school and girls and the Red Sox talked out, Denny mentioned Greymore. Billy frowned but did not reply. "I heard some guys at the barber shop one day talking about what he did. They said he didn't just kill 'em but he did some unnatural things." Denny paused, hoping that Billy wouldn't ask him what that meant, because Denny had no idea.

"Denny, I...I need to tell you something." Billy's voice was shaky and Denny couldn't read his expression in the firelight. "You have to swear you won't ever tell anyone." Now he looked up and Denny could see the seriousness etched on Billy's face. It was the face of an adult and the flickering light made it look more than a little scary.

"Come on, Billy, you know I..."

"Swear."

Denny looked at him again. His eyes seemed to be giving off the intense heat of the fire rather than reflecting it.

"I swear." It suddenly occurred to Denny that he really didn't want to hear what Billy was going to tell him.

"It's not true...what they say about Greymore." His eyes were like burning embers, aglow with conviction. "My dad says they blamed it on Greymore but he didn't do it. They were friends growing up, like you and me, real tight. My dad was the only friend Greymore had, because of the way he looks, you know?"

Denny nodded but didn't speak.

"Dad says there was no way he killed any of those kids. During the time of some of the murders they were together, that's how Dad knows for sure. They blamed it on him 'cause they couldn't find the real killer and because of what he looks like."

The weight of what Billy said seemed to be pushing on Denny's chest. Questions were popping into his head faster than he could ask them. "Then who did kill all those kids?" was the one that finally came out.

"My dad doesn't know. He says he goes over that summer in his mind over and over and it's like there's something there, something he's missing. He testified in Greymore's defense and it pretty much killed him in this town. He lost a lot of friends, and a lot of respect. Some folks still give Dad a hard time about it, especially now that Greymore's back." Billy fought to hold back tears. "Sometimes I think that's why he moved so close to the lake, to try to figure it out. Anyway, Crawford told my dad that Greymore would have been in for life without his testimony. He says if there's any more killing my dad should be held as an accomplice."

"That bastard, no wonder his kid is such an asshole."

Billy wiped his eyes and looked up at Denny. "Do you believe me?"

"Why wouldn't I?"

"Nobody else ever believed my dad."

A sudden flapping noise made both boys jump as the owl left its perch in search of dinner, leaving the night silent except for the crackling of the fire and two young voices. "Why do you think the killing stopped after they arrested Greymore?"

"Dad can't figure that out but I think there's something he isn't telling me."

Denny stared at the fire trying to think of what to say next. He reached back and grabbed another log and tossed it into the flames, sending fireworks of sparks in all directions. "I was wondering why your dad let you come. Everyone else is so afraid."

"Why did your mom let you come?"

Denny looked down at the fire. "She's getting worse. I don't think she really knows what's going on anymore. I could have told her I was going out to assassinate the president and she would have told me to have a nice time. If she bothered to say anything at all."

"What are you gonna do? If she keeps getting worse, I mean."

"I don't know. I was thinking maybe Father McCarthy could help...we used to be pretty religious. Except if Mom ever found out she'd freak out even worse. She hates him." He quickly filled Billy in on the confrontation the other night but stopped short of mentioning the tear-filled talk with his mom. "I think he could help..." he repeated, but had nothing else to add.

The fire began to lull the boys to sleep. They decided to pack it in so they could get an early start for the caves. Once inside the tent, away from the fire's heat, they noticed that the night had cooled considerably. They climbed into their sleeping bags and quickly drifted off to sleep.

(14)

DENNY WOKE up slowly, at first unaware of his surroundings. When he realized where he was, he slipped quietly out of his sleeping bag and out of the tent. It was morning, barely. The sky was brightening but the sun hadn't yet appeared over the horizon. Denny slipped his sneakers on and went into the trees to take a piss. He decided he was done sleeping and started walking back toward the old building shells. The dew on the leaves sparkled in the silver-gray light. Birds were beginning to chatter up in the trees. Denny walked on, not wanting to get too far from the campsite, but enjoying some time to himself. All of the anxiety he'd been feeling had lifted. Spending the night out in the fresh air, away from the cloying hopelessness of his house, had done wonders. He walked with a carefree step, enjoying the sweet smell of pine that hung in the still air.

He reached one of the foundations and climbed down into it. He began moving some of the rubble around, thinking he might find a souvenir, an old belt buckle, maybe. Nothing as cool as a gun, most likely, but you never knew. He had moved several pieces of the old foundation and was about to give up when something caught his eye. Down below some of the larger chunks of concrete, something metallic shined in the growing light. He moved as much as he could, then went and got a sturdy branch and pried some more pieces away. The object was still unreachable, trapped below three large hunks of cement. He found a longer branch to give him more leverage and began working on moving the masses of cement.

By the time he had uncovered the object, the sun was fully up and Denny was bathed in sweat. It turned out to be a large ring attached to a chain. The other end of the chain was imbedded in a large, rectangular cement slab set in the floor of the foundation. It took a moment for Denny to realize he had uncovered a door in the floor of the foundation. He thought about going back and getting Billy but decided to open it and take a quick look before going back. He slid the branch through the ring and began trying to pry the slab open. He pushed with all his strength, the branch bending under the stress. But the slab wouldn't move. He would need help. He scurried out of the foundation and headed back to camp. As he walked back he wondered about the door. Was it some underground storage room, possibly still full of ammunition?

Half an hour later after they had packed up the tent and eaten a quick breakfast, Denny and Billy were staring at the door. "I've been thinking, maybe they had something rigged to open the door. Like it would hook on the ring and they could crank it open."

Billy looked at the wall of the foundation and moved away some branches that had fallen into it. "I think you nailed it, Denny. Look at this." Two rods extended from the wall above the door. "I bet something was attached here, a crank or pulley or something."

"Yeah, I guess so. But how are we going to get it open?"

"Maybe with both of us we can pry it off." They found the longest branch that would fit through the ring and tried to get the cover open. The slab wouldn't budge.

"It's probably too thick to come off at an angle. We need to lift it straight up." As he said it, Denny began moving the branch so that the ring was closer to the middle of it. Then he lodged one end of the branch into the top of the foundation. "If we can lift this end of the branch, the cover will lift straight up." Billy joined him at the free end of the branch and they began pushing up on it. The branch began to bend and the ring was cutting into the bark. Suddenly a loud cracking noise drowned out the boys' groaning and the branch moved up with a jerk. Denny thought the branch had snapped but when he looked over, the cover was swinging slowly from the branch. It turned out it wasn't the weight of the cover that prevented them from getting it off initially, it was simply stuck in place by years of the elements. They moved sideways, holding the branch over their heads until the cover was no longer situated above the opening, and then let it down. They quickly ran over to look down the hole and were immediately assaulted by the smell coming from it. Both boys stepped back, coughing and gagging.

Denny remembered the time his father had forgotten to take a bag of groceries out of the trunk. In the bag among other things was a pound of hamburger. Denny had gone to get something out of the trunk a couple of days later and almost threw up when he opened it. This smell reminded him of that, but not exactly. Like there was another smell just as bad that he couldn't identify mixed with that rotten meat smell. They covered their mouths and noses and stepped closer for a look. Rungs of a ladder were cemented into the side of the shaft leading down into the darkness. They moved back before risking taking a breath or talking. "What are we going to do now?" Billy asked, still with a look of disgust on his face. The smell was noticeable even back where they stood.

"Maybe the smell will get better now that the cover is off. Or we can try tying our shirts over our faces and see if we can stand it."

Billy looked like he was considering both ideas. "Why don't we leave it open for a while and look for the caves and then come back and see if it smells any better?"

Denny thought about it for a moment. He wasn't sure he wanted to go down there at all, smell or no smell. At least looking for the caves would put off for a while having to climb down that ladder into who knows what. "Okay, let's go. We can leave the tent and stuff here. All we need is flashlights and some rope." They took what they needed and set out toward the caves. The day was already heating up even in the cover of the trees. They found what they were looking for shortly after. They had slept that night within a half mile of the entrance without even knowing it. It was sheer luck that led them to the opening at all.

After following the directions Billy's father had given them they figured they were in the right area but couldn't find the caves. They were on a fairly steep hillside with the lake visible in the distance at the bottom of the incline. That's when Billy saw a big snake, and thoughts of the cave evaporated as he decided instead to catch the snake. The snake quickly slithered away into a dense patch of bushes. Billy crashed through the bushes in pursuit just in time to see the snake slip into a gap in the rocks. Billy thought there might be a whole nest of the things in there so he began moving some of the loose rocks. He pointed his light between the rocks and discovered the cave. The way it was concealed, if it hadn't been for that snake, they never would have found it. And maybe they'd have been better off.

(15)

WALTER "BUGSY" Cronin climbed into his ancient van and began driving toward the outskirts of town. He wasn't nicknamed Bugsy because of any resemblance to the famous gangster that built Las Vegas, but simply because bugs were his life. Bugs and any other pests that needed killing. Bugsy was Haven's exterminator, had been for over thirty years. He had been expecting this call ever since he heard Greymore was fixing up the old house. A house can't sit for that long without being lived in. And if it ain't lived in by people it sure as hell will be by the critters. Bugsy referred to all of his victims as critters regardless of whether he was exterminating ants or a nest of snakes under an old shed. Critters. He expected Greymore's house to be infested with several different kinds of 'em and was prepared for everything from termites to squirrels.

When he told the boys down at the Witch's Hat where he was going today, he'd just about heard it all. "He deserves to live with the rats" and "I hope the goddamn bugs eat him alive" and "you couldn't pay me enough to go out there." But Bugsy paid them no never mind and went about his business. He knew Greymore's parents and had met Paul a few times when he had to go out and spray for termites or set some traps for mice. The kid was tough to look at, poor bastard, but that didn't make him a killer. Not as far as Bugsy was concerned. He judged people by the way they treated others and nothing any of the Greymores ever did made him think bad of them.

The boys said he was too naïve but this way of thinking had got him through sixty years on God's green earth and he wasn't about to change now. Not on that no good Cody Crawford's word especially. So when Paul Greymore called and asked if he could come out and check the place out, Bugsy said "Sure, Mr. Greymore, I can be out there tomorrow, first thing. No, I don't need directions; I took care of some critters there for your folks years back."

As he drove through town he thought back to the last time he had been out there. Damned if it wasn't 1961, just before all the trouble started. Had some hornets nesting in their attic that time. Hot as a bastard it was that day. Carol Greymore had mixed up a big pitcher of lemonade and made him sit down and have a glass after he came down from the attic. "It's hot as the blazes up there, Mr. Cronin, and I won't let you leave until you sit yourself down and cool off with a drink." She always called him Mr. Cronin and the husband always called him Walter. Paul was home that day and they had had a long conversation about fishing. Paul was always fishing or out on the lake. Never had many friends because of his face, so he kept to himself. But he had talked a blue streak about fishing that day. Bugsy had mentioned hunting season and the kid had gotten quiet. Said he couldn't figure out how someone could kill an animal for sport. Bugsy remembered feeling funny since he killed all kinds of critters just about every day. So they kept talking about fishing until Bugsy finished his drink. Then he thanked the Greymores and went on his way. Seems it wasn't too long after that the parents were dead and Paul was in jail.

As he turned off Main St. and headed along West Border Road, something began to bother him. Something wasn't quite right. There was also something familiar about the *wrongness* that Bugsy couldn't put a finger on. When he turned onto the unpaved Hillview Street, the feeling intensified. Like something you see out of the corner of your eye but not long enough to tell what it was, this was something hiding in the corner of Bugsy's mind but he couldn't quite see it clearly. It would come to him later, he thought as he pulled into Greymore's driveway, always does when you stop trying. Greymore was replacing some spindles on the front porch and walked over to meet Bugsy. "Thanks for coming on such short notice, Mr. Cronin, especially on a Saturday. I really appreciate it."

Bugsy shook hands with him, "No trouble at all, Mr. Greymore, and you call me Bugsy, or Walter if you prefer, like your dad did. They were nice folks, your parents. I never did tell you how sorry I was." He began gathering supplies from his van as he spoke.

"Thank you, Walter. I wasn't sure when I called if it was you or if you had passed the business on to a son."

Bugsy chuckled, "No, it's just me. Both of the boys got too educated for killin' critters. And for living in Haven, for that matter."

"Do you still do any fishing, Walter? I remember you telling me some spots to try when I was younger but...I never got the chance." His voice trailed off as he said the last few words.

"No, I guess you wouldn't have. I fish quite a bit since the wife passed on, keeps me from spending too much time down at The Hat when I'm not working." He slammed the back door shut and the whole van rattled.

"I'm sorry to hear that, Walter."

"Thank you, Mr. Greymore. Now, where shall we start?"

"Please, call me Paul. And we can start anywhere you like; I think I have every kind of pest known to man."

Two hours later Bugsy was back in the van having finished work at Greymore's. Greymore was right; he did have just about every critter Bugsy had ever been called upon to exterminate. Except mice, of course. That crazy old nag next door had so many goddamn cats nobody up on Hillview would ever have mice again. Greymore sure seemed like a nice enough fella, though. Not a child-killer, not in Bugsy Cronin's book. No way, Bugsy thought. Christ, after everything that happened in '61, hadn't people even begun to talk about Greymore maybe killing his own father earlier that same year? The poor mother had up and died just weeks after Greymore was sent away. Heart attack, they said. More like a broken heart, Bugsy figured. Greymore had a pitcher of iced tea made when Bugsy was finishing up, just like his mother had made the lemonade years back.

As a matter of fact, a lot of things were beginning to feel like that summer, including the weather. Bugsy reached in his pocket for a hanky to wipe the sweat from his brow and as he did a squirrel bounded in front of the van. The squirrel froze when it saw the van closing in on it. Bugsy instinctively stepped on the brake and swerved to the right. But it was too late. Bugsy felt the thump as the tires went over the animal and could almost hear the wet squish as the squirrel's innards were forced out through its skin. He pulled the van over to the shoulder of the road and climbed out to make sure the van wasn't damaged. *That one was free*, he chuckled to himself, as he got a shovel and scraped up the remains of the squirrel into one of the barrels he kept in the back of his van. As he did, something clicked in his head. He jumped back in the van and retraced his route out to Greymore's.

When he had driven the roads slowly he was sure he had figured out what seemed wrong earlier: not one piece of roadkill for miles out toward Hillview. This time of year the side of the road was usually littered with carcasses of skunks, squirrels, raccoons, possum and other critters. Sometimes even a deer or a fox, and just once, a moose. Now that he had discovered what was itching him all day, he began pondering what it meant. It seemed that he remembered something similar several years back, maybe that same summer he visited the Greymore's parents. Instead of going home he drove over to the Witch's Hat, Haven's local watering hole. A few drinks might just help him solve this little mystery.

(16)

THE TWO friends worked quickly moving the rocks away from the mouth of the cave. They scrambled inside as soon as the opening was large enough and began shining their lights all around. "Look at the size of this place!" Billy's voice echoed strangely in the cave. There wasn't much light and their flashlights weren't strong enough to offer much help. They could see the cave was fairly large and seemed to slope downwards to a smaller tunnel. "Let's see how far in it goes." Billy said as he began walking toward the back of the cavern.

"Wait a minute, Billy. This might be dangerous." Fear began to creep up Denny's back. He felt like he did when he was in the cellar the other day.

"Don't be such a chicken. We have to see where it goes."

"Billy, the cave could go in different directions once we start out. All I'm saying is, we need to leave a trail."

"Okay, you're right. How about we get some sticks and strip the bark off one end. We'll leave the bare end pointing the way back."

Twenty minutes later they entered the tunnel armed with sticks to mark their trail. The tunnel quickly narrowed to the point they had to walk single file and the ceiling was only a couple of feet above their heads. Denny's apprehension grew with every step; he felt like the tunnel was closing in on him. He switched his flashlight off because Billy was leading the way. The tunnel darkened considerably with only a single light.

"What did you do that for? I can't see shit now."

"I don't want to be stuck down here when both flashlights' batteries go dead. If yours dies it's time to turn around."

"Oh, good thinking."

Denny wished he had brought a sweatshirt; it was much cooler in the cave. Then he noticed something else. "Billy, do you smell that?"

Billy sniffed around in the air. "Yeah, smells just like when we opened that door out at the old building foundation only not as strong."

"Maybe the smell is in our clothes and we only notice it because we're in such a small place." But as they continued the smell grew more noticeable. The tunnel turned and twisted, always sloping down. They came upon a spot where the tunnel opened up into a small room-sized cavern. Two tunnels exited the cavern, one on each side. The larger of the two seemed to stay level while the second, smaller shaft continued the downward slope of the original tunnel. "Maybe we should head out and come back another time with more stuff, extra flashlights and things."

"Let's keep going for a few more minutes. They must lead somewhere." Billy took a few steps into one tunnel, then the other. "The smell seems much worse in the bigger tunnel; let's follow the smaller one for a while."

Denny followed Billy into the mouth of the smaller tunnel and into the darkness beyond. His heart was thumping loudly in his chest to the point he thought he heard it echo in the tunnel. He wanted to turn around and run back until he was out into the safety of daylight but his pride wouldn't let him. What would Billy think? They came to several other forks in the tunnel, always choosing the one that continued to slope down, and always leaving a stick to point the way out. Eventually the ground began to level off and the tunnel widened. They came around the next bend...and into a dead end. The tunnel just stopped. It looked like a cave-in had spilled rocks and sealed off the tunnel. Denny felt panic seizing him. What if there was another cave-in and they were trapped? How far underground were they? And nobody knew exactly where they were. As Billy climbed on the pile of rocks, Denny began taking some deep breaths, trying to remain calm.

"Denny, come over here for a minute. Listen." Denny climbed up on the loose rocks and cocked his head to one side. "Do you hear it?"

"I hear something but I can't make it out."

"Its water, it sounds like dripping or splashing or something." He began rolling rocks from up on the pile toward the floor of the tunnel. "Come on and help me!"

"What if the water comes pouring into the tunnel?" Denny swallowed hard. Billy stopped moving rocks for a minute, head cocked to one side, and then started again.

"These aren't piled tight enough to hold water back. Come on!" Reluctantly Denny began dragging rocks from the pile, always checking to make sure they had a clear path out of there. After a few minutes Billy pointed his light into the gap where they had moved most of the rocks from. "Holy shit, Denny! Quick, move these rocks over here!" He began frantically moving rocks from the wall. Denny helped without knowing why, the physical labor keeping his mind off his fear. Now Denny could hear the sound of splashing water. Billy shined the light again and then began pushing the rocks instead of pulling them. The rocks disappeared into the darkness. Denny could see the hole materialize in the dim light as Billy pushed more and more rocks out of the way.

Billy squirmed through the hole and Denny followed him. When Billy shined the light ahead, Denny gasped in astonishment. They were in a huge cavern. The light dimmed before it could reach the far walls but the most amazing thing was not the size but the fact that the floor of the cavern was mostly water; they had found an underground lake!

Denny switched his light on and they moved over to the edge of the water. One side of the water just ended at the wall of the cave while the side they had emerged on had a rocky shore that was partially covered with whitish rough sand. They slowly followed the water's edge to the far side at least thirty yards away. At that side another huge tunnel led into the rock. About ten feet above the lake on that side water poured in from a gap in the rocks, accounting for the splashing noise that had led them to the discovery. Both boys began exploring the cave, shining their lights along the edge of the water and along the shore. "Denny, come look at this!" Billy's voice echoed through the cave. Denny joined him at the edge of the lake and followed his beam of light. Floating along the side of the lake was a small red and white object. It took Denny a minute to recognize it as a fishing bobber.

"The water pouring in must be a run-off from the lake! We must be right down at ground level. I wonder if there's another way out through that big tunnel."

Billy nodded and went over to the entrance to the larger tunnel. Both boys moved their lights along the entrance when suddenly Billy's winked out. He shook the flashlight but the beam would only blink dimly for a second and fade out. While he was doing that, Denny continued to shine his beam along the floor of the tunnel. His light caught something and he moved it back for a better look. When he did, his breath caught in his throat. He tried to say something to get Billy's attention but not a sound would come out. His eyes were riveted to the object his light had found. Finally he gasped to get his breathing started again and shouted, "Billy!"

While he waited for Billy to make his way over he flashed his beam around and his panic grew. "What's up?" Denny jumped at the sound of Billy's voice.

"Look," He shined his beam around the tunnel so Billy could see the bones that littered the floor. Not little fish bones; big animal bones. He moved his light further and it fell upon the half-submerged ribcage of what might have been a deer.

"Denny, what the hell kind of bones are they?" Denny could hear the fear in Billy's voice that matched his own.

"Some kind of animal bones, big ones."

"Like human animals?"

"I don't know. Shit, look at this." Denny shined his beam back toward the shore of the lake. He bent down and picked up a handful of the white powdery covering and let it run through his fingers.

"What is it, Denny?" Billy sounded on the edge of hysteria.

"I thought it was some kind of sand but it's not. It's ground-up bone."

"That's it. Let's get the hell out of here!" They both moved quickly back to the small opening they had made in the rocks and slid through one at a time. Then they began their ascent from the cave. Denny led the way with his flashlight but had to stop when he heard Billy go down behind him. "Wait up, Denny, I hurt my leg."

Denny went back and shined the light onto Billy's leg. He'd tripped and opened up a big gash on his knee. It was bleeding freely and was caked with dirt and gravel. Denny cleaned it out as best he could. With nothing else to use, he took off one of his socks and tied it as tight as he could around the knee, covering the cut. It quickly soaked through but Billy said he was okay to go on. They had no trouble finding the sticks they had left behind but the going was slow. It hadn't seemed like much of an incline going down but both boys were gasping for breath. They slowed down again, partially from fatigue and partially because they were calming down the further they got from the lake.

"Denny, you're a smart kid, what was all that?"

"I don't know, Billy. Maybe some animals drowned in the lake and their bones came through the run-off we saw draining in there." He tried to sound more convinced than he really felt. He knew one thing, he was going to the library as soon as possible to read up on caves and see if it's normal to find bones in them.

The rest of the walk out was in silence and without incident. Denny was happy to see the sunlight streaming into the cavern. He was beginning to feel like a mole after a few hours with only a flashlight providing light. They decided to cover up the entrance the way they found it and they marked a few of the trees near the cave. Billy pulled the bloody sock from his knee and tied it to the branches above the entrance so they could find it again if they wanted to. Not that Denny could think of any reason he would ever want to go back in there.

They made their way back to the building shell and found that they had no desire to explore where the door led, not today anyway.

Billy bandaged up his knee, which had bled all over his lower leg and sneaker, and was still bleeding pretty good. "Might need a couple of stitches, maybe we better head back." They moved the door back into place and scattered a few rocks over the slab. "Maybe we can come back up here tomorrow and check this out." Billy said, sounding half-hearted.

"I don't know. I think my mother has a bunch of stuff for me to do," Denny lied. The sight of all those bones had thrown a good scare into him. He had conjured up images of being trapped down there and his flashlight giving out. In the total darkness he would hear splashing as something crawled out of the water and slithered toward him. He felt once again like he was back in his cellar that day when the water started gurgling. He shook his head to try and rid himself of such thoughts and cursed himself for being such a wimp.

"Actually, my dad mentioned something about making sure I'm around tomorrow too."

Denny heaved a sigh of relief. He was off the hook and wouldn't have to lie again about having things to do. "Let's get going and get that knee taken care of. Besides, I'm starving." They gathered up their equipment and started the hike back, Billy limping noticeably. *The trip had been exciting*, Denny thought, *a lot more exciting than I had planned. A different kind of exciting, anyway.*

PAUL GREYMORE checked himself in the mirror one last time. *Enough stalling*, he thought, *it's time to go.* He had anguished over everything in preparation for tonight. Half an hour over which pants, finally choosing a pair of jeans. Should he bring wine? Flowers for Mrs. Cummings? What if Joe wasn't home? The only quick decision was the long sleeve shirt, and that wasn't a decision at all.

He finally left the rectory and started the cross-town walk to the Cummings' house. Father McCarthy was on an overnight retreat in western Massachusetts and wouldn't be back until late the next evening, leaving Paul to find his own way around. The night was still, the warm air heavy. Not even the slightest breeze moved through the trees. The town itself was as still as the air. In spite of the heat, there were no kids outside playing, no parents sitting on their porches having a beer or a smoke. Doors were shut tight, holding back whatever dangers existed in Haven, then Greymore realized *he* was the danger they feared. He reached the walkway and hesitated for only a moment before going up to the porch. Taking a deep breath he knocked on the screen door. The seconds stretched endlessly until a face appeared in the door. The boy's eyes widened at the sight of Paul before he composed himself. "Can I help you?"

Paul took a step back, blinking. It wasn't the boy's reaction that startled him, he had seen that a thousand times. It was the fact that he was face-to-face with the same twelve year old boy that had become his best friend a lifetime ago. It took Paul a second to figure out that this must be Joe's son. "Is your dad home, son? I'd like to speak with him for a minute."

"Sure, I'll go get him." The boy bounded off into the house and Paul turned to look out over the road as he gathered his thoughts. He and Joe had been close and suddenly lost all contact after the trial. He decided right then and there that if Joe sent him away tonight, he would leave Haven forever.

"Can I help you?" This time it was the adult version of the face he knew so well that greeted Paul.

Paul turned to face his old friend. "Hi, Joe."

"Paul, I'd heard you were...back, but I didn't expect to hear from you." The words stung Paul with their cold ambivalence.

"I've been fixing up the old place and I thought I should stop by when I heard we were going to be neighbors..." His words trailed off. This was going worse than he feared. He could feel the awkward silence building like a summer thunderhead.

"Neighbors? You mean you're actually staying in Haven? I thought you were just fixing it up to sell..." He couldn't read the expression on Joe's face. Was it fear?

This was it. The final humiliation. To have his ex-best friend believe that he killed all those people. He could never stay here now. He felt his eyes begin to fill up and his face redden. "I'm sorry I bothered you."

Then anger began to replace his shame. Anger that after everything else he lost, the list would include his friend Joe. The boy that had accepted him unconditionally when all the others turned away from his ugly face. It wasn't fair. "Just explain one thing, Joe. Why did you testify for me and then never answer any of my letters once I went to prison?"

Joe's face shrunk into a portrait of confusion. "Letters? Paul, I sent you dozens of letters but you never answered them. I finally drove up there one day but they said you were refusing visitors."

Paul was stunned. He staggered over to the porch swing and slumped down, holding his head in his hands. Someone must have intercepted all of his mail, in both directions, except for McCarthy's. Crawford! He had taken away seventeen years of Paul's life and now to find out he had also stolen seventeen years of friendship. It was just too much.

Joe stepped out onto the porch and sat beside him. "Paul, I'm sorry. After you never answered my letters and refused to see me...I didn't know what to think."

The both sat in silence, lost in their own thoughts.

Joe spoke again. "Paul, there are stories that you almost killed the Crawford boy on your first day back. Is that true?"

"Yes."

"Good, I can't stand the little bastard."

Paul looked up and saw his old friend smiling. He couldn't help but to smile back. "Crawford must have had them stopping my mail from getting in or out. Joe, that means I've never really thanked you for testifying for me. It meant a lot to me."

"A hell of a lot of good it did." Both men burst out laughing and Joe reached out to shake Paul's hand. Then Joe's face clouded. "My God, Paul, if only I had tried harder to contact you. All these years..."

Paul shook his head. "Crawford wouldn't let it happen, no matter how hard you tried. I realize now just how much he hates me and how much he's taken from me. He's actually the reason I'm here, he stopped by to welcome me back to Haven...so to speak."

Joe stood up and pulled Paul up with him. "Come on in and meet the family, Paul. They've heard so much about you for the past seventeen years it's only fair."

DENNY SAT in the stifling confines of his bedroom brooding over another silent dinner with his mother. He had tried to engage her with stories of him and Billy in the caves and what they found. He knew most parents, *normal parents*, would freak out when they found out their kid was messing around at an old army base or in some underground caves, but she didn't bat an eye. He was actually hoping for a lecture on the dangers he had put himself in, hoping for *any* reaction, but tonight she was gone. Now, even after writing in his journal, he still wasn't ready for sleep.

He suddenly felt very alone. He knew it wasn't just his mother, but Bear's disappearance that was making him feel this way. But knowing that didn't help. He pulled a flashlight out of his desk drawer and flicked it on and off three times, aiming it at Billy's house. They had been doing this for years, since they realized their bedrooms faced each other. They had both learned Morse code and often stayed up well into the night "talking." He waited a few seconds and repeated the signal. No response. Billy was probably downstairs with his family, watching television in the living room. It only made Denny feel worse to picture Billy in such a normal setting while he sat by himself in the dark. The alarm clock by his bed told him it was almost 11:00 PM. Outside his window, the moon was hanging low over the lake, illuminating the area clearly. Sudden movement caught his eye. He leaned forward trying to focus on the shoreline. He could make out the ripples spreading out from the shore, but could see no further movement. He watched for a few minutes but the water was motionless now. He crawled into bed; the breeze from the fan was now blowing directly on him, giving him a chill and sending him under the sheets to get comfortable.

He still didn't feel tired and grabbed a book he'd taken out of the library. He lay in bed and started reading where he had left off the other night. The book was a factual account of the witchcraft hysteria that had swept Salem in 1692 and resulted in the execution of nineteen people, eighteen by hanging and one pressed to death. Denny was appalled that what he was reading had really happened. How could these people have done this? Many of the executed were done so based on the accusation of *children*, without any substantial evidence. As engrossed in the reading as he was, Denny began to doze and the book slipped face-down on his chest.

As he drifted off to sleep the fan made a strange screeching noise, then stopped. Denny waited and heard it again, above the normal hum of the fan. He realized the sound came from outside, not from the fan. The screeching stopped again. Denny waited but this time the sound did not return. He thought about getting up to see if he could see anything, maybe signal Billy. If it had come from down toward the lake he might have heard it too.

The thought came on him, probably out of loneliness and worry: what if it was Bear? The urge to go out and look for his dog was overwhelming. He fought it, knowing it was unlikely, knowing Bear was probably gone. He felt the sting of tears, felt empty. He decided to listen for a few more minutes. No more sound came and the constant hum of the fan lulled Denny back to sleep. If he had gotten up to take a look, he would have seen a light blinking frantically from Billy's bedroom window.

Denny opened his eyes to find himself staring up not at his ceiling but at the faces of his father and brother. They were both dressed in strange black coats and white shirts. Denny felt his breath stick in his chest at the sight of them. In a dark corner of his mind was the knowledge that this was a dream but he could not find that now.

"Dad, Jimmy," he gasped, "why are you dressed like that?"

They both stared down at him, scowling. Then they bent down. Denny thought they were reaching to help him up but when they stood, they each held a large rock. Suddenly Denny realized why he was having such trouble catching his breath. His gaze drifted from the faces of his family to his own chest. On top of him was a large rough-hewn board, covered with more rocks like the ones his father and Jimmy now held. For a fleeting moment Denny thought they were pulling the rocks off of him until they silently reached down and placed the rocks they were holding on the existing pile. He let out a groan as more air was squeezed out of his lungs and he was unable to draw any more in. "Why?" he squealed. But they were already bending over and placing more rocks on him, moving synchronously. The next time they stood up, it was no longer his dad and Jimmy; it was Dale and Cody Crawford. Neither spoke or wavered their gaze from him as they labored to pile the rocks higher and higher, heavier and heavier. Denny heard the last puff of air wheeze from his body as the world began to close in on him. Through his blurring vision only the growing heap of rocks was visible, and then it too grayed out.

Denny awoke abruptly, gasping for air. He felt something on his chest and struggled to get hold of it and toss it away. He sat up in bed trying to catch his breath, soaked in his own sweat, twisted up tightly in damp sheets. He glanced across the room at the book he had just thrown. The vividness of the dream came back to him and he began to shiver. He fixed the sheet and pulled it tightly around him, unable to shake the chill he felt despite the sweltering, humid air. He thought of getting up to change into pajamas and shut out the light but the thought of falling back asleep terrified him. He glanced at the clock and heaved a sigh of relief. The sun would be up in another hour or so. Denny remained awake until it did, only then allowing himself to drift back to sleep.

(19)

LATER THAT night Paul settled into a chair on McCarthy's back porch to reflect on the evening. The years had melted away as they talked until it seemed like Paul had only been gone for seventeen days instead of years. Joe's wife, Tina, was charming and his son was as bright and witty as Joe had been at that age. His daughter was harder to figure out. At times she seemed genuinely interested in Paul's stories of his time in prison but then she would come out with a snide remark and make Paul wonder if he imagined her interest. Julie had caused a few uncomfortable moments. It was clear there was tension between her and her parents. She wasn't outwardly rude or disrespectful, really, just defiant. Mercifully, when she was picked up by Dale Crawford, he didn't come in but only beeped his horn and revved the engine of his Mustang impatiently.

Paul had stayed long after Tina and Billy had gone to bed, talking deep into the night with Joe. Eventually the conversation wound its way around to the summer of the murders. Joe confessed to spending a lot of time that fall trying to figure out what really happened. He told Paul that he had visited him in the hospital after Crawford found him with the girl. Paul had been heavily sedated, still badly wounded. Joe said Paul was in and out of consciousness, mumbling and raving when he was semi-awake about something in the lake. Joe had put it off as shock from injuries or the drugs. That is, until he saw Paul's wounds.

According to Joe it was never in the papers and never mentioned at the trial as to the extent of Paul's injuries. "Christ, Paul, it looked like someone took a cheese grater to you," Joe recalled, "and your legs were covered with welts, all in a straight line, like huge bee stings. Damnedest thing I ever saw." Joe had organized a make-shift search party with his buddies under the pretense of finding more bodies. "We searched that lake for weeks and I used some of my college savings to hire divers. I really thought they'd find something." He told Paul tonight he didn't mean bodies but something else. When Paul pressed him on what he meant, he changed the subject, a distant look in his eyes. Paul wanted to keep him talking, wanted to tell him about his memories of that last day on the lake and trying to save the girl, but then Julie arrived and she and Joe got into it pretty good. She was drunk, maybe high, too. Paul had said goodnight before it got too ugly and walked home, expecting Dale or Cody, or both Crawfords to be waiting for him. Fortunately his walk back to McCarthy's was uneventful.

Now as the inky black began to fade to gray, Paul began to wonder. Not that any of his thoughts made any real sense but things were beginning to fit. His memories of that summer, his injuries, his ravings at the hospital, could it all mean something? He was suddenly glad to be far away from the water's edge. Just the thought of being within reach of the lake sounded ominous to Paul. *Within reach?* He considered that for a moment when a sudden breeze whispered though the trees in McCarthy's small yard, murmuring threats instead of promises. Paul shuddered in the clammy heat of dawn and went in the house to a fitful sleep.

"DENNY!"

The sound of his mother's voice snapped Denny out of a sound sleep. He had been dreaming of ice-skating on the lake with Julie. They were holding hands and skating toward a bonfire on the shore. There were others there, drinking hot chocolate and waiting for the New Year's Eve fireworks. His dad and Jimmy were off to the side passing a hockey puck back and forth on the blue-glass surface of the ice. But now he was back in his room, alone, and the dream was already starting to fade. He rubbed his eyes and looked at the clock: it was only eight o'clock! Why would his mother be waking him up so early on a Sunday? Had she thought about returning to church?

"Billy's here, are you up?"

"Be right down!" he called. He quickly threw on a pair of shorts and a t-shirt, slapping his Red Sox cap on his head as he left his room. When he got downstairs his mother was on her way out to hang a load of laundry on the line. Billy was sitting at the kitchen table looking like he was about to burst.

"Hey Billy..."

"You are not gonna believe this..." he looked out the window to make sure Denny's mom was out of earshot. "Guess who was at my house last night?"

Denny knew his friend was itching to tell him some big news.

So of course he pretended he wasn't interested. He walked to the cabinet and got out a box of Frosted Flakes. "I don't know. The Beach Boys?"

"Very funny. It was...wait a minute; maybe you wouldn't be interested after all."

Damn, Denny thought as he poured the cereal into a bowl then got the milk out of the fridge, *he always has the upper hand.* "Alright, alright, I'm not even awake yet. Who was it?"

"Paul Greymore."

Denny stopped with the carton of milk poised over his bowl and turned to Billy. "The Butcher was at your *house*?"

Billy frowned. "Don't call him that, okay? He came to visit my dad. You aren't going to believe this..."

Denny's mom came back in from the yard with the empty basket. She paused, as if about to say something. The moment dragged on and Billy gave Denny a questioning look. Denny just shrugged hopelessly and sat at the kitchen table to eat his breakfast. Finally she moved past and they heard her footsteps going up the stairs.

"He's moving back into his house!"

Denny almost spit out a mouthful of cereal, as a knife of cold, deep fear pierced his heart. "He's moving back?"

Billy was grinning. "Relax, scaredy-cat, he's not a killer. He's actually a really nice guy. And his face isn't that bad, you kind of get used to it and it makes him...interesting."

Denny was nodding slowly. "You're sure? Your *dad* is sure?" Denny was mentally counting the number of steps between his house and Greymore's. It wasn't a very big number.

"Yeah, he told us last night. He's moving back as soon as his house is fixed up."

Denny shook his head. "No, numbnuts, are you and your dad sure he didn't kill those kids?"

"My dad was already sure, even before Paul's visit, I already told you that." He went on to tell Denny about Crawford blocking the letters his dad and Greymore tried to send to each other and how Crawford even stopped his dad from visiting Greymore.

"So all this time your dad thought Greymore wasn't writing back and Greymore thought your dad wasn't returning his letters?"

"Yeah, and *man* were they pissed when they figured it out."

Denny crunched the last bite of his cereal thoughtfully, then raised the bowl to his mouth to down the sugary milk. A brief image of the Cat-woman flashed through his mind fleetingly. In the distance a dog barked. Denny turned his head toward the door but knew it wasn't Bear's bark. "I guess we know where Dale gets his assholeness from."

Billy giggled. "Is that even a real swear?"

Denny put his bowl in the sink and slapped Billy on the back. "It will be. Get Webster on the phone and I'll have it added to the dictionary." He let loose with a jaw-cracking yawn.

Billy punched his shoulder. "What are you so tired about? I tried signaling you last night to tell you about Paul and you didn't answer."

Denny shrugged. "That's weird; I tried to signal you around eleven. Then I fell asleep and had some crappy nightmare. I was just falling back to sleep when you came and woke me up again." He could never tell Billy about the dream he had with Julie in it.

Billy was never the one to let an opportunity to rank on someone pass him by. "Was it the one where you piss your pants at school and they send you to the nurse and you have to wear a diaper for the rest of the day?"

"Good one, but I already wear a diaper so that doesn't happen... again." Both boys cracked up. "I thought you had stuff to do today?"

"Not until later. You?"

"Yeah, my mom wants me to help her put the winter clothes up into the attic later." He looked down, hesitating, unsure of how to ask Billy for a favor, then he just blurted it out. "Will you come with me to talk to Father McCarthy?"

"Thinking about becoming a priest since you'll never get laid anyway?" Denny felt his face begin to burn as he blushed. He looked at Billy and saw the flash of memory in his friend's eyes. "Oh, hey... yeah sure. I'm sorry, man, I forgot..."

Denny's heart lifted, knowing as much as they ranked each other out, each would take a bullet for the other if it came down to it. His eyes drifted to the bandage on Billy's knee and thoughts of the caves came back along with a shudder.

"Thanks. Let's go before I chicken out." Denny yelled up to his mom and the boys headed out the door into the heat.

They rode their bikes into town, having most of the streets to themselves in the early-morning quiet of a Sunday. Downtown Haven was essentially closed on Sundays. Other than the spa and the Oakhurst convenience store, every window was dark and had a *Closed* sign on the door.

Just off of Main Street, on the cleverly named Church Street, stood Holy Trinity Church. The majestic white building was the pride of Haven. It was fronted with gleaming pillars and crowned with a spectacular bell tower, surrounded by an emerald green lawn and exquisitely manicured trees and shrubs. It was a postcard-worthy scene in every season, equally beautiful encircled by spring flowers or cloaked in a fresh coat of snow.

When they approached the church they immediately realized the flaw in their plan when they saw the streets and the parking lot full of cars. They had arrived just after the start of nine o'clock mass.

Billy wiped sweat from his forehead and looked up at the hazy sky. The unrelenting heat and humidity might actually break, he thought. Ominous clouds were building on the horizon. "Got any money? We can go grab a doughnut at the spa and come back after?"

Denny checked his pockets and came out with enough change to get them each a doughnut. "Jackpot."

They rode back to Main Street and parked their bikes out front. Denny hesitated for a second before moving toward the door. Billy looked back. "Wake up, dummy, this is the part where we go in and actually buy the doughnuts, then we eat them."

Denny swallowed hard, struggling to control his emotions. "This...this is the last place Jimmy and my dad were before..."

Billy stood in front of him and awkwardly put a hand on Denny's shoulder. "I'm sorry, Denny, I didn't know. Let's just go wait in front of the church, the priest always comes out after mass to yuck it up and bless babies and stuff, right?"

Denny cracked a grin even though his eyes felt ready to spill over with tears. "No, it's okay. Let's go in." Billy pulled open the door and a set of chimes hanging on the door announced their arrival to the mostly-empty shop. May, who owned the shop with her husband Teddy, greeted them with a sad smile when she recognized Denny. They sat at the red, round, plastic-covered stools at the counter and ordered honey-dipped doughnuts. Billy started spinning his stool around as May walked over to get their doughnuts.

"Oh, shit." He muttered.

Before Denny could ask what was wrong, he was surrounded by Dale and his gang. They had been hanging out at a back table of the Spa when Denny and Billy arrived.

"Well, well, are you boys skipping church, or have you decided to become Jews?" As always, Buddy, Chuck and Tony giggled at Dale's wit.

Denny glanced nervously at Billy, not seeing a way out of this without a beating. "Why don't you guys just leave us alone?" he offered.

"Why don't you guys just leave us alone..." Tony mimicked in a girlie voice. Tony Costa was the youngest of Dale's gang, and the smallest, but he thrived on having muscle behind him and was always mouthing off. "Why don't you make us?" He stepped closer and Denny saw how much he enjoyed playing the bully.

Billy slid off his stool. "How about just you, Tony? How about Dale lets you off your leash for a while, and just you, me and Denny go outside?"

The rest of the gang started hooting and hollering. Denny was at once amazed at both the balls Billy had, and the glimmer of doubt in Tony's eyes. Denny thought again of his brother and how he would never allow anyone to hassle him like this, on or off a playing field. Without thinking about it, he slid off his stool so he was face-to-face with Tony. "Yeah, Costa. How about it?"

The moment dragged on. Then a door banged behind them and Teddy stormed around the counter. "What is going on here?"

Teddy Stavros was a hulking Greek who looked like he ate more doughnuts than he sold. But everyone in Haven knew that beneath his girth there was a lot of muscle. Teddy was the winner of the Haven Day Strongest Man contest for five straight years, and last summer he had put on a charity event where he wrestled a bear. Everybody said the bear was toothless and declawed, but Denny didn't know too many people who would step in the cage with it regardless.

Costa was looking back and forth between Denny and Billy, the doubt in his eyes edging closer to fear. He finally turned to Crawford for help, but none was there.

It was Denny that spoke. "Teddy, Dale and his friends don't believe you wrestled a bear. We tried to tell them the story, but you always tell it best, and Billy and I have to go meet Father McCarthy. Would you mind if they hung out for a few minutes while you told them about it?"

Teddy was no dummy and he played along smoothly. "Of course, of course, gather around boys!" He put a pair of meaty arms around Costa and Crawford and herded the four of them back toward the booth. He turned and winked at Denny, and he and Billy gave him a thumbs-up and silently mouthed their thanks. May handed them a bag with their doughnuts and offered a smile as well.

Out on the sidewalk, they agreed that a visit to McCarthy now would be too risky since Crawford knew that's where they were supposed to go. "Billy, that was pretty ballsy of you to face down Costa like that."

Billy just shrugged as he got on his bike. "I'm tired of those guys; besides, I knew you'd have my back. Did you see him? He was actually scared of us!"

Denny grinned, "Yeah, and I think Crawford is a big enough shit that he would have let us kick Tony's ass."

Billy nodded, "Probably, but then the rest of them would have killed us. Let's go to my house and eat those doughnuts." They both rode away into the darkening day as Teddy animatedly told his tale and Crawford stared after them with murder in his eyes.

(21)

THE HEAT did break that day, beaten into submission by a wild thunderstorm. The boys barely beat it home from town before the wind picked up and distant rumblings of thunder began. Soon after, flashes of lightning cut through the dark afternoon and the rain began to fall. Once it started, it looked like it might never end. For two weeks the spring rains ranged from a cold, miserable drizzle to drops the size of grapes to viscous wind-driven thunderstorms. The most talked-about storm brought golf ball-sized hail with it.

Denny spent those endless two weeks avoiding Crawford's gang at school and moping around the house. The only good times were spent on Billy's front porch playing games of Risk or Monopoly and hoping to get a glance of Julie. He had resigned himself to the fact that Bear was gone and this made being a prisoner in his own house even worse. His mother drifted in and out of lucidity and seemed to be withdrawing even during the times she was herself. The worst of the two weeks was Mother's Day when Denny gave his mom a card and a plant and she barely noticed. The plant was already wilting, the card unopened still. On Sunday, two weeks to the day he and Billy had gone into town to talk to Father McCarthy, Denny decided to try again.

After lunch, he called Billy but there was no answer. He remembered Billy saying something about visiting relatives. The rain had tapered off to a misty drizzle and the day was warming up. Haven had exploded into color with all of the rain. Trees were filling out, grass was greening up, and flowers were growing. Denny got on his bike and started the ride to town alone. He saw no sign of Crawford or any of his gang, and by the time he arrived in town, the sky was actually starting to clear. The gray clouds were thinning, parting for the blue sky to make an appearance. Denny's mood lifted as he took a deep breath and knocked on the rectory door.

For some reason, Denny felt the urge to jump on his bike and pedal furiously home, or anywhere else. Suddenly this felt like a bad idea and Denny didn't want to have the difficult conversation he knew was ahead. If Father McCarthy hadn't opened the door when he did, Denny might just have bolted. But as soon as Denny saw him, his doubt melted away and he felt a faint hope that things might just work out.

The old priest was sipping a cup of tea when he opened the door and Denny saw surprise register in his eyes. "Dennis, is everything okay? What brings you here? Is your mother with you?"

"Everything is fine, Father...well actually it's not. My mother isn't here; she's why I'm here..." Denny felt his face flush, unable to articulate everything that had been pent up inside him for so long.

"Please, come in. Can I get you a drink?"

Denny hesitated. The rectory seemed sacred, not a place for a sweaty kid. Plus, he'd been trapped inside for two weeks and *needed* to be outside. "I could use a drink, but I...could we talk outside?"

McCarthy smiled. "Sure, I'm tired of being indoors myself. I'll mix up some lemonade and meet you around the side of the house; there's a picnic table there."

Denny nodded, feeling oddly like McCarthy had read his mind about the weather. He made his way around the side of the house and sat at the picnic table which was in the shade of a massive old oak. Good thing, because once the sun finally broke through the cloud cover, the heat began to rise. The ground was steaming as the rain dried. McCarthy came out carrying his tea and a huge, ice-filled glass of lemonade. He seated himself across from Denny and sipped his tea.

Finally, Denny spoke. It began in fits and starts but he quickly felt at ease and the whole story came out, interrupted only by gulps from his lemonade and an occasional comment or question from McCarthy. By the time he finished, his glass was empty and the ice was melting quickly. Tears were streaming from Denny and the last part, when Denny told McCarthy of his fear that his mother might just disappear into her own mind, came out in choking sobs.

McCarthy was silent for a moment. He looked to the sky—whether admiring the beautiful day or asking for guidance, Denny didn't know. "Dennis, do you know the definition of faith?"

Denny wiped the tears from his face, not sure if he was about to receive a religious lecture. "Believing in God?"

McCarthy nodded slowly. "The dictionary defines it as 'belief in something that is not based on proof or reason.' When you were younger, you believed in Santa Claus?"

Denny smiled. "Sure, of course."

"Some people think that God is the Santa Claus for adults. The concept of an all-powerful being sitting on a throne in Heaven, orchestrating everything that happens to everyone isn't much more far-fetched than a guy riding around in a sleigh pulled by flying reindeer delivering presents to every child in the world in a single night. Well, the ones on the good list anyway. And as a child, you did have proof of sorts; the presents showed up."

Denny nodded, still unsure what this had to do with his mother.

"Dennis, your mother lost her faith. The accident that took your father and brother...to her it was like waking up and seeing her parents putting the presents under the tree and eating the cookies she left for Santa. She took it as proof that God doesn't exist. *Can't* exist, because what God would let her loved-ones be taken away so brutally. By a man of the cloth no less."

"But I still don't know how to help her. How to fix her. I came here because of what happened at my house. I thought...after seeing her reaction..."

"Dennis, I'd be happy to talk to her. And I believe you are on the right track with your thinking. She *is* broken. Who wouldn't be? Kids are far more resilient than adults. You find out Santa Claus isn't real and you move on; that particular faith is one you grow out of. This is very different of course. Grown-ups are sometimes harder to fix. What your mother took as proof that God doesn't exist was merely one of the countless events that sparked the phrase 'God works in mysterious ways.' Faith can be very hard to restore once it is lost. But I promise you this, I will help you in any way I can. You don't have to be in this alone."

Something that Denny had been holding together inside broke. He began to cry uncontrollably. But these were cleansing tears. Some of the pain he'd been harboring was expelled in those tears, replaced by a growing sense of hope. When he was finally able to speak, he looked into Father McCarthy's eyes and said "Thank you." It wasn't much but it was all he could manage.

Denny stayed for another hour, planning the next steps with Father McCarthy. They agreed that Denny would begin to go to Mass himself for a couple of weeks before telling his mom. McCarthy would drive him home after Mass in a couple of weeks to try to talk to Janice. When Denny finally began the ride home, the sun was back in control of the weather and the humidity was sneaking back as well. Denny didn't care, because for the first time since the accident he felt like things might be alright, like he and his mom could be a family again. As he passed the school, he realized summer vacation was just a few weeks away. *This is going to be the best summer ever*, he thought.

He couldn't have been more wrong.

{22}

PAUL FINISHED unpacking his few belongings and closed the bureau drawers. He was finally beginning to feel like he was out of prison... beginning to feel *free*. The old house was really shaping up and this was to be his first night staying there. Joe had stopped by a few times to give him a hand and their friendship had picked up right where it left off. For the two weeks it rained, they had gotten the inside work done. The past week had been sunny and clear and even the outside and grounds were coming along nicely.

Paul went downstairs and wandered through the silent rooms. He still noticed that closed-up smell, but it was fading. Much stronger were the smells of cleaning fluids and fresh paint. He looked around making mental notes of what still needed to be done. His gaze fell on the stack of books he had borrowed from Father McCarthy's collection. He picked one out and took it out to the back porch to read.

The night was unseasonably warm and the air in the house still felt stale even after the house had been open all day. At least on the porch, new screens replacing the old, torn ones, the air was fresh and there might be a stray breeze to enjoy. He sat down on an old rocker that he had pulled out of the cellar and refinished. His mother used to sit in it on nights like this when Paul was young, sometimes falling off to sleep in it. The next morning she would always complain of a stiff neck or a sore back and Paul and his father would exchange knowing glances of the cause. She would always deny falling asleep out there and it became a running joke in the house. Paul smiled to himself at the memory. It's funny he hadn't thought any such thoughts the entire time he spent in prison. While some of the other inmates dwelled on their lives "outside," Paul rarely thought about it and never spoke of it. It was as if he was trying to keep the Paul Greymore in prison a separate entity from the one who existed before. Now that he was out the memories seemed to be all coming back to him slowly.

He began reading the novel he had brought out to the porch with him but immediately began to feel drowsy, lulled by the whispering voices of the night. To Paul, the faint rustling of leaves or splashes in the lake was music. The sounds he had become accustomed to falling asleep to were the slamming of steel doors or the screams of other inmates who were falling victim to the unspeakable acts that go on in the dark cells. He awoke suddenly, not knowing if he had been asleep five minutes or five hours. It must have been a while because the moon was now high in the sky, its glow shimmering on the waters of the lake. The night was still comfortably warm yet a chill passed through Paul. Another memory was trying to surface but it wouldn't quite come. Paul had a strange urge to go down to the shore of the lake but at the same time this thought terrified him. He shook his head, trying to clear the fragments of sleep from it. He longed for a cigarette but refused to break his vow. He finally gave in to the lure of the lake. It was as if the lake was pulling him toward it. Somehow he knew the memory that was teasing him was related. He left the screened porch, the door slamming behind him, echoing loudly in the night. The night was beautiful, the sky crystal clear, a welcome sight after the weeks of rain. Paul's sense that something was not right grew as he approached the lake but he could not stop himself from continuing toward it. The night was eerily quiet, none of the usual sounds of crickets or bullfrogs he was accustomed to. Paul struggled to bring the memory forward. Another night, long ago, just like this one. The strange urge to go to the lake, the ominous quiet... suddenly the memory hit him, not in bits and pieces but in one thunderous blow. He felt dizzy, overwhelmed. He crouched down, now at the edge of the water, and let the memory wash over him.

HAVEN

Paul awoke from a terrible dream, immediately unable to recall what it was about. Knowing he would not be able to fall back to sleep right away, he threw on his jeans and a T-shirt and went downstairs. He poured a glass of ice-water and carried it out to the screened porch. He was instantly aware of the unusual silence. On many nights he would be unable to sleep and would come out and sit on the porch for a while and the night would be alive with sounds. Crickets would be chirping, bullfrogs croaking, moths bouncing off the screens. Tonight there was none of that. The ice chinked against the side of the glass as it melted, shattering the unearthly quiet. Suddenly there was another sound. It came from the lake. It sounded to Paul like someone jumping into the lake but yet not quite like that. He slipped into his sneakers and stepped out into the night. The yard was dark, the half-moon hidden behind a restless curtain of clouds. Another noise made Paul jump. This one was off to his right. It wasn't a splashing sound this time but something crashing through the woods off to his right. Not exactly crashing, Paul thought, more like sneaking.

Paul stood riveted to the spot, intently listening to the cracking of twigs and branches. He relaxed as he realized whatever was out there was moving away from him. He had a sudden urge to follow it to find out. The woods were very dense around the lake and he knew he would make too much noise that way. His eyes fell upon his canoe and he began moving toward it. He could still hear rustling off in the woods. He quietly pushed the canoe into the water and hopped in. He slipped on a life jacket and pushed off in the direction of the noise.

Paul was not sure how long he had been following the sounds but he figured he was almost to the far side of the lake. At the slow pace he was rowing and because he was sticking close to the shore he figured he must have been out for over an hour. Suddenly the noise stopped and Paul stopped rowing, keeping his oar in the water to avoid making a splash. He sat silently in the canoe, waiting. It occurred to him that he might not really want to see who was out in the woods, but he pushed the thought away. He remained motionless, waiting for movement. His muscles began cramping because of the awkward position he was in. He thought he caught a movement along the shore in front of him, realizing that shapes were beginning to form around him. He looked up and saw the clouds thinning, allowing dim moonlight to filter through. He couldn't stay hunched over holding the oar any longer and risked sitting up, pulling the oar into the canoe as quietly as he could. When he did, a shape began to distinguish itself from the rest of the darkness on the shore. The dim moonlight brightened as the clouds separated and Paul realized he was staring at a deer drinking from the lake. He felt the air rush out of him and suddenly felt very tired. He had stayed up half the night on this great adventure and it turned out he had followed a deer halfway around the lake. He felt foolish and positioned himself to turn the canoe around and head home. The moon again disappeared behind the clouds leaving Paul in darkness again, but the eastern sky was beginning to change from inky black to a grayish blue. As Paul dipped the oar back in the water, something crashed through the woods where the deer had been. He figured the deer had run off but then the sounds turned into a chaos of rustling and something that sounded like growling. He turned in the canoe and stared into the blackness, leaning forward as if this would give him a better view. A sound unlike any he had ever heard rose above the rest and the other sounds stopped. He realized he had been listening to a struggle. He blinked frantically, willing his eyes to adjust to the darkness. There was more movement in the woods, different again. This time Paul recognized the sound of something heavy being dragged along the ground. He leaned forward even more, threatening the balance of the canoe and was able to see movement, black on black, toward the shore. He now heard small splashes and other slippery noises and when a sliver of moonlight broke through the clouds, he saw the deer pulled into the water and out of sight.

He sat motionless in the canoe. Panic threatened to overtake him as what he saw began to sink in. His mind buzzed, trying to comprehend what could take down a deer so quickly and also lived underwater. His thoughts turned to crazy stories of alligators living *in New York City sewers and he wondered if something like that was possible. He stared at the spot where the deer went in but the water had stopped rippling and there was no sign of anything breaking the surface anywhere. The sky was beginning to lighten and the lake took on that dreamy, surrealistic appearance Paul had seen many mornings waiting for the sun to rise. It suddenly clicked what the sound he had originally heard was. It wasn't something jumping into the lake but something coming out. Something that Paul followed around the lake until it found the deer. Something that was in the dark waters below him. He sat there until the sun was well over the horizon before he had the courage to row home. Even then, in the light of day, he was sure with each stroke that something was going to come out of the lake and take him under.*

He jumped back from the water's edge, the fear returning as quickly as the memory had. There was more, of that Paul was sure. The rest of the memories would come back to him about that summer. After this one, Paul was not sure he wanted to remember anymore. A chill ran through his body and he went back to the screened porch. He sat down and went over the events in his mind. *What did he think he had seen?* He recalled the other memory that had hit him on his first day back, and he knew they were related. Whatever had dragged that deer into the lake was the same thing he had tried to kill later that summer. But what was it?

Paul turned and went back inside, locking the door behind him. Then he went back to bed, and was still wide awake when the sun rose.

(23)

DENNY ALWAYS felt silly carrying a gift. Walking down the hill to Billy's house Saturday afternoon he felt like the eyes of the world were on him, and the people who those eyes belonged to were pointing and laughing. He didn't know why, but presents seemed like girl stuff. Of course Denny loved receiving gifts—that was a different story—and man, would he love to be getting the one he was holding. He adjusted the awkwardly-wrapped package, trying not to sweat through the wrapping paper, thinking how this would look on the shelf in his own room.

The week since Denny had visited McCarthy had been uneventful at school, dragging the way warm spring weeks do in school. Tomorrow he would go to mass for the first time and he was cautiously optimistic that his plan would work and his mother would be saved. The sound of a screen door slamming did not disturb his daydream, but the sound of the voice did.

"Are you heading to Billy's birthday party?"

The voice sounded normal, but before Denny turned to see who it came from, he realized that he was passing Paul Greymore's house. Icy fingers of dread squeezed his chest, making it suddenly hard to breathe. His mind's eye glanced away from the present he was holding to a newspaper headline: *Butcher Claims Another Victim: Killer's Neighbor Found Dead In Lake.*

Keep walking, he thought, *pretend you didn't hear.* Over the deafening sound of his own blood pumping through his veins and the beat of his own heart he heard footsteps rapidly approaching.

"Hey, you must be Denny? Billy's friend?"

Denny was caught in the vise grip of panic. The world began to float in front of him, shimmering in the heat of his fear. As much as his brain was screaming at him to run, he found himself turning to face the voice. Every horror movie he had ever seen, every comic book he had ever read, every nightmare he had ever awoken from shaking and sweating, suddenly ran through his mind in that split second. Then he was face to face with the Butcher, and his fear dissolved as quickly as it had formed. Paul Greymore was scarred and disfigured, yes, but he was human. He was smiling as he approached Denny—not a creepy spider-to-the-fly smile, but one that started in his blue eyes and drew the corners of his mouth up in a way that made the scars less important.

"I'm Denny O'Brien. It's nice to finally meet you, Mr. Greymore."

Denny found himself smiling at the comical expression of surprise Greymore registered. Clearly, he had expected Denny to cringe at the sight of him, or even run away. Greymore quickly regained his composure and held out his hand.

"My pleasure, Mr. O'Brien, any friend of the Cummings family is a friend of mine. Please, call me Paul."

"Then you can call me Denny." he grinned and shook Greymore's hand. The grip was cool and firm and Denny could feel that scaly presence of scar tissue. The package slipped from his left arm but before it could hit the ground Greymore had snatched it out of the air and was holding it out to Denny.

"Sounds like a puzzle, or maybe a model?"

Denny took the package back, "It's an X-wing Fighter model. From *Star Wars*."

Greymore nodded. "Sounds pretty cool, though I haven't seen the movie yet."

The two had started walking side by side down the dusty dirt road toward Billy's house.

"Do they show movies in ja..." He caught himself too late,

realizing how obnoxious his question was. To his surprise, Greymore chuckled. Denny looked up at him and saw an expression of sheer amusement on Greymore's face.

"It's okay, Denny. They show movies alright, but nothing you've ever heard of. All old black-and-white junk. Musicals mostly. Nothing violent, I guess they are afraid of getting the inmates all worked up and starting trouble. But I have heard a lot about it and sure would like to see it."

They reached the Cummings' driveway and heard voices coming from the backyard. Instead of going up the walk to the door, they went directly out back. The scene was exactly what Denny expected, yet it wasn't. The yard was festooned in standard birthday fashion; balloons, streamers, gifts piled on the picnic table. Mr. Cummings was already manning the grill while Mrs. Cummings flitted around with drinks. The only thing missing was the people. Other than Billy's family, the yard was empty. Billy spotted them—not very hard to do—and waved them over.

"Hey, Billy, happy birthday." Denny said as he reluctantly handed over the gift. His eyes scanned the yard, quickly finding Julie. She smiled and waved; Denny's heart almost exploded as he gave a quick wave back and looked away. Julie was wearing tight white shorts and a pink tank top. Her skin already had a mid-summer tan. She took his breath away.

This didn't escape Billy. He rolled his eyes and shook his head. "Thanks, Denny. Hi, Paul."

"Happy birthday, Billy." Greymore reached into his pocket and pulled out a rumpled envelope that he held out for Billy.

"Thanks. Do you guys want something to eat?" Billy put the envelope on the picnic table but his eyes kept sneaking back to Denny's gift. Denny had been friends with Billy for long enough to know this; Billy heard the rattle of the gift and knew it was one of the Star Wars models. His goal now was to get the food requirements out of the way so he could get to the gift-opening.

"Sure, what's your dad grilling?"

>> <<

The sun slowly made its descent toward the horizon as the party began to break up. Despite the sad fact that Denny and Greymore were the only non-family to show up, Billy seemed pretty happy with the day. A few parents had dropped gifts off, expressing lame regrets for their kids, citing conflicts because of Memorial Day weekend plans, but most didn't bother. It was plain and simple and obvious to everyone; Haven was afraid, and Paul knew it was him they were afraid of. At first he apologized profusely to Billy and his family but was quickly shushed each time. Eventually he gave up and enjoyed the day as well.

After a huge spread of barbeque, followed by the traditional cake and ice cream, Billy finally got to open presents. Unlike many boys his age, he saved his most coveted gift, the model from Denny, for last. He patiently waded through the parade of "adult gifts," clothes and such, until Denny's gift and the envelope from Paul were the only ones left. He opened the envelope, his face unable to hide the look of polite acceptance, the expectation that there was nothing more than a cheap Hallmark sentiment inside. When he pulled the Red Sox/Yankees tickets out of the card, it was clear Denny's X-wing Fighter was taking second place for the day.

Billy was a huge baseball fan, as most 12…now 13-year-olds are, and had been to Fenway to see a few games. But never had he been in the stands for a game versus the arch-enemy Yankees. The rivalry had reached epic proportions after a huge bench-clearing brawl a couple of seasons earlier, and the Yankees had edged the Sox by three games last year to win the division. Hopes were high in the spring of 1978, as they are every spring in Boston, for a World Series title. The '75 team had come oh-so-close, but that's for horseshoes and hand grenades, his dad used to say. Nobody remembers the second place team.

Denny felt a twinge of jealousy—not so much over the fact that Billy was going to see the game—but that opening the X-wing Fighter became a formality. Billy thanked him, sure, and he would love building it, but the Red Sox tickets stole the show. Paul seemed to pick up on Denny's disappointment. "Hey, Denny, Billy was too excited to notice, but there's an extra ticket in there for whoever he wants to take." His eyes twinkled a summer-sky blue and he gave Denny a wink. Suddenly Denny forgot all about the X-wing Fighter himself. He was thinking more about a Lou Piniella-Carlton Fisk rematch.

A few of Billy's aunts and uncles from out of state called, and while Billy was on the phone Denny talked with Greymore. It was strange; no matter how nice and friendly Greymore was, Denny would occasionally feel the unmistakable twinge of fear pulling at his gut. Greymore would sometimes get a look in his eyes that made all of the horror stories told about him seem very possible. In his heart, Denny had already decided none of it was true. But those eyes, when Greymore spoke about prison or being a kid...

They talked for a long time about Paul's workout ritual in prison and the changes it brought to his physical and mental strength. Denny was tired of his role of the 98-pound weakling. He had no father or big brother to help him at home and was bullied constantly at school. Mr. Donnelly, the school's "cool" Spanish teacher, once told him he had "a very punchable face" and that's why he was picked on. With a set of the rippling muscles like the ones Denny noticed stretching Paul's shirt, things might just change. It made Denny think of the set of dumbbells collecting dust in his brother's old room.

Feeling more comfortable with Greymore, Denny began telling the story of how he and Billy had found the burned out buildings from the old army base and from there the caves. He went into great detail about the location of the cave entrance, how Billy had found it chasing a snake, and how they had marked it with a sock. He was about to get to what he considered "the good part" of his story—what they had found inside the caves—when his thoughts were interrupted by the unmistakable growl of a glasspack muffler. Denny knew immediately that muffler was attached to Dale Crawford's Mustang.

Dale burst through the gate and strutted into the yard like the party was in his honor. Julie must have warned him that the usual beep or revving of the engine wasn't going to cut it to get her out of Billy's party. He whipped off his mirrored sunglasses, probably hand-me-downs from his dad, Paul thought, and grabbed Julie. He kissed her hard then started heading back toward the gate with her in a half-hug, half-head-lock. He hadn't said a word to anyone, hadn't even acknowledged anyone else was there. Julie wriggled free and tried to push him away. Dale gripped her by the upper arm and started dragging her toward the gate. Joe was over there in a blur, calmly putting his hand on Dale's chest while saying something to him. Dale looked down at the hand, looked back at Joe, then pushed the hand away and took a step closer to Joe. Greymore stood quickly and took a step in their direction. Dale saw the movement and gave Greymore an ugly look, then said something to Joe, put his sunglasses back on, and stormed out of the yard. Joe turned to Julie and put his hands on her shoulders. Incredibly, she shrugged him off and went after Dale. A minute later the Mustang roared to life and the scene was over in a screech of burning rubber. Billy's mom watched the entire scene with a look of painful sadness and burning anger. Denny watched her and thought there might just be a hint of understanding in that expression.

Joe stood for a moment with his head down, then walked back to the party. "Teenagers" he said with a smile, but the hurt was clear in his eyes, and things began breaking up shortly after. Denny and Paul helped Joe and Billy carry the presents inside, then said their goodbyes and headed up the hill together. "Did you really mess up Dale's face, Paul?"

Paul hesitated for a minute before answering. "Sometimes you're forced into a situation and you have to do what's right. For some reason, with me, it always comes down to violence. Joe and I met as kids and became friends as a result of a fight, it was part of life in prison, and it continued the minute I arrived back in Haven. The answer is yes, I messed him up. I probably shouldn't have done it, but at the same time he's lucky that's all I did." He said it with such a tired, resigned voice it sent a chill through Denny despite the summer-like heat. They were walking in the shadows and the lighting made Greymore's scars more prominent. He had that faraway look in his eyes and once again Denny thought about some of the Butcher stories. Is that what was going through Greymore's mind?

Paul snapped back to the present and sensed Denny's uneasiness. "They were giving me a hard time at the gas station. That I could live with. Then one of them insulted Father McCarthy, intimidated him. I could tell Crawford was the leader so I went after him. Another valuable lesson I learned in prison I guess." He chuckled to himself but it came out like a bark. "Anyway, it was over pretty quick. I'm sure the way it's being told makes me look like the crazy, deformed child-killer back to his old tricks."

Anguish. It was the only word Denny knew to describe the depth of sadness in Paul's voice. He never really understood the meaning of the word, the depths of emotion it signified until that moment. He would never forget it now. "Actually, that's exactly how it's being told. I figured you'd be ten feet tall and carrying an axe in one hand and someone's head in the other." It was out before he even knew he was going to say it. Paul stopped walking and looked at Denny for a second, then burst out laughing. Denny couldn't help but join in. Greymore actually doubled over, unable to control his laughter, and Denny had tears running down his face before he got a hold of himself.

"Thank you, Denny. I haven't laughed like that in...well I don't know if I've ever laughed that hard!" They had reached Greymore's house and Paul held his hand out to Denny. While they shook, Paul tightened his grip for a moment. "It's been a pleasure to meet you, Denny. I hope we see more of each other."

"Well I only live a few houses up...I'm sure we will. I'm back and forth to Billy's all the time."

"Great, see you later, neighbor."

As he headed up his walk, Denny heard him whisper "axe in one hand and head in the other" and begin laughing again. Smiling himself, Denny headed home.

(24)

DENNY PORED over the faded pages of the book as most kids his age would have studied a comic book or a *Playboy* smuggled from their big brother's room. He jotted a few notes in his spiral notebook then glanced at the lengthening shadows outside. The librarian gave him an impatient look as he returned attention to the book. *She can wait a few minutes to close up tonight*, he thought. The book was a collection of essays written by local writers compiled in 1939. The librarian had told Denny in a very condescending tone that the book was considered rare, that's why it was in the Research Room and could not be checked out. And that is why Denny was furiously copying passages from it.

Talking with Paul at Billy's birthday, almost getting to tell him about the caves, reminded Denny he had research to do, but the library was closed on Sunday and Monday for Memorial Day. Denny had gone to church on Sunday as planned and realized how much he had missed the Sunday masses. He looked forward to following through with the plan he and Father McCarthy had laid out over the coming weeks.

The day at school had dragged, Denny had spent it lost in thoughts of solving the mystery he and Billy had stumbled upon. The book he was riveted to now he had originally grabbed in hopes of finding some information about the caves in the area, but one essay proved far more intriguing. It was written in 1931 by a local farmer/

writer named Jacob Whiting. Apparently Whiting's entire family, along with much of Haven's population was wiped out by a plague that swept the area in the summer of 1927. Young Jacob had heard talk after the plague died out and did some investigating. What he found at first was no secret concerning the origin of Haven.

The town was founded by a group of suspected witches who fled Salem during the trials to avoid prosecution and possible execution. Hence the name "Haven." The town grew, families moving in from all around who knew nothing of the town's history. With that growth came the inevitable: politics. The town leaders were all descendants of the original founders. When another group opposed them to gain control of the town, they simply let it slip to the unsuspecting towns-people that there were Salem witches running the town. A lynch mob of angry townsfolk remedied the problem by hanging several of the town elders for witchcraft. Before their demise one of the "witches" allegedly put a curse on the town, condemning it to "suffer great tragedies every cycle until an acceptable sacrifice was made."

Whiting went on to discuss some of his further research which he claimed supported the curse. Working backwards from his family's deaths in 1927, he was able to find examples of the curse's tragedies roughly every 17 years (apparently a "cycle" or generation back in Puritan times was 17 years). There was a major drought in 1910 which caused a bad crop and left many people to starve in the bitter winter that followed. In 1893 a hurricane devastated Haven while leaving surrounding towns untouched. Whiting stated that records became hard to obtain any further back but the pattern was clear— every 17 years Haven would suffer a radically high death rate.

Denny made a few more notes before closing the book, and then thought about Whiting's claims. He realized almost immediately that, coincidence or not, the pattern had continued. The fatal explosion at the ammunition facility occurred in the summer of 1944. Denny already knew that the child killings kept the pattern going in 1961. That would mean this year would be another one.

The realization left Denny feeling suddenly cold. The usual comfortable library smell that he loved was now choking him. He had to get out of here and tell someone, but who? As he gathered his notes together his anxiety grew. By the time he had returned all the books and newspapers to their proper shelves, he was sure he was being watched. He could feel eyes burning into his back. He turned quickly to the window and for a moment he thought he saw the pale, white glow of a face disappear to the side but it was getting so dark he couldn't be sure.

He stepped out into the diminishing twilight, the heavy door slamming behind him. It was still hot and sticky. Dark clouds sailed across the sky, threatening to break the dry spell. *Thunderclouds*, Denny thought. He walked quickly down the tree-lined path from the library and turned on to Elm Street. And suddenly he was surrounded.

"Hey, smart boy. Getting an early start on your summer reading list?" Dale Crawford's remark was met with snickers from his gang. The usual suspects. Chuck Brantley, a thin, bookish kid who looked out of place running with Crawford. Buddy Dentner was blessed with the same athletic genetics as Crawford but he worked at it, religiously lifting weights and jogging to stay in perfect ass-kicking shape. Tony Costa was chubby and slow and dimwitted, but there was strength in numbers. The four tightened the circle around Denny. He thought it was best not to answer and maybe he could get out of this alive. His eyes were drawn to the scar on Dale's cheek and he had to suppress a grin, knowing that Paul had put it there. They closed in on him slowly. "Shouldn't you be home at this hour, Denny? Mommy might worry. Might think the Butcher got you."

Denny backed up until he felt the bushes that lined the library grounds pressing into his back. He glanced quickly up and down Elm Street but there was not a car coming in either direction. As far as Denny could see the street was deserted. "But that freak won't get you, will he? No, I saw you and your pussy boyfriend Billy hanging out with him." With that Dale put a big hand on Denny's chest and sent him reeling back into the hedges. Denny ended up tangled in the bushes, his feet awkwardly sticking out in front of Dale. He looked up and in the fading light saw something in Crawford's eyes. His stomach clenched and he suddenly felt that this wasn't going to be just a run-of-the-mill Dale Crawford Beating. Suddenly terrified, he shot his foot out with all his might and kicked Crawford squarely in the balls. Crawford's eyes bulged almost comically with pain and shock and he uttered a breathless groan before crumbling to his knees. Denny quickly rolled over backwards through the hedge and leaped to his feet on the other side, still clutching his notebook. He heard Dale yelling weakly as he sped across the library lawn. He immediately noticed the lights were out inside. He had left just before they closed. The librarian might still be in there but by the time she got to the door Crawford would have dragged him away. He heard them crashing through the bushes behind him and yelling for him. He dodged trees and picnic benches and darted around the side of the library as distant thunder rumbled above him. Sweat rolled down his face, partly from the heat of the night, mostly from fear. He crashed through the hedge at the far side of the lawn and stumbled to the ground on the sidewalk of Cedar Street. He scrambled to his feet. If he could get over to Stadium Road there'd surely be one of the beer-league softball games breaking up or some people walking their dogs. Before the thought could turn to action he was hit from behind.

The tackler pinned his arms to his sides so the full force of Denny's landing was absorbed by his chin on the cement. Lightning bolts erupted in his head and the slick coppery taste of blood quickly filled his mouth from where he bit through his lip. He was roughly turned over and felt knees pressing into his shoulders as his mind swam. He tried to squirm free but he was too dazed and Buddy outweighed him by a good twenty-five pounds. Buddy was the best athlete in Crawford's gang; he must have run on the sidewalk along the hedges while the others followed Denny across the lawn. He heard the others make their way through the bushes and their shadows engulfed him as they towered above him.

"You little shit! You're gonna pay for that in a bad way." Buddy hissed. Then Dale arrived, walking rather stiffly.

"Hold him good, boys. Watch those legs." Dale knelt down beside Denny, near his head. "Wouldn't have got very far in football if you let yourself get taken down like that in the open field,

O'Brien. Your brother would have broken it. Now let's get down to business. You see this?" He leaned closer so Denny could see what he was pointing at. It was the scar on his cheek. "That's from the deformed maniac that you and your little faggot friend are buddies with. Jumped me from behind, the crazy freak did. I gotta get a message to him." Denny heard a click and suddenly Dale was holding a knife in Denny's face. Denny squirmed frantically and tried to kick but the others held him tight. The blade inched closer to his face and he could almost feel heat coming from it. Like it was an extension of Dale, of his rage. A brilliant flash of heat lightning momentarily silhouetted Crawford, making him appear demonic. Then the blade touched skin and it was no longer hot but icy cold. Denny was motionless as the blade etched a groove in his cheek.

"Dale, what the heck. Are you crazy?" Chuck Brantley cried. "I thought we were just gonna scare him, beat him up a little?" Denny felt on the brink of hysteria, certain Dale was going to kill him.

"Shut up, Brantley or I might do you next." Brantley shut up. "Now we match, fuckface. You show this to the freak. You tell him who did it. Got it?"

Denny was numb, unable to respond. Dale grabbed his hair and nodded his head for him, sending streams of hot blood in different directions up and down his face. "Yes, Dale, whatever you say." The others chuckled dutifully, though more hesitant than before. Denny closed his eyes and when he opened them they were gone. Above him a few stars twinkled as the clouds began to break.

(25)

"AND THE others held you down while Dale did this to you?" Denny nodded. He reached up to touch the wound on his face but the priest grabbed his hand and gently put it down. "We just got it cleaned and the bleeding stopped. If you touch it you're liable to open it up again."

Denny had not known what to do when he sat up and felt the hot blood streaming down his face. He bunched up his shirt against the cut, scrambled to find his notebook, and ran. He ended up at Father McCarthy's doorstep. He had only wanted someone to help him, maybe drive him home, but McCarthy had managed to coax the whole story out of him, including Dale's threats toward Greymore. The priest had immediately called Greymore to warn him in case Crawford decided to follow through on his threats tonight. Greymore was on his way over to McCarthy's now, more to avoid any situation that would send him back to Braxton than out of any fear of Crawford and his gang.

Denny felt uncomfortable now that he had calmed down. He looked around the priest's humble home and began to reshape his opinions. He had always assumed priests spent all their spare time praying around candle-lit altars and blessing rosary beads or something. To see McCarthy's walls lined with regular books instead of bibles made him seem human to Denny. He got up and went over to the shelves, his love for books overtaking his shyness. He was surprised to see the diversity of the titles. "Excuse me, Father, but I didn't think you could read about this stuff."

McCarthy laughed, "My superiors don't understand it or approve of it but they cannot forbid it. Are you interested in mysteries, Denny?"

"I really love to read all sorts of books, but mysteries are my favorites. Especially when they're really scary and have monsters in them." He suddenly remembered he was talking to a priest and shut up, feeling his face redden.

"Those are my favorites, too. I have several you might want to borrow. These over here," he pointed to an entire row, "are real life mysteries, or so they say. The Loch Ness Monster, Bigfoot, UFOs, that sort of thing." Denny looked over the collection and onto the next shelf where his eyes fell on a thin, worn volume. It was the same one he had read in the library earlier that night.

"Have you read this one, Father?" he asked.

"No, that shelf is for books I haven't found time for yet. That particular book just arrived last week. It's very rare." Denny was about to mention the article about Haven when someone knocked loudly at the door. Denny jumped and his eyes widened. "Relax, Denny, it's only Paul." The priest opened the door and Greymore stepped in.

"Hi, Denny, how..." his words trailed off when he saw the fresh cut on Denny's face, his scraped chin and swollen lip. He quickly moved toward Denny to examine the wound. Denny watched his eyes change from a deep sky-blue to a blue-green that churned like the winter ocean, finally hardening to a cold ice-blue as he inspected Crawford's handiwork. "This is my fault, Denny. I'm so sorry this happened. I'm going to have it out with the Crawfords once and for all!" He turned and strode toward the door. There he was met by McCarthy.

"You'll do no such thing, Paul, unless you have hopes of returning to Braxton before the week's end!" The old priest put a hand on Greymore's chest and to Denny he seemed to grow larger. "Just settle down until we figure out what to do."

HAVEN

Denny watched as the two locked eyes for what seemed like a very long time. Greymore's filled with fury and vengeance, McCarthy's with righteousness and concern; both gleaming with power. Finally, Greymore lowered his gaze and slumped into the chair next to Denny. His eyes had changed again; this time Denny saw a more profound emotion than before in them, the same anguish he had seen in them on the day of Billy's party. Greymore put his head in his hands and closed his eyes. Denny was relieved because the gut-wrenching pain he had seen in them was too much to bear yet impossible to turn away from.

It was McCarthy who finally spoke. "We need to stay calm and rational. We can't let our emotions get in the way of clear thinking."

"But, Father, look at what they did to him. Because of me." He looked to Denny like he might cry. "We can't go to the police for obvious reasons. What can we do?"

"We'll think of something, Paul. First, we need to get Denny squared away." McCarthy turned to him. "I don't think you'll need stitches but it might not hurt to have a doctor tell you that."

Denny suddenly felt like someone let the air out of him. The events of the evening were taking their toll on him. His adrenaline rush was gone, replaced by a bone-deep exhaustion. He heard Father McCarthy talking to him but he had trouble concentrating on the meaning of the words.

Suddenly McCarthy was shaking him awake. "...alright, Denny? Are you alright?"

"I'm fine. What's the matter?"

McCarthy looked relieved. "I thought you might have a concussion the way you went to sleep so quickly. Did they hit you on the head at all? Maybe when that boy tackled you?"

"No, nothing like that, Father. I just got tired all of a sudden. Too much excitement, I guess." He started to say something else but his mouth wouldn't let the words out. Through the haze of sleep he heard Greymore call the Cummings and have Joe call his mother to say he was sleeping there. Then he felt himself being carried by two strong arms that he knew didn't belong to Father McCarthy. He forced his heavy lids open and looked at Greymore's face. Up close the scars were worse. The skin looked like melting wax. But it was the eyes that captivated Denny again. They had softened to a blue the color of a pair of faded jeans. In them Denny saw a look that he couldn't recognize. He knew he had seen it before and he struggled with the seduction of sleep to identify it. As Greymore gently placed him down on McCarthy's bed and covered him up, Denny drifted off. He dreamed of his father carrying him to bed after he had fallen asleep watching television.

OFFICER ROBERT Ortiz took the call Wednesday afternoon and instinctively made the sign of the cross when he hung up. The entire town had been on the edge since Paul Greymore's return but this was going to raise all kinds of hell. A boy was missing.

Mike Noonan was supposed to be home immediately after school to go to the hospital to visit his grandmother. When he did not show up his mother began calling his friends and discovered he had not been in school that day. That was when she called the police. Ortiz went directly to Chief Crawford's office and knocked quietly. He knew the Chief would go after Greymore once he heard the news.

Ortiz, only a child himself at the time of the killings in '61, had done quite a bit of research when Greymore's release became imminent. Frankly, he was not convinced Greymore was guilty. There were too many holes in the story. Ortiz considered Crawford the kind of guy who would convict a man because of his looks, just as he judged Ortiz because of his ethnicity. He entered the office and sat down opposite Crawford.

"What's up, Ortiz?" Crawford mumbled without looking up from the file he was reading. Greymore's file, no doubt. The man was obsessed with the case.

"We just got a call from a Mrs. Joyce Noonan from over on Stadium Road."

"I know her. So? What's her problem?"

"Her son Mike is missing. Has been since he left for school this morning." Crawford's head jerked up from the file and he stared hard at Ortiz for a moment. "I thought you might want to handle this one yourself."

Crawford quickly closed the file and stood up. "You go get the report from Mrs. Noonan; I'm going to bring in Greymore."

"Shouldn't we wait until...?"

"Go get the report, Ortiz."

Ortiz opened his mouth to argue but the look in Crawford's eyes made him swallow his retort.

"Yes, sir."

Crawford watched Ortiz go, then collapsed back into his chair. He knew what he had to do, what was *expected* of him, but he needed a little help. On top of the papers from Greymore's file that were strewn across his desk was a photo of the final victim from the '61 murders, Mary Larsen. This was no grisly crime-scene photo, however, but a glossy third-grade school picture used in the newspapers following her death. She was a beautiful little girl; her smile seemed brighter than the rest of the faded photo, leaping from it. Her radiant blue eyes held Crawford's gaze. To him, they weren't smiling but accusing. *Why didn't you get there sooner? Why didn't you save me?* The only answer Crawford had was in a flask in his top drawer, and he reached for it then; it was the help he needed.

He had been the one to find the missing Larsen girl and finally put the pieces together that led to Greymore's conviction. How many times had he replayed that day in his mind? How close had he come to being in time to save the girl? It haunted him. Shit, he thought, is there any man alive that this *wouldn't* haunt? But there was another voice that fought to be heard from its sealed-off room in his mind. Somehow, it managed to escape its prison and poke at Crawford.

What if you had saved her, Chief? What stories would she have told? Would she have damned Greymore, or would she have led everything to a different ending? And just what were those marks on her and Greymore, Chief? Would they have been a part of the story? Yes, I think they would have been a big part of it.

Crawford knew of only one way to silence the voice. He closed his eyes and took a long drink from the flask. The liquor burned his throat and stomach, but sent the voice back to its room, slammed the door on it and slid the deadbolt into place. It would get out again. It always did.

But I didn't get there in time, he thought.

And the rest, as they say, is history. Crawford was the hero, Greymore the psycho, and Haven was safe. His career took off and here he was, the great Chief Crawford. He pulled another newspaper photo out of the pile, this one of himself. He was shaking hands with the Attorney General outside the courthouse on the day of Greymore's conviction. He was in uniform, the short-sleeve shirt clinging to his muscular frame. His eyes were clear and determined, his face serious above his square jaw. Here he was, indeed. But just how did he get from *that*...to this? Everything in between seemed to be a blur, half a lifetime in a fleeting blink. He shook his head. Shit! How long had he been sitting here? He took another greedy gulp from the flask, threw it back in the drawer, and headed back to the scene of the crime.

OFFICER ORTIZ left the office and drove out to Stadium Road. The scene he found there sent a chill down his spine. There was a group of men gathered in front of the Noonan home, apparently forming a lynch mob. As soon as Ortiz pulled up, they gathered around his car. Ortiz stepped out and was greeted with angry shouts. *Good Lord*, he thought, *all they need are torches and pitchforks*. He raised his arms and gestured for the crowd to quiet down. "What's going on here, folks?"

A giant red-faced man stepped forward. "We're going out to do what should have been done seventeen years ago."

Ortiz tried to remain calm. He was 5'8" and weighed in at 160 pounds soaking wet. Not exactly the imposing figure necessary to quiet down a mob. He spoke with authority he didn't feel, "I don't know exactly what you mean by that but I'm sure you folks aren't thinking of doing anything stupid like taking the law into your own hands, right?"

The red-faced man stepped closer to Ortiz and leaned forward, looking down at him. "The law is the law and justice is justice; sometimes that don't mean the same thing."

Ortiz moved his hand toward his holster. "I'm not going to play games with any of you. We have a report of a missing child that I'm here to follow up on. If you want to be of any assistance, form a search party. Obstruction of justice is a serious offense." His gaze never wavered from the larger man's.

This seemed to make sense to some of the crowd and they began talking among themselves.

Red-face spoke again. "You damn well better follow up, Officer; we will not have our children disappearing again."

Ortiz met his stare, and then turned to the crowd. "Begin forming groups of four. I need to get a statement from Mrs. Noonan and then I'll assign territories to each group." He brushed past red-face and went to the Noonan residence. Joyce Noonan was upset but holding herself together. Her husband was on his way home from work and from what Ortiz could gather, theirs was a stable home, no reason to think the boy ran away on his own. He took the necessary information as quickly as possible, eager to get back outside and make sure there would be no riots. Red-face was gone, probably on his way to Greymore's. Ortiz called Crawford on the radio and told him to expect trouble, then began organizing the men into a search party. "We don't have a lot of daylight to work with so we're going to have to move fast." He ended up with six groups of four and quickly instructed them where to go and what to look for. "If you find anything, *anything* at all that looks suspicious call the station immediately and an officer will meet you. Otherwise send the lead man from the group to the station at six o'clock. Nobody out past six, understand? I'll be coordinating from the station and try to arrange dogs and a helicopter. Good luck."

Ortiz watched the men split up and head out in search of the missing boy. He had hand-picked one group from the men he knew and sent them out to search the woods around the lake. At least this would cut down on the likelihood of any trouble out there. Crawford probably would have dragged Greymore in before anyone got out there anyway. This was bad. He jumped in his cruiser and headed back to the station. When he got there he would work on getting bloodhounds out and a chopper at first light. On a sudden impulse, he pulled over at the first pay phone he saw and made a call that had nothing at all to do with choppers or dogs.

(28)

PAUL GREYMORE thrust the shovel into the dry earth, and then jumped with both feet onto the spade. Turning over the soil in his yard was going to be no easy chore. The dirt had hardened to a crusty clay-like substance from the relentless heat of the sun. *At least it will be some exercise*, Paul thought as he moved to drive the shovel into the ground again. He had stripped to the waist, the ungodly heat overpowering his inhibitions about his scars. If they can stand my face then they can sure as hell stand the rest of me. Muscles rippled as he turned over another shovelful of sunbaked earth. His skin was beginning to cook as well, highlighting the whiteness of the scars that covered him. As he bent to pull a rock out of the last heap of dirt, he heard the car pull into the driveway.

His first thought was that it was Father McCarthy but when he turned he saw an older model pick-up truck shaking to a stop. The second thing Paul noticed about the man was how red his face was. The first thing was his size. The man was easily taller than him, probably six-three or six-four. He had broad shoulders and big, beefy arms, and he was approaching with a look that told Paul he wasn't with the Haven Welcoming Committee. Paul tensed and positioned himself in case there was trouble. "Hi, what can I do...?"

The man's anvil-like fist stopped him in mid-sentence. He was able to react quickly enough so that the blow only glanced the top of his head as he ducked. In the same motion he brought his fist up squarely into the larger man's gut. He heard the *whoosh* as the air emptied from the man's lungs. The man was still able to get a meaty hand on Paul's throat as he gasped to refill his lungs. Paul chopped at the wrist that held his throat but was unable to break the grip. The man's hand was like a vise. He had recovered enough to grasp Paul's neck with his other hand as well. The world began to fade as the man tightened his grip. Paul was able to pry one of the man's rigid fingers from his throat and he gave it a twist that pulled it from its socket. The man winced but did not relinquish his grip. Black spots began to dance in front of Paul's eyes in a ballet that only he could see. As his focus began to narrow, he shot out his leg with a quick snap-kick. There was a horrible crunch, like that of a good-sized tree branch snapping as Paul's kick landed on the man's knee, bending it back in a way that God did not intend. The man went down in a heap, finally letting go of Paul's throat. Paul stumbled backwards and landed in the dusty soil he had been turning over. As he struggled to stay conscious and replenish his oxygen-starved brain, another car pulled into the driveway.

At first Paul feared it was others like this big guy coming to finish the job. But it was worse. Chief Crawford ambled slowly up the driveway, gun in hand. Paul glanced at the big man on the ground. He had been trying to crawl toward Paul, his leg flapping uselessly behind him, but had stopped. He was now leaning down on his elbows immobile, an expression of immeasurable pain on his ashen face. Crawford sauntered over until he stood directly in front of Paul. The expression on his face was an open book to Paul. He was going to kill him right here. Either blame it on the big guy or take the credit himself, saying Paul was going to kill the other man. "Larsen, look what you gone and done, you killed the Butcher." Crawford never took his eyes from Greymore as he spoke.

Larsen. The name seemed familiar to Paul.

The man's expression changed from one of horrific pain to one of horrific pain and confusion. "Cody, what are you..."

Crawford moved slowly and picked up Greymore's shovel, never taking his eyes or his gun off of Paul. "Yep, saw the whole thing as

I was driving up. Saw him swing the shovel at you," with a quick movement Crawford swept the shovel in an arc that landed squarely on the side of Larsen's face, "you had no choice but to shoot him 'fore he finished you off."

Greymore was too stunned to react. Larsen had dropped flat and rolled over onto his back holding his broken face. Crawford reached down and withdrew a small pistol from under his pant leg. Greymore had heard other inmates telling stories about cops who carried such guns. Unregistered weapons cops could use at their discretion when they needed some physical evidence. Throwaways or throwdowns or something, they called them. If you listened to the inmates every one of them was wrongly accused of their crime by a cop who planted such a weapon on them.

Crawford dropped the pistol on Larsen's chest. "For what he did to little Mary," he muttered.

Greymore remained motionless. His choices weren't very good; charge Crawford and probably get shot or wait for Larsen to shoot him. *Mary Larsen.* She was the one Greymore had tried to save that day on the lake. This must be an older brother. "Crawford, I was trying to save her, you prick. Tell him how you found me carrying her out of the lake. *Tell him the truth.*"

Paul watched Larsen as he stared at the gun on his chest through one good eye and one swollen one. Paul could see the hatred in them, burning like a torch for seventeen years. But he could see something flicker behind the rage: doubt. Even a man burdened with the loathing Larsen held for Greymore would have a hard time shooting an unarmed man while the Chief of Police watched. Hatred is one baggage that can be carried quite easily for seventeen years but the thirst for vengeance is more passionate and short-lived. Or so Paul hoped.

"Do it now Larsen, or by God I'll beat in your skull with the fucking shovel and shoot him myself!"

Paul watched both men. The wrong word, *any* word, would most likely get him a bullet in the chest. Larsen took his eyes off the gun and stared hard at Greymore for a long time. He squinted, an expression of confusion seeming to take over his face. Then he turned and met Crawford's gaze. Larsen winced and with a look of resignation closed his fingers around the handle of the gun. Paul tensed, ready to lunge at the big man. Then Larsen tossed the weapon in the crusty dirt at Crawford's feet. "Do it yourself. Killing is what I came here for but not like this."

Crawford's face twisted in rage as he raised the shovel. The blaring of a car horn stopped him in mid-swing as Father McCarthy's sedan screeched to an abrupt halt in front of Greymore's house.

The old priest leaped out of the car with the agility of a man thirty years younger and marched over to the three men. "What in the name of God is going on here, Chief?"

Crawford stood there with the shovel poised over his head and his gun pointed at Greymore. His expression was an ugly mixture of a cornered rat and a snared rabbit.

"Got an extra bullet for the priest?" Larsen sneered. Crawford grunted with disgust and threw the shovel across the yard.

"You're under arrest, Butcher, we got a missing kid. Quite a coincidence, wouldn't you say, Father?"

Paul froze when he heard Crawford's statement. Could it be true or was Crawford just using it as a way of getting Greymore alone to finish what he had started here? His eyes met McCarthy's and he was relieved not to see the same look he had seen at the gas station on his first day back. He stood stunned as Crawford grabbed him roughly and handcuffed him.

"I'll meet you at the police station, Paul, after I see to an ambulance for Larsen."

Paul nodded at the priest as he was led away by Crawford.

PAUL GREYMORE sat huddled in the corner of the 10 x 10 cell shivering in the rancid hot-box. The bars seemed to be closing in on him. His stomach felt like it was twisting around itself, threatening to add to the stench of vomit that already hung heavy in the air around him. He knew the feeling would pass, it always did. Other prisoners talked of the feeling. It was really just a type of anxiety attack, Paul had discovered when doing some reading. Just an excess of adrenaline in the bloodstream. Sounded logical enough when he read about it, but when it actually happened, logic took the express train out and he was sure he was either dying or going crazy. He pulled his knees up tighter to his chest and felt, no, *listened* to his heart beat. Fight or flight they called it. He could do neither.

The ride to the station had gone as expected. Crawford spent the entire ride telling Greymore what a sick piece of shit he was and how this time he would never see the outside of Braxton's walls again. Paul had sat silent, staring at the scenery outside the cruiser's windows. The free, unobstructed scenery. His silence had only added to Crawford's opinion that he was a psycho and sent him on another tirade. Paul had tuned him out completely by then.

It was the arrival at the police station that had caused Paul's panic. It was a mob-scene; the street was full of frantic Haven residents. Paul was reminded of the old Creature Feature movies where villagers would storm the castle to kill the monster.

Crawford had to slow the police car down to a crawl as the sea of people parted before it. They were screaming, banging on the car, even spitting on it, while Crawford continually threatened to stop the car and let them have him. He could hear them yanking on the door handles. The pounding on the windows was so violent Paul was sure the glass would give. The looks on the faces of the people was the worst part of it. Pure hatred, sheer malice.

When the car finally pulled up near the station, they had to wait for other officers to come out to help get Greymore inside safely. Even with the protection of several officers pushing the crowd back, Paul was jostled around, grabbed at and spit on. Once, a strong hand had gotten hold of Paul's shirt and pulled him toward the crowd. Before the police were able to break the man's grip and push the crowd away, Paul had taken several punches and a woman had opened a claw-like gash on his cheek. During the entire time, shouts and screams of "freak" and "child-killer" and "pervert" mixed with the angry death threats. If the mob had gotten to him, Greymore was sure they would have torn him apart.

Now he sat, his panic ebbing away like the tide. He was beginning to become more aware of his surroundings, the stink of piss, the angry shouts still coming from outside, the pain in his swollen throat. He had no idea how long he had been there. He stood up and stretched, his heart no longer trying to beat out of his chest. There was no window to the outside and the bars faced a wall that prevented him from seeing anything going on in the station.

He had declined his phone call knowing that Father McCarthy was on the way. The only other person he would have considered calling was Joe but he didn't want to involve him. He knew their friendship had already caused Joe enough problems.

When the old priest was led into the cell Paul sat quietly, waiting for him to speak first. "I know you didn't do it, Paul", McCarthy almost yelled as if reading Paul's mind and trying to cast out the doubt and fear that hid there. Paul almost smiled.

"What will it take for you to believe I did do it?"

"I know you, Paul. You are no more a child killer than I."

Paul kept his gaze focused straight ahead as he spoke, concentrating on the words "HELP ME" that were carved into the wall of the cell. "What if I am?" he said finally.

"What are you saying, Paul? You're being irrational."

"Think about it, Father, there hasn't been anything more than an occasional bar room brawl or domestic dispute in seventeen years, right? Within weeks of my return Haven is rocked by the disappearance of another of its children. My limited knowledge of statistics tells me this is no coincidence."

"Then there must be something more than a coincidence going on here, Paul. I take it as a personal insult that you think I spent all those years visiting you, befriending you, in vain. I have more faith in my judgment than you do, apparently."

Paul sat silent, idly wondering what tool had been used to carve into the concrete wall as he tried to form his thoughts into words. "What if I don't know what I'm doing, like a split personality or blackouts? Something like that." Paul finally raised his eye to meet McCarthy's and was surprised to see the man smiling.

"Stop doing this to yourself, Paul. Are you forgetting the airtight alibis you had for some of the '61 disappearances? How does this theory explain that piece of the puzzle?" Paul was beginning to feel stupid. And confused. For a while he had actually been listening to that little voice that was screaming in his head. *What if you really are the Butcher?* A voice that sounded an awful lot like Chief Crawford. "I'm not the only one trying to help you, Paul."

Greymore stared at the priest. "I know, Joe has been great..."

"I'm not talking about Joe." McCarthy looked around and then moved closer to Paul. "Do you think it was just a coincidence that I arrived at your house when I did?"

Paul opened his mouth to speak, but realized he had no answer.

In a barely audible whisper, McCarthy told Paul of the strange phone call he received, telling him to get to Greymore's house. "I didn't know the voice, but whoever it was may have saved your life."

Greymore was puzzled. Other than Joe Cummings and McCarthy, he was sure everyone in Haven wanted him dead or back in Braxton.

"Have you ever considered another possibility, Paul? Perhaps almost as crazy as the rest of your ideas, but then again..."

Paul frowned, unable to grasp where the priest was going with this. "But what else..."

"Maybe you're being framed," whispered McCarthy. "Maybe they couldn't catch the real killer in '61 but when they found you at the lake with the girl in your arms, the case was solved. Maybe the real killer knew when he had it made and just moved on."

"That doesn't explain the present." Paul muttered, his mind frantically calculating what the priest was suggesting.

"This is true, but what of the present? Kids run away all the time. Maybe the original killer is obsessive enough to follow you back here. Maybe there is a copy-cat killer." He paused, and then lowered his voice. "Or maybe there is a reputation at stake."

Paul raised his eyebrows in disbelief. "Are you accusing..."

"Shh, Shh. Enough for now, Paul. I'm merely presenting alternatives. You're not the only one who has thought about this for seventeen years."

"Obviously not," Paul laughed. But his mind was racing, rewinding seventeen years—recalling the hatred he had felt at the trial—back to the present when only a few hours ago his very life had been threatened. Could Cody Crawford hold such a vendetta?

(30)

MOLLY SHEEHAN jogged quickly to her car, keys jangling in the quiet dusk. She glanced nervously toward the lake. She couldn't see the twins, but she could hear them laughing and hear Lobo barking excitedly. They're almost ten years old, she told herself, and they are both strong swimmers. Besides, they won't go in the water until I get back, just like I told them. She had parked the old Country Squire on the shoulder of East Border Road. It wasn't legal, but it gave her quick access to the lake, and they wouldn't be here long. A few cars went by, but it wasn't really busy. She thought again of the boys and the lake—it was starting to get dark, and anything could happen.

Normally at this time of the evening, they'd all be sitting around after dinner to watch television together. But when Rich called and said he was stuck working a double, she'd had it. The heat was getting to all of them and she couldn't stand the thought of cooking dinner and trying to entertain the kids all night and get them to bed. So, she made sandwiches, packed a picnic dinner, and headed to the cool waters of the lake. That will tire them out, she thought, and they'll be asleep in the car on the way home.

What a dummy, she thought, leaving the cooler with the sandwiches and sodas in the back of the wagon. Instead of dragging them all to the car and back, she'd left the boys playing Frisbee with the dog down by the water. Damn! Of course the tailgate lock was stuck. As she fumbled with the key, jiggling it in the latch, she wondered how many times had she told Rich to fix this? Before she could get really worked up, the lock clicked. She grinned to herself and swung the back gate open. Suddenly a scream pierced the stillness and Lobo began barking. She couldn't stop the grin from spreading to a full-blown smile, thinking about what kind of silliness the boys were getting into. She'd be down there in a minute, laughing along with them.

Then another scream ripped through the dimming light, and Molly realized the boys weren't horsing around. Lobo's barks had turned into guttural howls and she could hear furious splashing. Oh my God, one of the boys is drowning! Molly ran like she'd never run before, slowing for a second when Lobo's howl turned to a yelp of pain, then nothing. Dread closed in on her like the night, and she flew to the water's edge.

Freddie stood frozen on the grass holding the Frisbee by his side and staring at the horror by the lake's sandy shore.

Eddie's body was literally in pieces. The autopsy would later show that his limbs had been torn off his body, not cut off. Molly acted quickly, knowing that if she could put the pieces back together, Eddie would be okay. *All the King's horses and all the King's men*, she thought, as she placed his arms by his torso. After she put his legs back where they belonged, she couldn't figure out why Eddie was still lying there. Just lying there like he was dead or something. Then she had it, his arms were switched! She put the right and left arms in the proper place. *All the King's horses and all the King's men.* Then she waited.

And that's how Officer Nelson would find them. Molly sitting on the ground by Eddie, fully expecting him to get up and finish the game of Frisbee. Lobo's head and front paws were sticking out of the water near Eddie's crudely reconstructed body. The rest of Lobo wasn't in the water; it wasn't anywhere. He would also find Freddie standing in the very same spot, still holding the Frisbee, his bathing suit sagging in the back filled with a load of his own shit. If Nelson hadn't been cruising East Border Road looking for kids drinking or parking in the usual spots and seen the wagon parked illegally with the back gate hanging open, they might have stayed that way all night.

(31)

MCCARTHY WASN"T allowed to stay and Paul wasn't allowed to leave. Crawford had seen to it that the judge would at least delay long enough to keep Paul overnight before setting bail. *If he even allows me out on bail*, Greymore suddenly thought. He shook his head, knowing this kind of thinking would only induce another panic attack. He tried to focus on what Father McCarthy had talked about. Another killer returning when he found out about Greymore. A copycat killer. The real killer long gone but Crawford perpetuating the Butcher story. As the evening wore on, these theories began to sound less and less crazy. Paul began to analyze the facts, after all, what else did he have to do? Most intriguing was the mysterious phone call that tipped off McCarthy. Who besides the priest and Joe could Greymore consider an ally? And who would know that Crawford was on his way...except another cop...

In any of the situations McCarthy had presented, there was a killer out there that had done all of the killings back in '61. Paul had been found with the body of one child in his own backyard. He had come from the lake in his canoe with her, that much he was sure. But what about prior to that? Where had he been? How had he gotten the girl away from the killer? And most disturbing of all, why couldn't he remember? From the front of the police station, none of which Paul could see from his cell, a flurry of activity was occurring. Doors were opening and closing, loud, urgent voices came in clips, and a moment later the screech of tires and wail of sirens.

Paul heard none of it. His eyes were closed tightly, childlike, as he concentrated on that day. The storm had been almost biblical. The rain was blinding it came down so hard. Over seven inches in a two-hour period he later heard. Lightning touched down all around. The almost continuous earth-shaking thunder. He breathed slowly, almost in a trance in his effort to remember. It hadn't rained all summer, literally. The storm had come from nowhere, unexpected, unpredicted. That was it, something about the storm itself held the key to the memory. The day had been the hottest of the hot. The temperature hovered near the one hundred mark, as did the humidity. It was unbearable. But what was it that made this so important?

Paul dozed fitfully while trying to summon the memory. When it finally came, it came as suddenly and powerfully as that storm so many years ago. He sat up straight in the bunk, disoriented by the memory and the unfamiliar surroundings. His eyes again found the desperate message carved into the cell wall. He was drenched in sweat and shaky. His heart pounded. He thought for a minute it was another panic attack when the events of the day in 1961 came back with a clarity that stunned him.

It had been the hottest day so far. No end in sight to either the heat or the drought. The weathermen had given their usual "chance of late afternoon thunderstorm" forecast, but that had become more of a hope than a prediction. Paul was out on his screened porch, hoping for the slightest breeze to come by, but the air was motionless. Heavy gray clouds loomed over the lake, but no more threatening than any others did that summer. He had already been in the lake for a dip. A momentary relief from the sweltering heat. He had showered, made a pitcher of lemonade, and parked on the porch. His parents were away visiting relatives and wouldn't be home until late that evening. As he sipped slowly, suddenly drowsy in the oppressive heat, a movement on the lake caught his eye. A rowboat floated on the glassy surface. Paul picked up a pair of binoculars he kept on the porch. It was a woman and a young girl, probably trying to escape the heat. As he drifted off he wondered if they were any cooler out there. He thought about taking his canoe out later as his eyes slipped shut.

HAVEN

A deafening clap of thunder jarred him from his brief sleep. He glanced at the clock, amazed that only thirty minutes had passed. The change in the weather seemed impossible. A cool wind was whistling through the screens. Black clouds rolled across the sky, so low it looked as if the sky was falling. A flash of lightning reached down into the trees. Paul heard the cracking of branches where it hit but that sound was quickly drowned out by another explosion of thunder. A movement on the lake caught Paul's attention. The mirror-like surface of a half-hour ago was now in turmoil. The wind whipped the lake into a frenzy of waves. Something touched Paul's memory and he grabbed his binoculars. The woman in the rowboat, now barely visible, was struggling in a futile effort against the surging water. The relentless wind, which seemed to be getting colder with each gust, was spinning the boat around like a toy. Then the rain began. Not as a sprinkle which would slowly turn into a heavier shower but as a torrential, drowning rain. Visibility quickly became a memory and as the skies darkened, Paul lost sight of the rowboat. Frantically he scanned back and forth over where the boat should be. A gust of wind sent a picture crashing to the floor behind him. In a dazzling flash of lightning, Paul was able to spot the boat again. In his brief glance it looked as if the woman had surrendered the oars in favor of huddling with the young girl who was probably scared to death. Paul kept the binoculars trained on the same spot as thunder shook the house. His hands ached from his grip, intent on not losing the right spot. When the lightning came again, it came in a blinding series of jolts, touching down all around the lake. In the sustained light from the multiple flashes, Paul was able to see the boat again. What he saw was burned into his mind. A dark shape was hanging over the bow of the boat, and as the light disappeared into a rattling quake of thunder, the boat flipped over.

Paul kept the glasses trained on the spot but as the lightning danced before him, he was unable to pick up the boat or its passengers again. He bolted into the house to call the police and threw the phone to the floor when there was no sound in the receiver. The lines must be down. Instinctively he grabbed his Buck knife from the *table and hooked it on his belt. Without another thought he sprinted outside; slipping across his yard, he quickly untied his canoe and leapt in, paddling furiously in the raging water.*

The howling wind and swirling water threatened to flip the canoe at any time but Paul was somehow able to keep it afloat. With every flash of lightning, the mental image of the rowboat flipping over, that strange dark shape hung across the bow, filled his mind. He kept his house in sight as he paddled, picturing the spot where he had last seen the rowboat. The cold wind bit at his rain-soaked body, but the effort of rowing was causing Paul to break into a sweat. His back and arms were already getting sore before he had even covered half of the distance. The thunder was constant, ranging from a low, threatening rumble to an earth-shaking crescendo. Jagged spears of lightning ripped across the black curtain of sky.

Paul stopped rowing and tried to scan the surface of the water using the binoculars, but visibility was next to nothing. He grabbed the oars and again began the seemingly futile task of rowing against the swelling lake. He turned occasionally to try to spot a couple of landmarks he had used to roughly triangulate where the rowboat had flipped. The looming hulk of the mental hospital on one side and a giant pine, a full twenty feet taller than others surrounding it, on the other side. Paul knew that even if he could spot these and stay on course, the chance of finding the boat or its occupants was slim. Nevertheless, he forged ahead, a sense of purpose driving him. Just as he was about to turn to get his bearings again, the canoe slammed to a halt, sending Paul rolling backwards. The back of his neck hit the front seat of the canoe hard, sending a shower of sparks into explosion behind his eyes. He quickly sat up, expecting the canoe to be torn to shreds by rocks. What he saw caused him to blink in surprise. It was the bottom of the rowboat that he had hit! The canoe was essentially run aground on top of it. Paul quickly began to search the water for the woman and the girl, his eyes darting frantically back and forth.

If it weren't for the bright orange of the life jacket, he never would have seen her. Twenty feet away floated the limp body of the little girl, held above water by the Day-Glo vest. Paul dove into the water without hesitation. He was a strong swimmer, having grown up on the lake, but the combination of the rolling waves and his aching arms and shoulders made even this short swim a struggle. He reached the girl, so intent on saving her that he no longer heard the sounds of the storm. Every part of him, every nerve and muscle, was focused on saving this girl. She was unconscious but he could feel a weak but regular pulse. Grabbing the front of her vest, he began kicking furiously back toward the canoe. Getting back was much worse. The canoe seemed to move further away with every stroke Paul took. The extra drag of the girl on his depleted muscles was agonizing. Finally, he reached the two boats.

He let the girl float for a moment as he clung to the half-sunk rowboat, trying to catch his breath. He still had to get her into the boat, find the mother, and row them all to shore without tipping over. It wasn't going to be easy. He hauled the girl up next to him and found he could easily roll her onto the bottom of the rowboat. From there, he climbed into the canoe and was able to bring her onboard while the canoe was still lodged against the rowboat. He laid her down in back with her head resting on another lifejacket. As he was about to push the canoe loose from the rowboat, a thought struck him. He dove back into the water, kicking down past the edge of the rowboat and coming up under it. There was not enough of an air pocket under it for Paul to resurface, but he began feeling his way around what was the floor of the small boat. As his lungs began to beg for air, his hand felt something and he grabbed it before swimming back to the surface. He burst from under the lake, gasping for air, feeling dizzy. In his hand was another orange life vest. As he crawled back onto the rowboat and into the canoe, the lightning charred picture of the girl and her mother huddling in the boat flashed again in his mind. This time he noticed the life jacket on the little girl and that there was not one on the mother she was clinging to.

He glanced down at the girl who lay motionless on the floor of the canoe. She was dressed in shorts and a matching t-shirt and she was barefoot. In his mind's eye, Paul could see the little girl taking off her sneakers so she could hang her feet in the cool water over the side of the boat. Just a carefree day on the lake, trying to get relief from the oppressive heat. Paul leaned over to feel her head for any injury that might explain her unconsciousness and found none. Her strawberry blonde hair was pasted to her head but there was no sign of bumps or bruises. Her skin was somewhat sunburned across her shoulders and on her face but her legs...Paul squinted in the driving rain. The girl's legs had slid under the rear seat of the canoe when he had laid her in. Now he could see something there that wasn't a sunburn. Leaning over precariously in the pitching canoe, Paul saw a row of strange marks across both of her legs. Angry red welts with a white center, like giant bee stings, ran in perfectly straight lines across her legs. Paul gently put his hand on one and could feel heat radiating from her otherwise cold skin.

Get to shore! The thought shook him with its intensity and raw instinct. All around him, the storm had gotten worse. The sky was completely black; the silver-gray rain was a blinding sheet between him and safety. He had let instinct and adrenaline take over since he had first seen the rowboat go over but for the first time, he was afraid. Something was wrong, something worse than this storm and a little girl whose mother was probably dead. Something much worse. A vivid image of his mother came, and he knew despite every instinct, every fear and every rational thought, he had to try one more time to find the little girl's mother. Before he could talk himself out of it, he filled his lungs and dove into the ocean-like surf. He swam under the rowboat and all around it, tiring quickly but suddenly obsessed with not leaving the girl motherless.

A sudden stinging sensation on his calf changed his thoughts in an instant. His lower leg began going numb and he felt a tugging, like he was snagged in weeds of some sort. He began pulling himself up onto the rowboat when the tugging became more insistent. Panic seized him and he began to flail his legs when he remembered the birthday gift his dad had given him when he turned thirteen.

"You're a teenager now, almost a man. Old enough to have this"

Clinging desperately with one arm to the rowboat, Paul deftly reached to his belt and whipped out his prized birthday gift: a Buck *knife. Flipping open the blade, he slashed blindly toward the vines he felt gripping his ankle.*

Paul sat rigid in the suffocating heat of his cell. His body was soaked with sweat yet he suddenly felt chilled, weak, like when a fever has just broken. He had never remembered any of those events before and yet he now knew there was more. He closed his eyes and placed himself back on the rowboat. He pictured the injured girl lying motionless, the raging storm, felt the pelting rain, willed himself to remember…but it was no use. The memory was done. Whatever had happened from that time until he had gotten back to shore was still locked somewhere in his mind. He tried once more to go back in his mind, to play out the rest of the memory, but it was no good.

He caught the sounds of voices drifting in from the station. A phone was ringing and Paul could see the reflections of bubble-lights ebbing and flowing like a silent blue tide. For a brief moment, a dark cloak of dread threatened to wrap itself around him—the missing boy was found dead…what else could cause such a stir at this hour…whatever this hour was—but he pushed it aside quickly. The memory was too important to be lost in the whirlpool of panic that was trying to pull him in.

Despite the frustration he felt for not being able to remember the rest of that day, Paul felt relief. His memory was finally coming back. Maybe it was being back in Haven that had triggered it. He lay back down on his bunk when the meaning of his memory hit him. He had been so caught up in the fact that he actually remembered something that he had completely ignored the enormity of *what* he had remembered. What were those marks on the girl's legs? What was that strange shape that had been draped across the bow of the rowboat? Paul felt suddenly very alone and vulnerable. Answers to these questions teased him from the dark corners of his mind but would not show themselves. Paul was not so sure he wanted to remember any more.

The stress of the day and his restless night began to take its toll. The murmur of voices and strobing blue light were all his exhaustion needed and he slipped back into a dreamless sleep.

(32)

ORTIZ HUNG up the phone, the irony of the situation hitting him like a hammer. Mike Noonan was home, safe and sound. He had blown off school, taken the bus to Malden Station, hopped on the Orange Line to Boston, and walked the rest of the way across Boston to the Fens. He sat in the bleacher seats watching "The Spaceman" Bill Lee get knocked around by the Blue Jays, giving up six runs in just two-thirds of an inning. Bob "The Steamer" Stanley came out of the bullpen and pitched shutout baseball for the rest of the game. Fred Lynn, Noonan's hero, went 2-for-4. All in all, it was still better than a day at school. He was sunburned beyond recognition, and having spent his return fare on hot dogs and soda, had made his way back to Haven on his thumb. He was eventually picked up by an off-duty State Trooper who drove him home.

Ortiz felt the blood rising in his cheeks. Since Nelson had radioed in from the lake, it was all hands on deck: the scene had to be secured, teams were out searching the woods around the lake, the family was being questioned, the husband brought in from work… and the Noonan boy had been forgotten. He shook his head, thinking the timing of it all might just be a blessing in disguise.

The Statie had brought the Noonan kid home just after seven. The parents, thinking that State and local police actually communicated with each other, assumed Haven PD would know the boy was home safe. If not for Noonan's father having too much to drink and calling to thank the police just now—Ortiz looked at his watch and saw it was after two o'clock in the morning—they still wouldn't know. And wouldn't *that* have been embarrassing when they finally got around to investigating.

But if they *had* found out earlier, Greymore would have been released immediately and had no alibi for the killing at the lake. As it stood now with the Noonan kid safe and Greymore being locked up during the Sheehan murder, there was no way Greymore could be a suspect. Crawford would have no choice but to let him out in the morning. Ortiz knew it wouldn't change what Crawford thought of Greymore, but he'd have no justification for keeping him locked up.

Ortiz knew Crawford would see it only as a roadblock to keeping Greymore behind bars. Sure, Greymore had to be set free...for now. But it didn't answer the real question: who was responsible for the Sheehan murder? Such a brutal killing, so similar to the string of murders in '61. Ortiz couldn't shake the feeling that the real killer would get away as Crawford just put his blinders on and tried to find a way to pin it on Greymore, despite the fact he was locked safely away in Crawford's cell at the time of the murder. Instead of being relieved that at least one more child in his town was safe, Crawford would be incensed that he couldn't fulfill his obsession of putting Greymore back in Braxton forever. He sighed heavily and went in to talk to Crawford.

(33)

PAUL WAS surprised to see the young officer approach the cell with keys in hand. "What, no breakfast today?"

A tired smile crossed the officer's face as he inserted the key into the cell lock. "Not unless you're cooking it yourself." He swung the door open wide and stepped aside for Paul to pass. "Come on up front and I'll get you your belongings. Oh, by the way, I'm Robert Ortiz, pleased to finally meet you, Mr. Greymore." He offered his hand.

Paul was momentarily taken aback. He had been treated with nothing but contempt and derision, yet here was a police officer actually treating him like a human. He shook hands, feeling dazed. Was this guy being serious? Or was his civility some kind of set up? "Why am I being released? Did somebody post bail?"

Ortiz held his eyes for a long moment, and then glanced back toward the office. He leaned close to Greymore. "There have been, ah, new developments. The charges are being dropped." He turned and walked back to the front of the station. Speaking in a louder voice, he added, "I just need you to sign a couple of forms and I can release your belongings and get you on your way."

Greymore took the hint to not follow up with any questions about the "developments." Was he being baited? He felt the stares of the other officers in the station; their loathing was like a physical force. He was used to it. "Can I use the phone to call for a ride?"

Ortiz turned. "No need, Mr. Greymore, I'll be happy to drop you back home." Ortiz made a production of getting the paperwork together and making sure Greymore accounted for each item that was returned to him. Finally they made their way outside, away from the cloying hatred of the police station. The heat was brutal, even though it was barely ten o'clock. The sun smoldered dully behind the thick haze, sure to burn through by noon and raise the temperature even more.

Greymore opened the back door to the cruiser and heard a snort from Ortiz. "Mr. Greymore, you are not under arrest anymore. You can sit up front, I don't bite."

Feeling half-foolish and half-suspicious, Greymore slipped into the furnace of the passenger seat. Ortiz pulled out of the parking lot, headed toward the lake. Greymore felt the young officer's frequent glances, felt himself being sized up. "Can I ask you a question, Officer?"

"You just did." Ortiz responded with a grin.

For the first time Greymore felt at ease, no longer wary of Otriz's motives. Growing up as an outcast, Paul had developed a keen skill for reading people. Spending seventeen years in prison had honed that skill to precision. "If the charges are being dropped, that can only mean the child turned up, someone else confessed, or another child went missing while I was in custody."

Ortiz looked at Paul thoughtfully. "You might have made a good cop, Mr. Greymore..."

"Please, call me Paul."

"Okay Paul. One of your scenarios didn't happen."

"I don't understand..."

"Well, you gave three scenarios for why you are being released. Nobody confessed."

"Officer Ortiz, I'm sorry but you're not making a lot of sense."

"No Paul, I owe you an apology for being evasive. It's been a hell of a long night and I'm so tired I doubt I'll be able to sleep." Ortiz took a slow breath, then glanced again at Greymore before continuing. "Two things happened last night. Mike Noonan was brought home safely. He ditched school and went to the Sox game. Spent all his money and had to thumb home. Staties picked him up and drove him back to Haven. Happy ending, right?"

"Yes, but I gather the second thing wasn't so happy?"

"No. A boy and his dog were killed last night at the lake. Not just killed...I'm sorry, I can't go into detail. Let's just say things are starting to look a lot like 1961. Damn, I really shouldn't have said anything."

Paul saw a look on the man's face that seemed both angry and helpless at the same time. "Why *did* you say anything, Officer Ortiz?"

They pulled into Paul's driveway and Ortiz put the car in park. He took a long look at Paul before answering. "It seems to me, Mr. Grey...Paul, that you got a raw deal. Something doesn't sit right with me about your case. I've read all the reports, even talked to a few folks, unofficially. Just a gut feeling. And you never heard this from me, but the way Chief Crawford obsesses over you...I don't know, gut feeling. Don't make me regret telling you. And by the way, please call me Robert."

Paul nodded, then opened the car door and got out. Then he leaned in and reached his hand across to Ortiz. "Thank you, Robert."

Ortiz shook his hand. "You're welcome...but what are you thanking me for?"

"For being decent. I don't get that a lot." He shut the door and walked slowly toward the lake, not turning as Ortiz gunned out of the driveway. Now at least he knew who made the phone call to Father McCarthy yesterday.

(34)

FOR THE few hours when Mike Noonan's "disappearance" was the focus of Haven PD, one officer had sat and called the departments of towns within a fifty-mile radius to alert them to be on the lookout for a missing boy. Eventually someone on the Bristol Police force remembered the DeMarcy case and did some investigating.

The news of Tony DeMarcy's disappearance had spread through the school quickly, as all good stories do. Denny glanced around the hall as Billy made his way toward him through the crowd. Denny could pick up snatches of conversation as other students rushed by.

"I heard the Butcher got Tony…"

"…and Crawford's out for blood…"

Denny had heard the rumors first thing this morning but it wasn't until lunch that he had been able to get any details. He and Billy were in separate afternoon classes.

"What'd you find out?" Billy asked as he opened his locker.

"It looks like Tony thumbed down from Bristol to hang out with Dale and the gang a few weeks ago. For whatever reason they didn't hook up. A kid matching Tony's description was seen in a canoe on the lake that day. Nobody's seen Tony since."

"Shit. Crawford is gonna go after Paul."

"I know. We've got to do something. I can't help thinking that there's some connection to the tunnels we found. I think we should tell your dad."

Billy looked blankly at him. "What connection? And what could my dad do about it?"

Denny shook his head slowly. "I don't know but I can't stop thinking about it. I guess we could go in and take another look around..."

"You're the boss, if you think it's worth a try..." he paused for a minute, "To tell you the truth, it scares the shit out of me to go back in there."

Denny sighed. "I'm glad it's not just me being a wimp. It didn't feel right in there. But we have to do this for Paul and for your dad."

"Alright. First thing in the morning we'll go in."

Out in the bright sunlight of a steamy spring afternoon, the caves lost some of their threat. They planned the next day as they headed to the bus area. "This time we'll bring spray paint to mark the trail, and extra flashlights, and if..." Suddenly Denny was being pulled roughly around the corner of the school, away from the hordes of students, into the shadows. He and Billy found themselves pinned against the back of the school, surrounded by Crawford and his gang. Tony Costa, Buddy Dentner and some other punk Denny didn't recognize stood flanking Crawford. The cut on Denny's face began to itch, as if recognizing its creator.

"You didn't think we were done the other night, did you O'Brien?" Crawford sneered.

Denny felt panic beginning to take him over, clear thinking going right out the window. Billy pushed Tony Costa's hands off of his shoulders and took a step forward, "Leave us alone, Crawford. We didn't do anything."

Buddy stepped forward and shoved him back hard against the wall, "Leave us alone, Crawford," he mimicked in a girlish voice.

Crawford leaned in closer to Denny. Close enough for Denny to smell cigarette smoke on his breath. "We look like twins, eh Denny-boy? What would your big brother say if he saw you now?"

Denny's mind was buzzing but now with something more than fear. Maybe it was Crawford mentioning his brother or maybe he had finally had enough of being pushed around. But now his head was filled with a blood red anger he had never felt before. "Yeah,

Crawford, it's like looking in a fucking mirror. One of those fun-house mirrors they have at the carnival where I know I look normal but my reflection looks really fucked up. You know what I mean?" From miles away he heard Billy inhale sharply, and then begin to laugh. Crawford's face twisted in surprise and rage and he sent a wild fist at Denny's face. To Denny, pumped full of adrenaline, it looked like it was coming in slow motion. He ducked quickly and for a split second relished the sound of Crawford's fist smashing into the solid brick school. Then they were on him.

Buddy had his arms pinned while Crawford hammered him repeatedly (with only one hand, Denny noticed). He writhed and squirmed but couldn't break free as Crawford continued to throw punches. Crawford stood up and reached into his pocket; a deafening click told Denny what was coming. The next instant Crawford was reeling forward, throwing his arms up wildly to save from smashing his face into the brick schoolhouse wall. Crawford turned, murder in his eyes, and stood face to face with Stubby, the bus driver. Stubby deftly moved his cigar from one side of his mouth to the other, "Put that blade away before it becomes your after school snack."

Crawford stared at him, his face twitching. Stubby held his eyes, all the while maneuvering the cigar in his teeth, looking calm as ever. Finally, Crawford folded the blade over and slipped it in his pocket. He turned to Denny, "This isn't the end O'Brien," then nodded to his gang and walked off. Stubby appraised the damage, apparently decided everybody would live, then turned and headed back to the bus.

Billy heaved a sigh of relief. "Nice going, Denny, did you take your brass balls pills today? Good thing you were careful about what you said or you would have pissed them off."

Denny cracked a nervous grin, "What's up with Stubby? I never knew he could talk."

Billy punched him on the shoulder and they headed toward the bus laughing.

>> <<

Denny sat at his desk that evening looking out at the lake, trying to make sense out of everything. The tunnels had something to do with this whole mess, but what? He thought back to the first time they were in there, closing his eyes and willing a mental picture to show him something. All those bones; something was wrong with the idea that the animals had been trapped in there. He thought of the bone dust on the floor of the cave, shuddering at the memory of the sound it made when he stepped on it, like sea shells at the beach crunching underfoot. He fast-forwarded to finding the larger bones in the cor-ner. That was it! He grabbed his journal and started making notes before he forgot. The last line he read out loud.

"If the animals were all trapped in the cave at the same time, why were some bones whole and others reduced to dust?" Denny lay down in bed but the thoughts of the caves held sleep at bay for most of the night.

(35)

BUGSY CRONIN made a few more colored marks on the map and used a pencil to roughly connect the dots. "Goddamn, will you look at that." he whistled to himself. He had spent most of his free time the past few weeks driving through the streets of Haven, just looking. He couldn't even bring himself to tell the gang down at The Hat what he was looking for. Not after the razzin' they gave him after he visited Greymore's house. He had filled them in on his observations about the lack of roadkill only to be met with laughter and sarcasm. "Maybe the Butcher couldn't find anything better to eat so he drives around the streets collecting them," "Yeah, check his barbeque. Maybe you'll find something there."

So how could he tell anyone that he had spent the last couple of weeks driving around Haven and taking body counts of small woodland creatures? But as crazy as it sounded, something was going on. He stared silently at the lines he had drawn on his map, representing the areas he had found to be unusually clear of road-kill. The lines traced almost perfectly over the roads that bordered Triangle Lake.

Two hours and six beers later he was driving slowly on Hospital Hill Road. Bugsy was the only person in Haven besides the police and fire departments authorized to drive this road. After the state mental hospital had shut down a few years back, the town decided to close the entire road since nothing else was on it. Too many kids coming up to drink and screw around. Somebody was bound to get hurt. So they gated the access road. And Bugsy had a key.

He had gone through his records for the past few years and found no lack of calls to the Triangle Lake area until he went back as far as 1961. Then he had discovered the same situation as he had now…very few calls to remove roadkill from any of the roads in the Triangle Lake vicinity. Mysteriously few, one might say.

He pulled his van behind one of the small cottage-type buildings that surrounded the main hospital. Many of the state hospitals had adopted the theory that housing some patients outside of the actual hospital-proper increased success rates in mental patients. The medical treatments took place in the main building but the patients were supposed to have the feeling of home, or a safe place, living in these cottages. From what Bugsy had heard, some of the "treatments" sounded worse than the mental illness itself. And the other things that had taken place in that hospital, the things that finally led to it being shut down, well, Bugsy didn't even want to think about that.

Downing the last third of his beer in one long gulp, he grabbed the old canvas bag from the passenger seat and climbed out of the van. He unhooked a heavy-duty flashlight from his belt and headed for the path that led down to the lakeshore. He knew from experience that the lake at night should be very active this time of year. He should have no problem spotting several different kinds of critters; maybe even a deer or two. He just wanted to know what was going on. He found the path and started down, sliding and stumbling. The path seemed steeper than last time he'd been down it, a few years back. Then again he was younger and probably a bit more sober that time.

He climbed across some larger rocks that were part of the path and when he jumped off on the downhill side he lost his footing on the loose ground. He desperately tried to regain his balance but it was too late. He cried out in pain as he tumbled down the incline, branches and bones cracking, until he slammed to a stop at the water's edge, flat on his back. "Shit! Maybe I shouldn't have had that last beer. Or the one before it, for that matter." He tried to sit up but the pain shooting through his legs made him flatten right back out on the damp ground. Above him the sky was littered with stars. Bugsy remembered his mother telling him when he was just a youngster that God pulled a big shade across the sun and sky so people could sleep. Stars were just little pinholes in that shade that let some sunlight through. Used to tell him that just as he drifted off to sleep...

He was awake suddenly, not sure if he had passed out or not. He heard rustling off to one side and tried to roll over to see what was making it. His legs were a symphony of pain. He could feel the swelling, felt like his skin would just split from it. "Least I'm not paralyzed," he muttered. He tried to see where his flashlight had dropped but couldn't find it. Knowing he had another one in his bag, he moved his arm cautiously to where the bag had landed. The bushes moved again over to his left and he thought he could make out a shape as he tried to move his head further over. He reached in his bag feeling around for his flashlight when his hands closed on something else. He pulled out the gun as a large dark shadow separated from the darkness and moved toward him. "I must still be pissin' drunk. Or in shock." The shape paused at the sound of his voice, and then moved suddenly on him. Ignoring the searing pain in his legs he sat up and fired at the figure, emptying the gun's chambers. The shape moved closer. It was now very clear to Walter "Bugsy" Cronin why there was so little roadkill in the area. Crystal clear. If only I could tell the boys at The Hat, wouldn't they shit themselves, he thought as he did just that. He felt himself sliding along the ground and realized the pain was gone from his legs. They really do look like little pinholes in a shade, he thought just before his eyes and lungs filled with lake water.

PART II

(36)

THE OLD man took a swallow from a paper-bag-covered bottle and settled down against the side of the building. *Thank God for summer,* he thought as he pulled a bunch of newspapers toward him. Now he could relax and enjoy reading them instead of stuffing his clothes with them to keep warm. Years of living on the streets had made him thankful for small things and wanting for little. He considered this to be a perfect night, a full bottle by his side and a stack of the day's newspapers to read. "Not that there is anything worth reading about," he mumbled as he flipped through the first pages and took another drink from his bottle.

When his eye caught the headline, his hands began to shake even before he went back and read it again. He placed the paper on his lap and gulped greedily from the bottle, knowing it would not help him prepare for what he was about to read. Wiping his mouth, he picked up the paper and quickly read the article, then began reading it again slowly. He had prayed this day would never come but somewhere deep inside him he knew it would. A car horn outside the alley made him jump and he snatched up the bottle and drank again. He reached into the pocket of his shabby overcoat and pulled out a piece of plastic. Protected inside the plastic was another article. He wanted to preserve this one until the day came that he needed it, so he had taken it into Zayre and had it laminated in one of those machines. He looked at the date in the corner of the article and then at the date of the paper he just read. *Seventeen years goes by fast,* he thought.

Once more he read both articles:

From the *Boston Sun*, June 2, 1978

Retired General Found Dead

General Hamilton Gunlinger was found dead in his California home early this morning. Sources state the sixty-seven year old Gunlinger apparently died of a self-inflicted gunshot wound to the head. Gunlinger was a decorated soldier who spent most of his military career in biological research, a field in which he was a reputed genius. A bit of a mystery surrounds the incident due to a strange suicide note and a newspaper article found by the body. Sources say the handwritten note included phrases referring to "an experiment that got out of control" and "playing God." The rest of the note was allegedly a rambling apology for "the damage done and that yet to be done."

The newspaper article found with the suicide note was clipped from a recent edition of the *Haven News*, a publication from a small Massachusetts town. The article tells of the murder of a young boy from the town and implies a connection to the recent release of Paul Greymore from Braxton State Prison. Greymore was convicted of murder in 1961 for the death of Mary Larsen, an eight-year-old Haven resident. Greymore, nicknamed the Butcher, was believed to be responsible for the disappearances of almost twenty children that year. Coincidentally, Gunlinger suffered a tragedy in Haven, Mass. in 1944 when his entire base was wiped out in an ammunition explosion while Gunlinger himself was off-site. "He never really got over that," an anonymous source is quoted as saying, "it was the only black mark in his entire illustrious military career." Private services will be held.

HAVEN

From the *Haven News*, August 30, 1961

REIGN OF TERROR ENDS
Local man believed to be "The Butcher"

Haven—The summer-long terror which has plagued the small town of Haven may have come to an end last night. Paul Greymore, 18, was arrested for the murder of eight year-old Mary Larsen, also of Haven. Details are sketchy but apparently Haven Police Officer Cody Crawford found Greymore carrying the lifeless body of the girl behind Greymore's house and made the arrest. Greymore reportedly had serious wounds to his head and body, the cause of the wounds is unknown. He is currently listed in stable condition at County General Hospital under tight security. Greymore will be charged with Larsen's murder and is suspected of being responsible for the disappearance of almost twenty children in the Haven area this summer.

The old man stuffed both articles in his pocket and slowly got to his feet. He shambled down the alley and handed his bottle to another street person, who looked at the bottle suspiciously before taking a drink. He continued on out of the alley into the city streets. The night was quiet, only the sounds of light traffic coming from the highway. He walked slowly at first, then faster. The city seemed larger to him, overwhelming. The enormity of the situation hit him and he felt dizzy. He suddenly understood the futility in trying to drown his past with cheap wine. The realization jolted him and he knew what he would do, what he *must* do. Something he should have done seventeen years ago. He reached involuntarily to his chest and slid his hand between the buttons of his old flannel shirt. His fingers found the key he kept on a chain around his neck and grasped it tightly. He was going home.

(37)

THE EARLY morning fog was already burning off when they arrived at the caves, promising another sweltering day. They dropped their book bags, filled with flashlights, spray paint and extra batteries, and quickly uncovered the entrance. Denny had told Billy of his new theory while they had hiked through the woods, and of his almost sleepless night. "To tell you the truth Denny-boy, I never even thought of that and I still didn't sleep much myself."

They had no problem descending through the tunnels, always stopping to mark their trail with bright red spray paint. At most of the forks they quickly spotted their sticks from their last trip and knew which branch to follow. Soon enough—*too soon*, Denny thought—they were at the entrance to the cavern which held the run-off from the lake. They took a few minutes to make the gap in the rocks larger, Denny remembering too clearly how trying to squirm back through last time had seemed to take an eternity, all the while expecting something to wrap itself around his legs and pull him back. Once inside they shined their lights around.

"Let's not spend too much time in here, I think we've seen all there is to see," Billy suggested.

Denny bent over the pile of bones that had sent them scrambling last time. "I still can't tell what these are. There's too many of them. I think it might be a few different kinds of animals all piled up."

"Which means..." Billy whispered.

"Which means unless some deer decided to shack up with maybe a couple of raccoons and a fox or two, somebody piled these bones here." The thought sent a shiver down Denny's back.

"Maybe there was an old Indian tribe that used to live here, do you think the bones are that old?"

"Could be. Let's take a look at that big tunnel." The possibility that all of these bones were intentionally piled here was unnerving. The amount of dead animals it would take to coat the floor with so much bone dust was unthinkable. Denny quickly headed for the larger tunnel, hoping there would be no more bones in there.

The large tunnel quickly narrowed to more of a hallway size with many small "rooms" to each side, all littered with various bones. Many of the rooms had another tunnel leading out from the far end. The boys followed these randomly. "Do you notice that smell getting stronger again?" Denny hissed.

"I thought it was your breath," Billy replied, followed by a nervous snicker.

They entered the next room and were repelled by the stench. "What the hell..." Billy quickly pulled his shirt up over his face.

Denny did the same. "Let's head back."

"Wait." Something had caught Denny's flashlight beam. Something shiny across the cave. Keeping his shirt across his mouth and nose he slowly made his way across the large, circular room.

Before he could relocate the object, he heard Billy off to one side. "Oh, shit. Oh, Denny."

Denny quickly scampered over and shined his light next to Billy's. His stomach rebelled at the sight, threatening to launch this morning's Frosted Flakes all over the cave floor. In the twin beams of their light lay a human skeleton. Fragments of leather laid next to it, maybe the remains of shoes or a belt. Denny's mind whirled, wanting to shut down. He squeezed his eyes shut, willing himself not to panic like he did last time.

"Denny, let's go, let's go and never come back," Billy whined, "We'll tell Sheriff Crawford and that will be the end."

Denny opened his eyes and tried to focus in the impenetrable darkness. "Wait, let's think about this, Billy. This body has been here for a long, long time. It's no worse than finding more animal bones." He hoped his voice sounded calmer to Billy than it did to his own ears.

"Denny, this ain't no fucking Indian. Look at this. It's a kid, Denny." his voice wavered near hysteria.

Denny looked again and knew Billy was right. The skeleton was approximately their size. "One more thing and then we're out of here," he turned and scanned his beam along the far side of the cave. There! A metallic reflection winked back at him. He scurried across the cave, dodging other partial skeletons along the way. He bent down and located the object that had caught his beam. He picked it up and held it to the light, somehow knowing deep down what it was.

A single word bounced back at him from the small silver rectangle and suddenly the cave was like a merry-go-round. Denny leaned over onto his knees, trying desperately to stay conscious. He was dimly aware of Billy behind him. Billy's hand on his shoulder. Billy shining his own light on the small silver tag at the end of the chain. Billy muttering something when he read the word "BEAR" on the dog tag.

Denny forced himself to shine the light down at the skeleton. It was definitely the right size. The shiny white of the bones began to pulsate in and out of focus and Denny felt himself being pulled away. He stumbled along, letting Billy lead him until his head began to clear. He had no idea how far they'd gone when he stopped and grabbed Billy's arm. "I'm okay now, are we going the right way?"

"Beats me, I just wanted to get you the hell out of there before I had to carry you out, which I practically did." Billy's voice had regained some of its natural confidence.

Denny was aware only of the cold metal in his hand and the rotting stench of death that permeated everything around him.

"Okay. Let's keep going. As long as we're heading uphill, we should be alright." They went on for what seemed like hours, careful to mark their trail, growing more afraid every time they came upon one of the marks they left.

When they had to stop to replace the batteries in Billy's flashlight, Denny began to feel panic creeping back over him. "We're going in circles, Billy. We'll never find our way out," he was close to tears.

"Don't, Denny, don't you go fuckin' losin' it on me now!" His voice betrayed his attempt at bravery, but still Denny felt better knowing Billy was in control. "We just keep heading uphill. We took a few wrong turns, that's all," he screwed the cap back on his light. "Let's go."

They walked for another eternity when something along the far wall of the tunnel they were in caught Denny's eye. It was just a lighter shade of black against a black wall, but Denny recognized it immediately. "Billy, the ladder!" Against the far wall were rungs imbedded in the stone, leading up. Billy shined his beam upwards where a circular cut-out was clearly visible. Billy scaled the ladder quickly and a moment later blinding sunlight filled the tunnel. Denny scampered quickly up the ladder, blinking in the bright light, letting its warmth pour over him. Never had the sun felt so good. They quickly put the cover back over the hole and sat down at the edge of the foundation.

The sun was high in the sky, making it probably after noon. They had been down there for over four hours! Denny couldn't think of anything worse than what had just happened, except for the day he found out about Jimmy and his dad. Without warning, that memory invaded his head. The news that there had been an accident. His mother crying, telling him his big brother was dead. His father confined to the hospital bed, death waiting to take him. Never getting the chance to say goodbye to either of them. He held the dog tag up and read it again. Tears streamed down his face, etching lines in the dirt, and his body shook with sobs.

He felt Billy's arm on his shoulders. Billy had been with him through it all. "It's alright, Denny."

Slowly Denny got control of himself, smearing his face as he wiped the tears. "I don't think it will ever be alright, Billy." He slipped the dog tag in his pocket. "Let's go."

(38)

THE OLD man walked into the bank like a sinner walking into church. He felt like the eyes of everyone else were burning through him, not wanting to be in the same building as the smelly old man. *Did that woman just pull her child a bit closer? Did that man's nose just wrinkle in disgust? Yes to both, I believe. But I'm just a drunk who needs a drink, and paranoid to boot.* He had cleaned up as best he could in the public bath house at Carson Beach, but there was only so much a man could do after so many years on the streets. He made his way quickly to the safe deposit boxes. With badly shaking hands, he removed the chain from around his neck and looked at the key. It amazed him that he'd worn it for all these years, yet never thought about it. Until he read that article, he wasn't sure he even knew the key was there. Was that even possible? He held it close to his face and read the number stamped on the side: B391. It took him a few minutes to find the corresponding box, and a few more painful seconds for his trembling hands to ease the key into the lock. Before he opened the box he hesitated.

He had been a street person for more years than his booze-addled brain could recall. Until the story in the paper about Gunlinger, his life before the streets was a blur. The article had tripped a switch in his head, but the lights were slow to come on, they were still warming up. The key around his neck was the first step, but he honestly had no idea what he would find when he opened the box. He closed

171

his eyes and let out a long breath, thinking about the bottle he had given away the night before. Finally, he swung the door open wide, and when he realized what the box held, his eyes opened wider. The box was full of cash. Not small bills either. Packages of twenties, lots of them. "What...where did I..."

He grabbed one pack and quickly stuffed it in his pocket. Suddenly sure he would be robbed, he slammed the door of the safe deposit box shut, drawing confused and somewhat annoyed stares from the other customers around him. He stuffed the key in his pocket and hastily retreated, frequently looking over his shoulder, certain he would be followed and jumped, losing the money and the key. Losing whatever waited for him back in Haven.

Two hours later, dressed in new clothes and carrying a duffel bag containing more clothes and toiletries, all purchased at Woolworth's, he returned to the Post Office and emptied the rest of the cash into the duffel bag. Three other items tumbled into the bag along with the stacks of money. Moses reached in and fished them out. Two of them were metal canisters with what looked like spray triggers. They looked almost like whipped cream cans. He placed them carefully in the duffel bag. The other was a small billfold. He opened it and found a driver's license with the name Frank Rodman and a picture of a young man that looked familiar. When he moved the license closer to examine it, he realized with a wave of despair that he was looking at a picture of himself. A much younger (and sober) version of himself. He slid the billfold in his pocket, thinking again about the lifetime that had passed him by. His mouth suddenly felt like it was full of cotton, his throat like sandpaper. He wanted...no, he *needed* a drink. Just one, he told himself, and he made his way next to the nearest liquor store. As he reached for the door with a violently trembling hand, a vision hit him with such clarity that he froze, his arm stuck in mid-flight to the door handle.

He saw the younger version of himself, the one in the picture, wearing a white coat, a lab coat, and safety glasses. He was leaning over a table, holding a beaker of liquid just above the lick of a flame from a Bunsen burner. He poured the bubbling liquid into a test tube that held a small amount of powder. As the mixture began to smoke, his eyes widened and he began furiously writing in a log book.

"Pal, you comin' or goin'?" A young man with a toothpick hanging out of the corner of his mouth and slicked back hair was waiting to get into the store.

"Pardon me...sorry..." He stepped aside and let the man pass. The tremor in his hands spread until his entire body was shaking. It wasn't for need of a drink this time, it was something worse. He realized the vision wasn't a vision at all, but a memory. He had been a scientist, and a damn good one. He had been a well-respected member of a research team at a company called BioHealth in Cambridge. He had helped discover...something. A breakthrough in cough medicine, or decongestant...it was hazy. But that's where the money came from. Before he gave it all up, or before the bottle took it away. When he was able to get the shakes under control, he turned away from the liquor store and began walking toward the bus station, afraid of the once-drowned memories he felt fighting their way to the surface of his mind.

{39}

ROBERT ORTIZ'S body tensed involuntarily as he picked up the phone. "Haven Police, Officer Ortiz speaking." Every time the phone rang he thought the worst; another child missing or dead. "Okay, I'll check it out." Not this time, he breathed. He quickly strode into Crawford's office. "Just got a report that there's a van parked up on old Hospital Hill Road behind one of the state hospital buildings. Might be Walter Cronin's."

Crawford didn't even look up. "Bugsy's probably doing some fishing or sleeping one off. Go get him out of there and make sure the gate gets locked."

"Yes, sir." Ortiz grabbed his hat and headed out to his cruiser. Crawford is burnt, he thought to himself, spending way too much time on Greymore. He glanced up at the sky as he walked across the black desert of the parking lot, hoping to see rain clouds. Weathermen had mentioned a chance of showers but it didn't look likely. He hopped into the inferno that was his car and headed for the lake. Weathermen had been predicting showers for days. It was becoming more wishful thinking on their part than an actual forecast. It seemed most areas were at least getting scattered showers but not a drop had fallen in Haven, not even a threatening cloud lately.

Ortiz pulled over when he arrived at the open gate to Hospital Hill Road. He checked the chain and found the padlock hanging open. It must be Cronin, he thought, he's the only other person with a key. Sure enough, there was Cronin's van, parked behind one of the old cottages. Either the caller had taken their dog for a walk up Hospital Hill or maybe the van was visible from the lake.

Ortiz stepped out into the blazing sun and walked beside Cronin's van. Looking inside he noticed several empty beer bottles in the front, but Cronin was nowhere to be seen. Ortiz walked around the other side of the van and noticed what looked like a path leading into the woods. Crawford was right on both counts, thought Ortiz, fishing first, sleeping it off later. He stepped onto the path and headed down toward the lake. He had no problems following the path. The advantages of youth and sobriety made the trip uneventful compared to Bugsy's. Still, he noted the steep incline and loose footing, wondering how Cronin had made it considering his age and the empty beer bottles. He was sweating through his uniform as the ground began to level out.

As soon as he reached the bottom, he felt that same feeling he always got when something was wrong. Whether it was his cop's instinct or just a burst of adrenaline, he knew it well. The trigger this time was the flashlight at the bottom of the path. Ortiz's mind immediately began processing this information. The flashlight meant Bugsy had been down here last night or very early this morning. The way it was thrown down on the ground was mildly alarming. Maybe he dropped it without realizing. Ortiz walked over and picked it up. The flashlight switch was on and the light was out. Cronin had been here in the dark. He quickly began a visual search of the surrounding ground and his body pumped out another surge of adrenaline. A few feet closer to the lake was a gun. Knowing he should get back up to the car and call for back-up, he walked over and bent down to look at the weapon. Just an old .38, but what would Cronin be doing down here at night with a pistol? A quick inspection showed the gun had been fired recently, all chambers empty. Clearly if he was going to do any hunting, he would have brought a rifle. And why was this stuff here on the ground? Where was Cronin? The heat was unbearable; with the sun reflecting off the lake it felt twice as hot. Ortiz stood and looked at the rest of the area. He frowned as he circled a small section of ground near the water's edge. The ground was disturbed, as if something heavy had been dragged out of the water. *Or into it*, the realization came abruptly.

Ortiz was suddenly uncomfortable. Something was very wrong with this whole scene. "Cronin! Walter Cronin can you hear me! Bugsy!" His voice echoed eerily across the lake's expanse. Ortiz made a cursory search of the rest of the area, noticing how thick and impassable the woods quickly became. *He's dead*, the voice inside his head called, *he's in the lake just like all the kids*. Ortiz shook his head, trying to suppress his fears and suspicions and act rationally. Looking out across the lake he could see the few houses that bordered the other side. One of those is Greymore's, he thought. Won't that just fit right in with Crawford's theory.

The climb up was considerably more difficult than going down. There was no way Bugsy would have made it, Ortiz thought. He was breathing hard and bathed in sweat when he reached the top. He leaned over with his hands on his knees for a minute, wishing he had thought to take a drink from the lake before he came up. His mind was still actively working on the possible scenarios that occurred here. Could Bugsy have stumbled down the incline at night and gotten hurt? Emptying his gun in hopes of someone hearing the shots? Lying in the hot sun all morning until he finally had to drag himself into the water to escape the searing heat? Ortiz's analytical mind dismissed this immediately. What could he be doing with a handgun in the middle of the night? It simply made no sense. Just like a lot of things these days. It would make perfect sense to Crawford, though. Greymore came over in his boat and killed Bugsy, dragging the body into the lake. Ortiz stood and looked again across the lake; the reflection was blinding off the water. It would be too easy for Crawford to make that story believable. Ortiz needed to find out more before reporting in; otherwise he might not have the opportunity.

He went back to Bugsy's van and climbed in the driver's side. The heat was suffocating, with an underlying stench of dead meat and chemicals permeating the air. Ortiz glanced back at the multitude of plastic containers and wondered how many of them had dead animals in them. The thought of how nasty Bugsy's job was made Ortiz feel a little better about what he was doing. Laying traps and spraying for bugs wasn't so bad, it was the picking up of the roadkill that turned his stomach. He re-focused his thoughts on the front of the van. There was a stack of folders and papers on the passenger-side seat, under several empty beer cans. Ortiz began flipping through the pages. Mostly work orders and receipts, nothing of any help to explain what he might have been doing out here last night. The last folder was different.

There were handwritten notes on many pages that looked like they were torn out of a notebook, and also a map of Haven. Ortiz studied the map and tried to make sense of the notes scrawled along the margins. Bugsy seemed to be keeping track of all the places he had to pick up roadkill. He even had them dated. There was a red line drawn along Hillview Street, West Border Road, and Chestnut Street where there seemed to be no markings to indicate he had any pick-ups. Ortiz frowned, his mind kicking into high gear, totally oblivious to the furnace he was sitting in. He went back to the pages of notes and started correlating some of them to the map. Once he figured out Bugsy's process, it was pretty easy to follow. From what Ortiz could see Bugsy had been doing a bit of detective work on his own. The result of that seemed to conclude that there was an unusual lack of roadkill being reported along the roads that bordered the lake. What significance could that have? Could the wildlife that lived in the thick woods be responsible for eating any of the animals hit by cars? Ortiz figured Bugsy would have thought of that right off and not bothered doing any of this. He found another page of notes stuck in the back of the folder. Bugsy had made a matrix of all the years going back to 1960. Very detailed and methodical, Ortiz thought. Along the top were simply Hillview Street, West Border Road, and Chestnut Street with the years running down the left hand column. Scrawled across the very top of the paper were the words "March through May counts." Ortiz quickly scanned the numbers filled in across the fields. Bugsy must have kept very detailed records through-out the years, Ortiz thought with a bit of admiration. He looked at the numbers again, thinking he had missed something the first time. Going back over it, he was coming to the same conclusion that Bugsy did, as was evident by the underlined numbers on two of the rows of data. One was for this year, where the numbers were in the teens for the total number of pick-ups on those streets. The data was fairly consistent for almost every other row, with the counts generally in the high thirties to low forties. All the way down the page until he was almost at the bottom, where Bugsy had underlined another row of numbers in the low teens. Without even looking to the left margin, Ortiz knew what the year would be. What could this all mean? His eyes wandered to the left and confirmed it: 1961.

At the very bottom was a single word underlined in red. While Bugsy had compiled a nice set of data, he too had no resolution. The word was simply, "*why*?" He gathered all the papers and stuffed them into the folder, taking it with him back to his car. This warranted a visit to Bugsy's house. Maybe there was something more there that led Bugsy to come out here at night with a gun and empty it, but into what? He had seen no evidence of blood, granted he hadn't really looked for it. Tonight he would swing by the Witch's Hat and talk to some of the regulars that Bugsy hung out with. Hopefully, Bugsy himself would be there to answer all of the questions he had, but his instincts told him not to expect it. Maybe he had shared his theories with some of his drinking buddies. Which begged another question: was Bugsy out here alone last night? There was only one flashlight and all of the empties and the folders were on the passenger seat, leading Ortiz to believe Bugsy was alone. He pulled out of the parking lot and started down the driveway, one hand on the radio. Should he report in or check out a few things first? He tightened his lips and slowly slid his hand off the radio. He couldn't fill in Crawford yet. There was something very strange going on. But what if Bugsy had wandered into the woods and was still alive but hurt? He couldn't live with that possibility, even though every bone in his body told him Bugsy was dead, in the lake. He grabbed the radio and called in a missing person report, requesting a search party. At least it wasn't a little kid, he thought to himself, followed by a prayer.

(40)

THE OLD man sat motionless on the bus, ready at any moment to jump out of his skin. The bus itself sat motionless in the Callahan Tunnel, mired in Boston's infamous traffic. At first he thought it was the fact that he hadn't had a drink in over eight hours that was making him jumpy, since this was the first time in half a lifetime he had gone that long without a drink. At least while he was conscious. Strangely, though, he did not even *want* a drink. It was the immobility that was driving him crazy. The need to get back to Haven was overwhelming. The impending sense of dread that had overtaken him since reading the article about Gunlinger and the murder in Haven was unbearable. The worst part about it was he didn't know why.

He had scoured the newspapers looking for any news concerning Haven, and finally found what Gunlinger's mysterious suicide note had alluded to. There was a grisly killing that took place: a boy and his dog were dismembered while swimming at the lake in Haven. Greymore was mentioned as being in custody, but the details were sketchy and the article mentioned an earlier disappearance where the missing child turned up safely. He would get the story straight when he got there. Either way, he was not able to draw any connection between any of this and a reason for Gunlinger to eat a bullet.

His memory of life before being a street person had faded to the point he could not distinguish real events from alcohol-induced hallucinations. But the fog was strangely beginning to clear. Bits and pieces of reality were slowly rising from the haze. He knew he had been in the military because of Gunlinger and the tattoos on his arms. Now he remembered the base in Haven. There was more, though, more to his life in Haven than just being stationed there. But he couldn't pull it through. Exhaustion began to take its toll. He had walked most of the morning to get to the bus terminal and had to wait there for three hours for the first bus to Haven. He had felt exhilarated, a sense of purpose. But the adrenaline was wearing off and his head pounded with the effort of trying to recall the life he had drowned in decades of cheap booze. His head nodded forward as sleep overtook him.

When he awoke he was unsure of his surroundings. He had dreamed fitful dreams of laboratories and experiments. Of being in the woods, running, a huge explosion echoing behind him. He looked out the window and noticed the smoggy city stench had been replaced by fresh country air, the buildings by trees. He also noticed his memory was becoming as clear as the air around him. That's when he began to wonder if he was making a big mistake. The incidents he was remembering, if they were true, were worth burying in his mind. The bone-deep chill he felt told him that they most certainly were true and that there was more where they came from.

He pulled the newspaper articles out of his pocket and read them again. This time they began to make sense. Moses had been a scientist for a highly secret division of the Army. The "ammunition depot" in Haven was just a front for his division, led by General Gunlinger. Their work had been in gene research. The cover of the ammunition depot had worked out perfectly. He knew now that Gunlinger had intentionally destroyed the base, killing everyone on it. He didn't know how he managed to get off the base or if he even knew of Gunlinger's plan.

He remembered stumbling through the woods of Haven and he vowed to avenge the deaths of his friends and fellow soldiers. At some point the realization hit him that trying to expose Gunlinger would undoubtedly lead to his death and his accusations would become the ranting of a madman. A few planted incident reports in his files would show him as unstable and the cover-up would be complete. He had seen it dozens of times and, God forgive him, he had participated in it on more than one occasion. Always for the good of the country, for national security, he had told himself. He knew deep down it was for personal gain or survival.

He had crept through the woods, wanting to see his family. Family! The revelation shook him. He had a wife and daughter in Haven. He had been afraid to go to them. He feared for them more than for himself. If they knew he was alive they would be in serious danger. He made the decision to get away for a while, until he felt it was safe. Once he was away he realized the only way to keep everyone safe was to let them believe he had been killed in the explosion. He read about his own funeral in the paper, tears streaming down his face as he thought about the pain his wife and daughter must be going through. Fresh tears burned his cheeks now as he thought of his wife and little Jan. Sweet little Jan growing up without a father. His beloved Catherine having to fend for herself and their daughter. The guilt and shame had been too much back then and he fell easy prey to the bottle. It wasn't just those emotions, it was fear too. Everywhere he turned he saw people he suspected of being Gunlinger's spies looking for him. As the years slipped away so did his character. His drinking and paranoia led to problems at work and he was eventually fired. He took menial jobs that fit in better with his drinking schedule, eventually losing those too. At some point he put all of his cash and his fake identity into the safe deposit box and faded into the street life of Boston. Almost as disturbing as the memories themselves were how quickly they were returning the closer he drew to Haven.

He wiped his face and smiled feebly at the woman sitting across from him who stared at him. She looked away, probably thinking him just another drunk judging by his appearance. He had no idea of the fate of his family and the realization sickened him. Anger welled and mixed with the swirling revulsion and aching grief he felt. Half of his life had been spent trying to wipe out the memory of Gunlinger's act, but he had also erased his own existence. He struggled to regain his composure and think this thing through. He had been drawn to Haven after reading of Gunlinger's suicide, even before he had remembered he had once had a family there, had a life there. Was his subconscious responsible for setting him in motion before his conscious mind caught up to it? He didn't think so. He read the articles again. An experiment that got out of control. Playing God. As the sign for the Haven exit flashed by the window unnoticed, he began to remember the experiment.

(41)

ORTIZ SMILED to himself as he walked into the dim, smoky bar. While his eyes adjusted he saw the reaction that was universal anytime a cop walked into a bar: guilty stares from the patrons and a suspicious *"now what?"* look from the bartender. It was not crowded, it was barely five o'clock, just the regulars passing time with tired old stories and illogical political theories and the barroom staple of Red Sox talk. Ortiz suspected that Bugsy would have been an active participant had he not gone missing.

The searches at the lake for the past two days had turned up nothing. Ortiz himself had helped search Bugsy's house and had found nothing remarkable. The house was small and looked like it had once been well-kept, but those days were sliding into the past. The furniture was looking threadbare, a few years past the "lived in" look that was generally accepted. A thin layer of dust coated the family photos that decorated the walls. The sink was half-full of dirty dishes, not to the point of total disregard, but enough to clearly state that washing dishes wasn't a priority. All evidence of a lonely old man just getting through the days.

The only area that was in any state of order was a small room off the kitchen that Bugsy evidently used as an office. The furnishings consisted of a battered old desk with a leather chair and a pair of dented metal filing cabinets. Ortiz swallowed hard as his eyes scanned the dozens of framed pictures of Bugsy's family. There was

185

no rhyme or reason to how the pictures were arranged, somehow making it even sadder.

Ortiz had spent a couple of hours meticulously searching the files but it seemed like anything Bugsy had discovered was either left in his van or was still with him. *At the bottom of the lake.* The thought had come unbidden and Ortiz remembered having a similar thought after finding Bugsy's gun and flashlight abandoned on the shore.

Now Ortiz's only hope was that Bugsy had, at some point during his amateur investigation, shared his theories with his drinking buddies. There was a group of three older men at a table in the back, pitchers of beer and bowls of pretzels littered the surface, while the men spoke earnestly. Ortiz recognized them and knew Bugsy hung with them. He suspected that their conversation would ordinarily be filled with good-natured ribbing and easy laughter, but not tonight. These were no ordinary times in Haven. Ortiz signaled to the bartender to set up a couple fresh pitchers, and walked slowly over to the table.

"Evenin' gentlemen, mind if I join you for a bit?" His timing was perfect as a waitress delivered two fresh pitchers of beer. The men looked at him without guilt or suspicion, but with an expression of mild alarm. They figured he was here to give them bad news.

John Shields, Haven's lone accountant, answered for the group. "Pull up a rock, Officer, we're not going anywhere." The other two, Charlie Nasmith and Scotty McMann, murmured greetings. Charlie was sales manager at a Ford dealership in Danvers and Scotty worked for the town Parks and Recreation Department. In fact, he *was* the Parks and Recreation Department. John waited for Ortiz to get settled before speaking again. "Is this about Walter or Greymore?"

Ortiz was confused for a split-second before recognizing Bugsy's given name. "What gives you the idea I'm here for either?"

John smiled. It was the same smile he probably gave his customers who were trying to claim too much for charitable deductions on their tax returns. It said "cut the bullshit."

Ortiz needed information and game-playing wasn't going to cut it with these guys. "Have you guys seen Walter for the past couple of days?"

The three men exchanged glances and it was all the answer Ortiz needed. They looked concerned, if not plain scared. Scotty topped his mug off from one of the pitchers and Ortiz saw a slight tremble. "He hasn't been around the last couple of nights, Officer. I haven't seen his van around either and there was no answer at his house today."

Ortiz quickly realized that John may be the leader of the group, but Scotty was a closer friend to Bugsy. "Please, call me Robert. I'm here on my own time."

Scotty nodded. "Is Walter in trouble, Robert? Is he hurt?"

"I don't know. We found his van parked up behind the State Hospital. It was empty, looked like he might have hiked down to the lake."

Scotty slammed his mug on the table and all three men waited to hear what he had to say. "You didn't find him, though, did you? He's gone, isn't he Robert?"

Ortiz nodded slowly. "It looked like he'd gone there at night. I found a flashlight down by the water." Ortiz knew Crawford would pitch a fit if he found out what he said next. "Do any of you know if Walter owned a gun?" Ortiz, of course, knew it was Bugsy's gun. That was easy enough to check out. It was his and he was licensed, no crime there.

The three men again exchanged glances. Charlie spoke for the first time. "What's going on here, Offi...Robert?"

Ortiz slowly moved his gaze from one man to the next, landing finally on Scotty. "I also found his gun by the lake. It was empty, fired recently. Walter saw something that night and emptied his .38 into it, and now he's gone. I'll be damned if it didn't look like he was dragged into the lake."

"Good Lord..." Scotty put his face in his hands. Nobody spoke for a long moment until Scotty finally sat back with a desperate sigh. He looked at Charlie, then John, both giving a nod, urging him to spill it. "Walter's been acting strange the past week or so. He said there is something going on in Haven, something that has nothing to do with Greymore. He's been spending a lot of time driving around the streets by the lake at night."

Ortiz grabbed an empty mug and poured himself a beer. It was grounds for suspension to be drinking in uniform, but it was the furthest thing from his mind. He took a long drink. "The roadkill."

The three men stared at him, then nodded almost in comical unison. "You know about it?" Scotty asked.

"Only by putting the pieces together of what I found in his van. He might have made a good cop." He looked around the table and saw sad realization in their eyes. Their friend was gone. "I need your help. Off the record. There's too much focus on Greymore...something's missing. Did he say anything else? Any theory he had about the roadkill or the lake? As crazy as it might sound, I need to hear it."

John and Charlie were shaking their heads. "No, he just kept going on about how there were no kills to pick up near the lake this year." Charlie frowned. "Wait! He also mentioned it had happened before. Back in 1961, same year as the other killings, Greymore again..."

Scotty cleared his throat, then took a long pull on his beer. "There's more. After you guys left the other night, Walter and me stayed for a few more. He told me..." Scotty looked around, either afraid to break his friend's trust or to repeat the bizarre theory. "He told me he thought Greymore was innocent. Now...and back then. Said he knew Greymore's folks and they were good people. Said Greymore himself had him up to get his house ready. Said he's good people, too. Swore on his wife's memory there was no way Greymore did any of the killing."

Ortiz waited. John and Charlie were shaking their heads slowly, maybe not wanting to believe their friend had been losing his mind right in front of their eyes. "Scotty, if he believed Greymore was innocent, did he have an idea of who was responsible?"

Scotty looked up with haunted eyes. "He thought there was something in the lake. Something that ate animals...and people. I just...I laughed at him." He looked pleadingly at Ortiz. "He said he was going to prove it. He was...he was going to go looking for it. He was right, wasn't he? And now it got him too..."

John and Charlie gaped at Scotty, then turned to Ortiz. "Robert, I think Scotty here is pretty upset. Surely, I mean, you're a police officer. This kind of talk…it's crazy. Isn't it?" John clearly wanted to hear an answer that would fit in his world where everything was debits and credits. Something that made sense, that balanced out on the bottom line, that *added up*.

Ortiz finished his beer, unsure of what to say to these men. What he believed was that Bugsy's theory was a lot closer to the truth than Crawford's. But that kind of talk would have him out of a job in no time. On the other hand, to shoot down Bugsy and portray him as a drunk or half-crazy old man, that was just wrong. "I appreciate all of your honesty and cooperation tonight. As I said, I'm here on my own time, but if this conversation were to be repeated, it would still impact a police matter. My being here unofficially would only muddy the waters in Crawford's eyes. Whatever is going on in Haven, I will get to the bottom of it, on my own if I have to. That I promise you." He looked pointedly at John, then the others. "Can I count on your discretion until my investigation is complete? For Walter?"

All three men nodded and mumbled their agreement. Ortiz held Scotty's gaze a moment longer, feeling a silent understanding pass between them. He nodded, threw a twenty on the table, and walked out.

(42)

THE OLD man got off the bus at the same gas station where a few short weeks ago the inevitable series of events were set in motion when Greymore and McCarthy had innocently stopped for gas. He wandered over to the pumps, wiping perspiration from his brow. The man pumping gas wiped his own forehead with a dirty rag and stuffed it back into his pocket. "Hot enough for ya?" he asked amiably.

Immediately the old man placed the face and the rambling voice. He was the spitting image of an old friend, Matt McCauley. Matt was a writer for the *Haven News* and had been the person he had been supplying information when things had started to go bad. He had been afraid to look him up after the explosion. But Matt would be his own age now. It hit him then that he was a generation behind and this was probably Matt's son. Most of the adults he met would likely be children of people he had known back then. The thought saddened him, the realization that he had missed seeing his friends marry and have children. Missed seeing those children grow up and have kids of their own. My God, I could be a grandfather. The thought was staggering and he blinked back the tears he felt, pretending to wipe sweat from his eyes. "Too hot, too early, I'm afraid. I'm looking to stay in town for a spell, any recommendations?"

The man finished pumping and made change for the driver, watching him pull away. "There's the new Holiday Inn right up the road here, but I'd say your best bet would be to get a room at old

Betty Chandler's place. She'll whip you up some of the finest home-cooked dinners, no extra charge, and you'll still pay less than the Holiday Inn. Unless you're looking for air conditioning and a pool, then of course Holiday Inn would be the way to go."

His mind was working fast. He needed to find out a lot of information in a short time. Getting it from a local was the best way to do that. If he could hook up with Matt McCauley he could get everything he needed. He would have to reveal his identity to Matt but it would be worth it. Better than the endless hours at the local library. "Chandler's sounds just fine, I'm sure this heat will pass soon enough. And the home-cooked meals I could definitely use," he laughed. "You know, you remind me of a guy I used to know, last time I came through these parts."

"You don't say! Who might that be?"

"His name was Matt McCauley." Mossy watched the man's face open up. "I met him when I was stationed at the old base here in town, back in the early forties it must have been."

The man stared off for a moment before offering his hand to Mossy, "I'm Chris McCauley. Matt's son."

Mossy grabbed his hand and pumped it furiously; "I'm..." he almost faltered and gave his real name, "Frank Rodman, pleased to meet you. How is old Matt, is he still in town?"

Chris's face clouded and he cleared his throat, "My father was killed on the base. There was an explosion in '44. Everyone was killed."

Mossy shook his head slowly. How could this be? He struggled with what to say next. "Matt wasn't in the service when I knew him. I was transferred before the explosion. I lost a lot of friends in that disaster, I just never knew he was one of them." At least I can be honest about something, he thought.

Chris smiled a faraway smile. "He was on the base for an interview. He was writing for the town paper. My mom says there was a lot of talk back then about the base. My father was going there to try to break a story. Talk was that it was more than just an ammo depot. My father had a source on the inside. He was going to interview

General Gunlinger, the guy in charge of the base. Turns out my dad was on to something. This guy Gunlinger just killed himself. Made some weird comments in a suicide note." Chris shook his head "I don't remember my dad at all. My brother and I were just rug rats when he was killed."

Mossy couldn't blink back the tears this time and they ran slowly down his face. That bastard Gunlinger really covered his tracks. He even set up Matt to be on the base the day of the explosion. "Your dad was a fine man and a brave one too. I'm truly sorry to hear about this."

"Thank you, Frank." Chris wiped his own tears away and glanced at his watch. "If you want to hang here for a bit, I'd be happy to drop you off at Chandler's. I'm closing in about twenty minutes; you can grab a cold drink and the paper and save yourself a walk or cab fare."

"I'd be much obliged. You're sure it's not out of your way?"

"Not at all. I haven't seen Betty in a while, anyhow. I'll introduce you," he smiled slyly, "it'll be just about supper time by then." He winked and headed toward the office.

He tried to absorb everything during the short ride through Haven. How it had changed! Many of the old farms were gone, new housing developments now stood where the barns and pastures used to be. The amount of stores in the center of town was overwhelming. Many of the streets had changed to the point where he didn't even recognize them. Chris chatted the whole time, like they were old friends. He talked mostly about people in town, some whose names rang a bell. Mossy tried to steer the conversation to the present situation. "I thought I saw a story in the paper about a murdered child."

Chris turned to look at him, frowning. He could feel Chris's eyes trying to read his expression. He tried to keep his face open, friendly. Chris turned back to watch the road. "Terrible thing, it's like sixty-one all over again."

"Sixty-one, what is that?"

"Nineteen sixty-one, when this happened before." He wiped his glistening forehead again, "It was hot as blazes that year, just like this, and now it's starting all over again." He banged the steering wheel with the palm of his hand, making the car swerve slightly to the side of the road. Mossy waited, giving him time to continue on his own. He didn't want to seem too curious and draw any suspicion.

"I was nineteen and my little brother, Jake, was eighteen. Irish twins, as they say. Bad things started happening in Haven, kids disappearing, some found all torn up, some never found. A bunch of us went out to the lake to do some fishing. There was me and Jake, my girlfriend Lori and her little brother, Kevin, and one of Kevin's pals, Willie Decker. They were only nine or ten, just little guys. We always traveled in a pack by then, safety in numbers as my mom used to say. Anyway, Lori and I wanted to go over to the rocks and dive in to cool off. It was hotter than Hell that day. Little Kevin and his friend stayed down at the shore, fishing. Jake said he'd stay with them. He was half-cocked but promised to keep an eye on them. We older kids had been drinking a bit. What else would a bunch of teenagers be doing on a hot summer day?" he looked at Frank, his eyes begging understanding, if not forgiveness, "Anyway, Lori and I were diving in, having a good time, fooling around a little on the rocks, when we hear screaming. We get back down there as fast as we can and Willie's gone.

"Kevin was hysterical, ranting about Willie being taken by a monster. Jake was drunker than we thought, said he slept through most of it." He paused to wipe his face again, tears instead of sweat this time. "All I heard was that Willie was in the water. Lori and I dove in and kept going under, thinking we could find him, save him, but Willie was gone. We finally had to give up before we drowned ourselves. I grabbed Jake and made him tell me everything he remembered. He said he was half awake and Kevin told him he was going into the woods to pee. He thought he dozed off again and was dreaming when he heard Kevin screaming. I remember going over to Kevin; the kid was probably in shock. I knelt down in front of him and asked him what he saw when he came out of the woods. He said he saw a monster come out of the lake. When it touched Willie he fell asleep and the monster dragged him into the lake. Then he just started crying and shaking.

"When they finally caught the guy, it was easy to see why the little kid thought he was a monster. His face all fucked up like that. He is a monster. The Butcher. People figured he wore Scuba equipment, came out and injected Willie with something, then took him. The crazy part is that Kevin never believed it. He actually testified in the guy's defense, swore it was a real monster that took his friend. A lot of weird things went on that summer. A long time later, when Jake was really drunk one night, he told me he didn't sleep through the whole thing. He said he woke up when Kevin first screamed. He said Kevin was right. He never said anything more about it, drunk or sober. Though it's hard to find him sober even if you tried. Now this guy is back, out of prison, and kids are dying again."

"I'm really sorry, Chris, I didn't mean to bring up all these bad memories. I was just trying to keep up the conversation. I'm very sorry about your brother." Mossy was stunned. He thought of the impact his life had had on this one man's family. How many other families were ruined? Like a stone dropped in a pond (or *lake*), the ripples just kept spreading wider and wider. He shook his head, trying to maintain his composure. And what about the guy they call the Butcher? After rotting away for all those years to finally get out and face the same fate all over again? He had to do something. "Do the police really think this guy would come back here after all that time and start killing again? He'd have to be insane."

"Don't you think it's insane to kill children anyway?" Chris snapped.

"Of course, but the killer was so clever to have eluded the police before. Why wouldn't he move to a town where nobody knew him if he was going to kill again? That's all I meant."

"I know. The same question bothers me. It just doesn't make sense. Over twenty kids disappeared back in '61. Almost all summer the town lived in fear of him. He would certainly know that if he came back and another kid disappeared, he'd be the first suspect. I just don't get it. Maybe he is just crazy."

"What about your brother, is he still here in town?"

"In and out of the drunk tank, mostly. Most everybody thinks its guilt, blaming himself for not watching those kids and letting Willie get taken."

The old man licked his parched lips, "Is that what you believe, Chris?"

He waited as Chris struggled with the question. "No. You'll probably think I'm either crazy or a drunk myself but I believe he's trying to forget something. Something he saw that day at the lake."

(43)

DENNY SAT in the small set of bleachers at Memorial Park watching Billy warm up for his baseball game. Joe often took him along whenever Billy had a game. Tonight, Billy's cheering section was one bigger; Paul Greymore sat on Denny's right with Joe and Tina next to him. Billy kept glancing over, as if expecting trouble. Denny knew why. It was obvious from the minute they stepped out of the car that they weren't welcome. The blatant stares and the people whispering to each other and sometimes pointing were not his imagination. Nobody wanted Greymore in Haven, let alone at a park full of kids. Not a single person had actually said anything yet, but the family seated in the same row of the bleachers got up and moved when they saw Paul coming.

When the game started, people had something to focus on besides Greymore. Denny watched with a mixture of emotions as Billy played flawlessly at third base, fielding everything that came near him and making throws cleanly to first base. Now, in his first at-bat, he stung an opposite-field double down the right field line, sending Frankie DeLeo all the way home from first. As happy as Denny was to see Billy do well, there was a tinge of jealousy. Denny loved the game, loved to play the game, but had shied away from try-outs again. He avoided all organized sports, unaware of the real reason: his brother's memory. What if he wasn't as good as Jimmy? Worse yet, what if he was *better*? Billy tried to convince him, Joe had even offered to take him to try-outs this year, but Denny always had an excuse. Now, watching the game, he knew he would have made the team. He wasn't as good as Billy, not quite, but he was good enough.

His reflections were interrupted as angry shouts came from the crowd. Denny's heart lurched, thinking people were finally screwing up enough courage to confront Greymore. But that would come later. Now it was just a bunch of kids who wandered across the outfield causing a delay in the game and the shouts from the spectators. Before Denny's heart could settle back into its proper place in his chest, he realized it wasn't just some random kids, it was Crawford and company. And he would recognize those long, tanned legs anywhere. Julie Cummings was with them.

Denny could see Julie trying to pull Crawford off the field, but he was too strong. Then he grabbed her arm and twisted it, shoving her roughly away.

"That son of a..." Denny turned to see Joe trying to get up but Paul and Tina were holding him from either side telling him to stay calm. Finally the group reached foul ground and the game could continue. On second base, Billy had his hands on his knees and his head down. He looked like a kid who was out of breath after legging out a double, but Denny knew him better than that. He wouldn't be winded in the least: he was humiliated by his sister's bad choice of friends. For that, Denny hated Crawford even more.

By now the group had made their way to the stands. Denny recognized Tony Costa and Buddy Dentner, the usual suspects in other words, flanking Crawford. Chuck Brantley was noticeably absent from the party. In fact, Denny hadn't seen Brantley with Crawford very much since the night at the library. Whether Brantley had seen enough that night to smarten him up, or Crawford had kicked him out of the gang, Denny didn't know. Either way, Brantley was better off for it. Denny felt sick, wishing he was anywhere but where he was. *Something's going to happen*, he thought. *As sure as I can smell rain in the air sometimes, I smell trouble right now.* Dale and Julie were arguing loudly and Denny could see her eyes darting in their direction as they fought. Eventually Dale noticed too, and when he turned and saw Denny and Greymore sitting with the Cummings, Denny knew just what kind of trouble he smelled.

"Well, well, look who's here: the freak and the geek." As always, his hyenas laughed.

Denny felt Greymore's body tense next to him. He could almost smell ozone in the air now, like a thunderstorm was close. As much as it must have hurt Joe to see his only daughter with that creep, he saw the immediate danger in what could happen if Greymore got a piece of him. He would be on his way back to Braxton: do not pass go, do not collect two hundred dollars. Joe stood and turned to Greymore, putting a hand on his shoulder.

"Paul, stay here with Tina and Denny, let me handle this." Paul was staring at Dale, staring hard, but he gave Joe a barely-perceptible nod. As Joe turned and started down the stands, Denny jumped to his feet.

"Denny, stay here." Paul's voice was insistent, but when Denny looked in his eyes, he saw what looked like understanding.

"I can't, Paul, not this time. Okay?" Again, this time with a look of resignation, Paul nodded.

He slipped through the crowd and made his way down the stands, catching up to Joe. He glanced at Billy, who had completely stopped paying attention to the game and in a bizarre role-reversal was standing on second base watching the action in the stands. Joe turned to see Denny and his eyes quickly darted to Greymore then right back to Denny. With his lips set in a grim line, he turned back toward his daughter. Crawford, with his gang in tow, had started up the stands despite Julie's increasing protests, and now they met halfway up as Denny took his spot next to Joe.

"Julie, go sit with your mother, Mr. Crawford and I have something to talk about." His eyes never left Dale's. Julie was looking down, probably afraid of what she might see in her father's eyes, probably not wanting to look at Crawford at all for putting her in this situation. As she tried to move past Dale, his hand shot out and grabbed her arm.

"I don't think I want my girl anywhere near that child-killing freak." Dale sneered.

"Take your filthy hands off her, Crawford, she's as sick and tired of your shit as I am." Before Denny knew he was even thinking them, the words were out of his mouth.

Crawford's head snapped in Denny's direction. His face began to redden and he screamed a single word. "You!"

Denny saw a look in his eyes that went a few steps beyond anger. Maybe just a step or two away from crazy. Crawford shoved Julie away and stepped toward Denny. Denny's senses seemed heightened as he waited for Crawford's attack. Behind Crawford, Denny saw that Billy had wandered off second base at the sound of Crawford's voice. The pitcher spotted it too and he whirled and threw a strike to the second-baseman, who tagged Billy out. The crack of the ball hitting the glove was as crisp as a gunshot. Denny saw Julie's eyes widen and in that split-second he thought he saw a spark of concern for him in them.

Finally, he saw Dale's wrecking ball of a fist arcing toward him. Before the jaw-shattering blow arrived, Joe's hand shot out and caught Crawford's fist in his. Billy raced off the field toward the stands. Joe's eyes remained on Dale's as he squeezed Dale's fist. Crawford winced and now Denny saw the fear in his eyes. Dentner made his move, stepping around Crawford to get to Joe. Denny waited until he was close, then swung. It was a wild punch, but it was fueled by years of being bullied, and it landed squarely in Dentner's unsuspecting gut. Dentner doubled over, the air leaving his lungs in a violent reverse gasp. As he desperately tried to breathe, he stared at Denny with an expression that said *you did this to me?* And before he could get any air, Denny swung again. This was a left-handed swing that had none of the fury or power of his first punch. But it was enough. It connected with a sickening noise to Dentner's ear and he went down silently, still unable to suck in enough air to utter a whimper let alone a scream. Costa moved fast, grabbing Denny roughly by the shirt and landing a glancing blow to his head. Out of nowhere Billy came, batting helmet still on, hitting Costa in the small of the back in a flying tackle. Costa bent awkwardly before slamming into Denny, sending them both crashing to the stands. Billy was flailing wildly at Costa who was struggling to throw Billy from his back. Denny was pinned under both of them, helpless to do anything but watch the scene unfold. Dentner had regained his ability to breathe and when he touched the trickle of blood dripping from his ear, he looked at it quizzically, then reacted. He threw Billy and Tony aside and pounced on Denny's chest, his knees grinding Denny's shoulders into the rough wood of the stairs. Before Dentner's punches began raining down on him, Denny saw Billy suffering the same fate. Costa had ended up on top of Billy's and now had Billy's arm twisted behind his back while he took wild swings at Billy's head with his other hand.

Denny fought off as many of Buddy's punches as he could but his arms were going numb with Dentner's weight pressing down. Suddenly the weight lifted and Denny saw Paul holding Dentner's shirt collar in one hand and Costa's in the other.

Through it all, Joe continued crushing Crawford's fist. He stared Crawford down the entire time.

Tina had made her way through the crowd and was holding the sobbing Julie in a protective mother's hug.

"Crawford, if you ever lay a hand on my daughter again, I will end you. Are we clear?"

Crawford swallowed hard and nodded.

"Say it."

Crawford winced and Denny could clearly see the frightened child that hid behind the bully. "I…I won't touch her again…ever."

The crowd, initially stunned by the scene and content as spectators, began to stir. A group of the men had gathered in a circle around them and muttering began to turn to louder voices. Finally, inevitably, the mob started closing in.

"Hey, get your fucking hands off those kids!"

Paul let go of their shirts and held his hands up, trying to show he was only trying to help. Costa and Dentner shrunk away behind Crawford. Paul helped Billy and Denny up, trying to ignore the rising voices in the crowd.

Joe stared at Crawford for another long moment before letting him go. Crawford pulled his hand back, opening and closing his fist, as if surprised it still worked.

A burly man lumbered closer to Greymore. A couple other guys moved in next to him. Joe stepped in front of the big man. "Henry, no need for this to get any worse. That piece of shit," he moved his chin in Crawford's direction, "ever put his hands on your Becky, you'd have the same little chat Dale and I just did, right?"

Joe turned to one of the others, "Sully, you have a son a year or two younger than Billy. How would you like Dale Crawford and his little gang messing with him?"

Sully and the third man looked up at the big man, Henry, for direction.

Joe went on, "This has nothing to do with Paul Greymore. Those kids are too old, too big, to be picking on Billy and Denny. And nobody but chickenshit bullies put their hands on a young girl. Paul just broke it up. You saw it the same as everyone else here did." He spoke this last line loudly. "Okay?"

The big man, Henry, thought about it for a minute. It was a long minute and the murmurs began again. In the distance a siren wailed. He looked at Greymore curiously, then back at Crawford. "Sure, Joe. We just want to watch the end of the game."

Joe nodded, put one arm around Tina and Julie, the other around Billy, nodded at Henry and the others, and headed down the stairs. Denny felt Greymore's arm on his own shoulder and followed Joe down. Only when they were almost back to the parking lot did they hear Crawford's screams.

"This isn't over! This is NOT over!"

As they piled into Joe's car, the approaching siren grew louder and somewhere deep in his heart, Denny was sure this was not over, not even close.

(44)

MOSES BLAAKMAN, known now as Frank Rodman, was sure he'd made the right choice about his lodging five minutes after meeting Betty Chandler. She would be a bottomless pit of information—that is, if her non-stop chit-chat didn't drive him crazy first. He listened patiently to her life story.

Betty Chandler had moved to Haven just a year after the events of '61 were through. She and her husband had retired from New York, having sold a fairly successful catering business. Real estate in Haven, needless to say, was going cheap. Betty's husband Greg had heard a rumor there were plans for building up Haven into a resort area—golf, activities on the lake—and figured on making some investments. The stories were not accurate, but Greg and Betty fell in love with Haven and bought a big old Victorian in the center of town. Minor restorations and renovations, and they had a bed and breakfast. It never really made them any money, but in truth, neither cared. They loved the area and loved people. Anyone that did happen through town stayed with them and raved about the meals. Greg passed on quietly in '71 and Betty decided to keep the place running.

Chris's timing was perfect and he worked himself into a dinner invitation after introducing "Frank" and Betty. Over a delicious meal of baked ham, beans and potato salad (which Betty apologized at least a hundred times wasn't something more) the talk made its way from the usual "where are you from, how long will you be in town" back to the return of Greymore and the missing children. "Well," Betty breathed, "if you ask me, there's something very weird going on here, and I don't mean that Butcher nonsense either." Frank was immediately interested in hearing more. He was trying to figure a way to prompt her to continue, but Betty Chandler needed no prompting. "Chief Crawford's on the verge of a nervous breakdown, and that boy of his, nothing but no good."

Chris looked up from his plate. "What's going on with Dale?"

Betty was in constant motion, refilling drinks, wiping the table, picking up plates, and always ready to say more. "He's been getting caught drinking, getting in fights, and I heard," here she pauses, ever the storyteller, "he even got into a fight with that Paul Greymore. Didn't win that one." She chuckled, seeming to enjoy this fact more than she probably should.

Chris looked up again, frowning. "Now how on earth did you hear about that, Betty?"

Betty looked momentarily annoyed—to think anyone would question her ability to find things out—but this passed quickly into a knowing smile. "Don't you worry about how I know, young Mr. McCauley, but I do know."

Chris shook his head. "Well I hope you've got it right before you go spreadin' it around to anyone with two ears."

Now she really was getting annoyed—no—pissed off. "I don't think I like what you're suggesting, Chris."

Chris looked torn—wanting to really tear into an argument—but not until he finished his dinner. He took a couple more quick bites while he contemplated his reply. "I think you know perfectly well what I'm suggesting, and why. Let's just say it wouldn't be the first time you've told stories that were not a hundred percent...accurate." He quickly followed this by shoveling three more forkfuls of potato salad into his mouth, as if afraid Betty would tear the plate away from him in anger.

To Frank, this was beginning to look like an old and familiar dance. Betty's smile hardened and her eyes narrowed as she stared at Chris. He didn't seem to notice, being so focused on his meal. "You'll never let that go, will you? What's done is what's done and I can't change it. I said my sorrys to you and I meant them. But don't you come into my house, sit at my dinner table, eat my food, and try to give my houseguest the idea that I'm some old busybody who spends her days whispering about every little this and that, no matter if they're true or not. That is not what I do and you know it, Mister McCauley."

Chris looked like the embodiment of an ad for "the guy who went too far." Whether he was upset about accusing Betty or just afraid he'd jeopardized any future dinner invitations, he backed down. Wiping the last remnants of beans from his plate with a slice of bread, he looked sheepishly from Frank to Betty, suddenly aware of the uncomfortable tension he had ignited. "I'm just saying I was there and I know exactly what happened and I want to make sure you do too."

Frank cleared his throat, and both Betty and Chris's heads snapped in his direction. Betty's look was victorious, Chris's was relief. "Sorry," Frank mumbled, "Would you two like me to step out?"

Betty-the-hostess quickly returned. "Don't be silly, Mr. Rodman. You might even be interested in hearing this." She gave Chris an I'm-going-to-tell-it-my-way-and-God-help-you-if-you-interrupt-me look, then proceeded to relay the story of Greymore's return. At the same time she somehow cleared the dishes from the table and reset it with apple crisp and dessert plates.

Chris nodded a few times during her story, but was now more interested in the dessert menu. "My, my, Betty, but you have outdone yourself on all accounts. That apple crisp looks wonderful, and you must be in cahoots with either Dale or Greymore to know so much about what happened. Or maybe you were hiding in the back of Father McCarthy's car?"

Whatever little storm had brewed between them had passed for now. Frank was intrigued by the drama that had already unfolded in little old Haven. "Well it certainly sounds like this Crawford kid needed a hard lesson."

"Truth be told, Mr. Rodman? He's had his share of hard lessons living with that man as his father. Not one to spare the rod, Chief

Crawford. In the line of duty or at home. Doesn't mind the drink, either, from what I hear." She served the apple crisp as she spoke. "Not that Dale didn't have it comin' to him, of course."

Frank pondered the recent events as he gobbled down the best apple crisp he could ever remember eating. It seemed that for such a small town, Haven was full of tension. He needed to keep them talking and get as much information as he could. "Betty that was far and away the most delicious dessert I have ever had. I'm about ready to bust." Betty beamed and waved him off, but it looked to Frank that she was waiting on the compliment. He made an exaggerated stretch after he pushed his plate away and wiped his mouth. "Chris, you mentioned the lake on the way over here." This bought Chris a questioning look from Betty. "Probably all built up with big houses and overpriced gift shops by now."

Chris was on his second helping of apple crisp, so Betty jumped in. "No such thing, Mr. Rodman, still as quiet and beautiful as ever. Too far off the beaten path for most. Too much tragedy for the rest. A lot of people, including myself, don't care for the lake. It's pretty enough, but so much bad luck in this town has centered around the lake. Too much to be a coincidence if you ask me."

This was exactly what Frank was hoping for. "Yes, Chris mentioned some of what happened back in the sixties, and I saw the story of a murdered boy just the other day. Terrible thing."

Betty nodded slowly, a faraway look in her eyes. "Oh, there was that, and it was probably the worst, but it seems there's always something. I guess you have to expect a drowning here and there, and some fool skating too early or late in the season and falling through the ice, but..." she shivered and wrapped her arms around her, as if sympathizing with those who had gone through the ice. "It's like it's everything around the lake, too. Like it's the center of something bad. Greymore's own parents, that awful hospital up there on the hill, that poor O'Brien fellow and his son getting killed in that accident, then the priest. How tough it's been for Jan and little Denny since then. You know, she refuses to set foot in a church since the funeral. It seems like too much for one town."

Frank felt the room shift. The kitchen swam in front of him, black dots appearing and disappearing. It just couldn't be. *Jan*. He suddenly wanted a drink and to be back at the Boston Common drinking it.

"Mr. Rodman, are you alright? My Lord, you look like you've just seen a ghost. Mr. Rodman?" Betty had a towel damp with cold water before he could even speak. He pressed it to his forehead, closing his eyes as if that would block out his thoughts. He had to know.

"I'm fine, thank you, Betty. It must be this heat. I'm sorry to interrupt." Somehow he kept his voice even and conversational. "This Jan, did you say O'Brien?" Betty nodded and he plunged forward. "Some folks I met way back had a little one named Jan, different last name, I can't recall..."

"Blaakman." It was McCauley who answered, looking at Frank suspiciously now.

He tried a smile, shaking his head. "No, that wasn't it, I'm sure." He brought the towel back up over his face. His stomach was trying hard to push dinner back up. His mind was flashing backward and forward—thirty-four years back, forward to the present—just a fleeting second in his mind, but for some it was a lifetime. The anguish his daughter must have suffered, losing her husband and child. For his grandchild, here and gone, and never knowing him. It was too much. He slumped down on the table unable to think, unable to move. Far away he heard chairs scrape and voices calling someone named Mister Frank Mister Rodman. One thought, one word, was echoing in his mind, blocking out everything else. Somewhere in a deep hidden crevice, he knew it should be "Jan" or "family" or "grandson"—but no. DRINK. If he didn't get a DRINK...a DRINK would make it go away...a DRINK would make it better. He felt hands pulling him up, wiping his face with a cold cloth, someone now lightly slapping his cheeks.

"Frank, Frank, should we call a doctor?" Chris looked at Betty, and her expression mirrored his own. "Frank, come on, are you okay?"

He squeezed his eyes shut tighter, willing his stomach not to empty itself. DRINK. He tried to focus on not throwing up or passing out, tried to keep that word DRINK out of his head. How tough it's been for Jan and little Denny since then. Denny. Jan. She was alive. Her other son alive. Probably still in Haven. DRINK. DENNY. DRINK. JAN. DRINK...

NO! He couldn't go back to that life. Yet? No, NEVER! He had a daughter and a grandson.

"I'm okay." He muttered.

He blinked a couple of times and took the towel from Betty and wiped his face. "Really, I'm okay now. I don't know...maybe the heat...maybe coming down with a summer cold."

He looked up at Betty and Chris. On their faces he saw concern, but something else—suspicion.

"I'm sorry; I don't know what came over me." He had to keep them from thinking he was anything but someone passing through who stopped to look up a couple of old acquaintances. Based on this evening, he knew he would be the subject of conversation all over town by morning with these two gabbers.

"I'm afraid I haven't been completely up front with you folks about my visit to Haven." The look that passed between Betty and Chris almost brought a smile to Mossy's face. He had them. They were practically salivating at the prospect of better gossip than some old guy almost passing out at dinner. "You see, I was in the military back in '44." He paused—what had he told Chris already? "I was at the base before the explosion. I was there for an inspection, strictly routine stuff. Walk around, make sure proper procedures and safety measures were being followed. The thing is, the inspection went fine, but I had the strangest feeling the whole time I was there." Betty and Chris were riveted. Perfect. "It was almost too good. Everything in its place. These inspections were unannounced, and we almost always found a few little things to report. Documentation not available, log books not up to date, nothing flagrant usually or even remotely dangerous, but *something*. Not this time. It was like they knew we were coming." He paused, partly for effect but more to conjure up the rest of the tale.

Chris spoke first; he had some skin in this game. "Isn't it possible they did know you were coming? I mean, there must have been leaks, even in the military." He spoke logically but his eyes told the real story. He knew his own father had gone to the base investigating something; he wanted it not to be in vain. He wanted something to be wrong. And, of course, something was.

"I thought about that, too. There are a couple of reasons why it doesn't seem right. First off, we were never questioned after the explosion. It seems that an accident like that happens so close to a safety inspection that was passed with flying colors, the investigation itself would be called into question. Did we cut corners? Did we miss something? Were we bribed? But nothing. Myself, or anyone else on the inspection team—never questioned, never consulted. Doesn't that seem strange?"

Chris was nodding; Betty was looking from Chris to him, wanting the story to go on. "It sure does. Especially because of what I know of my dad wanting to investigate. There was something going on." He spoke with conviction. He spoke like an ally. "What else? You said there were a couple of things?"

"Some things people said while I was there, on the base. Part of the inspection involves personnel interviews. Nothing obvious, but looking back after the explosion, I just don't know."

Betty might as well have been sitting there with pencil and paper. You could almost see the wheels of her memory bank turning, filing all of this away for later. "What kinds of things?"

He shook his head, not sure how much to tell. "Some of the soldiers seemed spooked, you know? Some talked like they were afraid of the base commander, but others were afraid just to be there. They talked about noises, late night activity around the lake. The place was an ammo depot, not a training facility, what were they doing at night? Some even thought people were disappearing. They mentioned a couple of guys who were suddenly reassigned. But they could never get in touch with them. I looked into it; the records were all intact, transferred, a security clearance too high for me to get any details. Then the explosion. No survivors. Not a single person off-site? Nobody on leave? Nobody patrolling far enough away to live through it?" He shook his head again, not having to feign the grief and frustration he felt.

"My father didn't think it was an ammunition depot." Chris looked to Frank, then Betty. "Weapons. He thought they were testing some new super-weapon. Maybe nuclear. It would explain a lot, the secrecy, especially the explosion. I was too little to remember but my mom told me all this."

Betty looked about ready to burst. He felt torn between the satisfaction of getting these people on his side and getting information and the fact that he was using them. He was no better than Gunlinger: whatever means necessary to reach his end. But if his end was for the good of the town, to clear an innocent man's name, did that make it alright? Self-doubt and the need for a drink began making a play, but Betty, God bless her, just kept talking.

"I'll tell you one thing; someone needs to get to the bottom of it. Haven is too nice a town to survive much more of this. People's spirits break, the good folks leave and soon all you're left with are the thugs and drunks and rowdies. Then where will we be? Now that poor Sheehan family, the funeral tomorrow is going to be a tough one."

It was a soapbox speech if ever he'd heard one, but one look in Betty's eyes confirmed that she meant it. Chris sat nodding and he could see the same pride for his town that Betty was verbalizing. And he knew that while Betty didn't know it, the "someone" she mentioned that needed to take action was sitting right in front of her. It was a daunting responsibility but it was also the first time in a very long time that anything but a cheap drink actually got him excited. He needed to make things right, if not for the town then for his family. For himself. Then the moment of exhilaration passed and left him tired to the core. He had a funeral to go to in the morning. "Betty, you've got yourself a beautiful spot here and I'm sure things are going to work themselves out. Everything happens in cycles: war, peace, the economy...everything but the Red Sox...they're a constant, I guess."

Betty and Chris took the bait again and the mood lightened. The next half hour was all baseball and he soaked it in. This is what could have been, he thought. "Well folks, I've had a long trip and that was the finest meal I've had in...I don't know how long." Wasn't that the truth. "Now I need a hard bed, a soft pillow and about ten hours of sleep."

Betty the innkeeper took over, shooing Chris out and getting him settled in one of her guestrooms. The room was perfect and even though the night remained hot, he slept the sleep of the righteous. Or at least the exhausted.

(45)

FATHER MCCARTHY looked out over the congregation, feeling every day of his 72 years. Funerals were a part of being a priest, but the funerals of children were something he would never get used to, not if he lived another 72 years. The shining casket was so small, too small, but the pain it inflicted was immense. His eyes found Molly and Rich Sheehan and he felt their grief. They looked nothing like the happy young couple that attended Mass faithfully, always holding hands and smiling, their two boys in tow. Their faces were lined with loss. The distance between them in the pew told an old story: grief-stricken parents looking for someone to blame and ultimately finding each other. He made a mental note to pay them a visit in a week or two to see how they were coping.

As he was about to begin the service, the door at the back of the church opened and a blinding slice of sunlight pierced the gloom. McCarthy watched as the silhouette resolved into an old man as the door closed behind him. It was nobody McCarthy recognized, probably a distant relative, he thought, and began the service. When it was time for the eulogy, Rich Sheehan made his way clumsily to the dais, already sobbing; his eyes held the hollow look of heavy sedation. He did admirably well, speaking with a dreamy, loving joy of both his boys, bringing sad smiles to the faces in the crowd as he related a couple of amusing stories about his rascal sons. Molly was stoic throughout, making McCarthy wonder who had it worse;

Molly for being there or Rich for not being there. His question was quickly answered.

As Rich finished his prepared speech he paused and looked at the casket, then at Molly. "My last memory of Eddie is kissing his sleeping forehead before leaving for work on the day he died. My wife, my poor Molly, has a different scene to remember. I can close my eyes and see his face, puffy with sleep, rolling over after my kiss. What Molly sees..." His voice broke and fresh tears were streaming down his face. "What Molly must see when she closes her eyes...it haunts me. Because what she sees is my fault, for not being there, for not being there to save my son..." His knees buckled and he collapsed to the floor, sobbing uncontrollably. Molly couldn't hold back her emotions. First a single tear rolled down her cheek, then she was at her husband's side trying to console him, her own grief pouring out in her tears.

She helped him down from the altar and he stopped abruptly in front of the casket. He placed one hand gently on it.

"I'm so sorry, Eddie. Why..."

Then Molly and other family members carried his sagging form back to the pew. McCarthy looked into his eyes and immediately looked away. The pain and guilt were something he didn't want to see. How Rich could survive this, he didn't know. McCarthy again looked out at his congregation. They were waiting for something to make this better, waiting for *him* to make it better. He stepped up to the podium and cleared his throat. He cast his eyes over the anxious crowd and they found the old man sitting in the back. He was sitting with his head in his hands, shoulders shaking, clearly crying. At that moment he looked up and his eyes met McCarthy's. In those eyes, McCarthy saw the same anguish and shame he had just seen in Rich's eyes. Then the man got to his feet, and without looking back, exited the church. As the blazing shaft of sunlight narrowed with the slowly closing door, McCarthy began to speak.

Later, at the cemetery, McCarthy found himself scanning the crowd for the old man. He silently cursed the weather. As much as people complained about cold, cloudy, drizzly days for funerals,

McCarthy would take it over this every time. This was a day for picnics and beaches, cook-outs and cold beer, not a day for burying a child. The sun was relentless and he was sweating profusely. The humidity made it seem like he was breathing with a hot pillow over his face. Everything felt as moist and rancid as an armpit. But the Sheehans had gotten themselves together and were holding hands as they each dropped a handful of dirt on their son's casket. The hollow, scratchy sound it made always made McCarthy shudder. It was the sound of finality, of an ending, not a happy one. Molly and Rich hugged and McCarthy thought they might just get through this after all.

As the service concluded and he invited the mourners back to the Sheehan's house, he caught a movement out of the corner of his eye. It was the old man, he had been there after all, watching from a distance in the shade of a stand of old pines that bordered this side of the cemetery. McCarthy finished, had a few words of consolation with the family, and made his way toward the old man. Clearly this was no relative or he would be with the rest of the family.

McCarthy knew that murderers sometimes went to the funerals of their victims, and he had a gut feeling that this guy had something to do with whatever was going on in Haven. As he strode across the thirsty grass, the man turned and began walking away. He wasn't hurrying, McCarthy didn't even think he had seen him coming, he had apparently just decided it was time to go. McCarthy caught up to him on the other side of the pine grove. "Excuse me, sir?"

The old man stopped, hesitating for a minute before turning to face McCarthy. When he did, McCarthy realized the man was older than he had first thought, and his eyes were still clouded with the same look he had seen in the church. Up close, McCarthy saw it wasn't the fresh, unfamiliar look of new loss that Rich Sheehan carried, but an older, well-acquainted look of a lifetime of pain. The man met his gaze and a hint of a smile touched his weathered face. "Lovely service, Father."

McCarthy was taken aback. He wasn't sure exactly what he expected by confronting the old man, but he felt immediately disarmed by the man's open expression and calm voice. "Thank you. I'm Neil McCarthy, are you a relative?"

"No, just an old man with bad timing, I'm afraid. I went to the church to think, maybe to pray. I didn't realize there was a...service."

McCarthy was instantly back on his guard. *The man is lying.* He wasn't sure how he knew this, but he was sure of it. But for some reason, McCarthy was not afraid and pressed on. "So...you decided to come to the cemetery to think or pray, not realizing the service would end up here?" He tried to keep his voice light but it came out as what it really was: an accusation.

Instead of getting angry, the man's face seemed to sink. "I'm sorry, Father. Lying is obviously not one of my better skills. I read about the boy in the paper. I don't really know why I came...I'm not a relative, not a friend of the family. I'm nobody."

"Do you have a name...Nobody?"

The man seemed to relax, perhaps sensing McCarthy was not an enemy. "For now, you can call me Frank Rodman. Later, well, we'll leave that alone for the time being. I'm staying at Chandler's for a bit." He extended his hand.

McCarthy shook hands with him, his instincts telling him that as strange as the man was acting, he had nothing to fear. "Pleasure to meet you, Mr. Rodman. I apologize for...stalking you, but these are strange times in Haven. I feel it's my responsibility to do my part to keep it safe."

"Strange times, indeed, Father. About to get stranger, I fear. A pleasure meeting you. Now, if you don't mind, I need to seek refuge from this heat. It really was a beautiful service." He turned and began walking.

McCarthy's instincts told him that this man knew something and not to let him go. Before he could speak, cries from back at the grave site drew his attention. He turned and saw some people forming a circle around someone on the ground. It could have been Molly Sheehan but McCarthy wasn't sure.

Torn, but knowing his responsibility was with the funeral, he addressed the stranger. "I guess I need to get back, Mr. Rodman. Perhaps we'll speak again sometime."

HAVƎN

The old man stopped and turned to face the priest, his mouth again dancing at the edge of a smile. "I believe we will, Father." Then he was gone. McCarthy slowly walked back to his car, thinking about how familiar the man's face was but unable to place the resemblance.

(46)

DENNY TOSSED his books into his locker, slammed it shut, and turned to leave. His eyes tried to look everywhere at once. He and Billy were dead, it was just a matter of time. After the scene at Billy's game, he knew Crawford meant what he said: it wasn't over. They would get him, Billy too, it wasn't a question of "if," it was a question of "when." Denny expected to be more afraid then he felt. As he walked down the hall, waiting for the sound of footsteps running, the strong hands grabbing him, it was more a sense of resignation he felt. In a way, he just wanted it over with. But he knew when the time came, he would be plenty scared, and with good reason.

School let out an hour later than usual, thanks to a mandatory safety assembly. Denny left the school and walked slowly down the steps. The bus waited on the other side of the parking lot, a yellow safe house of sorts. Denny knew Stubby would not let Crawford on the bus. All he had to do was cross the lot and he'd be safe right to his doorstep. Billy had baseball practice and would get a ride home from there. He'd be safe, and if Denny could make it to the bus on his own, they'd both be okay, at least until tomorrow. One day at a time.

When he turned and began walking in the opposite direction, toward Haven Square, he was surprised himself. His heart was beating too fast and he felt his face and hands tingling he was so keyed up. If he turned and ran he could still make the bus. Every logical fiber of his brain was screaming at him to do just that. But anger and adrenaline were in charge, and he walked slowly and steadily toward town. Fear and logic had ruled for too long. A strange sense of calm overtook him as he heard the bus grind its gears and pull away. No turning back.

He left school grounds and wandered down side streets in a meandering route to town. The day was sunny and hot and he was in no rush. In many of the yards he passed, crocuses and tulips were bursting on the scene. The trees had filled with brilliant green leaves and lawns had shed their brown winter coats in favor of green themselves. Birds chirped loudly and a few dogs barked lazily when he passed. People were out, welcoming the spring. They cleaned leaves out of their flower beds and raked up last year's mulch. Everyone had a smile and a wave, and Denny eagerly returned each one. This is how it ought to be, he thought, this should be life in Haven.

He reached Main Street and paused. Going left would take him toward the library and the ball fields where Billy practiced. He could browse books for a while, then watch the end of practice and catch a ride home. Going right would put him in Haven Square. It wasn't much, boasting a Woolworth's, the Grand Theater, and a bunch of other stores including a pizza place and ice cream shop. Denny knew Crawford and his disciples would likely be in one of those two places. The hobby shop was also in that direction, and that was Denny's second favorite place (the library, of course, taking first place), and for the second time that day his feet carried him away from safe harbor.

Haven Collectibles was an irresistible mix of the kid's world and what Denny considered the good part of the adult world. Denny stepped in, the chime above the door jingling in his arrival. Mr. Goetts looked up and smiled, waving him over. Enjoying the dimness created by the tinted-glass windows, the cool of the air-conditioned store, and the slightly dusty, somehow *mysterious* smell, he ambled over.

"How are you, young Denny? Did Billy like the X-wing?"

"I'm fine, Mr. Goetts. Yeah, he loved it—who wouldn't, right?" Denny grinned.

"Indeed. What do you think of these?" He gestured toward some coins laid out on a piece of black velvet that he was about to put in the glass display case.

Denny moved closer and saw that they were all Buffalo Nickels. "Wow, those are cool!" Denny didn't know enough about coins to collect them. He had a book that could hold every penny from 1909 until 1985 and had a few holes beyond that to write in the dates after '85. Denny never understood that—did the people that made the book not know what years came next? Denny's had plenty of holes left to fill but that was the extent of his collection. But he did know that the nickels Mr. Goetts was adding to the display case were something he wouldn't mind collecting someday.

"Yes, they are...cool. I just received them in a shipment from down south."

To Denny, "down south" could mean anything from Saugus to Florida, but it was interesting to think about how Mr. Goetts got all the coins and stamps he sold. The counters on this side of the store were filled with them. Why he had never thought to ask Mr. Goetts the last thousand times he'd been in the store was a mystery. "Where do you find them?"

"Sometimes there are trade shows in the bigger cities: Boston, Providence, Hartford, and New York of course. But you won't get any deals there. I have people who keep their eyes open for me all over the place. Flea markets, yard sales, things like that. Sometimes you only get onesies and twosies, but sometimes, usually at an estate sale, you hit the jackpot. Part of the items are the former owner's collections. Sometimes amateurish, sometime very substantial. This one was somewhere in between. However, this particular gentleman had an affinity for Buffalo Nickels and wheat-back pennies, which are always quick sellers. My contacts know what I'll pay for them, so they get them as cheap as they can and sell them to me. And I sell them to the lovely residents of Haven and its surrounding towns. For a slight profit, of course."

Denny nodded slowly. "So it's their job to just go around to these yard sales and look for coins and stamps for you?" He wondered idly if there might be any such coins that found their way into the caves under the lake.

Mr. Goetts smiled. "Not their only job, I'm sure. But I certainly don't have the time to do it myself. And I'm always looking for a deal, so if you should come across any interesting finds, you bring them to me first, eh?"

Denny blinked; it was like Mr. Goetts had read his thoughts. "Sure! Maybe I'd get enough for the Dracula model."

Mr. Goetts laughed. "Maybe you would. Now go, I know what you came to see. But don't forget to keep your eyes open." He winked.

Denny made his way slowly to his real destination, taking in the rest of what the store had to offer. Aside from the coins and stamps in the glass counters that took up one side of the store, a set of shelves in the middle of the floor held a different set of treasures: elaborate kites; Lionel trains; small, hand-painted figurines of soldiers and cowboys; and several unmatched plates and cups with intricate designs. Denny moved to the other side of the middle aisle and glanced at the dizzying array of Testors paints that filled the shelf. It was a cursory glance at best; before he would need paint he would need something *to* paint. He turned slowly and couldn't hold back a smile.

The entire wall was lined with shelves that contained every possible model you could think of. Every sports car, every airplane, every battleship (even Cousteau's Calypso, another one Denny had his eye on), and of course every glow-in-the-dark Aurora monster model. Frankenstein, The Wolf Man, The Phantom of the Opera, The Hunchback of Notre Dame, and next on Denny's list, Dracula. Then his gaze caught another in the collection and he shuddered. The Creature from the Black Lagoon. Could something like that really be in the lake? A monster that came out and snatched kids? It seemed as unlikely as a vampire or a man that turns into a wolf. But wasn't the Phantom of the Opera just a guy with a messed up face...like Paul? His mind began to wander and the good mood that had filled him since he walked away from the school evaporated. Hideous images of monsters and bleeding, suffering children filled his head. These faded and it was his father in a hospital bed, connected to machines that kept him alive, still dying. He mumbled his goodbye to Mr. Goetts and stumbled into the blinding light of the afternoon.

He craned his neck nervously in both directions, sure he would see Crawford, and even more sure that Crawford would see him. He felt dizzy, disoriented. Why had he decided to walk to town in the first place? He could be home, safe and sound, watching television, or reading. Doing anything besides waiting to get his ass kicked again. Shaking his head and cursing his own stupidity, he started walking quickly toward the ball fields. He thought he might still make it there in time to catch a ride home with Billy. The tilting angle of the sun offered a different opinion. With every step he expected to hear his name called and to hear the gang overtake him. He looked over his shoulder, hating himself a little every time he did it.

The streets seemed much less crowded than they had and Denny wondered if he'd been in Goetts' store longer than he thought. It seemed closer to dinner time. *No*, his mind screamed, *it's late because you strolled here from school like you didn't have a care in the world.* This wasn't the Great Oz voice that sometimes helped him out. This was another voice that liked to mock him and berate him for his weaknesses. This time it was right. He got to the fields and felt a gnawing begin in his gut. The park was empty, cast into shadow by a random cloud floating across the sky. It would be a long walk home.

He leaned against the tall chain-link fence for a few minutes, mentally mapping out the safest route home. Finally, he pushed himself away and turned to start the trek, and felt his luck run out. Heading in his direction, probably coming from the ice cream shop or the pizza place after all, were Crawford and Buddy. Denny turned quickly, his mind trying to calculate a new route home, but Tony Costa was coming from that side. *They must have been watching for a while, giving Costa time to get around the other side*, Denny thought, *and now I'm screwed.*

Without a second thought, he scrambled up the fence and jumped off the other side, breaking into a sprint as soon as his feet touched the ground. He heard the yells and the sound of the fence as the others climbed in pursuit. He waited for the panic to set in, but still he felt calm. He was scared, he knew they'd really mess him up this time, but it wasn't the mind-numbing terror he expected. *Maybe you're not such a pussy after all*, the Great Oz murmured. Denny actually grinned while he ran for his life; maybe I'm not. The healing cut on his face itched, as if objecting, but he ignored it.

He knew he couldn't outrun them if they were close, but if he had enough distance and turned it into an endurance contest, he liked his chances. He dared a look behind him and saw his three pursuers about forty yards behind, spaced widely across the field. The gates leading to the street were at either corner; if he angled toward either of them, he would be helping close the gap with one of his pursuers, Buddy or Costa. Once Denny chose a direction, they would converge toward him. He kept his pace as he crossed the field. One thing was sure, he did not want to get caught here, on the empty fields with no one in sight to help. He hit the fence on the far side in full stride and launched himself over, barely keeping his balance when he hit the sidewalk. Now it was decision time. Buddy, the fastest of the gang, was coming from the far left, Crawford was following Denny's own route, and Costa on the right.

He broke right, wanting to keep as much distance as he could between him and Buddy. The sun had dipped below the tree line to the west and the streets were lined with shadows, a possible ally now that he was off the open field. As he sprinted by the gate at this end, he still had twenty yards on Costa. He heard Crawford hit the fence, then land on the other side with a grunt. Buddy would be the furthest back. He crossed the street and cut left down the first side street he came to, bolting up the first driveway on his right. It was a risk: if there was a dog or a fence to slow him down, they'd be on him. His luck was back, there was only a low chicken-wire fence separating the driveway from the backyard. Denny hurdled it and sprinted across the yard. He heard voices behind him as Crawford's gang united and three sets of footsteps grew closer. There was a stockade fence around the rest of the yard but the stringer rails were on this side, making it easy to climb. He was up and over quickly, landing in the next yard where he found himself in a maze of small fir trees. He was winded now, and the yard was a maze of shadows. A new plan was forming: hide here and wait them out.

He found the largest of the firs and squirmed through the low branches to get as close to the trunk as he could. The smell of pine was overwhelming. Denny heard voices on the other side of the stockade fence. He considered running but decided to stay put and see if they got sick of looking for him.

"I swear he came up this way," Costa gasped, out of breath.

"Could that little fuck have gotten over the fence that quick?" Buddy growled.

"Let's spread out. I'll go up this street and check the yards. Buddy, you're fastest, you go back around Oak Street in case he didn't cut down this street. Tony, you go over the fence in case he did go that way."

"But why—" The sound of an open palm striking Costa's face silenced his whine.

"Shut the fuck up and find him. Or I'll fuck you up instead."

Denny heard footsteps retreating and finally the sound of Costa making his way over the stockade fence. Luck was with him again; Costa was the dumbest and laziest of Crawford's minions, fueling Denny's hope that he might just get out of this with his face intact. He remained still as Costa wandered around mumbling, halfheartedly looking for Denny.

A sudden urge to giggle took Denny by surprise. He remembered a time back in second grade when he and Costa were both in Mrs. Nolan's class. Battleaxe Nolan was a terror. She was old and fat, really fat, but she took shit from no one. Costa wasn't a thug back then, just a class clown who didn't know when to keep his mouth shut. He'd been on Battleaxe's nerves all day and she'd finally had enough. She didn't like to punish the bad kids in the ways most teachers did. She rarely kept kids after school and never sent them to the principal or called their parents. Her disciplinary measures were based solely on humiliation. And boy was she good at it. She'd already moved Costa's desk right next to hers but that didn't stop his nonsense. So she dragged him by the earlobe around to her desk, and made him sit on her lap. "If you're going to act like a baby, Anthony, that's how I'll treat you." She cradled him in her flabby arms like an infant, actually rocking him back and forth, goo-goo-ga-ga-ing at him. When she squeezed his earlobe until he did what she wanted—suck his thumb—he broke. He sat on her generous lap sucking his thumb with tears and snot running down his face while the rest of the class laughed.

If Costa hadn't been such a jerk, Denny might have felt bad for him. Now, he pictured the teenage version of Costa suffering the same fate and couldn't control himself. He began giggling into his hands, trying to stifle the sound, but it only turned it into a snort. Costa was dumb, but not dumb enough to know trees didn't make that kind of noise. He was still muttering when he stepped in front of the tree Denny hid in. With no alternative, Denny squirmed out of his hiding place, his clothes caked with sap and smelling of pine. He took one look at the dopey expression on Costa's face and fell into a full-on laughing fit. He should have been scared, hell, he should have been terrified, but that look, that slow-witted, open-mouthed look of stupidity, was too much. It was the same look he wore before Battleaxe made him suck his thumb.

"You think this is funny, shit-for-brains?"

Denny looked at him, then laughed in his face. He was literally doubling over he was laughing so hard.

"You won't be laughing for long. Crawford is gonna waste you."

Denny's laughs subsided into a hiccup as he stared at Costa. "Why don't you do it yourself, asshole?" The words were out before Denny had even thought them. *Touché*, the Great Oz commented. It was the scene at Teddy's Spa playing out again. This time Costa didn't have Buddy or Crawford, but he didn't have Billy or Teddy.

Costa's face was an open book; he did not expect this. He was not used to one-on-one fights, he was used to the mob mentality Crawford inspired and ganging up on outnumbered opponents. He had the size and weight on Denny, but his eyes were full of doubt. Denny took a step toward him, and Costa's eyes flicked back and forth, no doubt hoping to see Crawford or Buddy coming to the rescue. Denny saw what was about to happen—Costa was going to yell that he found him, and that would be the end. Lights out, party over.

For no reason other than to prevent this, Denny swung. There was no real hate in the punch, not even anger, just calculated self-preservation. His fist connected squarely with Costa's mouth and he felt Costa's lips mash against his teeth. Blood was flowing before Denny's second punch came, a flailing roundhouse that grazed the top of Costa's head. With blood flowing freely down his chin from his mangled lips, Costa lowered his head and charged. Denny knew once Costa got his hands on him, he would be overpowered. Costa would sit on him, squeezing the breath out of him until the others arrived to finish him off. He sidestepped the oncoming tackle, at the same time putting everything he had into a mighty uppercut. The punch, combined with Costa's forward momentum, landed with a sickening crunch to Costa's nose. Yet another memory flashed in his mind at the sound: being out to dinner for his mom's birthday. His dad had splurged and ordered lobster. The sound it made when Dad cracked the tail was the same sound Costa's shattered nose made. His head snapped backward, blood already spraying from both nostrils, and he sprawled awkwardly into the tree Denny had been hiding in. He rolled off the branches, landing on his back. Denny pounced, not willing to lose the advantage. He dug his knees into Costa's shoulders with all of his weight. Costa's face was a wreck. Blood was pouring from his mangled nose and his shredded lips. His eyes were twin windows of terror. He couldn't speak, only making gurgling sounds and coughing on his own blood. He shook his head back and forth, eyes wide, waiting for more blows.

"You listen to me, Costa. I've had enough." He slapped him hard in the face to make sure he was listening. "You tell Crawford to stay away from me and Billy. And Paul Greymore. I've had enough." Suddenly the situation hit him, and he felt hot, salty tears burning his eyes. He was shocked at the damage he'd done to Costa, but part of him wanted to do more. "Do you understand? I've had enough!" Costa nodded, spraying droplets of blood back into his hair and forward to the front of his shirt. Denny cocked his fist back, feeling his entire body starting to tremble. He relished the fear on Costa's face, how he squeezed his eyes shut waiting for the pain. But in the end he couldn't do it. He climbed off Costa and stood over him. "You tell Crawford. No more." Then he turned and walked away through the pines. The smell to Denny was the smell of Christmas, and a memory rose unbidden. *He and Jimmy tore through presents while their mom and dad watched, snapping an occasional picture, both smiling and sipping coffee. With wrapping paper and bows flying, neither noticed Dad slip away. "Open this one next," Mom said with a sly grin, pulling a small gift wrapped in silver paper from behind her chair. The boys exchanged glances and both ripped at the paper together. Denny held the leash in his hand and saw his own confusion mirrored on Jimmy's face. They heard the cellar door open and suddenly a small tornado of black fur with a red bow around its neck bounded into the living room. The boys exchanged another look, this one of utter surprise, then fell to their knees to play with their new puppy. When Denny looked up, his parents were arm in arm and Mom wiped a tear of happiness from her cheek. "Thank you Mom, Dad," Denny said quietly, then the ball of fur was on him and he and Jimmy were lost in giggles.*

He wiped a tear from his eye as he walked. He felt no glory in what he'd done, no sense of victory. But whatever he was feeling had to be better than what he'd have felt if they all caught him, if only a little. He reached the street, got his bearings, and started walking slowly home. If the others did catch him, he would deal with it.

(47)

CRAWFORD'S MUSTANG sat idling in the shadows of the trees surrounding the lake. Aerosmith was playing on the tape deck but none of the three boys in the car paid any attention. Crawford and Buddy were turned around in the front seats, waiting for answers from Costa. Crawford drank greedily from the half-empty pint of whiskey, then passed the bottle back to Buddy. "I'm going to ask you one more time, you fucking 'tard, what happened?"

After the three had split up, Crawford and Buddy met back at the park, finding no sign of Denny. They waited impatiently, then went looking for Costa. Eventually, they went back to the pizza place and continued the search in Crawford's car. They finally found Costa a few blocks from his house. He'd been sneaking along the side roads, lumbering from behind a parked car and trying to hide behind a tree when he saw the car coming. Crawford and Buddy jumped out and grabbed him. Then seeing the mess that was his face, threw him in the car, stopped at the liquor store, and headed out to the lake to figure things out. Crawford knew, and he knew that *Costa* knew, that where they were parked was where Eddie Sheehan was killed.

Costa hadn't said much, other than he wanted to go home. The longer Crawford waited for an explanation, the more whiskey he took in, and the more pissed off he became. "This is it Costa. Spill it, or I'm going to drag you down by the lake and tie you to a fucking tree. If the Butcher doesn't get you, something will."

Costa looked shell-shocked, but at the last threat, he broke down and started sobbing. "Just take me home, Dale, please. My nose is broken, I think, and I...just take me home."

Seeing Costa's weakness was like pouring gasoline on the flames of Crawford's rage. He tried to control it, knowing at some level that he was capable of going too far and maybe killing this fat piece of shit. What made it easier was knowing there would be no retribution: Costa would just be another victim of the Butcher. He took a deep breath and spoke as calmly as he could. "Sorry, Tony, that's not an option right now. Once you tell us how O'Brien got away, I'll take you home and Mommy can fix up your stupid face. You have ten seconds. And I count fast. One...two...eight..."

"Alright!" Costa sobbed. "O'Brien did this. I found him and he sucker-punched me. He's gone crazy, Dale, I swear. He's not the same kid. He told me to tell you he's had enough and to stay away from him and Billy and Greymore."

Crawford burst out laughing. "He said that?" He took the bottle back from Buddy, took a swig, then gave it to Costa. "Well, Buddy, what do you say? I guess we better leave them all alone."

Buddy laughed. "Yeah, maybe we should move out of Haven just to be safe." He snatched the bottle from Costa and drank. Crawford glared at Costa. "Maybe you're just turning into a pussy like Brantley."

"No, Dale, I swear, he got me by surprise, that's all. We'll get him next time."

Crawford nodded. "That's more like it, Tony. Let's get you home and cleaned up."

>> <<

After he drove the others home, Crawford cruised around town, sipping what was left of the whiskey. He knew better than to go home too early himself, and run the risk of having to face his father. Cody Crawford had always ruled the house with a loud voice and a quick hand. Sometimes that hand held a belt, sometimes a lit cigarette. But lately it had been worse. His father was drunk most nights, and the abuse—verbal and physical—was getting out of hand. Dale hated his father but feared him more. He thought his father was going insane. And he knew it was Greymore's return that was causing it.

As the whiskey found his brain, the idea that Dale could fix all this by taking care of Greymore himself began to turn into a plan. He could picture finding Greymore by the lake with his next victim, the way his father had so long ago. In Dale's fantasy, he would save the kid, square off against Greymore, and beat him in a life-or-death fight to the end. His father would arrive at the scene and realize what had happened, pulling him in for a hug, telling him how proud he was.

When he came back to the real world, he was shocked to see he was on Hillview Street, idling in front of Greymore's house.

(48)

CHERYL PEROIT looked down at the small bundle she was holding with a twinge of emotion. Was it sadness? Anger? She wasn't sure. Whatever it was tugged at both her heart and her mind. She had come out to the lake with a purpose and now it was time to put up or shut up. From where she sat beneath the shade of a towering pine tree, the lake looked so tranquil. She shuddered despite the searing heat at what she had come to do. Just then the baby in her arms squirmed and let out a small cry. Cheryl looked down at the newborn just as he opened his porcelain blue eyes. He's hungry, she thought, I guess I can at least feed him. She lifted her shirt and let the baby nurse. The feeling was strange to her still. She reveled at the similarities of the circumstances that put her into this situation and the results of those actions.

How she had screamed in ecstasy in the back of Chuck Brantley's van and screamed in pain at the birth of the resulting child. How Chuck had tongued and sucked the same breast that was now being suckled by his son. And how Chuck didn't even know the baby existed. What would the point be? He was going nowhere and would have said it wasn't his kid, so she had dumped him when she realized she was pregnant. Twice she had called a clinic about getting an abortion, but both times she was unable to go through with it.

It had been easy for her to hide the fact she was pregnant. Who was going to notice? Certainly not her parents, who probably spent more time wasted than she did. So she simply wore bulky sweaters as she began to show during the winter. She was slightly heavy to start with so by just watching her diet, she was able to maintain her weight, although in the end it was all baby and Cheryl herself was as thin as she had been in years. How did I let myself get here, she thought to herself. Two years ago she had been an honor student thinking about college and life outside of Haven. Then she had met Dale and Chuck and all the rest of the gang and before she knew it, she was a burnout. Getting high before school, drinking after school, then onto bigger and better things like cocaine and speed and God knows what else she took when she was fucked up. Then to really hit rock bottom by getting knocked up by Chuck Brantley. Just this once without a rubber, he had pleaded with her. She was so coked out and horny herself that she had given in. And here she was.

She looked down again at the baby with a mixture of emotions. He had dozed off while feeding and she gently laid him down on the grass and pulled her shirt back down. He, she thought. She didn't even have the decency to name him. But what was the point? Making sure he was still asleep she reached into her jeans and pulled out a small plastic bag. Her hands shook as she unrolled it. She withdrew a small spoon from the bag and carefully dipped it into the white powder. She had already done some before coming out here but couldn't help herself, she needed more. At rare times when she wasn't stoned, Cheryl realized she had a problem. But at times like this, she had no problems, only solutions. Here goes another solution, she thought as she inhaled the cocaine, and then dipped the spoon back in and snorted again. By the time she had rolled the bag up and put it back into her jeans, she could feel the effects. She looked out over the lake again but now it seemed different. The water looked dark and foreboding. Despite the crystal blue sky and vibrant green of the woods surrounding the lake, everything looked dark and brooding.

"You are really fucked up now, Cheryl," she said aloud without realizing it. She picked up her son and stumbled down to the edge of the water. She squinted as she emerged into the ultra-bright sunshine, feeling the heat on her flesh. The baby squirmed but did not awaken.

She laid him down in the grass by the shore and sat on a nearby rock. It's party time, she thought. Once this is over, I'll get off the shit, start going back to school, and get the hell out of this town. It will be like none of this ever happened. Without waking him, she tied a cord around the baby's ankle. Already his skin had begun to turn a brighter shade of pink in the scorching sun. "Shit," she muttered. She had left the backpack up by the tree. She struggled to her feet and walked quickly up the slight incline to retrieve it. The tree seemed much further away than when she had walked down to the shore, as if it was moving further away with every step closer she took.

Finally she reached the tree, the shade a welcome relief. She reached into the pack and pulled out the ten pound weight she had taken from her basement, a remnant of her father's get in shape kick that had lasted about a week. That'll be longer than my baby lasts, she thought. Also in the pack she found a couple of cans of beer she had forgotten about. One for now and one for when the job is done, she thought. She put the weight down and cracked one of the beers, quickly slurping up the warm foam that oozed from the top. As she drank she thought of how easy it would be. Just tie the other end of the cord to the weight, Mom and baby go for a little swim, and only Mom comes back. Nobody will ever know.

Then it hit her, an unseen force, a voice booming inside her head, echoing through every crevice of her conscience. She dropped the can of beer and choked on the mouthful she was about to swallow. Foam sprayed from the can on the ground and from her lips. *You are about to kill your own son!* Suddenly her stomach recoiled and she doubled over, sinking to the ground, spewing hot vomit onto the grass. You could name him Carl, just like your grandfather. God, how she had loved her grandfather, why did he have to die? A distant cry brought her back to the situation at hand. She looked down to the shore and could see the baby squirming and crying. Its face and arms were bright red, already sunburned. Cheryl scrambled to her feet, almost losing her balance but steadying herself against the tree. "I won't do it, I can't do it!" she muttered. Suddenly it all seemed so clear. She could get help caring for Carl until she finished high school. Then she could work during the day and take college classes at night. She could do it. "Carl, oh my God, what was I thinking?"

She started down the slope toward her son when her foot caught a root and turned her ankle over sharply. She heard a snap, like the breaking of a thick twig and felt a white-hot pain shoot up her leg. She looked down and could see her broken ankle already beginning to swell. "Carl," she sobbed, and started crawling down the slope. Suddenly the water turned to a whirlpool at the shore in front of the baby. With a huge splash, a large black shape erupted from the lake and was on the baby. Cheryl saw what looked like...what are those things an octopus has...tentacles, wrap around its small body and in seconds the crying had stopped. Cheryl had stopped crawling, staring in disbelief at what was happening. It's just the coke, she told herself, that and the shock of breaking your ankle. Just get down there and get your baby out of the sun before he cooks. She stood, ignoring the grinding pain in her ankle, and began to run down the incline. The creature turned in her direction and she stopped. It has to be the coke, it has to be. It looked at her, then back at the baby with eyes too intelligent to be something she cooked up in a drug-induced haze. Then it slipped back into the lake, the cord around the baby's leg dragging behind, disappearing under the swirling water.

"Nooooo!" she screamed. "Carl, my baby!" She stumbled to the water's edge, sure that she would find her baby still there in the sun and all this was just another hallucination. But when she finally got there, hands and knees torn and bleeding, her ankle looking like a swollen sausage, Carl was indeed gone. The impossibility of what had happened swept over her. Overcome by shock, panic and cocaine, Cheryl collapsed at the edge of the lake.

{49}

MOSSY STOOD motionless, staring out across the lake. The distant trees shimmered in the scorching heat and the only sound was the gentle lapping of the water kissing the shore. The view was breathtaking. The shoreline was surrounded with lush, green foliage. The azure sky was brilliant and cloudless. The water was inviting; he could almost feel its coolness relieving him from the blistering heat. The thought of going into the water caused an inadvertent shiver. Mossy continued to roll everything over in his mind. The conversation with Chris had both added to his confusion and started to stir more memories. The lake played a huge part in this whole thing. And whatever it was…it was happening again. The funeral had been horrible. He had kept his composure talking to the priest, but it had taken every ounce of will not to find the nearest bar or liquor store.

Some of the things that Moses had started to remember were now becoming clearer, as if they were deep in the lake themselves and were coming closer to the surface. *It's not memories buried under the lake, is it Mossy? It's secrets you've been hiding from all these years, all the wasted years. And something worse, oh yes, something much worse.* Mossy swallowed hard and shook his head to exorcise the voice that was haunting him. He was suddenly parched, his hands and face breaking into a cold sweat. No drinks, he told himself. He held his hand up in front of him and was saddened to see the tremble in it. He was just a weak old man, and a drunk to boot.

Why had he come back? He could have kept on doing what he had been until he met the same end as most of the homeless; freezing to death, drinking himself to death, or getting killed by another homeless person, probably over a bottle. The yearning for a hit right now was overwhelming, almost dizzying. Mossy bent down and splashed the cool lake water onto his face. When he reached in to do it again, a memory came back so clear and fast that he jerked his hands out of the water and stumbled back away from the water's edge. He landed on his butt about ten feet from the lake, still staring across, letting the memory fill him.

A much younger Mossy stood at the edge of the water. It was the lake, yet it wasn't. He was inside, in a cavern, standing next to another man, both dressed in military uniforms. They were staring down into the black water expectantly, each holding a small flickering lantern. Other lanterns hung along the back wall of the cavern creating dancing shadows. The only sound was the splashing of water down the rocks and into the lake and the occasional shuffle or clearing of the throat from one of the men. Finally the other man, Tony Scibelli, spoke. "Do you think it survived the transition? The environment was very controlled in the tank; any number of bacteria in this water could prove fatal."

"Nonsense," Mossy snapped, "we exposed it to several strains of bacteria and also introduced amounts of lake water into the tank gradually. It survived."

A sound caused them all to jump slightly. But it wasn't from the water, it came from behind. A tall man, his face still hidden in shadow, emerged in the dim light. Yet they both knew who it was. They snapped to attention immediately.

"At ease, men," the man said, his tone almost inaudible, echoing strangely in the cave. "Status, please."

Mossy waited a moment, hoping Tony would answer but knowing he himself was expected to. "No sign yet, sir, but I'm confident..."

"How long has it been?"

"Almost four hours since the migration. We know from its behavior that it will go into a type of hibernation when stressed."

"*Pull it,*" Mossy's superior ordered.

Mossy was crushed. He knew the creature was fine, it just needed time to adjust to its new environment. "*Sir, I think it's a little premature...*"

"*Pull it, Scibelli,*" his voice still low, but more commanding, impossible to disobey.

"*Yes, sir.*" Tony replied, moving slowly toward the water. When they had transitioned the creature to the lake, they had attached a line to it for just this reason. There was always the possibility their work would fail and the creature would not survive the uncontrolled habitat.

Tony stepped forward, his shoes disappearing into the dark water. He lost his footing momentarily, almost falling but managing to regain his balance with an awkward movement, one foot coming out of the water and then splashing back down.

He reached down and grasped the line, pulling hand over hand. Mossy watched as the slack line tensed then grew limp again. Soon the frayed end of the heavy cord dangled from Tony's hands.

"*Goddammit! Didn't you check the line?*"

"*Of course. This is the heaviest line we have. I don't understand...*"

A sudden ripple caused each man to take an involuntary step backwards. A splash erupted closer to the shore, then a blur of movement. Tony screamed and fell in the ankle deep water, dropping his lantern; the flame extinguished with a hiss as it submerged. The shadowy darkness near the water's edge became thicker with just the single lantern. Mossy moved closer to Tony, who was now thrashing wildly, splashing water everywhere, and still screaming. Mossy saw another black movement and suddenly Tony was jerked into knee deep water and spun around so that it looked like he was trying to crawl back to shore, his grasping hands unable to find sure grip as he was pulled in deeper. As soon as it had started, Tony's screaming stopped, as did his struggling. The sudden quiet was worse than the deafening echo of the screams. Tony's body went limp, doing the Dead Man's Float on the surface of the shallow water, and then it was gone, pulled soundlessly under.

"I guess it just needed a little encouragement. Good work, Blaakman."

Mossy was still staring at the spot where Tony had gone under. He couldn't believe what he had just seen. Never in the lab had the creature been so fast and so vicious. "I think we should take termination steps, sir. We..."

The General moved closer to Mossy, towering over him. In his eyes, Mossy saw determination and victory. And something else. Something that looked a little like insanity. "That is not an option, Blaakman. Do you read?"

Mossy swallowed hard. The wrong answer would probably get him shoved into the water to join Tony. Knowing he was sacrificing something else to save his life, he answered slowly. "Loud and clear, sir."

Mossy jumped to his feet and scrambled further away from the water's edge. That was almost thirty-five years ago, he thought, it has to be dead. He squinted, looking hard across the water. It looked darker now, foreboding, even in the blinding sunlight. Mossy shivered, his body dripping cold sweat. The memories had finally come and now he was damned. All of the ugliness and pain and guilt knocked Mossy to his knees in the dry grass. His stomach recoiled and all he wanted was to be back on the streets of Boston with a full bottle and a head empty of these memories. He longed to splash cold lake water on his face, but couldn't bring himself to get any closer to the edge.

(50)

ROBERT ORTIZ finished typing the final portion of the incident report, put all the pages in a folder and walked it into Chief Crawford's office. Crawford didn't even look up as Ortiz dropped the folder into his IN basket. Ortiz shook his head and turned to leave, disgusted at Crawford for being too obsessed with Greymore to see what else was going on around him.

"What's that all about, Ortiz? I don't have time to read it right now." His tone was abrupt, distracted. He still hadn't looked up from the file he was reading.

Ortiz summarized the report, knowing Crawford would have it filed without ever reading it. "Eighteen-year old female. Cheryl Peroit. Medical exam validates her story that she recently gave birth. She is hospitalized with a severely broken ankle and appears to be in shock. Drug scan shows traces of alcohol and excessive amounts of cocaine. She was in possession of cocaine and there were a couple of cans of beer by the lake where she was found."

Crawford's head snapped up. "She was found by the lake?"

"A couple of fisherman came across her on the west side. She was unconscious and they were afraid to move her. By the time the ambulance got there she had come to. She went crazy trying to run into the lake, broken ankle and all. She was high as a kite. They had to restrain her and sedate her. I'm on my way back to the hospital to question her when she comes around."

Crawford stood and moved around to the front of his desk, color rising in his cheeks. "That name rings a bell. I think she goes with one of Dale's buddies. What about the baby? You said she had recently given birth. Is the baby okay?"

"That's the worst of it, Chief. When she was flipping out, she was screaming about the thing that had taken her baby. That's why she was trying to run into the lake. She said her baby was dragged off by a monster."

Crawford stared at him blankly. "So, have you found the baby?"

"Not yet. We're dragging that part of the lake and we've got a couple divers in. Her parents and her friends that we've found so far didn't even know she was pregnant."

"What! How can they not have known? Christ!"

"One more thing, Chief. There was also a ten pound weight found on the shore and some rope in her backpack. It's possible she drowned the baby herself. We'll know more either when she comes around or when the search team comes up with something."

"Just what we fucking need right now!" Crawford's face was beet red. He was pacing rapidly back and forth in front of Ortiz. "Get over there now. Make sure you're there when she wakes up and find out what the hell happened. I'm going to go find Greymore."

Ortiz felt his own face grow warm, tingling with sudden nervousness. "Greymore? What does he have to do with this?"

Crawford stopped pacing and stood in front of Ortiz. He locked eyes with him and Ortiz matched his stare. He didn't like what he saw in those eyes. Hatred, anger, madness? Nothing good. Not for the first time, lately, he thought he caught a whiff of alcohol on the Chief's breath. This Greymore thing is making him crazy, he thought. "Doesn't it seem suspicious to you that a baby disappears, once again in the vicinity of Greymore's house? Don't you think somebody fucked up on coke could see Greymore as a monster? Christ, the guy is a monster. Make sure you're there when she wakes up and find out if it was Greymore. Update me as soon as you hear from the search team. I'm going to find out where Mr. Greymore has been today. If he doesn't have a story I like, I'm bringing him in."

Ortiz opened his mouth to argue, but again Crawford's eyes made him change his mind. Nothing he could say would change what was going to happen. "I'm on my way. Docs say it might be another couple of hours and she might not be very lucid but I'll be there. Jameson is in charge of the search team. As soon as I'm updated, I'll track you down. Phillips is following up with more of her friends. He might end up talking to Dale, unless you want to take care of it."

Crawford seemed to relax a little. For a minute, he had looked like a tightly stretched wire, ready to snap. "Let Phillips handle the questioning. I want Greymore. I want to know immediately about any reports of kids missing. I don't care if they're five minutes late from school or their mother says they were abducted by aliens. I want to know about every one. This could blow and send the town into a panic and we need to be prepared for it. Try to keep it out of the papers for a day if you can. Understand?"

Ortiz understood all too well. "Yes, sir. I'll be in touch soon. Do you want back-up on Greymore?" Ortiz didn't like the thoughts of Crawford handling this alone.

"I'll call if I do but I'm not concerned right now. Let's keep the resources focused where they are now." He brushed by Ortiz on his way out of the office. When he got to the door he stopped and turned to face Ortiz once again. His face had returned to its normal blotchy complexion and his eyes had lost the fire of a few moments ago. "You understand it's our job to do what's right for the people of this community, don't you, Robert? That sometimes we need to make decisions for the greater good?"

Ortiz swallowed hard and cleared his throat considering how to answer. Before he could, Crawford was gone. It was beginning to seem much worse than Ortiz had thought. "He's never called me Robert before," he said aloud. His gut told him something bad was coming. He thought about getting someone else to cover the hospital and tracking down Greymore himself. Not for the safety of the town, but for Greymore's safety. It would mean his job to disobey a direct order. He was torn between his sense of duty and his instincts. He stopped to check something in the files before leaving the office.

He made just one brief stop before heading to the hospital to question Cheryl Peroit.

>> <<

Greymore dozed peacefully on his favorite chair on the screened porch. Father McCarthy had picked him up and treated him to lunch. There was still plenty to do around the house but the big meal combined with the heat had sapped his motivation. A short while ago he had heard police cars and an ambulance over across the lake, but wasn't able to see much because of the trees. Whatever it was, it didn't look good. He thought about heading over to find out more but the thought of Crawford being there made it seem intolerable. Instead, he had let the heat deplete his strength and ambition and kicked back in the chair. His eyes snapped open at the first ring of the phone. His life had been controlled by bells for seventeen years; it would be hard to ever sleep through an alarm clock or a phone ringing again.

He grabbed the phone on the second ring, assuming it was either Joe or Father McCarthy. "Get out of the house now, Greymore," the voice on the other end of the phone rasped. It was clearly somebody trying to disguise their voice.

"Who is this?" Paul demanded.

"Someone who doesn't believe all the stories. Crawford is on his way and you don't want to be there. Trust me." The phone went dead. Greymore slowly placed the receiver in the cradle. He couldn't make out the voice at all but he had an idea who it was. If Paul had learned one thing in prison, it was to trust his instincts. Right now his instincts were telling him to get the hell out of there before Crawford got there. He tried calling Father McCarthy and Joe but there was no answer in both cases. He moved quickly out of the house and down to the lake. Without thinking about where he would go, he hopped into his canoe and began paddling out, wanting to be around the bend of the lake before Crawford showed up.

As he paddled he began to size up the situation. Why would Crawford be on his way over? That answer came quickly as Paul remembered the activity across the lake earlier that day. There must have been a disappearance and that's why Crawford was coming. Sure, Paul had been with Father McCarthy for a good part of the day, but would Crawford even wait for an explanation? Or maybe Crawford would just lock Paul up and not allow him a phone call. The thought of it made Paul angry and scared at the same time. He could not spend another night in a cell. Not one. He had broken a sweat rowing and he was safely out of sight of his own house.

As disturbing as the phone call was, Paul felt a sense of relief. More than that, he was actually happy. Someone in this town besides Father McCarthy and Joe believed in him. Paul knew it was the young police officer, Ortiz, that had made the call. The man had treated him with respect the morning he drove Paul home. He must know Crawford is losing it. Paul shook his head, sending beads of sweat flying off of his face. Sooner or later, probably sooner, he would have to find a way to get Crawford off his back.

He was rowing in good rhythm now, moving steadily across the lake. The burn in his back and arms felt good. He lengthened his stroke, feeling the muscles strain, just like the old workouts in the prison yard.

At first, everybody had wanted to fuck with him. He was a scrawny kid with a mangled face who was convicted of killing kids. Even with the assortment of scum that called Braxton home, Paul was at the bottom of the food chain. A pervert. At a loss for anything else to pass the hours, he began lifting weights. It quickly became an obsession. Most would look at it as a release, but in fact it was just the opposite. The stronger he got, the angrier he got. He had been beaten countless times during his first few months, to the point he had considered suicide. He was able to put an end to that, pris-on-style justice. That was when Father McCarthy started visiting. His savior. McCarthy had kept him sane. He continued his workouts in the yard. He continued to gain strength pretty quickly, handling impressive amounts of weight for someone his size. It just wasn't in his metabolism to become bulky. It was deceiving to see his wiry frame lay down on a bench and start putting up two hundred an fifty pounds. Though still thin, he was all muscle, not an ounce of fat on him. There was always someone looking for a fight, though. He didn't win them all, but he did earn respect.

Now he felt that same energy coursing through him, fueled by contempt. His strokes were long and powerful, propelling the canoe faster and faster across the lake. His whole body was screaming but he continued in a frenzy of anger and adrenaline. His mind swirled, he pictured the prison goons coming for him, but now they all looked like Crawford. Faster and faster he paddled, cutting through the calm water, leaving a turbulent wake behind him. Only when he saw that he was approaching the opposite side of the lake did he allow himself to stop and cruise into shore.

He slumped forward in the canoe, spent. He gasped, trying to feed his starving lungs. His whole body was shaking, both from exertion and frustration. Would it ever end? Could he ever have a life without somebody after him? He knew his only choices were to figure out what was going on or get out of town for good. The first seemed impossible; the second was to admit defeat. He pulled the canoe up onto shore, still gasping, bathed in sweat. The woods were strangely quiet around him. The heat scorching. He started walking into the cool of the trees. His body had gotten what it needed, a grueling workout. Now he needed to clear his mind. He would hike into the woods and go over it all again in his mind, hoping this time something new would surface. He started into the trees, hopeful that he would find an answer.

(51)

MOSSY STEPPED hesitantly through the doors of the Haven Public Library. He stood for a moment as his eyes adjusted to the light. Though sufficient, it was dim in comparison to the glaring sun that remained high in the sky outside. After the incident at the lake he had gone back to his room, blanketed with despair. The temptation to stop at a local liquor store for a bottle had been overwhelming. Somehow he had forced himself to go straight back to his room. He had crawled into bed and been overcome with emotion. He had shuddered under the blankets, consumed with hate, anger, shame and guilt. His body wracked with the mental anguish he felt and the physical need for a drink. Finally, he had fallen into a fitful sleep. When he awoke, his mind was swimming with another new memory, as if it had come to him in a dream. He knew immediately it was real and was filled with a new sense of purpose. He felt an unnatural calm as he showered and shaved and put on clean clothes. He couldn't erase what he had done in the past, as no man can, but he could put an end to it.

Though he had cleaned up and looked more than presentable, just another older man spending a lazy afternoon at the local library, he felt as conspicuous as if he was wearing his street rags and carrying a brown bag in the suspicious shape of a bottle. Filled with resolve, he walked confidently past the desk, nodding to the woman who was stamping the cards of returns, and continued on into the research room. The library hadn't changed in all the years Mossy had been away. Of course it had been remodeled and painted and the furniture updated, but it was still the same. Mossy took a deep breath, letting that delicious smell of the books, of knowledge, fill his senses. As a boy, he had spent countless hours on days like this in the library soaking up anything he could get his hands on. He longed to go to the stacks and just grab a book and sink into one of the soft couches and drift wherever the book took him. But he had another reason to be here. Maybe someday, after this was over, there'd be time for imagination. Not now, though.

He began looking at the volumes on the shelves, quickly familiarizing himself with the system in which they were arranged. It wasn't long before he found what he was looking for. Among the many titles under the World War I category, he pulled a single book from the shelf. It was entitled *The End of the Great War*. He held it for a moment, afraid to open it. Afraid that what he thought to be a real memory might just be something his own imagination conjured up to help him through his pain. Finally he took the book over to a nearby table and sat down. He opened to the table of contents and found a chapter called Submarines: Monsters of the Deep. It couldn't be his imagination. Here was the exact book and chapter he had remembered. But that only proved he had read this book; the real proof remained to be seen. With trembling hands, he flipped open to the chapter. Swallowing hard, his mouth and throat like sandpaper, he began to turn the pages, his eyes moving up and down each page, more frantically as he turned each page and didn't find what he was looking for. When he came to the end, he shook his head and started over. It had to be here. After his second time through, he slammed the book shut. His stomach rolled and he felt dizzy. It was impossible. His mind could not have invented this whole thing.

The memory that had come to Mossy in his room, the one that had saved him from returning to his old life, was a spin-off of the one he had about the underground cave. When the experiment had started, it had been exciting. A little scary but ultimately good. When he and Tony had begun to realize that Gunlinger had different motives for the product of their work, the two had taken matters into their own hands. They had done research of their own, followed by exhaustive experimentation, often lasting throughout the night, even when they had full days of work to do after. But they had done what they set out to do. They had discovered a simple fail-safe to end the experiment if it got out of control. Mossy had written the formula in this book, in this chapter. He put his head in his hands, staring down at the book that he had thought to be his salvation. How could it be? The canisters he found in the safe deposit box were proof that it wasn't some booze-induced false memory. Suddenly his eyes widened as he read the cover. At the bottom of the book were words that were magical to Mossy. "Fifth reprint" was stamped on the lower part of the cover. Quickly he flipped to the copyright page and found what he was looking for. This edition of the book was printed in 1965—twenty years *after* Mossy had written in it.

His momentary relief was replaced by a new sense of dread. The original must be gone, replaced by this newer edition. He leaped up, overturning his chair in his haste to get back to the shelves. Luckily nobody else was in the research room. Mossy scanned the shelves eagerly, but he knew what the result would be.

"Can I help you?"

Mossy jumped at the sound of the voice behind him. It was the librarian. She must have heard the commotion and made no effort to conceal her dissatisfaction with the tipped-over chair.

"Oh, ah, yes, perhaps you can," Mossy stuttered as he bent to upright the chair. "I'm looking for an original copy of this book, printed in the forties. I did considerable research in it some time ago. Now that I read this volume, it seems to have changed. Is there any chance the original is still around?" He stopped, wondering if he sounded as absurd to her as he did to himself.

Apparently not. She moved toward the table to look at the title of the book. "We usually don't throw any books away unless they are in too poor condition, and even then we would donate them somewhere. We typically archive older editions if there are no significant changes; otherwise we keep both versions on the shelf."

"Oh, I see. Well, I've already checked the shelf but can't find it. Would you be able to check your archives?" He flashed a smile that at one time had quite an effect on the ladies.

She returned his smile, seeming pleased to have such a knowledgeable person in her library.

"Of course, I'll check right away." She strode off through a door between the stacks that Mossy hadn't even noticed until she disappeared through it. Mossy glanced up at the old clock on the wall. The hands seemed to be moving slower than real time. It seemed like an eternity before the librarian returned. In her hand was a very old, beaten up book. Mossy looked at the clock again, and realized she had only been gone five minutes. They must have a very efficient archiving system, he thought. She handed the book to him.

"This is the only other copy we have. It might be a little dusty. Please be gentle with it and return it to me at the desk when you are through with it." She smiled again and disappeared back into the main part of the library.

Quickly, Mossy flipped the book to the same chapter as before. There it was, just as he remembered. In black ink at the bottom of the page was a very long, seemingly meaningless string of letters and numbers. To anyone else it was gibberish. To Mossy, it was redemption.

(52)

ROBERT ORTIZ hated the waiting. So much of police work was not what you saw on television. The car chases, the shootouts, the grappling with suspects and grilling them in stark interrogation rooms; that stuff hardly ever happened. Mostly it was a waiting game. You wait for hours for the suspect to show up. You wait for calls to be returned. You wait for trial dates to get your shot to put some scumbag away. Today, Ortiz was waiting for the woman, actually the girl, in the bed to wake up. He'd been in the stuffy, sterile room for two hours carving a path between the window and the chair by the bed. Waiting

He rose again from the chair and retraced his footsteps to the window. Outside, Haven shimmered in the afternoon heat. People bustled around, bringing the sick into the hospital, taking the healed home. Most were unaware of the girl in the bed, Ortiz himself, and what was going on in their quiet little town. Below, in the parking lot, a boy on crutches was being helped into a car. On the street beyond, a woman dropped a bag of groceries and two boys jumped off their bikes to help her pick them up. Their normal lives ticked on, unaware of the girl and the cop.

In the bed behind Ortiz, the girl moaned softly. Ortiz turned and saw her peaceful, drug-induced sleep becoming fitful. Her moans grew louder and she began first shaking her head back and forth, then twisting her entire body from side to side. Before Ortiz could get to the side of the bed, Cheryl Peroit suddenly sat up, snapped open her eyes, and looked at Ortiz with one of the most alarming stares he had ever seen. It wasn't the foggy, confused look he expected. It was intense, full of questions, and full of fear. "Where is Carl?"

Ortiz felt his heart drop. The waiting wasn't the worst, he remembered. It was telling people about the death of their loved ones: in this case, her own child. But was she a victim or a perpetrator? "Miss Peroit, my name is Robert Ortiz, I'm a Haven police officer. I'd like..."

"WHERE'S MY BABY!" The woman—girl—began to take on a look Ortiz had seen before: the mixture of a memory she knew to be true and the desperate hope that it wasn't. Before Ortiz could stop her, she ripped the IV out of her arm and threw back the bed covers. On cue, a nurse and a doctor burst into the room and restrained Cheryl Peroit; their soft cooing and gentle pushing got her back where she belonged. "My baby?" The nurse and doctor assured her everything would be fine as they settled her back in bed and re-inserted the IV. Ortiz watched helplessly, reduced to waiting once again. "Where is Carl, where is my baby?"

"Miss Peroit, we were hoping you might be able to tell us that." Ortiz stepped closer, ignoring the disapproving looks from the hospital staff. "You were alone at the lake, unconscious and your ankle was broken. Do you remember anything?" At this, the doctor made his exit but the nurse remained sentinel.

Cheryl's eyes glazed for a moment, almost rolled back into her head, then filled with tears. "He's gone. The monster took him." Tears welled in her eyes, and Ortiz waited for the breakdown, but it didn't come. Cheryl remained calm, met Ortiz's eyes, and spoke again with the conviction of a person who is fully in control of their faculties. "It came right out of the lake, took my baby, took Carl. For a minute, it looked at me and I was sure it was going to take me too. Did you catch it, Officer Ortiz?" Her eyes remained wet, but no teardrops escaped.

Ortiz blinked. *How could a person sound so rational when what they're saying makes no sense whatsoever?* Then he thought of some conversations he'd had with Chief Crawford. To an outsider,

Crawford might sound like the voice of reason. To Ortiz, he was crazier than the proverbial shithouse rat. "Miss Peroit…"

"Please, call me Cheryl. Did you catch that…that thing? Did you get my Carl back?"

"Cheryl, as I mentioned you were found alone by the lake." Ortiz paused, not wanting to utter the next words. "There was evidence of cocaine. And there was rope. And weights."

To his surprise, the girl did not flip out. No hysterics, no denials, no ranting. Her calmness chilled Ortiz more than any of those reactions. "I did not kill my child Officer Ortiz. Something came out of the lake and took him. Yes, I did some coke. Yes, I went to the lake with every intention of…" Finally she broke. Her sobs were those of true suffering. Her body convulsed, like her entire being was trying to squeeze the liquid from her body through her eyes. And the tears came. The nurse swooped in, preparing to add a sleep-inducing cocktail to Cheryl's IV line. The girl saw what was about to happen and grabbed the nurse's arm. "No more drugs. Puh-puh-please?" The nurse shot another look at Ortiz. They must practice that look at nursing school, he thought. But she did not administer whatever was in the syringe. Not yet, anyway. Cheryl regained her composure as quickly as she had lost it. And suddenly she looked older to Ortiz. Just like that. A scared girl one minute, a…what scared adult the next. One who had experienced tragedy, seen the cold reality of the world. She wiped her eyes, blew her nose, and trudged ahead.

"I went to the lake to kill my baby. I know how that sounds, what it makes me. But I didn't do it. I couldn't. Something came out of the lake, Officer. In broad daylight, a monster came out of the water and stole my baby." Her eyes were holding Ortiz's gaze but he was sure she wasn't seeing him. Real or a drug-induced hallucination, she was seeing a monster take her child. "It was horrible. It had…tentacles, like an octopus. But it walked. I…" She paused, realizing how absurd, how drugged out her story sounded. She shook her head. "I saw it."

Ortiz waited. Silence was a cop's best friend when questioning a suspect. Guilty people couldn't seem to stand it, they had to keep talking to fill the void. And eventually they said something they wanted to hold back. But Cheryl remained silent, never breaking eye contact with Ortiz. A single tear snuck out of her left eye, blazing a wet trail down her cheek, and dropped to the white sheets. Silently.

(53)

DENNY SAT in the waiting area of Russell's Barber Shop, idly flipping through a battered copy of *Field and Stream*. Russell's was a mysterious glimpse into the adult world that somehow intrigued Denny at the same time it troubled him. It seemed no matter what day or time he came in, the same bunch of old guys were there talking about the same stuff. The Red Sox, politics, why don't they put a stoplight at the intersection of Main and Hartford Street: Denny felt like he was stepping into the rerun of a television show. Today was different, though. Denny sensed it as soon as he walked in and sat down.

He'd walked into town from school, knowing full well Crawford and his gang were out to get him. With everything going on, and after what he'd done to Costa, he wasn't afraid. Billy was at baseball practice and Denny was meeting him after his haircut and getting a ride home from Billy's dad.

The barber chair was currently occupied by Ray Jackson, one of the mechanics from Haven Auto Repairs (Foreign cars our specialty!). Denny realized he had never seen Mr. Jackson dressed in anything other than his Haven Auto greens with "Ray" proudly stitched above his heart. In a small town like Haven, you tended to bump into people pretty much everywhere: church (well, not for Denny), the grocery store, parents' night at school, and Denny had never seen another outfit on the guy.

Across from Denny in the waiting area, really just a bunch of chairs by the front window, sat Dom Moretti and "West End" Willy Seaver. Dom owned a television and watch repair shop in town and frequently did readings at Sunday Mass. In every town, there's a West End Willy. Nobody seemed to know much about him, including why he was called West End, he didn't appear to have a job, and he hung out in the barber shop or the coffee shop shooting the breeze all day. The odd thing about West End hanging at the barber shop was that he was bald as a cue ball.

Denny glanced up from his magazine, quickly looking down when he noticed Russell staring at him. *Here it comes*, Denny thought, *he'll stare at me for a while, dig through his mental phone book until he figures out who I am, then come out with, "You're the O'Brien kid, right?"* It amazed Denny that Russell could remember every person in Haven and who they were related to, but it unnerved him the way Russell gawked at him.

"You're Jimmy's little brother, right?"

At this, the rest of the guys turned to look at Denny. Sometimes Denny thought this was the worst part of being the brother left alive. Worse than the empty feeling and the heartache at missing Jimmy: the looks of others. Are they pitying me? Or are they thinking Jimmy should be sitting here instead of me? He felt his face turning red. "Yes, sir, Denny O'Brien."

"Good kid, that Jimmy. Helluva good athlete."

"Yes, sir." Now comes the rest. He'll ask me what sports I play and if I'm as good as Jimmy. Denny felt his face burning, felt the stares of the other men in the shop. His mind raced thinking of a way he could get up and out of the barber shop without looking like a complete jackass. But when he looked up, Russell was back to furiously clipping away at the wispy hair on Mr. Jackson's head and West End Willy had a finger cheerfully up his nose to the second knuckle. And an idea snuck into Denny's head, finding a crack in his grief and guilt over Jimmy's death: *maybe it's all in my head.* Before he could start analyzing just what *that* meant, the conversation around him veered off the normal path.

"What do you think Crawford will do about the Sheehan murder, about Greymore?" Dom asked.

Willy examined the treasure on the end of his finger, wiped it on the palm of his other hand, and began vigorously rubbing his palms together. Denny made a mental note to never shake Willy's hand.

"Mightn't have to do nothin'. Might be folks who take care of it for him," Willy offered. He spoke with an accent that Denny couldn't place. Somewhere south for sure. It just added to the mystery that was Willie. Maybe West End was somewhere in Texas, or the Carolinas.

Dom nodded thoughtfully. "You could be right on about that, Willy."

"Now don't leave us hanging," Jackson chimed in, "just what do you mean by that?"

Denny felt him staring again. He's wondering how much he should say in front of me. He brought the magazine closer to his face and began mouthing the words of an article about Large Mouth Bass, hoping the look on his face was one of intense interest. It must have been good enough.

"Coupla fellas in here over the past few days are talking about doing just that." Willy continued, "Sometimes folks get to talking big, but I got a feeling these guys weren't just flapping their gums, I think they mean business."

Denny flipped the page of the magazine, he wanted the men to keep talking and they wouldn't do that if they thought he was listening. He snuck a glance at Russell and saw him looking hard at Willy. "I think someone's gums are flappin' right now." The men all laughed, but Denny didn't hear any humor in Russell's voice, what he heard sounded more like a warning. One that Willy didn't pick up on.

"Folks think Crawford's gone soft. Too much time with the bottle to handle anything bigger than moving violations or breaking up brawls at the Hat. Might be that somebody has to do his job for him." With that off his chest, Willy went back to picking his nose.

Denny took another peek: Russell looked pissed. Ray Jackson was looking at Russell in the mirror with wide eyes that held a mixture of surprise and anticipation. Denny quickly went back to the magazine, sensing Russell about to check on him. After what seemed like an eternity, Russell spoke. "I don't think Chief Crawford would be too happy to hear that kind of talk. Funny you never mention it when he's in here for his weekly trim."

Willy pulled another winner out and began rubbing it into his palms. "I would have mentioned it, but the Chief was too busy looking through the envelope you gave him." He said it so casually, but it was a direct hit. Russell was seething. Jackson looked ready to jump out of the barber chair for fear of losing an ear.

"Willy, might be a good time for you to head out," Russell managed through tight lips.

Willy was already getting up. "Maybe so, Russ. I'm thinking about growing my hair out anyway." Dom and Ray cracked up, but Willy and Russell just glared at each other before Willy turned for the door. "But I'll leave you with this: there's other folks, me included, that remember a lot about when kids were going missing before. And when it ended up Greymore was behind it, things just didn't smell right." The bell jingled and he was gone.

Russell watched him go. "I think old Willy might have done some brain damage by sticking his finger a bit too far up his nose." The others laughed, but it sounded forced. "You're all set, Ray. Do you want the Al Capone?"

Ray snorted. "Of course, do you think I come here for your cutting skills and intelligent conversation?" That broke the tension and the laughter sounded genuine to Denny.

Russell chuckled as he opened a drawer and pulled out a device that looked something like an old belt sander but with rows of coiled springs where the belt should be. He slipped his hand into a leather strap on the top of the device and flipped a switch. Whatever the thing was, it started humming and Russell began moving it across Ray's shoulders, back and neck. Ray moaned and looked like he might just melt into the chair.

"Russell, I'll trade you my wife for that thing, straight up, right now." His voice sounded alien, vibrating. It reminded Denny of when his brother used to tap him hard and fast on the back and tell him to talk. It came out all weird, like Ray sounded now.

"No deal, Ray. Nothing against Mrs. Jackson, of course, but this is my secret weapon."

Finally, it was Denny's turn for his boy's regular. Most days, he would sit there with the napkin around his neck feeling too tight and the inevitable itch on his nose driving him crazy with his hands trapped under the barber poncho. Russell would ask him the usual questions and Denny would politely respond. But today was different, and what he had just seen had him burning with curiosity. "What's the Al Capone thing?" he blurted out before Russell could start his inquisition.

There seemed to be a new shine in Russell's eyes. Most people came in to shoot the breeze and gossip about Haven stuff. Not many took an interest in Russell or his profession. "Ahhh, you like the looks of that, huh? Or is it the name Al Capone that got you riled up about it?"

"Both, I guess." Denny replied, shyness taking over his curiosity.

"Well, that little beauty is called a portable massager. They were quite popular back in the twenties. After a shave and a haircut, important customers would get a massage. I call it the Al Capone because he insisted on the massage after his weekly cut. At least that's what the guy that sold it to me said."

Denny smiled. "Wow, that's pretty cool."

"Tell you what, young Mr. O'Brien. After I finish up with you up here, I'll try out the Capone on you. Better that than to have you come in here with your gang and shoot the place up." He gave Denny a conspiratorial wink.

As Russell began working on Denny's hair, the bell over the door jingled and in strode Jason Hamilton and Richie Lincoln. They were both seniors at Haven High and stand-outs on the football team. Jason was quarterback and Richie a wide receiver. At last season's Thanksgiving Day game, they hooked up for a 40-yard touchdown pass to win the game. The PA announcer, moderately famous in

Haven and surrounding towns for making up nicknames for players, called them "the Presidents." The nickname stuck and rarely did anyone speak of them as individuals anymore.

"I do not believe what my eyes are seeing" Russell squawked. "Do we have another victim of The Patron Saint of Barber Shops?"

Jason and Richie looked at each other with blank expressions. Almost simultaneously they flipped their long hair out of their eyes. It was almost eerie how similar they were; they were both tall and well-built with long brown hair. But it was their mannerisms that made them seem like they should be brothers instead of just friends. People said it was this weird link that made them so dominant as quarterback and receiver, because they almost seemed to know what the other was thinking. Some people just assumed they were queers.

"What do you mean, Russell?" It was Jason, but both boys were staring at Russell with equal confusion.

As the comb and scissors flew through Denny's hair, Russell kicked into storyteller mode. "Back in the sixties, when the Beatles first came on the Ed Sullivan Show, the country went crazy. Well, the country was already half-crazy because of President Kennedy being assassinated. But the Beatles, they made people crazy in a good way. But they were also the death knell for barbers. Kids saw those floppy mops and it was goodbye haircuts. I read that sixty percent of barber shops went out of business since the early sixties. Everyone wanted their hair long, like you boys."

Jason and Richie exchanged glances. "But what did you mean about The Patron Saint of Barber Shops, Russell?"

"I was getting to that. It was finally this year that things started turning around for this business. Let me guess, you boys want your hair cut short, above the ears, kind of feathered back?"

Russell had them. They both nodded, then flipped their hair back again. Denny thought it was an unconscious gesture that was going to look pretty stupid when they had short hair.

"Let me ask you another question: have you seen any movies lately that you really liked?"

Again they exchanged a look. "We saw Saturday Night Fever at the Grand a couple weeks ago." Richie said almost timidly. "That Vinnie Barbarino guy can really dance."

Russell barked out a laugh. "I rest my case, your honor. John Travolta, Vinnie Barbarino, Tony Manero...call him whatever you want. To us barbers, he is the Patron Saint. Just like in the sixties everyone wanted to be the Beatles, now everyone wants to be a disco king."

When Denny's haircut was done and the talcum was settling, Russell slipped his hand into the massage gadget and turned it on. Denny stiffened when it first touched his back, but immediately relaxed. It was a magical feeling that almost tickled but not quite, and it seemed to sap the energy out of his muscles. Denny felt like he was turning to liquid. In his own eerie vibrating voice, he said "Russell, if I had a wife I'd offer to trade her for that thing too."

That got Russell and Dom laughing so hard Denny thought they might actually fall on the floor and start rolling around.

Denny left the barber shop feeling great for the first time in a while. He loved the clean-cut feeling of just having his haircut, and the Al Capone might have been the best thing he'd ever felt. With the bell jingling behind him, he counted the money he had left, found enough for a milk shake at Leo's Drugstore, and headed that way.

When Denny arrived at the practice field, Billy was just finishing up and walked over to meet him. "Hey, Denny, my dad should be right along."

"Okay...Billy..." Denny had been thinking about what he'd heard at Russell's and was concerned for Paul's safety.

Billy knew immediately something was wrong. "Denny, what happened?"

"I think we need to tell Chief Crawford what we found at the caves." He quickly relayed what West End Willy had said about guys taking matters into their own hands. "I think they are going to do something. And soon. I'm scared for Paul."

"I think you're right. Let's go in the morning before school. I'll crash at your house tonight and we'll take our bikes. We can still get to school on time."

Denny was nodding. "Thanks Billy. I'd hate to see him get hurt after everything he's been through. Your dad is a good friend, just like you are, and Paul deserves another chance."

"You're not going to try to hug me, are you?" Billy said, then punched Denny's arm. "Let's go, there's my dad."

(54)

FATHER MCCARTHY snapped his head up quickly and looked around the room slightly confused. He picked the book off his chest and folded the page over where he had been reading before dozing off. The book was the very same one Denny had asked about the night he had shown up here after getting jumped by Crawford and his gang. McCarthy got up and went over to one of the bookshelves and traced a finger along the titles until he found what he was looking for. As usual, curiosity had gotten the best of him when Denny had mentioned this particular book. He had read through most of it before finding what Denny must have found, the story about the origin of Haven. Just as Denny had done, McCarthy did some quick math and concluded that if the curse held true, not that he believed in curses, Haven would suffer terrible tragedy this year.

McCarthy thought of everything that had happened since he had arrived in Haven with Paul. It seemed, curse or not, that the tragedy was already upon them. He shuddered to think what would have happened to Paul if they had not been together when the Peroit girl's baby disappeared. Crawford had shown up at McCarthy's door loaded for bear, clearly deflated when McCarthy told him that Paul had been there all day, preparing for a mandatory three-day seminar designed to re-acclimate long-term prisoners to society, then at lunch in town. Thankfully Paul would be in Boston for the next few days, away from the madness that Haven had turned into.

He pulled another worn volume from the shelf and carried it to his reading chair, willing himself not to look at the clock on the way by. He knew the night was more than half gone and he had barely slept. Not that this was unusual for him. He thumbed through the leather-bound journal until he came to the dated entries he was looking for.

He came to some notes from August of 1944, the year the Army ammunition base had exploded, killing everyone. Something had started scratching way back in his memory, trying to get to the surface when he had realized that based on the so-called curse 1944 was one of the years, like this one, that Haven would suffer. He flipped the page and found an article taped onto the page. Underneath it, in his own writing from so long ago, was the date and source of the article: *The Haven Sun*, July 29, 1944. McCarthy quickly read through the story, which was basically another account of the explosion and some possible explanations. There it was! That name; it rang a bell but he couldn't quite make the connection.

He read aloud, "General Hamilton Gunlinger issued an emotional, if somewhat confusing statement regarding the incident in Haven. 'I knew almost every person killed in that explosion, many of them I considered close friends. It puts a terrible burden on one's beliefs when something like this happens. You begin to ask yourself why God would do such a thing, so seemingly random and pointless. Then you realize that your faith is all you have to cling to. We are not privy to God's plan, nor can we try to supersede it with our own plans. That is now perfectly clear to me.'"

McCarthy scanned the rest of the article, which gave a brief biography of Gunlinger, and closed by saying he had transferred to a base in California when the decision was made not to rebuild the base in Haven. He reread the quotes from Gunlinger. What did that mean? Why was the name so familiar? McCarthy searched his mind for the answer, his gaze falling on the window across the room, where he could see the black night sky beginning to awaken to a lighter shade in the east. He would need to get some sleep; knowing the answer would come to him eventually. The way things were going in Haven he hoped it would come in time. He flipped through the journal, going forward in time from that entry. When he came to the final entry in December of 1945, he closed the book and went to the shelf to get the next series. The answer was here somewhere. McCarthy had kept a journal faithfully for most of his life. Somewhere there was a connection. As the sky outside went from a purplish gray to a flaming red-orange, McCarthy's journal fell to his chest and he slept fitfully, the answer to the riddle just out of his grasp.

He awoke shortly, refreshed after only a few hours of sleep, a new plan in mind. After turning on the kettle to make a pot of tea, he returned once again to his bookshelf. Instead of grabbing the next chronological volume, McCarthy skipped all the way to the latest journal he was working on. After adding a few heaping spoonfuls of sugar to his steaming cup of tea, he settled back into his reading chair, determined to figure out what was bothering him. Something about the explosion in '44 had started the gears moving but he couldn't quite make the connection. He started at the end of the journal, working quickly backwards from his most recent entries. It wasn't long before he found what he was looking for. As the tea cooled beside his chair, the article answered questions that had eluded him and robbed him of sleep for the night. It described the suicide of General Gunlinger and the strange note and newspaper article found with the body. The article talked about Greymore's release and the recent disappearances.

"Of course, how could I have forgotten this," McCarthy sighed aloud. The stress of the Sheehan funeral must have been weighing on him more than he thought. He sat back and closed his eyes, trying to decipher what it meant. Sitting up, he reached down to sip his tea, wincing at how cold it had already grown. He thought about a hot refill, but instead grabbed a pen that he always kept with his latest journal and began an entry for the day. Perhaps it would make sense written down, he thought.

August, 1944: Explosion at Haven's ammo base. Gunlinger survived, everyone else dead. Gunlinger makes strange quotes regarding "changing God's plans."

Summer, 1961: Disappearances/murders plague Haven. Greymore arrested and convicted for the murders.

May, 1978: Greymore released, disappearances begin again in Haven. Gunlinger commits suicide. Quoted in suicide note as "playing God." Found by the body was an article from the Haven Sun describing Paul's release and the new disappearances.

McCarthy read the lines over and over, and then began writing again:

Why wasn't Gunlinger on the base when the explosion occurred?
What is the connection between the killings in '61 and Gunlinger?
Why was Gunlinger monitoring the Sun? Couldn't be a coincidence that he stumbled on that article.

McCarthy was stumped. There had to be some sort of connection between Paul and Gunlinger, but what? Paul was just a child when the explosion happened, and then Gunlinger went to California. Could Paul's parents have known Gunlinger or had friends or family involved in the explosion, or with Gunlinger? McCarthy wasn't even sure Paul's parents lived in Haven in 1944. It would have to be somebody in that age range. Wait! He again flipped through his latest journal and found what he was looking for. The man he had met at the Sheehan funeral, Frank Rodman. He had said some strange things but with everything going on, McCarthy had forgotten about him almost immediately.

Shaking his head, he got up from the chair and walked slowly to the front porch. The heat was suffocating, even in the early morning. The air was still and heavy; it was like breathing underwater. McCarthy looked toward the sky, not an unusual pose for a priest. He was looking for rain clouds, however, not guidance. He decided he would talk to Greymore, confront him with the information he had when he returned from his seminar. Then, with Paul or alone, he would find this Frank Rodman.

(55)

JOE CUMMINGS sat at the bar of the Witch's Hat nursing a beer and glancing around nervously. He pondered the message he received at work just as he was getting ready to leave. His secretary had taken the call at the end of the day. She said it was Father McCarthy, pleading to meet him here this evening on an urgent matter concerning Paul's safety. She had seemed shaken up just from taking the call. Instead of trying to reach McCarthy or Paul, he had done as instructed. He had been here for almost an hour and there was no sign of McCarthy. Now that he had time to really think about it, why would McCarthy want to meet him in a bar of all places? As he waited the place began to fill up, Joe looking expectantly at every new person to enter, willing it to be McCarthy.

Something was wrong. He could almost feel the *wrongness* hanging in the smoky air. He was getting strange looks from some of the other men. Furtive looks, like they knew something he didn't. He glanced at his watch for the thousandth time and decided it was time to go. He headed for the pay phone to let Tina know he was on his way when another guy from the bar cut in front of him and grabbed the phone. "I'm gonna be a while, pal," he said with a stiff smile.

"I just need to make a quick call before I go so maybe you'd let me go first?" Joe answered jovially, trying to hide the rising fear.

"I was here first, pal, either wait or save your dime for later." Joe hesitated. He needed to find out what was going on. "You got a problem, pal?" He looked at the man, puzzled, and turned away. When he got to the door the man wasn't talking on the phone, just holding the receiver and staring at him. He stepped out into the night air and headed for his car. The parking lot of the Hat was dark, spotlights from the building losing the battle with the darkness that seemed to grow out of the surrounding woods. As he approached his car something seemed odd about the way it was parked. The reason for the strange angle of the car hit him and his whole body tensed.

When he got to the car he confirmed his suspicion—he had a flat tire. No problem, he told himself, probably ran over a bottle. He'd just change it and get home. He knew the spare in the trunk was good. Had to be a bottle, this was the parking lot of a bar, after all. It wasn't working, though; he couldn't convince himself that there wasn't something terribly wrong. His whole body was tingling with anticipation, fueled by adrenaline.

A dog barked off in the distance, the smell of stale beer and greasy hamburgers cooking over an open flame, everything seemed so intense.

The gravel crunching as he moved to the trunk to get the jack and the spare. The sound of the Hat's door opening and closing, opening and closing.

He had the trunk open and grabbed the jack and tire iron, the metal cool in his sweaty hands.

The sound of crunching gravel again, this time not caused by his own movements. Just other customers headed for their cars, god-dammit, that's all. Probably give you a hand and get you home faster.

But when he turned he knew he had been lying to himself. His instincts were right, something was very, very wrong. As the group of men approached he squinted to recognize them at the same time he tightened his grip on the lug wrench. The sound of their footsteps seemed deafening. Then the lights went out. For a moment he was in total darkness. His heart pounded and he considered running for the bar, or better the street; he had no allies in the bar. The darkness turned to blinding light as the high beams of a pick-up truck assaulted his eyes.

The men lined up in front of the truck, black silhouettes haloed by the headlights. He could see in their shadowy outlines that he was not the only one holding something. He thought he could make out a baseball bat and a chain and oh shit is that a gun? He thought of locking himself in his car but to what end. They'd get him anyway and he wouldn't have the satisfaction of taking a few swings before he went down. His fear seemed to dwindle, displaced by the resignation that he was in for a fight. "Evening, boys. Care to help a fella change a tire?" His attempt to sound nonchalant and cocky sounding scared even to his own ears.

The men began spreading out, forming a semi-circle around him, his car behind him. They began closing in. The gravel crunched, the dog barked in the distance. Joe reached back and slammed down the trunk. The action stopped the men momentarily and he saw his chance. He turned and leaped onto the trunk, then to the roof of his car. The men circled the car and finally one stepped on the rear bumper and onto the trunk. Joe smashed the tire iron to the man's knee with all his strength. The man's howl of pain sparked the others into action.

As they reached for him he swatted their hands and arms and fingers away, occasionally enjoying the sound of breaking bones. "I'm king of the hill you fuckers, try and take me down!" he laughed crazily. He swung the iron like a man possessed, hitting heads, arms, anything that came near him. He was beginning to think he might actually get out of this when a strange whirring sound caught his ears. His heightened senses recognized the sound just a split second too late as the swinging chain wrapped around his legs. Suddenly he was in the air, his legs yanked out from under him. His head and shoulders crashed onto the roof and he bounced awkwardly to the ground.

He tried to crawl under the car but they dragged him back. He kept swinging the iron and when he realized he no longer had it he swung fists instead. They finally got hold of him and he felt the grip of steel on his wrists, then a clicking sound. They handcuffed each hand to a door handle of his car as they beat him. "Handcuffs," he muttered. "Crawford! You bastard." The beating stopped and he knew he was right. He also knew that knowledge might have just gotten him killed.

"Finish it," a husky voice commanded, and the blows started again, until everything went black.

He had no idea how long he had been out for or what they had done to him while he was unconscious. He felt an arm fall numbly to the ground as the cuff was removed and he had a vivid image of Jesus being taken down from the cross. He tried to open his eyes and could only manage to get his left partially open. The right was either swollen shut or gone completely, he couldn't tell. He made out the shape of the man taking the cuffs off and realized that he was wearing a hood. "Am I dead?"

The man removed the second cuff and Joe's other arm fell to the ground and his whole body slumped further against the car. "Not this time. You best watch the company you keep, though. Next time you might not wake up. Worse yet, it might not even be you but that pretty little wife of yours. Or your son or that slut you call a daughter. Not that everyone hasn't had their shot at her already." The man giggled and Joe realized it wasn't a man at all, but a boy. He couldn't quite place the voice but it was familiar. He tried to kick the boy as he stood but his leg flailed uselessly. His clothes were warm and sticky. "Stay away from that freak, Cummings."

"Fuck you," Joe replied with nothing but tired resignation in his voice. The boy kicked him, then again, and Joe's world faded as the boy walked away laughing.

(56)

CRAWFORD SAT at his kitchen table with an empty bottle of scotch in front of him. The bottle had been nearly full when he first sat down. He was dressed in full uniform and there were only two other things on the table besides the bottle and a glass. One was a framed picture of his dead wife. The other was his service revolver.

Susan had been dead for almost thirteen years, since Dale was just a toddler, and Crawford had hardly thought about her in all that time. Being the local hero in a small town had afforded Crawford a lot of luxuries. He'd been young and handsome, built like a football player. Women had never been a problem anyway, but after nailing Greymore, they literally threw themselves at him.

Susan had been prettier than the prettiest. She hadn't thrown herself at him, hadn't really shown any interest at all. Perhaps that was what had attracted him. The thrill of the hunt. He had pursued her relentlessly, using his charm when needed, using his muscle to dissuade other suitors when necessary. Eventually, he won her over. They married quickly and Crawford thought he had it all. Looks, a great career, a beautiful wife. A few months after the wedding, Susan was pregnant with Dale. The icing on the cake, he had thought, a son. He could right all the wrongs his own father had done to him as a child. But when the baby came, it was a lot of work. Dale was colicky and suffered from chronic ear infections. He required constant attention, leaving little time for Susan to perform her marital duties. The little time they had, Susan complained of exhaustion. Cody began spending more time at the bar after work than he did at home. When he did come home, he was drunk and angry, a bad combination, especially for Susan.

The Greymore arrest was the last good bust he had made. And it preyed on him that maybe it wasn't so good. The wounds had plagued him, and Greymore's insistence that he was innocent and trying to save the girl seemed so damn sincere. But there were no more killings and with the help of the booze, it became easier and easier to silence his own doubts. But whether or not he was a good cop, that was harder. He found the solution to this was brute force. People opened up, did and said what you wanted with a little physical encouragement. He began to take this practice home to get what he wanted out of Susan.

One night, after he had broken up a bar fight, he came home and found Susan waiting up for him. She had been crying, and Cody thought something had happened to Dale. He'd been drinking and when she didn't tell him what was wrong the first time he asked, the second time he asked with his fists. He beat her badly, still stoked from the barroom brawl. Finally, she told him what was bothering her, and it was the last thing Cody wanted to hear. She was pregnant again. One brat was enough and she hadn't even gotten her figure back yet. Now another nine months of gaining weight and complaining, the end result being another screaming kid. It was too much. He began swinging and didn't remember stopping. When he came to, Dale was screaming in his crib, wet and soiled and hungry. And Susan was dead, her skull caved in.

Cody may not have been a good cop, but he was a good criminal. He immediately began calling friends and family, asking if Susan was with them. He explained that he had come home and found Dale asleep in his crib but no sign of Susan. Disposing of the body was not a problem: there was an old well on his property that had long been covered over. He threw Susan's lifeless body down it, along with some of her clothes and jewelry, followed by a few bags of lime. Then he covered the well and covered his tracks.

Susan had never taken to being a mother, he explained to sympathetic listeners. She missed her freedom. She had often left poor Dale sitting in his own mess until Cody got home. Her family argued vehemently that Cody was lying, Susan loved the baby, loved being a mother. But they were out-of-towners and their pleas went unheard. The official story was that Susan had just up and run out, taking some clothes and jewelry and cash. The outpouring of support Cody received was overwhelming. Neighbors and wives of other officers helped care for Dale. Cody stopped drinking for a while and played the role of betrayed husband and single parent.

All the while, Greymore haunted him. He had made deals with his connections at Braxton to make sure no mail got in or out. Greymore had no family so it wasn't difficult. The only one he couldn't keep out was that priest, but it hardly mattered. Everyone told the priest they were innocent.

Now Greymore was back and kids were getting killed again. Innocent or guilty? Crawford tipped the bottle to his glass but there was no more salvation there. He looked at the picture of Susan and felt a rare pang of guilt and remorse. How had he gotten here? What could have been? It was all spinning in his head, Greymore, the little girl he couldn't save, Susan, the baby that was never born…

He picked up the revolver, turning it in his hands. How could he ever make any of this right? Never mind right, he thought, he would settle for tolerable. He turned the gun again and stared down the muzzle. It was a black hole that held his stare. He believed that somehow it held the answers. He looked closer, not realizing his thumb was tightening on the trigger. Was there a light down there? Was that where the answer has been hiding all this time?

The room exploded with a crash and a flash of light. Cody's eyes were closed and he felt the gun being taken out of his hand. Now I'll never find the answer, he thought.

"Dad, what are you doing?" Dale's voice was frantic. He had walked up to the back door, sneaking in late after his business at the Witch's Hat, to see his father sitting there with the gun. He flung the door open and threw the lights on, the door slamming against the counter hard enough to smash the panes of glass, but his father had not moved, just closed his eyes. He pried the gun away and his father mumbled something about an answer, then put his head down and passed out. Dale would soon begin to wonder if it would have been better if he had just stayed outside and watched.

(57)

TEN-YEAR-OLD SEAN Jenkins loved fishing. But, man, did he hate getting up in the middle of the night to do it. As far as Sean was concerned, the fish weren't going anywhere so what would the harm be in sleeping a few more hours before trying to hook them? But when your dad says you can skip school to fish, why argue? His dad called in sick to work, telling Sean you just couldn't let days like this pass without fishing, and here they were. The sky was just starting to lighten in the east when Sean and his dad pulled the last of their gear out of the trunk. Sean's dad Harry, known at the Witch's Hat and numerous other bars in the greater-Haven area as Jenk, was adding what he lovingly called a "jump start" to his coffee thermos. In layman's terms, Jenk's jump start was a generous splash of whatever brand of Irish whiskey was on the sale table at Main Street Wine and Liquors. Sean watched his father with a combination of love and disgust that confused him. He already knew how the day would play out. Everything would be great through the morning as they talked and fished, but as the day wore on and the thermos emptied, Jenk's mood would shift to anger—at the heat, at the lack of fish, at the Yankees, pretty much at anything. If Sean played his cards right, he would nod at all the right times and answer any slurred questions thrown his way correctly and escape with a backhander or two. If he really screwed up, he might get a closed fist to his gut. Or worse.

By the time Jenk had finished his drink, he would be a sloppy pile of tears lamenting the loss of Sean's mom, Myra, who was "taken too soon to Heaven." What further confused Sean was the fact that his only memories of his mom and dad together involved yelling, screaming and the occasional thrown beer cans or wine glasses. Sean knew what to expect, this wasn't their first fishing trip since his mom passed from liver failure. What he didn't know is that it would be their last.

When they made their way through the woods to Jenk's latest "can't miss" spot—his cronies at the Hat were famous for giving him such tips—the sun was peeking over the horizon and Sean knew it would be another steamer. Some mornings at this time of the year the first job at hand would be to start a campfire to keep the chill off until the sun got high enough to warm things up a bit. But since the temperature hadn't dropped below seventy degrees at night in over a week, Sean got busy finding a couple of forked branches to stick in the ground and hold their rods up. Jenk began opening the tackle boxes and selecting hooks, weights and bobbers for them to use. Sean had his own ten-year-old wisdom on that process: hungry fish will bite no matter what's on the end of your line as long as there's a big, juicy worm involved. Sean had spent the early evening hours yesterday on his hands and knees catching "night crawlers," which he considered the top-of-the-line menu item for any self-respecting fish.

A few minutes later, already breaking a sweat, Sean and Jenk put their first cast of the day into the water and propped their rods onto the sticks that Sean had hammered into the soft ground at the shore. As was their tradition, they held their drinks high—Sean's a canteen filled with Cherry Kool-Aid, Jenk's with the not-quite-full thermos of high-octane coffee—and Jenk recited his official fishing toast. "The fish may bite, God may smite, we've got bait and drink, everything's alright!" Sean took a swig of his Kool-Aid and watched his dad take a greedy gulp from his own thermos. Jenk's Adam's apple moved up and down as he gulped, like a bobber getting some strong nibbles. He wiped his mouth with the back of his hand, and with an exaggerated breath, took a look across the lake. "Sure is a beautiful spot, huh Sean?"

Sean squinted out at the lake as well; it really was a beautiful spot. The sun was almost fully over the tree-line to the east and its rays danced across the calm lake. The only sounds were birds, frogs, a few lazy heat bugs, and the gentle lapping of the lake against the shore. His gaze finally settled on the motionless tips of their fishing rods. "Sure is. Hope it's as lucky as it is pretty."

Jenk laughed, a sharp bark-like sound that held no humor. "Well, Sully swore he pulled in a fifteen-inch trout at this very spot. Old Sully, mind you, is the same person that swears his wife is the spitting image of Sally Field. Now my eyes ain't what they used to be, but Becca Sullivan looks more like an acre of unplowed field than she does Sally Field." And so it began. Jenk would take so many different forks from the original conversation that he'd never find his way back. Sean tuned him out, thinking about Sally Field in *Smokey and the Bandit*. When Jenk found the road in his thoughts that led him to baseball, Sean began listening again.

"And the Yanks have a fucking shortstop—forgive me, Myra—who couldn't break two-fifty last year."

The constant apologizing to Sean's dead mother every time he swore was one of Jenk's most annoying habits as far as Sean was concerned. Either stop swearing or stop being sorry about it every time for fuck's sake. Sorry, Mom, he added with a sly grin.

"We have The Rooster at short. He almost hit .300 last year and made the all-star game. Position by position, Sean, we've got those pinstripe-wearing fuckers beat. 'pologize Myra."

Sean was already forming the opinion that his dad was as useless as a screen door on a submarine and didn't know squat about simple things like fishing, but he loved his Red Sox. Watched or listened to every game, studied the box scores every day. This year, thought Sean, this year might be different. He watched his dad take another lengthy sip from his thermos, and then let his eyes drift over to the fishing rods. It was already hotter than balls even in the shade and the tips of the rods hadn't so much as wiggled.

"Gotta go drain the vein," Jenk muttered. His dad had a healthy supply of phrases for just about all of his bodily functions. And

Sean had heard them all a million times. Sean watched him get unsteadily to his feet and wander off into the trees. Next would be the slurred speech and it would go downhill quickly from there. Sean looked at the sky, hoping to see a thunderhead moving in, but the sky was a brilliant blue and rain was as out of the question as Jenk staying sober. The sun was still low in the east and it was already time for a swim. Suddenly both rods jerked at the same time. Sean stared at the rods, sure that he had imagined it. Then the line slowly tightened on each rod, and both tips began to bend toward the lake.

"Dad!" He quickly snatched his own rod off the holder and reached down to ease the drag on his father's rod, allowing the fish to swim without pulling the rod into the water. He yanked back on his own rod to secure the hook while Jenk's reel buzzed furiously letting out line.

"You got a whopper, boy!" Jenk stumbled out of the trees and grabbed his rod, immediately tightening the drag. As soon as he did, the tip of his rod jerked toward the water. Sean was busy trying to reel in when both rods snapped back to normal and the lines went limp. "Damn, it snapped both lines!"

Sean glanced over, disgusted to see his dad hadn't bothered to zip up. He put his own rod back on the forked stick and went to get a couple riggings out of the tackle box.

"What in the hell..." Jenk was still trying to reel in but the line had gone taut again. "Must be caught on a log or..." Jenk's rod jerked mightily, bending almost completely in half.

Sean watched in semi-amazement as Jenk's arms flew straight out and he struggled to keep his balance. *Why doesn't he just let go?* Sean thought. The rod began to bend back to its normal position, then suddenly jerked again. This time Jenk let go—or it was pulled too hard for him to hold—but not before he lost his balance completely. He pinwheeled his arms and for a minute Sean thought he was going to stay dry. The blazing sun behind him gave his silhouetted shape a comical, almost cartoonish appearance. Then he teetered again and went face-first into the lake. Sean shook his head smiling as his dad struggled to his feet. "If you wanted to cool off you should have at least taken your shirt off!"

Jenk shook the water out of his hair, still struggling to keep his balance in the waist-deep water. He looked down into the lake with a confused expression on his face. "My foot's caught..."

The water around Jenk swirled and Sean saw a dark shape in the water. He started toward the lake to help when the water erupted. The splash was huge but Sean was able to see two things, neither of which made sense. A dark shape, impossible to see clearly because of the position of the sun, was looming behind his dad. The second thing was that the shape had tentacles. Then his dad's feet went out from under him, and both figures disappeared. The water eddied for a minute then it was smooth as glass as if Sean had imagined the whole scene. Finally, he reacted, running into the water screaming for his dad. Later, he would wonder why he was brave enough to do it, but in the moment he was running on pure adrenaline. The fear would come soon enough.

He splashed around, diving under the surface, yelling for his dad until he was too winded and hoarse to yell anymore. Then he began to cry. He felt like he might never stop.

(58)

CHIEF CRAWFORD sat in his office gazing intently at nothing. He was hungover to beat the band. In fact it felt like a marching band was playing a rousing beat inside his head. He had only the slightest memories of sitting at the table the night before. The beating of Joe Cummings at the Witch's Hat last night had him concerned. Cummings would be sure to ID some of the men responsible, and then there'd be hell to pay. He had enough to worry about with Greymore on the loose. He didn't need this shit. He tried to focus on the papers strewn in front of him on his desk. There were reports of all the disappearances from 1961, the court transcripts and an assortment of psychiatric evaluations done on Greymore before the trial and during his prison term. He had to make sure that when Greymore slipped, he'd put him away for good this time. *If he lives to stand trial*, thought Crawford. He was just getting absorbed in the testimony of Kevin Denneker when a disturbance from the lobby pulled him back to the present.

Annoyed, he got up and stormed out of his office to see what was going on, right hand instinctively going toward his hip. Officer Hudson was making gestures with his hands, trying to calm down a couple of nerdy kids who were obviously responsible for interrupting Crawford. "What's going on?" he boomed, hoping to scare the snot out of the little brats. Instead of cowering when they saw the Chief, they barreled past Hudson and ran up to him. They were both talking a mile a minute so that Crawford couldn't understand either one of them.

"Quiet!"

They both stopped mid-sentence, looking at each other then back up at Crawford. The band had picked up the tempo in his skull and the drums were echoing to the point he felt dizzy.

"What do you kids think you're doing, coming into my station and causing a ruckus like this? We have work to do around here." He eyed both kids, trying to attach names to their faces while waiting for an apology.

The skinny one took a step closer and cleared his throat. "We… my dog was missing…out by the lake…and all these crushed…"

"Slow down kid, first things first. What are your names?"

"I'm Denny O'Brien and this is Billy Cummings. We live over by the lake on Hillview Street."

Immediately Crawford's mind was working in high gear, band or no band. The Cummings kid should be at the hospital worrying about dear old Dad. "Son, do you realize your father is in the hospital while you're here spinning yarns?" He could tell immediately that the kid didn't know anything about last night, which in a way was a relief.

Denny vaguely remembered hearing the phone ring early that morning but his mother seldom answered it. Billy's face had gone pale and in it, Denny saw his own reflection from a few years ago. "The hospital? What happened? Is he alright?"

Crawford could see tears ready to burst out any minute. The O'Brien kid didn't look so hot either. Crawford put on his fatherly game face. "I'm sorry to be the one to have to tell you, Billy. Your daddy got in a fight last night, at the Witch's Hat…a regular barroom brawl…"

"A barroom brawl! My dad doesn't hang out in bars looking for a fight. Is he alright?" The kid's concern had taken a turn toward anger. O'Brien looked ready to pass out.

"He got beat up pretty bad but the docs think he'll be okay. Why don't I have one of the officers here take you over to be with your

Dad? I'll talk to Denny here about whatever was so important when you came in." He motioned toward Hudson to get a car ready.

"Denny, you stay here and…"

"No, I need to go with you, Billy."

"But what about…"

"We can tell Chief Crawford all about kids drinking by the lake some other time. I should go with you to the hospital."

"That's right boys. You take care of Billy's Dad and when it's all over, you get to tell your friends you rode in a real police car. If there's a problem with some kids drinking out by the lake, I'll be sure to take care of it. Don't worry about a thing."

Crawford watched as Hudson escorted the kids out to the parking lot. What a couple of losers, he thought. Coming into the Police Station to snitch on some teenagers having a few beers out by the lake. Crawford chuckled to himself. It was probably Dale balling Cummings' older sister. How ironic, he thought. He went back into his office to go over the court transcripts again.

Once they were out of Crawford's earshot, the boys began working on Hudson. Billy wanted answers about his dad. "Officer Hudson, how bad is my father? What really happened? You know my dad doesn't hang around in bars."

Hudson eyed them in the rear-view mirror for a moment. Denny could see beads of sweat on the older man's forehead. Clearly, he was torn between being a cop and his compassion for Billy. "Like Chief said, he got beat up pretty good. An anonymous call came in early this morning. He was laid out in his car behind the Witch's Hat out on the town line. The car had a flat and it looked like someone had rolled it into the woods. Your mom tried to call up to Denny's but there was no answer. We told the school to call us when you arrived, but I guess you never did arrive there.

"Your dad has a concussion and a lot of broken bones. The doctors say as long as there isn't any internal bleeding, he should be okay."

Denny felt nauseous, slumping against the car door. Memories of his own father's accident had been tearing at him since the mention of the word hospital. He tried to push away the image of his dad, bandages covering most of his head and body, tubes and wires sticking out of him all over the place. He shook his head to push the mental picture away. He had to stay alert. This whole thing didn't make sense, Billy's dad in a brawl at the Witch's Hat. "Who else was injured in the brawl?"

Hudson eyed him again in the mirror, his brow creasing causing balls of sweat to race down the side of his face. "That I'm not sure of, Denny. Mr. Cummings is the only one hospitalized that I know of." Denny thought he wanted to say more, but he didn't.

Denny could see Billy getting madder and madder. "Are you telling me my father was in a barroom brawl, beaten half to death, and didn't take anyone down with him? My dad could take on any three of the losers that hang around in the Witch's Hat and not even break a sweat. What the hell happened, Officer Hudson?"

This time Hudson would not meet their gaze in the mirror. "That's all I know for now, Billy. Maybe he was jumped or hit from behind. The doctors might be able to tell us more. We haven't found any witnesses yet." He pulled the car into a reserved spot by the main entrance to the hospital. "You boys take care, now."

Once inside the hospital lobby, Billy stopped and grabbed Denny's arm. "What were you doing back there? Why didn't you stay to tell Crawford what we found?"

Denny hesitated. Being in the hospital was playing games with his mind. It was still all too clear in his memory, as it probably always would be, coming into this same lobby with his mother. She was really his mother back then. Neither of them knew the extent of the injuries to his father. The police had already told them about Jimmy. They had gotten a ride to the hospital by officer McDermott. It was like an instant replay, time was disintegrating in Denny's mind and he thought for a moment he was going in to visit his father.

"...Denny? Are you okay?"

Denny returned to the present and tried to compose himself. "Yeah, I'm fine. I don't think we can trust Crawford. As soon as I saw him...did you see his eyes? They were all red and bloodshot and he kind of looked half crazy. If he finds out about the caves, he'll use it against Paul. Remember the story about how they caught him in '61? There was a canoe on the lake when they found Paul with that dead girl. Crawford'll say Paul was trying to get her into the canoe to bring her to his secret cave. It'll fit too nice with his suspicions. I think we need to figure something else out. Let's worry about it after we see your dad."

They spoke to a woman at the information desk and were instructed on how to get to Mr. Cummings' room. They would have to stop at the desk in the Intensive Care Unit as he was still in serious condition. The woman, who was wearing a huge smiley face button, did say that his condition was stable but she had no more details. They took the elevator to the third floor. For Denny it was an eternity. He couldn't remember even being on an elevator since his last trip to the ICU. The past and present began to blur once again in his mind. That final visit when they were told the inevitable. There was nothing the doctors could do for Denny's father. Tests showed no brain activity. He was essentially being kept alive by machines that regulated his heartbeat and breathing. Those machines would be shut down, with Mrs. O'Brien's consent.

The elevator came to an abrupt stop and the doors slid open. Denny and Billy went to the desk to ask about Mr. Cummings. The nurse on duty was a pretty blonde girl. To Denny she looked too young to be a nurse. She explained that Mr. Cummings had sustained a concussion but there seemed to be no brain damage. He had several broken bones, including his nose and a few ribs. There were multiple bruises and lacerations, many requiring stitches. She explained that it would be somewhat of a shock to see him because of the cuts and bandages but that there was no indication of any internal injuries. She also told the boys that normally only adults would be allowed in, and especially only direct family, but because of the circumstances, Mr. Cummings had convinced the doctor to let both Billy and Denny in. He had insisted on it, as a matter of fact. Then she led them into the room.

(59)

CHIEF CRAWFORD took a long drag on his cigarette, unsure of what to say to the boy. Interrogation was one of his favorite parts of the job. Give him a hard-ass thug trying to stay tightlipped about something and he'd break him. Give him the reluctant witness and Crawford would coax him into whatever statement was convenient to his case. But a kid...shit he couldn't talk to his own no-good son never mind some ten-year-old that had just watched his father murdered. *Allegedly.* Crawford knew Jenk was a hard, sloppy drinker and probably got heavy-handed when drunk. He saw the telltale marks of an abused kid. He ignored the similarities to his own life that stared him in the face and pushed out his cigarette in an overflowing ashtray.

"Sean, tell me again what happened, what you think you saw. Take it slow and think real hard, lying to a police officer isn't very good idea."

Sean winced, "I'm not lying. I already told you twice what happened." He jutted his chin at the tape recorder running at the end of the table. "Just rewind that and listen to it, I don't feel like telling it again."

Crawford smiled. The kid was trying to sound tough but was on the verge of tears. "Okay, let's talk about something else. Like the bruises on your back. And how you broke your arm in two places last year." Crawford had insisted the kid get checked out after he was

287

brought into the station hysterical about what happened to his dad. When the doctor mentioned the bruises, Crawford bullied him into looking up his records and found the broken arm. Crawford knew he had the kid. Sean dropped his eyes, the defiance stripped out of him by Crawford's words.

"I slipped on some wet leaves on the porch steps and landed on my back. Last summer I fell off my skateboard." His voice had gone monotone, robotic. Like he was reading a script.

"Sean, we both know how you go the bruises and the busted arm. I know...knew your dad. I know how he got when he drank and how much he missed your ma. It's not his fault; it's just how he handled his grief."

Sean looked at him with wide-eyed hope. His secret was out in the open and Crawford had played the concerned cop to perfection. Tears rolled down Sean's cheeks. "He...he didn't mean to h-hurt me, I just made him m-mad. He was always sorry."

Crawford looked up as Ortiz stepped into the room and nodded at him. *What the fuck is he doing here?*

The trap was set, now to spring it. "I know Sean. And sometimes you can only take so much. Sometimes you need to do some hurting of your own. He was going to hurt you again this morning, wasn't he? But this time you were brave, you'd had enough. Does that sound about right, Sean?"

The boy recoiled when Crawford's thinly veiled accusation hit him. His face, already red from crying, went deep scarlet. "You think I...hurt my own father? You think I killed my dad?" His voice was rising, but steady. "You stupid, shit-kicking bastard. My dad was right, you're a no-good country bumpkin redneck!"

Crawford felt his own blood rise. This wasn't what he expected. He had the kid and Ortiz made him clam up. He glared at Ortiz. "Get him out of here."

The boy was mumbling expletives in an eerie impersonation of his father. His face was angry, his mouth a thin slash. "Stupid, inbred piece of dogshit..." Tears continued to roll down his cheeks but he was no longer sobbing; Crawford could see he was straight-out pissed.

Ortiz was gaping at Crawford, wide-eyed and slack-jawed.

"You heard me Ortiz. Get the little shit out of my sight. Now!"

"My pleasure, *Chief.*" Ortiz spat back.

Crawford didn't even look up. In his mind he was seeing a different little boy with an abusive father. And wishing he'd had the balls to do what he accused Sean of.

(60)

DENNY SAT in the waiting room of Haven General pretending to read a magazine. Just as the pretty young nurse was opening the door for them, a doctor had bustled past them and overruled the nurse's decision to let a non-family member in the room until he was done with his rounds. Now, by himself in the too-bright lights of the waiting room, he couldn't concentrate on any of the stories, couldn't think straight. His concern for Billy's dad had him upset but his memories of his last visit to a hospital were torturing his mind. He'd sat in a room just like this, waiting for his father to die. In the same way that he loved the smell of the library, Denny loathed the smell of hospitals. The combination of medicines and disinfectants, the antiseptic white all around him, it all reeked of death to Denny.

He was interrupted by Billy whispering his name. "Denny, come on in. The doc is finished and Dad's awake. He wants us both in with him." Denny put down the magazine and entered the room of Joe Cummings. He moved slowly around the curtain that surrounded Joe's bed. The hissing of oxygen and beeping machines were causing Denny's mind to reel backwards. When he looked at the bed it wasn't Joe but his own father he saw lying there. His eyes filled with tears and when the image faded to reveal Joe, his own face a mask of black and purple, Denny's knees buckled and he dropped to the floor. He was vaguely aware of someone pulling him up and heard his name being called from far away. "Come on, Denny, wake up. If the nurse comes in now she'll boot us for sure!"

Denny opened his eyes and saw Billy crouched over him. He shook his head trying to compose himself. "I'm okay. Help me up, Billy."

"Are you alright, Denny?" The voice from the bed sounded like two pieces of sandpaper being rubbed together.

"I think I'm supposed to ask you that, Joe." Joe smiled and Denny's mind swam for a moment when he noticed the missing teeth and tracks of stitches around Joe's mouth. This time he was able to stay on his feet. "I just thought about my dad when I saw you lying there..."

"Oh shit, Denny, I'm sorry. I wasn't even thinking when I asked you to come here with me." Billy sounded close to tears.

"I apologize too, Denny, it must be hard for you," Joe added, ignoring Billy's language, "but I need you to hear this."

"I'm okay now, Joe, but you don't sound too good. Should we call the nurse or something?"

"It's just a bruised windpipe, sounds worse than it really is. But you should see the other guys..."

Denny smiled, knowing that it was really probably worse than it looked or sounded. And also knowing that there *were* a few guys somewhere who did look worse. Billy had told him that there were broken ribs and a serious concussion to go along with the multitude of stitches. As bad as Joe sounded, Denny had to hear what he wanted to say.

"Something's going on here in Haven, boys, but I guess you already know that much. Something bad, something that's too much like '61 to be a coincidence."

"You don't think Paul..."

Joe cut Billy off, "Of course not, but whatever killed all those kids is back. But it isn't Paul. I know that much."

"All the weird stuff did start to happen when Paul came to Haven." Denny hated himself for saying it as soon as the words left his mouth.

"I know how it looks, dammit, the same way it was back then. But it's wrong. I was with him in '61 when some of those kids disappeared. He was in prison when the first one was found dead this time. He told me something back then. I snuck in to see him at the hospital after Crawford found him with that dead girl. He was hurt bad. Worse than I am now, I tell you. He had some strange kind of marks on him, all around his chest and shoulders. Like big bee stings all in a nice straight row. He was delirious, or at least I thought so then. He was babbling about going back to the lake to make sure it was dead."

"What was dead?" Denny glanced at Billy and knew they were thinking the same thing. The caves, all those bones. How many kids did they never find that year? And all the years since?

Joe closed his eyes and Denny thought he had fallen asleep. "He didn't know, or at least he didn't say," he slowly opened his eyes, "but he was afraid. Paul had been through more and taken more shit than anyone I ever knew. But this was the first time I ever saw him afraid. I remember him sitting up, grabbing me by the collar and pulling me toward him. When I looked into his eyes I thought he might just have gone crazy, but it was terror I saw, not insanity. He said *'It might still be there, Joe'* then the nurses and cops came in. They dragged me out as they were giving him a shot. I heard him screaming *'Stay away from the lake, Joe, it might still be alive!'*"

"I got friends to help me search, even hired divers with some of my college savings to find out what he was talking about." He smiled, an ugly sight. "Your grandparents were not happy about *that*. Some people thought I was looking for bodies and that's why they helped. As the word spread around what I was really doing, nobody would help, and we hadn't found a damn thing anyway. That was the last time I ever spoke to Paul until he came back. I went off to college and he went..." His voice broke but he recovered quickly. "They blocked our letters from getting through and I just let him slip away like a bad dream." Tears were streaming down his face now but he made no move to wipe them away. "My parents sold the house while I was still away at school, they'd had their fill of Haven." He looked at Billy, then Denny, his eyes burning with emotion "Find Paul. Hide him from Crawford. Talk to him. Maybe things are starting to come back to him now that he's back. It's kind of funny. We're all back now, like a big fu…big reunion, and it started all over again." The last words faded and Joe's eyes closed.

"Okay, Billy, we have to go back to the police and tell him everything, then…"

Joe's eyes opened again. "Crawford did this, at least Dale was part of it. They handcuffed me while they…did this. You can't trust the police," Joe whispered. Denny stared at Joe, then Billy, the words sinking in. "Some of Dale's gang was there, too, Billy. They threatened Mom and Julie and you. I already sent them to Aunt Sarah's over in Malden, but you can stay with Denny. You need to help protect Paul, keep him safe until we can figure this out. I know it's too much to ask you son, but Paul doesn't have anyone…" Joe's eyes closed again. The boys waited for more, but eventually Joe's breathing slowed and the boys knew he was asleep.

"Billy, your dad's right, they'll go after Paul. And maybe Father McCarthy, too."

"Paul is in Boston for a few days so he'll be safe there. We'll start by going to Father McCarthy…"

Denny turned to head out but Billy grabbed his arm. "What is it, Denny? You saw the caves; you heard my dad's story. What is it?" he pleaded.

"I don't know, Billy, but nobody but us believes there's anything going on in this town other than Paul…the Butcher is back. We're on our own until we can figure out something better. Do you want to stay here with your dad for a while? You're safe here. If they wanted to…you know…do anything worse to him they would have done it."

"No, I'm going with you. I can't let Dad down. He risked everything to stand up for Paul seventeen years ago. I can't let that be for nothing. Let's go."

Denny took one last look at Joe, and then they headed out together.

(61)

GREYMORE SAT alone in his Boston hotel room, willing more memories to return. He knew part of what had happened, but he needed the rest. Needed it fast. The key memory was missing and his instincts told him time was running out.

Tina Cummings had tracked him down by phone and let him know about Joe's attack. He was sick, knowing it was payback for the incident at the baseball game. He also knew that if he hadn't spent the evening hiding in the woods before rowing back to his house at midnight, he would have been there for Joe at the hospital. He had walked right by Joe's house early that morning on his way to the bus station, oblivious of what had happened to his friend. He wanted to return to Haven immediately but he would be violating the parameters of his release. He was required to complete this post-release training. It was another blow he would have to endure. God, would it ever end? If only he had been there with Joe, to stand by his side and fight. It would have paid back an old debt, he thought. As hard as he tried, memories of 1961 would not come, but an older memory of Joe did.

His parents had moved here from the city when the doctors convinced them there was nothing else that could be done for him. Haven was very much the same back then as it was when it all went bad in '61. His parents had gotten in "on the ground floor" of what was going to be the next resort area. The small cottage was inexpensive, especially considering it was waterfront. The plan was to continue building modern luxury houses, extending Hillview Street deeper into the woods.

Development never started on the project. The decision not to rebuild the military base contributed to the bankruptcy of several Haven businesses and the resort project was dead. For Paul and his parents, it was just as well. The small house on the lake was heaven for them. His father, John, had saved wisely and made some decent profits on investments, and retiring to Haven in the summer of '55 was pure bliss.

John spent the long days on the lake with Paul, teaching him everything about the wildlife. Fishing, canoeing, hiking, the days were perfect. Paul would occasionally have a feeling that he was being watched, but shook it off as paranoia. Reality came to visit after Labor Day, time for Paul to start school. It was as bad as could be expected. Kids back then were no more accepting of anyone different than they are today. Paul was harassed, ridiculed and picked on daily. Again he felt like someone was watching him; this time he didn't write it off, just assumed it was another of the bullies waiting their turn. The teachers did their best to protect him, but even they were not entirely comfortable with his looks.

His parents were constantly at school, begging or threatening the staff to protect their son. They were considering taking him out and teaching him privately. He was miserable. He longed for the summer days spent on the lake. Then everything changed. He was sitting eating his lunch in the schoolyard, alone of course, while everyone else ate in groups or had already finished and were starting games of catch or just general roughhousing. He didn't even have to look up when the shadows moved across the table. It would be the same as every other day. Name-calling, stealing his food, maybe a little shoving. His stomach tightened. There were four of them, what was he supposed to do?

"Hey Greymore, save anything good for me today?" It was Jarrod Johnson. The kid outweighed his own IQ. He was tougher than the rest of the class by virtue of having had the experience of seventh grade twice already. Maybe third time was a charm, but not for ole Jarrod this day. "Come on, freak, give me something to eat."

Without even thinking about it, without considering the results even for a second, Paul shot out of his seat and delivered a fierce blow to Jarrod's nose. The sound was at once gratifying and revolting. For a terrifying minute, Paul thought the punch had no effect. Jarrod had staggered back a step, but that was it. He wiped a hand across his nose and it came back dry. He then wiped his eyes, which looked like they were starting to tear, then the floodgates opened. A deluge of blood from both nostrils. Jarrod tried to speak, but the flow of blood and his hands over his face trying to slow it down made his words unintelligible.

In the split second that that all happened, the other three made their move. Eric Foley and Gary DeNatale moved in on Paul quickly, trying to get a hold of his arms. Frankie O'Malley, perhaps the only one of the fab four with a lick of sense, took a couple of steps back, looked again at the swelling mess that used to be Jarrod's nose, and simply shook his head and walked away. Paul had for a fleeting moment thought standing up to Jarrod was enough, for an even shorter moment felt a bit invincible after doing one-punch damage to Jarrod. Then the adrenaline rush faded and the fear returned. By the time he realized what was happening, Gary had his arms pinned behind his back and Eric was punching him in the stomach. He squirmed and flailed but couldn't break free. Eric, now beginning to get carried away, feeling a primal bloodlust, began aiming for Paul's face. Paul was moving enough so that most of the shots glanced off the top of his head or hit his shoulders. Eric grabbed Paul by the shoulder, trying to hold him still enough to get a clean shot. Paul did the only thing he could, he slammed his head forward as hard as he could, waiting to hear the same sound his punch had delivered when his head crushed Eric's nose. Instead, he got a head full of sparks. The blow had landed on Eric's forehead: Eric's head was harder. This enraged Eric and he began to punch wildly, some now connecting with Paul's face. Not because they were better punches but because he was throwing so many, so fast, the odds were in his favor. Paul's eyes were blurring with tears and blood.

Then the punches stopped. Through his half-closed eyes, he saw Eric with an arm across his throat, his own arm disappearing behind him at a bad angle. Suddenly Eric was spun around, and Paul could see another boy in a blur of movement hit Eric with rapid-fire jabs that snapped his head back with each blow. The grip on Paul's arms loosened, and he made his move. He slipped out of Gary's grip and threw an elbow straight back. This time his aim, or his luck, was better as he heard the air forced out of Gary's lungs. Eric's head was still snapping back and forth under the flurry of punches from the other kid when Paul turned to face Gary, who was now struggling to get air, any air, back into his lungs. The weeks of torment had built to a crescendo and Paul used this moment to get retribution, at the expense of Gary's face.

It all happened in a matter of five minutes, from the shadows appearing on Paul's lunch until teachers were pulling Paul and his rescuer off of Gary and Eric. But the result was devastating, and to Paul, beautiful. Somehow, *right*. Jarrod's attempts to stop the blood had failed miserably. From his face to his elbows he was covered in red. Eric's face was a jigsaw puzzle of cuts and bruises. Gary's face was one big bruise already, and both of his eyes were almost shut. Paul's own head was split from his failed head-butt, and he had a few cuts from some of the early punches. The other kid—Paul finally placed him as Joe Cummings—was the only one unscathed. Except for his bruised knuckles. Unless you count Frankie O'Malley, who was taking it all in from across the yard, an amused look on his face. As Mr. Robertson, Paul's history teacher, dragged Joe back away from Eric, he felt Paul's stare, turned and gave a crooked smile and a wink. Paul couldn't help but to smile back.

From that point on, they were inseparable. Of course, two weeks detention helped them get to know each other. It was then Joe admitted that he'd been spying on Paul, both at home and in school. He wanted to approach Paul but was intimidated by his looks. He looked Paul directly in the eye when he told this, his face flushing with embarrassment. His honesty impressed Paul, helped create a bond. To Paul, the fight and ensuing detention were worth it. The harassment diminished. It didn't go away completely, probably never would, but it got a whole lot better. And now Paul had an ally or two. Frankie became much friendlier after that day, so did a lot of kids. But he and Joe had something special, something that twelve-year olds take for granted. They were best friends.

Greymore shook his head and tried again to call Joe at the hospital. He needed to talk to him, but once again he was told Joe was resting and was not to be disturbed. He wondered if Joe was hurt worse than Tina had made out, or if Crawford was once again keeping him isolated. The thought of Joe lying in a hospital bed because of their friendship was unbearable. Another reversal, he thought, remembering when he had been the one in the bed and Joe had visited him.

(62)

MOSSY AND Chris sat on the front porch of Betty Chandler's house as the sun set on another blistering day over Haven. Chris sipped slowly from a bottle of beer while Mossy nursed a glass of iced tea. What he was about to do was not easy; nothing is when you don't know what the consequences will be. But before he put his final plan in motion, he *had* to be sure.

"Chris, I have to talk to you, about your father." He hoped the few beers put Chris in the right mood for what he was about to hear.

"What about him?" Chris's tone was curious, with a hint of suspicion.

"I'm afraid I haven't been honest with you since I arrived in Haven. Perhaps once I explain you'll understand. If not, then I don't know what will become of me, of this town."

"Frank, what are you talking about? What does you being here have to do with my father?"

Mossy looked him in the eye, and for a second, he got the feeling Chris already knew everything. "Let's start with my name: it isn't Frank Rodman, it's Moses Blaakman. Folks call me Mossy, at least they used to."

Chris continued to meet his gaze. "Go on..."

"The truth is...I wasn't transferred before the explosion, I was off the base without authorization. You see, I was your father's contact. I was the one feeding him information. I...I am responsible for his death." He swallowed hard, taking a sip of iced tea, waiting for a reaction.

Chris sat back in his seat, took a long drag on his beer, and slowly nodded his head. "I knew something wasn't quite right about you, Frank...I mean Mossy. Why are you here, after all this time? Why are you dragging this all up again?"

Mossy exhaled, not even realizing he'd been holding his breath. "Because of what's happening in Haven, because of the children disappearing, getting killed..."

Chris jumped out of his seat and faced Mossy. His face was red; one hand held his beer bottle, the other was clenched in a tight fist. "You...you have something to do with this? You..."

Mossy held his hands up in a surrendering gesture. "Chris, please sit down and let me explain. When I'm finished, you're free to do whatever you think is right. But please hear me out."

Chris continued to stare at him, then his whole body seemed to sag and he sat heavily back in his chair. He sighed loudly and downed the rest of his beer. He reached toward the cooler to pull another one, then changed his mind. "I don't know if I want to hear this. Some things...maybe they should be left alone."

"I'm afraid this isn't one of them, Chris. If things weren't happening again in Haven, I wouldn't be here and we wouldn't be having this conversation. But we are, and at the end I'm going to ask for your help. The same way I asked for your father's help back then. Maybe this time it will have a better ending."

Chris nodded silently, then did reach in for another beer. "If my father trusted you, I guess that's good enough for me. I don't know how I can help, but go ahead and tell your story. After that, we'll see."

Mossy spoke for a long time, pausing only to refill his glass. He told everything, as best as he could, wishing more than once that his glass contained more than iced tea. Chris seldom interrupted, only to ask a clarifying question or two. *He has his father's nose for getting a story*, Mossy thought. Finally, he got to the end, to his plan to kill the creature. "I can't do it alone, and I hate to put anyone in harm's way, but I don't have a choice. I can't go to Crawford, he'll arrest me or throw me in the nuthouse. I have to make this right...at least as right as it can get at this point. It has to end."

Chris sat quietly, looking out at the horizon. The sun had set, it was almost full dark, and he took another slow pull from his beer. "Okay, I get it. But what do you need from me? Are you asking me to go into the caves with you?"

Mossy turned to face him, "No Chris, I couldn't do that. I am responsible in a way for getting your father killed, I couldn't ask that of you. What I need from you is confirmation. This whole thing, it's so unbelievable. When I tell the story out loud, it sounds even more made-up than when I think about it. I need to know I'm not crazy before I do what I'm thinking of doing. I need to know for certain that this whole thing isn't some fantasy, some form of insanity or alcohol-induced hysteria. I need to *know*."

Chris nodded. "It does sound crazy, I'll give you that. But I still don't know how..." Mossy could see it in his eyes when he figured it out. His face darkened and he started to shake his head.

"Chris, your brother is the only other person alive who has seen it. Please, I need to be one hundred percent sure. Then I promise I will leave you and your family alone."

Chris was still, lost in the possible ramifications of forcing his brother to face the horror of his memories. Then his expression softened. "Maybe...maybe if he talks about it...and someone believes him...maybe he can get better?"

Mossy felt the desperate hope in Chris's words. "Maybe so, Chris." He hated himself for using Chris's emotions as a means to an end. He knew better than anyone the grip the bottle could have. He doubted one conversation could heal that, but then look at where he was less than two weeks ago and where he was now. If that was possible, maybe anything was possible. "Maybe so, indeed."

Neither man noticed the movement of the curtain in the open window behind them.

(63)

MOSSY, CHRIS, and Jake McCauley sat huddled in a booth in the back of the Witch's Hat. Mossy already had doubts about how this was going to turn out. Jake was a wreck, so deep into alcohol and depression that it was impossible to tell if he was drunk or sober at any given time. Chris introduced them, telling Jake that he was an old friend of their father's. They talked for a while about Matt McCauley, Mossy sharing some stories about him and the fact that they were working on a story about the old army base. During the conversation, Mossy watched with a keen, knowing eye how many drinks Jake was putting away. Vodka was Jake's weakness, while Chris drank beer and Mossy nursed ginger ales. He waited for the right moment to turn the talk to the day at the lake.

"Jake, the story your father was working on had to do with an experiment I was involved with at the base. You see, it wasn't an ammunition depot at all, it was a research facility." Mossy watched carefully for any reaction from Jake. He seemed to be listening but he was as focused on his drink as he was on the story. "Jake, we were working on using DNA to alter the genetics of living creatures, to create new species." Jake continued to stare at his drink, but Mossy caught a darting eye movement and a furrowing of Jake's brow. He was getting through. He glanced around the bar, making sure nobody was in earshot before continuing. "It worked, Jake. We created a new life-form; part mammal, part reptile...it was an abomination."

Jake was shaking his head back and forth, slowly at first but starting to get faster. A mewling sound escaped his tightly-closed lips. "No..."

Mossy plunged forward. "Jake, listen. We were scientists but we were playing God. We fucked up..."

"No!" Jake smashed his glass on the table, burying shards into his palm and slashing his fingers.

The bartender stared over, one hand under the bar, no doubt reaching for a bat, or a gun. "Problem over there?"

Chris jumped up and approached the bar. "No problem, just a little accident. Can I have some towels to clean it up, and a couple more drinks?"

The bartender continued to stare over at the booth, trying to figure out if whatever was going on was worth the price of a couple of drinks. It was. He handed Chris some paper towels and started making the drinks. Chris brought the towels over and started cleaning the mess. Mossy helped Jake get the glass out of his hand and wrapped it tightly with paper towels. "He's going to need stitches."

Chris nodded, then went back to the bar top grab the drinks. When he returned, Jake took one in his good hand and downed half of it in one desperate gulp. He knew what was coming.

"Jake, I know what killed the boy at the lake that day. There was nothing you could have done. You were lucky you weren't killed yourself."

Tears meandered down Jake's face and his mouth turned into a humorless smile. "You call this lucky? Spending my days trying to forget the unforgettable? Spending my nights trying not to dream? Some luck. I wish it was me that day at the lake, I can't live like this." His eyes held the desperation of a man standing on the ledge of a building, willing someone to give him a reason not to jump.

Mossy reached out and grabbed his arm as he started to raise the drink to his lips. "Jake, what did you see? Please, if you tell me, I think I can kill it. Maybe if it's dead, and you know it's dead, you can try to move on."

Jake looked at him with an expression of such emptiness that Mossy knew it wasn't possible. "I glimpsed Hell that day. Does that help?" Then he downed the rest of his drink. "Can I get another one?"

Mossy took a deep breath, exhaling slowly. "Jake, listen, I know what you're feeling. Because I've been feeling it for over thirty years, trying to drown it just like you are. And for me, it wasn't one kid I couldn't save, it was...I don't even know how many."

Jake raised his eyes from his glass to meet Mossy's and in those eyes Mossy saw turmoil. There was a battle going on in there, alright. The old Jake, from before the incident, wanted to spill it all, just open the floodgates and finally let every bitter memory, every ounce of guilt, flow out of his mouth with his story. The new and improved Jake (just add alcohol!) wanted to have a couple of more drinks, maybe more than a couple, until the memories and guilt slid beneath the surface of the booze for another day. "I'll tell you what I saw on one condition. If you don't agree to it, I will never speak of it to anyone. I will sit here and drink until I pass out. I'll do that every day until death puts me out of my misery."

Mossy met his gaze. "What's the condition, Jake?"

"I'm going with you to kill it. Whatever your plan is, I'm in. This is not negotiable."

Mossy didn't blink and the lie came easily and convincingly as he slowly nodded his head. "Fair enough, Jake. As long as you know the stakes going in and that it's a long-shot that either of us comes out alive."

Jake sat back in the booth with a wry smile. "I've known the stakes since that day at the lake. And what I'm doing now isn't living anyway. Chris, please go get me another drink, storytelling can be thirsty business." Chris smiled, a real smile, and got up to go to the bar. Jake grabbed his arm on the way by. "Make mine what he's drinking, I've got to get my head clear if I'm going to be killing monsters."

Chris put his hand over his brother's and squeezed. "You got it, Jake. Two ginger ales and a beer for yours truly."

When Chris returned with the drinks, Jake's bravado was short-lived as he began to relate his story for the first time.

"As much as I've tried to forget that day, no matter how much booze I drink, I can't. I tried pot, too, but it didn't help. I guess I'm too much a coward to try anything stronger. Or maybe I just know how easy it would be to take too much of that stuff..." He paused, a frighteningly wistful look haunting his face, "Anyway, there are days I can't remember my own name when I open my eyes in the morning, but that day is as clear in my head as it was when it happened. It was hot, so hot all summer. Just like it is this year. No rain, no cool breezes, just heat and humidity. And dead kids." He took a sip of his drink, grimacing when he realized there was no alcohol in it.

He turned his gaze to his brother. "By the time you and Lori went over to the rocks, I was shitfaced. I don't think you or Lori had any idea just how drunk I was, otherwise you wouldn't have gone."

The implication hung there, an overripe piece of fruit left festering for so many years. Mossy couldn't tell if it was accusation or Jake's attempt to ease his brother's conscience.

"As soon as you guys were gone, my eyes started closing. I slurred something to Kevin about staying out of the water until you got back, then I stumbled over to a patch of shade, sat back against a rock, and passed out. 'Cept I wasn't *really* passed out. I felt so tired that I couldn't move, but I wasn't asleep either. I could hear you and Lori playing grab-ass over at the rocks; I remember being a little jealous, she was such a pretty girl. I was planning on sneaking over there to see if you could talk Lori out of her bikini, and I could catch a glimpse, but I was just so damn tired." A shy smile played at the corner of Jake's mouth and Mossy could picture him before this happened, a young, good-looking kid with his whole life ahead of him. Wanting nothing more than a peek at his brother's girlfriend's tits. Tears were starting to leak from Chris's eyes and Mossy suspected he was thinking the same thing. What could have been. The vise-grip of guilt tightened around Mossy's heart.

"Kevin and Willie were fishing, but I could hear them whispering. They were thinking about going in for a swim after all, but were afraid I would be pissed if I woke up. I could hear all this, but I couldn't find the strength to open my eyes and tell them not to go in until you and Lori got back. Willie...he was kind of a hard-ass for a little kid...he came right over to me, close enough that I could feel his breath on my face. 'Jake, can you hear me? Jake the snake, you old fart-sniffer, you awake?' He actually called me an old fart-sniffer. Man, the kid had some balls. Next thing I hear is him telling Kevin that I was out cold and then the two of them splashing into the lake." He wouldn't raise his eyes, and he took another desperate gulp of his drink, but it was still just ginger ale.

Chris had a look of surprise that just might deepen to anger if it could. Mossy remembered Chris telling him part of the story the day they met, and the little boys going into the lake under Jake's watch wasn't part of it. Chris opened his mouth to speak, but Mossy placed a hand on his arm and shook his head. Chris nodded, understanding that a confrontation might silence Jake.

"For some reason, when I heard them go in the water, I was scared. I managed to open my eyes and sit up a little. Why would I be scared? Both of those kids were better swimmers than I was. Why should I have been so scared?" He looked up, eyes shifting back and forth from Chris to Mossy, and back. His eyes were windows to a haunted soul. Finding no answers from Mossy or Chris, he shook his head and kept going. "At first they were fine, splashing each other, horsing around, kid stuff. Then the water...it started swirling behind them. They couldn't see it, but I could, and I knew why I was scared. Something bad was going to happen...was already happening."

Mossy felt like frigid water was running through his veins instead of blood. He was suddenly cold right to the bone. He knew what was coming. Knew exactly how this story would end. He'd known it all along, but to actually hear it...it made it more real.

"Kevin gave Willie a shove, knocking him down in the water, then started running for shore. They still hadn't seen the whirlpool behind them, that's what it was, a whirlpool. Willie got up and started chasing him. Kevin finally made land, got a few steps out of the water and turned to wait for Willie to come get him. That's when he started screaming. Willie was running after Kevin, that awkward, high-stepping run you have to do in the water, probably thinking

Kevin's scream were part of the game, when the lake behind him...
erupted. The whirlpool exploded with a splash...and this...thing...
was there. Willie turned and saw it, and started backing up out of
the water. The thing just watched, the whole time Kevin screaming
his head off. I started to get up...and it looked at me..."

Jake was now cringing in the corner of the booth. His eyes were
staring straight ahead, but he wasn't seeing Mossy or Chris or the
seedy surroundings of the Witch's Hat. He was seeing the lake and
two little boys and a monster about to take one of them. Mossy had
never seen a look of such terror.

"It looked at me and it started coming toward the shore. I couldn't
do anything. I wanted to grab Willie and Kevin and run...but I froze.
It kept coming and I could see how big it was. It had two arms and
webbed hands with huge claws...but it had tentacles too...and those
eyes. Willie was almost out of the water and started turning to run,
but one of its tentacles wrapped around his wrist and he never struggled...just slumped into the water. The whole time it was looking at
me, daring me to do something. I pissed myself, that's all I did, then
leaned back against the rock and waited for it to come for me. But it
didn't, it just backed into the deeper water dragging Willie with it.
The whole time staring at me and Kevin screaming bloody murder.
Then you and Lori came back...and I've spent every moment since
then wishing it did come back for me."

Chris was looking at Jake with such sorrow that Mossy had to
turn away. He knew when Chris's eyes turned his way, they would
contain hate and anger and disgust. "Christ, Jake...I'm so sorry. All
this time...why didn't you tell me?"

A wry smile filled with despair darkened Jake's face. "Would you
have believed me? Or just thought it was all a drunk hallucination?"

Chris nodded. "You're right...but now we know the truth. It's
back, what do we do? Tell the police? And everybody thinks it's
Greymore doing this..."

Mossy spoke. "I'm going to kill it, that's what. I'm not sure how
to help Greymore, but I am ending this once and for all." His voice
shook with anger and conviction. Finally he was able to look them

each in the eye. "Everything that happened is my fault. I helped create this thing. I thought it was dead, but when it killed all those kids in 1961, I should have come back. I grabbed on to Greymore being guilty like a drowning man grabs for a life preserver. Deep down I knew it wasn't him, that somehow that thing wasn't dead. Then the killings stopped and I was able to convince myself that Greymore was responsible...I've ruined so many lives..."

Jake was slowly nodding his head. "When do we do this?"

"You are not a part of this, Jake." Chris's voice began to rise, gaining another look from the bartender. In an urgent whisper he continued. "This is your chance to move on, to get your life back. You are not going anywhere near the lake."

Jake's reply was immediate and final. "That's not what Dad would have done."

Mossy's mission was clear; any doubt he harbored because of his alcoholism was gone. But there would be no more innocent victims, he would do this alone. "Jake, I need a few days to get some things together. When I'm ready, we go in to the tunnels under the old base and kill this thing. You are there to record the evidence. I'll get you a good camera and make sure you know how to use it. You can finish the story your father started." He was once again disgusted at how easy the lies came.

Jake was nodding. There was a glint in his eyes that wasn't there at the start of the night, a hint of the old Jake, perhaps.

"Now, if you don't mind, I need to go home and get some rest." The three men got up and left the bar, each lost in his own thoughts of what was to come.

(64)

DENNY AND Billy got off the Round-Up and staggered against a nearby tent laughing. Denny finally got himself under control. "That ride's the best! If I didn't think I'd puke, I'd get right back in line."

Billy started walking. "Come on, a nice piece of Fried Dough will settle your stomach." They ordered their dough and piled on cinnamon and sugar before devouring them.

"This is the greatest. How could they have even thought about canceling this?"

Even with everything else going on, the lure of the carnival was too much for boys to resist. Paul had been away in Boston, safe, scheduled to return later that evening. Joe was healing and should be released in a day or two, and Denny had avoided Crawford for the past couple of days. Denny felt...normal for the first time in a long time.

Billy shook his head. His mouth was caked with sugar. "I don't know, but it looks like a lot of people canceled it for themselves," He gestured toward the midway.

Denny looked at the thinner-than-usual crowd making their way from booth to booth. "You're right; this place is dead compared to last year. And hardly any little kids." A sudden jostling of people on the midway caught his eye. "Oh, shit. This could be a problem." Denny's sense of normalcy had lasted less than a minute; pushing their way through the crowd was Dale Crawford and his loyal subjects. They looked ready for action, shoving anyone in their path and taunting anyone who even looked at them.

Billy wiped the sugar off his face. "Let's head over to the other side. Maybe we can avoid them." They quickly ducked around the side of the Fried Dough cart and headed back toward the rides, away from the midway.

"This sucks, now we're going to have to worry about those clowns all night. I figured they'd be out boozing somewhere." They ended up in front of the Ghost Ship ride where a barker dressed as a pirate rattled through his spiel to try to get them in. The line was already pretty long since the ride was new this year. "I've still got some tickets left, let's check this out."

Billy dug through his pockets and also came up with some tickets. "We'll still have enough for one more Round-Up after this," he said with a grin.

Finally, they reached the front of the line. The Ghost Ship consisted of four-man cars that followed a track through the "ship." Beyond that, they could see nothing in the blackness. Just as they were climbing into the rear seats of the next car behind an older couple, angry shouts rose behind them. As their car moved slowly into the impenetrable darkness, they saw Dale and three of his cronies pushing their way to the front of the line. They would end up in the very next car! Denny quickly looked forward. It was impossible to see the people in the car in front of them, which meant Crawford couldn't see them. "Do you think they saw us?" Billy whispered in a shaky voice.

"I don't think so; as long as it stays dark in here, we'll be okay. Once it's over we either make a run for it or duck into a hiding spot at the end of the ride."

Black lights flickered on and off, momentarily illuminating the inhabitants of the Ghost Ship—skeletons, murderous-looking pirates, giant rats feasting on dead sailors—the usual. Denny paid no attention. He was desperately trying to remember where the exit from this ride would put them but it was no use; his fear was too overwhelming. From behind, Crawford's group was getting rowdier. It sounded like they were getting in and out of the car. The sound of breaking glass to their left. The lights flickered on another exhibit and it was covered with the glistening remains of a bottle thrown at it. Denny swallowed hard. They were really fired up, probably drunk, no telling what they would do if they came across Denny and Billy.

"Boo!"

The voice from behind made Denny jump in his seat. It was one of them right behind their car! The smell of alcohol blasted Denny as the voice erupted in laughter. "Hey Dale, I think these two just shit their pants!" Drunken laughter filled the air around them. The ride was almost over. Denny could see a patch of light up ahead. As they got closer, he could clearly see the people exiting the cars! They'd be spotted for sure.

"Billy, we have to get off the car," he hissed.

"We can't, what if there are wires and stuff around here, we can't see a thing."

"It's better than the alternative; they'll see us for sure. They'll chase us, Billy; you know they'll catch us." Denny's hand instinctively went to his face and traced the scar that Dale had given him. He grabbed Billy's arm. "Let's go." He waited for the next flash of black light, and then leaped into the inky blackness. A second later he heard Billy thud down next to him. They were between exhibits in complete darkness. They stayed crouched down as the next car went by. The smell of booze was unmistakable, even cutting through the smell of must and grease that filled the inside of the Ghost Ship.

They both lay still in the darkness, hoping against hope that none of Crawford's gang would decide to get out of their car. Denny almost jumped up and ran when he felt something scurry across his leg. It must have been a rat! And not a baby one by the feel of it. He swallowed hard, trying not to freak out.

Dale's car was passing them now, just a few feet away.

"Hey, gimmee that bottle!" Dale yelled, his words slurring slightly. "Hey, what the fuck? It's empty!" The bottle shattered against the wall behind Denny and his legs were showered with the shards of broken glass.

At least it will scare the rat away, he thought, still keeping his tenuous grasp on composure. Soon their car moved into the patch of light at the exit and Denny watched them get off the ride.

"That sucked!" one of the gang yelled.

"What kind of Ghost Ship was that? That bullshit wouldn't scare my grandmother!" They all laughed and shoved each other as they moved out of Denny's line of sight.

"Let's give them a minute to move on," Billy whispered, "and then we'll get out of here. They're really stewed tonight, maybe we should just head home."

Denny was crushed. As much as he feared Crawford and his gang, it would kill him to leave the carnival. He waited all year for it. To him, nothing matched the endless onslaught of sights, sounds and smells of the carnival. Except maybe a Red Sox game at Fenway. As scared as he was, he had hoped Billy would give him the courage to stick it out. But he knew Billy was right: if Crawford caught them tonight, there was no telling what the result would be. He sighed deeply as he got to his feet. "You're right, Billy. Let's go."

They walked sideways with their backs against the wall to avoid getting too close to the rails that carried the cars. Who knew what kind of shoddy electrical wiring might be lying around on the floor? They finally reached the end of the tunnel. Although they could clearly see everyone getting off the ride just in front of them, they remained hidden in the shadows. Just as they were about to step into the lighted exit, hushed voices made them shrink back into the darkness. It was Crawford and his gang waiting outside the ride! *They must have seen us and they're just waiting for us to walk right into them*, Denny thought. Denny felt fear taking over as he strained to make out what they were saying. Their conspiratorial tones made it difficult to make out and Denny was only able to catch snatches of the conversation when the cars stopped to let riders out. Then the next few words would be lost as the next car made its way to the unloading area.

"…Dad says he killed 'em all…"

"…already got Cummings real good…"

"...his kid and his little faggot friend..."

Denny edged closer, not wanting to hear but knowing he must. He inched as close to the exit as he could without being seen.

"We're going out there tonight to finish this once and for all. Cummings was just a warning. His geek kid and O'Brien I'll deal with later. Tonight is Greymore's last night as a killer. My dad can't do anything official because the Butcher always seems to have either Cummings or that priest as an alibi. But we don't have to be cops to throw a little party for that freak." The maniacal laughter that followed was worse than the actual words. It was worse than the rat running over his leg. Much worse.

Dale's crew finally headed out, apparently on their way to Greymore's house. Denny quickly relayed what he had overheard to Billy.

"We've gotta get to Greymore first. Denny, they might kill him. Chief Crawford will find a way to justify it, just like last time."

"Either that or they'll just make him disappear. Then they won't need a cover story. Let's go."

They made their way quickly through the sparse crowds, turning their heads constantly to see if they were being chased. Before they reached the exit, they ran squarely into a man who stepped from behind one of the trailers. Denny and Billy bounced off the giant and fell in a pile of arms and legs. The man towered over them, then reached down and offered them each a hand. He yanked them to their feet effortlessly.

"We're sorry, mister," Denny muttered. "We weren't looking where we were going."

An ugly smile crossed his face and he spoke with an accent Denny couldn't place. "No apologies necessary, boys. Now, how about you each hand over two bits and I'll bring you in to see an unadvertised attraction? It's a creature, of sorts, I bought while on the northern circuit, way up in Maine. I'm not saying it's a werewolf, but I'm not saying it ain't. But we have to keep it quiet, a lot of people are looking for this thing, and if certain people found out I had it, I might just disappear right along with it."

Denny looked at Billy with no idea what the man was talking about. "Sorry, mister, we really have to go."

The man looked crushed. "That's too bad. I like to find a couple of kids at each stop and let them see it. Just in case I do disappear, others will know. Maybe it doesn't matter in the end, but it makes me feel better, helps me sleep. You would be the first here in Haven."

Despite the urgent need to get away from Crawford and warn Paul, Denny was oddly drawn to see what the man was hiding. Billy, however, remained focused.

"Come on, Denny, we have to go." Billy pulled his arm and Denny stumbled after him. "Sorry mister, maybe next time," Billy yelled over his shoulder.

The last thing Denny saw was the big man trudging slowly back into the shadows of the trailer.

They exited the fairgrounds and made their way quickly through the parking lot. Denny suddenly grabbed Billy. "Wait, I have an idea. Find Crawford's car, we need to slow them down." Billy nodded and the boys snuck up and down the rows of cars until they spotted Crawford's Mustang. Denny bent down and unscrewed the cap from one of the tire valves. He grabbed a small, pointed rock and pushed on the pin, smiling triumphantly as the hiss of fetid, rubber-smelling air rushed by his face. "Billy, do another one in case he has a spare." Billy quickly went to work, pulling his house key out of his pocket to release the air. When both tires were flat, the boys looked around to make sure they hadn't been spotted, high-fived and headed out of the lot.

Two shadows hurried through the deserted streets of Haven as if the Devil himself were chasing them. In a way, maybe that was the truth. As the sounds of the carnival faded behind them, they raced down Main Street in a desperate effort to get to Paul before anyone else did. Denny's mind raced as fast as his legs. The Town Square was completely empty! Normally with the carnival going on, the square would be pretty desolate but the crowd at the carnival was sparse at best. Could everyone really be this afraid of the Butcher? The pounding of their footsteps, the heavy breathing and the buzzing of the overhead street lamps were the only sounds to break the unearthly quiet. Sweat poured from them as they turned down Forge Street toward the old Blacksmith Shop, one of Haven's historic landmarks.

The Town Blacksmith building was originally built back in 1805. The Kilgore family had served as blacksmiths for most of the surrounding towns for generations. Surviving members of the family still resided in Haven and had long ago donated the building and the grounds to the town to preserve. Denny had toured the building on a field trip, as had everyone else that grew up in Haven, and had been pretty impressed with the entire concept. During the tour, they had actually fired up the old oven and shown how horseshoes were made. Denny remembered standing close to the oven and feeling the searing heat from it that was capable of melting iron. The heat he was running through now seemed to rival that in its intensity.

Just as they approached the Forge building, headlights cut through the still darkness with the suddenness and intensity of lightning. Thinking as one, Denny and Billy dove headlong into the tall hedges that surround the Forge. They tumbled through the thick bushes, scratching skin and tearing clothes, and landed in a heap on the dry lawn on the other side. Denny rolled over onto his stomach, ignoring his torn shirt and bloody arms to catch a glimpse of the car. He heard Billy rustling around next to him. As he suspected, it was a police cruiser. The car trolled by, sweeping a spotlight across the sidewalk that they had been running on seconds before. Denny wasn't sure if they had been spotted running or if this was just Haven's finest doing their duty.

The car slowly pulled over to the curb just ten feet from where the boys crouched behind the bushes. Denny was sure they were caught, but then the flick of a match illuminated the inside of the car. They were just pulling over to have a smoke.

Denny and Billy looked at each other, helpless to move and too close to the open windows of the car to speak. It was too dark to make out who the officers were but it didn't matter: if they tried to get away it would look suspicious. They would have to wait it out.

Finally the officer flicked the butt to the sidewalk in front of them, played the spotlight once more over the old building, and the car pulled away. After the tail lights had turned onto Main Street and out of sight, Denny and Billy stood and brushed the dry grass and dust off themselves.

"I thought we were busted," Billy breathed.

"Me too. I wonder if it was Crawford."

"I don't want to know. Let's get going."

They cut through the back of the Forge grounds, across a large clearing that was also part of the property donated by the Adams'. Heat bugs buzzed in the trees above them. The occasional twinkle of a firefly was the only light visible from where they walked. A thick haze masked the moon and stars.

When they finally reached Hillview Street, it was as eerily quiet as the rest of the town. They jogged past Billy's house. Denny watched Billy out of the corner of his eye. Billy glanced at his darkened house with an expression of such pain and sadness that it made Denny feel like he'd just stepped off the Round-Up. None of this was fair. Billy's family was forced to move out of their home, while the rest of the town cowered in theirs. Worst of all, perhaps, seventeen years of an innocent man's life were wasted, and now the scene was being repeated. He slowed down and Billy slowed with him. "What if they have a patrol at Paul's house and see us?" he wondered out loud.

"So what, you live up the street, what can they do?" Billy tried to sound surprised at the question but Denny could tell he understood.

"They can do anything they want. Let's cross the street and stick to the woods until we get to the house."

They crossed the road and made their way into the outer fringe of the woods. These woods would take them all the way north into Maine, or in another direction to the border of Braxton State Prison a hundred miles away. They stayed low in the underbrush, ignoring the occasional scurrying sounds and crashing through the trees around them. They had both lived near the woods long enough to know the creatures that inhabited them, mostly chipmunks and squirrels but ranging as large as fox and deer and every once in a while a coyote.

HAVEN

The boys got to a point where they were across from Greymore's house and could see the road up past Lovell's. The houses were both dark and there were no cars in sight. "There's no lights on, maybe he's not back from Boston yet?"

A sudden thought hit Denny and he felt like he might cry. "What if they already got him?"

Billy shook his head. "No way they could have been here and gone already. Paul's probably not back yet or he's with Father McCarthy."

Denny nodded. "We'll wait at my house; we can see any cars coming up the road."

As the boys made their way up the hill toward Denny's house, it was his turn to dwell on the unfairness of life. They stopped directly across the street and Denny saw a light on in his mother's bedroom, knowing she was either reading or just staring off into space, waiting for sleep to come and save her from a few hours of thinking, another day closer to death. He swallowed hard at the thought and tore his gaze away from the house. Suddenly a rough hand was covering his mouth and pulling him into the bushes along the yard.

(65)

JULIE CUMMINGS swatted the hand off her butt for what seemed like the thousandth time. Dale was shitfaced, making him more obnoxious and more grab-ass than usual. They had just exited the Ghost Ship where Julie had spent the entire ride fending off Dale's groping hands. "Knock it off, Dale!"

"What's the matter, Jen? I thought we'd have a little fun before me and the boys take care of a little business later."

Julie was starting to get scared. Dale was starting to slur and the rest of the gang were all pretty drunk, too. All they'd been talking about was "getting Greymore." Julie didn't think much of it until she'd heard them talking about getting guns from Dale's father. She had ignored her mom and Billy when they said Dale Crawford may have had something to do with her dad's attack. Now she knew they were right.

She wasn't even supposed to be here. Her father was still in the hospital; Julie and her mom were staying in Malden. She told her mom she was going to the Meadow Glen drive-in in Medford to see a double feature with her cousins but had already made plans with Dale to come get her. God, she was going to be in trouble.

Dale again reached for her ass and she again knocked his hand away.

He and his friends just laughed it off. "Come on, baby, I thought you loved it," cooed Crawford. He reached for her breast and this time instead of his hand, she slapped his face. His hand instinctively went up to his stinging cheek, to the same spot the scar from the gas nozzle was. Then his eyes narrowed and his anger started to boil over, and he raised his hand to strike back. But Julie was too fast and too angry herself. She stepped closer to him, waving her finger in front of his face.

"Don't even think about it, you piece of shit! Just 'cause your friend knocked up Cheryl, don't even think you're going to come close enough to me to make that happen. And don't *ever* raise your hand to me!"

She'd had enough. Even before tonight she was tired of Dale and his friends. Always drinking and fighting and getting into trouble. And getting her into trouble with them. She was finished with them. She missed her old friends and how she used to get along with her family and her teachers at school. How had she gotten herself into this, she wondered. She wanted to be "cool" that's how. She'd decided her friends were too boring, too goody-goody for her, and she started hanging with Dale and his gang. Sure it had been fun for a while. Edgy, dangerous, all of the things she wasn't. She tried cigarettes and drinking, even smoked pot a few times. Then the newness wore off and she realized she was wasting her time, hell, wasting her *life*, with a bunch of small-town losers. She'd decided a while ago to break it off with Dale and ditch him and his friends and his stupid lifestyle. She was just waiting for the right time, and Dale had been good enough to supply all the reason she would need tonight. She had certainly been willing enough to experiment with booze and the rest, but getting felt up by some drunk yahoo police-chief's son was not her idea of trying something new. The new Julie was going to do her best to mend some fences and be the old Julie—starting now.

As good as it sounded, it wasn't going to be that easy. Dale's strong hands were suddenly pinning her arms to her sides and he was grinding himself against her. For the first time, Julie realized she may have gotten into something she couldn't handle. Dale backed her around the corner of one of the tents and his gang followed, glancing around to make sure nobody noticed them. He pressed his lips to her ear, darting his tongue in and out quickly before speaking. "You uppity little bitch, I knew you weren't one of us. But I figured I'd play things out with you until I got in your pants. I know it's what you want and tonight, you'll get what you want and so will I." She squirmed in an attempt to break free, feeling nauseous from both the stink of his breath on her and the situation she was in. "Guys, take a walk, come back in ten for sloppies." His crew snickered and disappeared around the corner, back to the lights of the carnival.

One thought overtook all of her reasoning: *He's going to rape me.* Him and maybe all the rest of them, too. Anger and fear battled for control of her next action. Rational thought was not an option. It was fight or flight. She was a Cummings, she chose fight. She brought her knee up as hard and fast as she could just as Dale had started kissing her neck. She heard the air burst from his lungs and felt the grip on her arms loosen. She was vaguely aware of a sense of satisfaction as he struggled to get a breath. "Bitch," He gasped.

Before he could utter another word, her knee shot forward again as she tried to jam his balls up into his throat. This time he went down to his knees before collapsing into a fetal position on the ground. Julie could feel the adrenaline ripping through her veins. She wanted to stay and tell him how dumb she felt. How she'd made a fool of herself to everyone she truly cared about for the last several months by being seen with him. But she knew better. She knew those apes wouldn't wait ten minutes, they'd come back in five hoping to get a glimpse of her ass. Choking back bile but not able to stop the tears from streaming down her face, she turned and ran. Back to her old life if it would still have her.

Julie felt better out in the bright lights and movement of people on the midway. That feeling was short-lived when the realization that she had no way to get back to Malden hit her like a hammer. Despite the crowds around her, she suddenly felt more alone than she ever had before. Loud voices from behind galvanized her into action. She didn't even bother to see if it was Crawford's gang or not; she began to run through the crowd with no destination in mind. She exited the fairgrounds and slowed to a walk on the deserted streets of Haven.

Normally there'd be people out walking dogs or people congregating on someone's porch to collectively escape the heat of being indoors. Tonight, there was no one. The Butcher had everyone too scared to be out. Not only were they inside, thought Julie, but no doubt their doors were locked too.

The thought of the Butcher should have scared Julie, walking alone through the dark empty streets, but it didn't. Since Greymore's return to Haven, Julie had heard nothing but horror stories from everyone in town—except her family. Her father led the charge and Mom and Billy were right behind defending Greymore whenever the name came up. Christ, even Denny O'Brien wasn't afraid of the guy.

The first night he'd come over to visit her dad, Julie had been a little unnerved. As the night went on, she began to sense there was more to Greymore than meets the eye. Despite his scarred face and the muscles that bulged beneath his shirt, there was a quiet gentleness, a kindness that Julie picked up on. And a sense of humor that had survived everything he'd been through. And all she did was treat the guy like shit. She felt smaller for that than she did for being Dale's girl. Judging people was something the old Julie was good at. And the old Julie was back. Her ability to see people for what they are made her behavior for the past several months even more embarrassing. What had she been thinking?

As she walked through the quiet streets, unaware that she was already heading in the direction of her house, her thoughts returned to Greymore and what Crawford and his thug friends had said. That they were going to "take care of business" and "get him." Tonight. She knew what she had to do. She quickened her pace; feeling a sense of resolve, she began to run.

AS JULIE rounded the corner and started up Hillview Street, her resolve began to ebb. She was physically tired, emotionally spent, and starting to get freaked out. The stifling heat and eerie quiet had teamed up to unravel the last of Julie's fraying nerves. As she approached her house, the temptation to slide into bed, turn the fan on and deal with life tomorrow was almost overwhelming. Her heart leaped with hope when she saw her dad's car in the driveway, then she remembered her mom saying it had been towed from the Witch's Hat to have the tire changed and the garage would drop it here.

"I thought we'd have a little fun before me and the boys take care of a little business later."

"Guys, take a walk, come back in ten for sloppies."

Thinking of it, of those words, brought the anger back. She resisted the pull of her own empty house and continued up Hillview Street toward Paul's. Without warning, a memory so vivid and so real, she actually shivered. Someone just walked over your grave, her Grammy used to say. More likely it was the silly Ghost Ship ride that brought it back.

When she was seven or eight, her dad had bought her a book about pirates a few weeks before their summer excursion to Cape Cod. Julie had been instantly captivated. That was just Julie's way: when she read about sharks she wanted to be the female Jacques Cousteau. Her dad had taken her to the New England Aquarium in

Boston to learn more. When she read The Swiss Family Robinson, she made her dad build her a tree house. That year, it was pirates.

They arrived late Saturday afternoon in Falmouth after sitting in endless traffic, her dad keeping a nervous eye on the car's temperature gauge. They settled in the cramped cottage, took a walk on the beach, went out later for ice cream. Julie spent a restless first night; the heat robbed her of sleep while visions of walking the plank owned her dreams.

The next day, despite her sleepless night, Julie was up early. She stumbled into the small kitchen, rubbing the sleep out of her eyes. Her mother was cracking eggs into a mixing bowl. "Can we go to the beach, Mommy?"

"Good morning to you too, honey. It's seven o'clock in the morning. Your dad went for coffee and Billy is still sleeping. After breakfast, the beach it is."

"Did you know that a ship captured by Black Sam Bellamy, called the Whydah, might have wrecked somewhere near Cape Cod? Daddy thinks we might find treasure!"

"Your dad has a great imagination, honey."

"But Mom, the ship went down in 1717 near here in a bad storm. The next day, over a hundred pirate bodies washed up on shore!"

"Oh honey, I'm not sure you should be reading that."

"Daddy picked it out for me at the library. He said it's educational and full of local history."

Her mother shook her head. "That sounds about right. But I wouldn't get my hopes up too much about finding treasure. Some people search years without finding so much as a single gold coin."

"They're call doubloons. And Daddy said we might get lucky because the Cummings family goes waaay back, and we might have a little pirate blood in us!"

"Oh, Julie..."

Just then Joe Cummings appeared with a Styrofoam cup of coffee and a twinkle in his eye. "Well shiver me timbers, if it ain't little Julie Cummings!" he growled in his best pirate voice (which really wasn't very good at all). To Julie it was Black Sam himself, bigger than life. She ran over and hugged his legs, not noticing how sandy they were. He scooped her up in his free arm and gave her a kiss. "Ready for a little treasure hunt?"

It wasn't the best beach day of the year, hot enough to swim but overcast with threatening skies in the distance. Her dad had already set up chairs and towels on his way back from the coffee shop. Staking a claim early turned out to be unnecessary with the gloomy weather, but it made getting there that much easier.

After the usual battles of slathering the kids with Coppertone, Billy started filling buckets with sand and making roads for his Matchbox cars. Immediately, Julie began asking her dad to dig for treasure.

"Slow down, Julie, let's do this right. There's a lot of beach here and we don't want to waste our time digging in the wrong spot." Joe ignored the skeptical look his wife gave him and pulled Julie's pirate book out of the beach bag. "Sit with me and let's take another look through this book before we start."

Julie sat patiently while her dad pored over each page. Suddenly, he got up and walked to the edge of the water. He made a production of walking a few paces back toward the chairs, changing direction after looking up at the hazy brightness where the sun hid. He pointed up, then traced a line with his outstretched hand back to the water and then toward the street. Finally, he walked back to within a few feet of the chairs, and called for Julie to get the shovel.

Julie attacked the sand like the Tasmanian Devil on Bugs Bunny cartoons. Sand flew everywhere despite Joe's urges for her to slow down. She had a decent hole going and sweat was beginning to drip down her head. Tina was looking curiously over the top of her book and even Billy had stopped construction on his Matchbox metropolis to watch Julie. She grunted with effort as her muscles began to tire, but the fierce determination on her face made Joe smile.

On one of her violent thrusts of the shovel, there was a sharp clink as metal met metal. Julie's eyes widened and she looked up at her dad with an expression of wonder and excitement that was possible only in a child. With renewed vigor she began to dig. Moments later she was in the hole brushing sand off an old, dented metal box. She looked up again at Joe and swallowed hard.

"Julie, you did it! Come on, climb out of there and let's see it!" He reached down for her hand. She hesitated for a second, afraid to let go of the box at all. Then she slowly reached up and let Joe pull her out of the sand. They both fell to their knees as Julie placed the box between them and her eyes widened again when she heard the contents rattle around. Tina Cummings joined them and Bill squirmed over to complete the circle.

"Daddy, do you think…"

"Only one way to find out, kid. Go ahead and open it."

With her hands shaking from exhaustion and excitement, she pulled on the lid. It resisted for a minute then flew open, scattering gold jewelry, coins, and pearls on the sand. Julie looked up again. "Daddy, can we keep it?"

"There's a law older than the pirates even. It says 'finders, keepers.' It's all yours, honey."

Julie picked up each piece of jewelry and each coin and examined it carefully before putting it back in the box. Billy quickly got bored and went back to his cars. Tina walked over to where Joe stood, placed her hand on his cheek, mouthed "I love you" and went back to her book.

Julie stood shaking, tears rolling down her face. She could remember nothing else about that week's vacation. Years later when she figured out her dad had set the whole thing up, the memory had become even more special. How could she have forgotten what a great dad he'd been? What a great dad he still was? She cursed her stupidity and made a solemn vow to herself to make it up to him. With frightening tenacity, she continued on to Greymore's house.

(67)

DALE CRAWFORD was pissed, and that meant someone was going to get hurt. He had pulled himself together before Buddy and Costa got back. He played it that he'd told Julie to find her own way home because she was being a bitch. He told them he'd get her later. "She'll be walking bowlegged for a week when I get through with her." This had been met with nervous chuckles from the others. "Tonight, we take care of Greymore. And he might not be walking at all when we're through." He didn't see the look that passed between Tony and Buddy. It was the same look Chuck Brantley had when Dale had put his knife to Denny's face. When they got to the parking lot and Crawford saw the flat tires, he went apeshit.

"That fucking little cocktease did this! She is going to pay!"

Buddy and Tony tried to calm him down but he was in a booze-fueled nuclear rage. Pain and destruction were the only things that would calm him down. He took the tire iron out of the trunk and began smashing the windows and lights on the other cars in the lot, all the time screaming about Julie. When he was too exhausted to swing the tire iron any more, he slumped down against his own car, looking around to find that Tony and Buddy had bailed. "Fucking pussies," he slurred. He threw the tire iron back in the trunk and slammed it shut, then began walking home.

He contemplated walking to Julie's before realizing she would have called Mommy for a ride back to Malden. Greymore was first on the list, he'd told the boys, and decided that's where he would go. Halfway across town, as he began to sober up a bit, the thought of facing Greymore alone began to sound like a bad idea. He had snuck one of his father's guns out of the house but had left it in the useless Mustang. No way he was going over there unarmed, he told himself, no telling what kind of weapons he might have at his house. "I'm not scared of him," he muttered. But he couldn't shake the thought of their first meeting at the gas station.

There seemed like nothing left to do but go home. Then he remembered finding his father at the table the other night staring down the barrel of his service revolver. "What the fuck is happening..." Again he thought he might have been better off just waiting outside to see if Mr. Tough Cop had the balls to pull the trigger. Then where would he be? Mother gone, father dead, too young to be on his own. They'd probably throw him in some group home or stick him with a foster family. It was a rare time that Dale Crawford actually thought about the future, and this was why. He suddenly felt completely sober and unusually hopeless.

Everything was fine before Greymore got here. Dale was the town badass, fully protected by the fact his father was Chief of Police. He had Julie wrapped around his finger and he had a gang that would do whatever he told them. Now, Julie was gone, Brantley had bailed after the night at the library, and now Tony and Buddy had both deserted him. "What the fuck is happening," he repeated. But all roads led back to Greymore. He would have to get his shit together, convince Tony and Buddy to help him, and finish that freak once and for all. It would put him back on top where he belonged and maybe help his father get *his* shit together for a change.

He'd had these thoughts before, but they were always in a haze of either alcohol or rage. Tonight, he felt oddly calm, his rage and most of his drunkenness left back in the parking lot. The thoughts that went through his head now, the precise step-by-step plans, had the razor-sharp focus found only in the true genius or the hopeless psychopath.

PAUL WAS startled by the knock on his door. He'd returned from Boston later than expected thanks to traffic and had walked home from the bus. He hadn't slept well in the hotel and the days had been long. He'd stretched out on his bed to rest for a moment and had fallen into a deep sleep until the knock awakened him. *Crawford* was the first thought that entered his mind. But Crawford wouldn't knock. He'd torch the house and drag Greymore's burnt bones out of the rubble. *Then who?* Before he could finish the thought or get half-way to the door, the knocks became a steady pounding. He threw open the door and the girl, in mid-knock, came stumbling into his arms. Paul caught her by the shoulders to keep her from falling. "Julie? Is something wrong? Is it your dad?"

She was out of breath and frantic. "Mr. Greymore…you have to get out…*we* have to get out of here."

"Slow down, Julie. What's going on?" Paul stepped onto the porch to look up and down the street. Seeing nothing unusual, he went back in and closed the door. "Take a deep breath and talk to me."

She took a second to compose herself before responding but still speaking in machine-gun burst between breaths. "It's Dale and his stupid gang. They're coming. To get you. And me too if they find me."

"Julie, I think…"

"No! We have to go. Please." The look in her eyes said more than her words ever could. The girl was afraid. For her life.

"Okay. I don't have a car; we can take my canoe across the lake and get back to town from that side. Father McCarthy will help."

"Let's go. Anywhere but here." She pulled him toward the back of the house.

Neither of them spoke as they prepared to get on the lake in Paul's canoe. Paul threw an empty canteen, some rope to tie up the canoe and a flashlight into a knapsack. Julie kept looking back toward the street, imagining the Mustang's growl as it screamed up Hillview Street. Finally, life jackets on, they shoved off. And it was then that Paul thought about everything that had been going on, and the part the lake played in it. Suddenly, this seemed like a very bad idea. He looked at Julie, saw the raw terror in her eyes, and began rowing. No turning back now. "Julie, what happened? It's okay, we're safe…from Crawford."

"He tried to rape me." Her voice was flat, head down, eyes shut tight.

Greymore stopped rowing, staring at Julie in disbelief. He knew the kid was bad news, a chip off the old block, but this was over the top. "That son of a bitch." He began rowing, this time with one oar, turning the canoe around.

"No, Mr. Greymore, what are you doing? You can't go back!" She lunged across the seat to stop him, threatening to dump them both into the lake. "They mean to kill you. They're drunk and there're three of them. I think they have guns. Please?"

Paul was seething. The atrocities he faced in prison were bad, but to him, hurting a child, and Julie *was* a child, was unacceptable. She held his eyes now, had to see the murder in them, but she wouldn't look away. He sighed deeply and nodded. She sat back down and he began rowing again.

"Mr. Greymore, I want to apologize for the way I acted the night you first visited my father. I was rude and you didn't deserve any of it. I'm sorry."

Paul wanted to interrupt, but he could see it was something she wanted…*needed* to say.

"I haven't been a very good daughter lately. Hell, I haven't been a very good person. I used to be good. I became a cliché, started hanging with the wrong crowd. My grades went down, my old friends stopped wanting to see me, I became a rebel. I thought it was cool. But I'm done with it.

"I thought about everything on the way over here. How I've been acting, how I've treated everyone. Especially Dad. Then I thought about Denny losing his dad. I can't even imagine what it was like. He was really close to his dad the way I am...or the way I used to be. With everything I've done, in my heart I know I can count on my dad for anything. I'm so afraid of how badly I've hurt him..."

"Julie, I think your dad would be really happy to hear this."

Julie wiped tears from her eyes. "I know. I'm going to see him tomorrow. I'm so afraid of what he thinks of me."

"Well, the Joe Cummings I know will probably give you a big hug and tell you he loves you."

Julie smiled, still wiping the tears away. "Thanks."

"Now, why don't you tell me what happened tonight?"

Greymore felt the old anger rising as she related the events that took place at the carnival. His prison instincts were telling him to find the punk and teach him another lesson, since the one at the gas station didn't seem to take. But he knew Julie was right; things were already too far out of control, and with Crawford's gang drunk, the situation could only end badly. And Braxton was not on Paul's list of places to visit anytime soon.

Paul stopped rowing and stared intently back toward his house. Paul was surprised by the distance they had covered; listening to Julie had made the time pass quickly. He had left lights on in his haste to get out and it was easy to pick it out of the darkness. The thing that struck him as odd was the lights on in the Cummings house. "Julie, your mom is still in Malden and Billy is staying with Denny, right?"

"Yeah, why..." She followed Paul's gaze and saw the lights. "The house was dark when I walked by, I'm sure of it."

Paul began rowing.

(69)

DENNY'S EYES darted to Billy and saw that he was in the same situation. "Don't struggle, boys, I'm on your side. I know what's going on. I'm going to take my hand off you now. Please trust me and don't run or scream." The hand slid away as quickly as it had come on. Denny whipped around to face the person, not sure what to expect next, never expecting what he saw.

The man was older, probably close to seventy. He had the face of someone who had not lived an easy life. Denny had never seen him before, yet there was something about him. He squinted in the dark to try to get a better look but he couldn't place him. Billy was first to speak. "What the hell do you think you're doing? Who are you?" He was tensed, ready to take a swing at the old man.

"Calm down, now. We need to have a talk, boys. I can explain everything and I'm going to need your help. I suspect you'll probably need mine as well."

Denny finally got his composure back, though still distracted by the nagging feeling that he should know who he was talking to. "What are you talking about? You'd better start by telling us who you are or we'll have the cops up here before you know it." He tried to sound brave and arrogant but it suddenly crossed his mind that this could be the killer.

"Neither one of us wants the police involved, Dennis. We both know that much."

"How do you know my name?" Denny was looking around, making sure he and Billy each had a clear path to run if it came down to it.

The man seemed to smile slightly, as if he knew what Denny was plotting and it amused him. "I'll get into all that soon enough but I'd prefer not to stand in the woods all night. Billy, can we go to your house and I'll explain everything there?"

Billy's expression of surprise that the man knew his name would have been comical in different circumstances. "Oh, sure. Nothing I'd love more than to invite a complete stranger to my house for tea while there's a murderer running around town!"

The man laughed out loud. It was a hearty laugh that was contagious enough to bring a grin to both Billy and Denny's faces. Yet it seemed like a laugh that was seldom used. "I know what you're thinking, son." The man paused, almost seeming to choke on his own words. His face tightened and his eyes grew distant.

It was a look Denny had seen countless times and suddenly he knew. "Oh my God. You're supposed to be dead."

The man's face crumbled and a tear moved slowly down his weathered face. "I'm sorry, Dennis. Maybe after I explain you'll be able to understand why I've done what I've done."

Billy's expression again bordered on comical, this time in its confusion. "Denny, what the hell is going on here?"

"Billy, I'd like you to meet my grandfather."

Billy took a step back and shook his head. "Denny, your grandfather was killed in an explosion thirty-five years ago. Remember, we went to the site?"

The old man wiped his face and smiled a sad smile. He held out his hand to Billy. "Pleased to meet you, Billy. Again, I'll explain everything. You can both call me Mossy."

Billy shook the man's hand hesitantly, "Mossy? I'd be more likely to call you moldy after having been dead so long." They all laughed at that.

Denny spoke slowly, carefully. "My mom...she doesn't know. Otherwise you'd be in the house and not crawling around in the woods." His voice came out more pointed than he had thought it would.

"I'm not ready for that, yet. I don't know if she is, either. I read about what happened to your father and brother. I'm sorry. I'm more sorry I couldn't be here for your mom."

"Couldn't or wouldn't?" Denny spat out.

"It's not what you think, Dennis. It's all about what's happening in Haven, how it all began. Let's go down to Billy's house. Please?"

The three walked along the woods again, in case a patrol car came by. Denny was surprised to see lights on at Greymore's, he must have just got back from Boston. He glanced at Billy and knew by his expression that Billy noticed the lights too. They crossed over at the bottom of the hill and went into Billy's house. It was one of Denny's favorite places to go. It was always so full of life, warm and comforting, like an old blanket. It was a family house and that was what Denny really loved, so unlike his own. But as they entered and flipped the lights on, it was as if a part of the house had died. It was so quiet and empty, a shell without a heart or soul. The whole night was beginning to play on Denny's nerves. The letdown of the carnival being so bad, the horror of overhearing Crawford's plans for Paul, finding out his grandfather had kept himself hidden for so long letting everyone think he was dead, and now to walk into one of his safe places and have it feel like a tomb. Denny felt deflated, defeated. The air was suffocating with the house having been closed up.

Billy was busy mixing up some lemonade while Mossy sat staring curiously at Denny. Denny felt extremely uncomfortable. His mind was reeling, filled with overlapping thoughts and emotions that he had no time to sort through. Finally, Billy brought three glasses of lemonade filled with ice and joined Denny and Mossy at the table. He seemed to be enjoying the whole thing.

"Okay, we're in the house, we've got refreshments, now let's hear a story."

Denny looked at him as if he'd gone crazy. He was enjoying this! He seemed on the verge of hysteria.

Mossy took a long drink from the glass. Denny watched as he placed the glass back on the table, not missing the tremor in the old man's hand. "I don't know how much you already know, but I'll start by saying this; Paul Greymore didn't kill anybody seventeen years ago, and he's certainly not killing anyone now."

Billy slammed his own glass on the table. "You scared the shit out of us in the woods up there to tell us that? There better be more."

"Hold your horses, Billy. There's plenty more. More than you'll wish you knew by the time I'm finished. I'm just trying to figure out where to start."

"The beginning is always nice." Billy said quietly through tight lips.

For the next half-hour Mossy sat patiently and told them everything he knew about the experiment at the base and the real reason behind the disaster that occurred there. Denny and Billy sat speechless through the entire story. "So when I realized what Gunlinger was planning, it was too late. I could save myself or stay and get killed with the rest of them. There was no middle ground and that's God's honest truth. If I could have done anything to save even some of the people, so many innocent people…" He buried his face in his hands. Denny looked down at his glass. He felt horrible. What must it do to a man to live with something like that? Denny again thought of his mother. Then Mossy continued. "I knew that they'd come after me if they knew I was alive. Worse than that, I knew they'd kill your mother, too. Gunlinger was crazy. He'd have thought I told her about the experiment and I swear he would have had her killed. Sometimes I'm surprised he didn't anyway. So I took to the streets. I created a new identity and worked as a pharmaceutical researcher in Cambridge for a while. I stayed close enough to make sure your mom was okay, but not too close. The only way I could have any peace was to drink myself into oblivion. So I did. That escalated to drugs, which I had access to at work. Including experimental drugs. I kept tabs on your mom for a while but pretty soon the bottle was more important. I lost my job, lost my will to keep dealing with everything and became a bum. I slept in the streets, stole tips off tables or begged money to buy another bottle. Pretty soon the whole thing was buried under so much cheap booze, there was nothing left for me to do except keep doing what I was doing. Honestly, I'd forgotten everything that happened until I read the article about Gunlinger. I guess "blocked out" is a better way of saying it. Or maybe some of the drugs I took screwed up my memory.

I've been arrested, beaten up over pocket change and almost froze to death more times than I care to think about. I heard the stories about the Butcher back in '61. I kept watching the papers, part of me knowing what was going on but the other part, the part so saturated in misery and two-dollar wine, convinced me it wasn't true. When they caught Greymore, I was able to tell myself he really did kill them all. Christ, there certainly hasn't been any shortage of people that have done just as much killing as they said he did. I kept watching and the killings had stopped. Until now. Look at this." He pulled the newspaper clippings from his pocket and handed them to the boys. Denny and Billy hunched together to quickly scan the stories.

Denny finished and looked at Mossy. "Why did you come back this time? If you believed it then, why not now?"

Mossy wouldn't meet his gaze for a long moment. When he finally did, Denny saw such pain in his eyes that he wanted to turn away, but he didn't. "I just had to. There are only a handful of times in every person's life that he has a chance to make a difference. I had one of those thirty-five years ago and I blew it. Because of me not coming forward, all those people back in 1961 died and another man went to prison for it. Now I have another chance. I'm an old man, Denny. This is my last chance. There's probably a nice spot by the fireplace reserved for me in Hell no matter how this turns out but I have to try. I have to do what's right. I don't know what else to say."

Denny felt tears in his eyes. This was his grandfather. He reached over and put his hand on the old man's shoulder, feeling him tighten as he did so. "There was nothing else you could have done. You or anybody else. Right, Billy?" Billy was looking pretty confused. Like he wanted to stay angry but couldn't. Denny knew they would have to work together. Billy would have to trust Mossy as Denny had trusted Paul.

Billy slowly nodded his head. "Right. I'm sorry you had to go through all this alone, but you're not alone anymore." Billy downed the last of his lemonade, uttered a loud burp, and said, "What's it gonna take for us to kill this thing, anyway?"

{70}

MOSSY SIPPED another glass of lemonade and tried to hide the tremors in his hands from the boys. He realized the absurdity of his little soap-box speech about doing the right thing as he was about to involve two children in a very dangerous undertaking. But he'd thought it through over and over and could come up with no other way of fixing this. McCauley was a more able-bodied ally, but he didn't know how to find the entrance to the tunnels. Once he was in, Mossy was sure he'd be able to find his way around, but to find the entrance he needed the boys. All of the other scenarios ended with him being arrested or thrown in an asylum. "For a while, we thought the experiments were valuable to both science and the security of the country. We were so caught up in Gunlinger's patriotic hype we almost didn't realize just how crazy he was." He picked up his glass to take a drink and realized it was empty. So was the pitcher. Billy got up to make a fresh one.

"There were signs, sure, but we were caught up, like I said. We actually created a life. You have to understand the magnitude of that. But eventually we started to see the cracks. It was like Gunlinger wasn't human, like there was something else wearing a human costume. At times we'd get a glimpse of the real Gunlinger. It was mostly his eyes. You can learn a lot from a person by reading their eyes. He fooled us for a while, like I said, but the times we saw through his mask were frightening." Billy came back to the table and filled his glass.

"When we finally realized that Gunlinger was insane, we knew we couldn't let him have full control of the experiment. We knew we couldn't stop him, he would have made us disappear and found other scientists to finish his madness. Instead, we made sure we could stop the creature if it came down to that. We engineered a weakness that Gunlinger didn't know about. A manufactured birth defect, if you will. It had to be simple enough that it could be accomplished without any hard-to-get poisons, but obscure enough that the creature wouldn't be killed accidentally. We were smart guys back then, good scientists, it wasn't that hard. The end result is an easy-to-make poison that is lethal to the creature but harmless to humans."

Denny interrupted for the first time since Mossy had begun. "How do you know it will work? I mean, did you guys build more of these things and test it?"

Mossy took another long drink. He fleetingly thought how good a shot of vodka or some rum would go down with the lemonade, but somehow the urge wasn't as strong as it should have been. "No, Denny, we didn't build any more of them. Gunlinger would have been on to us. Sometimes you just have to trust science. I know it will work. I know every cell that comprises that thing. It will work."

Mossy saw Denny and Billy exchange a look, and in that look he saw doubt. He couldn't blame them.

"Things progressed and Gunlinger's facade began to erode. I guess the real facade was his attempt to cling to his sanity. Anyway, I finally decided I had to do something. Tony wasn't convinced. I'm not sure if he was scared, or if there was some part of him that still believed in Gunlinger's vision of creating an army of these creatures. But I sure as hell wasn't going to be a part of it. I had been using my off-base privileges to make contact with a local reporter here in Haven. I hadn't told him much, but I'd been hinting that there was more to the base than an ammo dump."

"Is he still alive? In Haven? He could help clear this up!" Denny was excited, hopeful.

Mossy shook his head slowly, sadly. "No, he's dead. Either Gunlinger was on to me or it was just shit luck, but he was on the

344

base the day of the explosion. I'd decided that I was going to tell him everything but my timing was off, I was too slow…" He couldn't keep his emotions in check and the tears began to flow. He put his face in his hands and cried. Finally, he was able to go on. "The creature got a taste for blood, human blood. That's when I knew it had to end."

"What do you mean?" Denny asked.

Mossy looked thoughtful, a hint of a sad smile creeping across his face. "Throughout history, there have been several documented cases of animals attacking humans. Sharks, lions, tigers, even dogs. In some cases, the animal seems to acquire a liking for the taste, a blood lust. Have you ever heard of the Tsavo Lions?"

Both boys shook their heads.

"In 1898 close to 100 workers were killed building a railroad bridge across the Tsavo River in Kenya."

Suddenly Billy looked up. "Wait, I watched an old movie with my dad about that. Bwana something. I thought it was made up."

"It was very real. More recently, from the early 1930s until 1947, an entire pride of lions killed several hundred people, maybe as many as a thousand in Tanzania. They were called the Man-Eaters of Njombe."

"I don't understand," Denny interrupted "what does this have to do with the thing in the lake?"

Mossy again got a faraway look in his eyes. "I guess I better back up. To really understand, you need to know what the creature is. Gunlinger was a molecular biologist, and a brilliant one. He had theories that back then were considered crazy. The military was the only place where he could gain the power to test them. He recruited the top biology graduates from colleges across the country to perform his experiments. His goal was to develop a cross-species creature that could be used by the government as a weapon. It had to be intelligent and instinctual, violent and emotionless. And amphibious. His vision was to drop small armies of these killers off-shore and have them infiltrate coastal bases. No air attacks, no bombing, just a mindless army of silent killing machines."

Billy looked ready to either laugh or start screaming. "Mossy, no offense, but you're sounding a little crazy again."

"Not crazy at all, really. No crazier than Columbus thinking the earth was round. Look up the names Cohen and Boyer, and Paul Berg. They are research scientists forging the way for tomorrow's medicines. Recombinant DNA and gene splicing are all over the news. Gunlinger was way ahead of his time, that's all. It was the *result* of our experiments, I think, that drove him to madness.

"You see, we were way ahead of the research being done even today. We cracked the genetic code. We were able to identify DNA sequences for virtually every aspect of an animal, fish, insect... even plants."

"What do you mean by every aspect?" Billy was back up, searching cabinets, finding a bag of chips and returning to his seat. "Like eye color?"

Mossy nodded. "Eye color, any physical characteristic really, as well as defense mechanisms; its venom is a chemically-enhanced version of scorpion venom. Scorpions, like some spiders, inject venom that induces almost immediate paralysis. We re-engineered the creature's venom to have the same effect but to also sedate the victim to avoid panic. Squid-like tentacles for long-range delivery of the venom, bear-like claws for in-close fighting, lion's jaws, the eyes of a fly, the radar capability of a bat...it's a hideous patchwork of a thing, built for one reason: to kill. Which brings us back to the lions. Gunlinger was able to acquire the blood of one of the Tsavo lions. We identified the DNA sequence responsible for the human blood-lust and made it part of the creature's fabric."

Throughout all this, Billy continued munching chips and was now licking salt off his fingers. Denny watched him, thinking he would never be able to eat again after hearing about the creature in the lake. "Mossy, how could something so noticeable, and such a killing machine, go unnoticed for over 30 years?"

"Good question, Denny. The answer is simple: it slept."

Billy was now wiping his fingers inside the empty chip bag, then licking the crumbs from his fingers. "Slept? Are you saying it slept until

1961, woke up to snack on some kids, then went back to sleep until now? Did you inject this thing with some Rip Van Winkle DNA too?"

Denny uttered a choked laugh at this, and was surprised to see Mossy smiling as well. "Not exactly, Billy, but you're not far off. I've mentioned part of the creature's DNA was from a bear, a Black Bear to be exact. If you know anything about bears..."

"It hibernates!" Denny blurted out.

"Give the boy a prize." Mossy answered with a smile, pointing at Denny.

Billy noisily crumpled up the empty chip bag and tossed it in the trash. "This thing slept for...how many years? Why didn't it starve?"

"Another excellent question. I mentioned we sequenced plant structure...you've heard of the Venus Fly-Trap?" Mossy didn't wait for an answer. "A few of the 'suckers' on each of the creature's tentacles serve a different purpose than the rest. They emit an odor which attracts victims; in this case not flies but larger prey like mice, rats, frogs and the like. When they touch the source of the odor located at the center of the sucker, small, chitinous hooks trap the prey and the creature ingests it while still hibernating."

Denny cringed at the thought of it, pictured the sleeping monster feeding. "But why would you *want* it to sleep...I mean hibernate for so long?"

"We didn't want it to, not for that long. It was an unknown side-effect, if you will, of the Black Bear DNA and some other sequence. We did want it to have the ability to hibernate and heal, kind of like a medically-induced coma; that's why we engineered the ability for it to feed while sleeping. We certainly didn't foresee it hibernating for years. We never got to figure that flaw out. But we did know it would put itself into hibernation when it is injured or traumatized in some way. I figure the explosion in 1944 sent it to bed. It woke up in 1961 and something happened to it to put it back to sleep."

Denny looked at Billy and Billy returned his look. "Paul!" they exclaimed together.

Mossy looked confused. "You mean Greymore? The one they accused of the killings?"

Denny was nodding. "I'm sure of it. He was found with a dead girl in his arms but he was trying to save her. I bet he fought that thing and somehow hurt it enough to send it into hibernation."

Mossy nodded. "Well, this time we're not putting it to sleep, we're killing it."

(71)

THE CLOCK ticked loudly as Denny and Billy sat in the kitchen trying to make sense of what was going on. Mossy had left, walked back to Chandler's to get some sleep. "Denny...do you believe him?"

Denny looked intently at Billy, feeling a tiredness beyond his twelve years. "Yeah, I guess I do. It's crazy, but it makes sense. But what do we do now? Nobody else is going to believe any of it."

Billy nodded slowly. "My dad and Paul might..."

"No!" Denny stared at him. "If we tell them they *will* believe us. And you know what they'll do? They'll go in those caves themselves to kill it. We help Mos...my grandfather make the poison, then we get him to the caves. He's sure he can kill it."

"But maybe Paul and my dad could help. You can't expect an old man to take that thing on by himself."

Denny was torn, faced with a decision he was too young to make. Responsibility, retribution, fear...the once black-and-white images of right and wrong now fading to gray. Introducing Mossy to his mom could be what she needed to be healed. But if it happened before the creature was killed and Mossy died trying, she might be lost forever. To ask Paul and Joe to risk their lives to help Mossy was too much. Denny would never risk having Billy go through what he did when he lost his dad. And losing Paul would feel like he was going through it again. *Now where did that thought come from?* As cold as it sounded, Denny had to let Mossy fix this. If he failed...Denny would deal with that when…if…the time came. He explained this as best as he could to Billy. "Swear to me, Billy, swear you won't tell."

Billy nodded reluctantly just as the back door flew open.

"What the hell are you doing here?" It was Julie, followed by Paul.

Denny's heart had almost burst from fear, picturing Crawford and his gang coming through the door. Or something worse, something with tentacles. Once the fear passed, his heart continued to rattle against his ribcage in Julie's presence. "Julie…Paul…we came to warn you. Crawford and his gang…"

Paul held up his hands. "Julie got here first and warned me…"

Billy found his voice, "You're supposed to be at Aunt Sarah's…"

Paul again motioned for quiet and took over, quickly relating Julie's night. Denny felt his face burn and his heart grow icy. Whatever else happened, he would personally make Crawford pay.

Billy was enraged as well. "We left the carnival and Denny had the idea to let the air out of Crawford's tires. We should have burnt his fucking car…"

Paul looked at Denny, "You probably saved an ugly scene, Denny. Great thinking…if he had gotten here first…"

Denny's pride swelled at Paul's words, but it was the look of gratitude and admiration on Julie's face that made his face burn brighter.

Billy continued excitedly, "Then when we got here and you weren't home, Paul…"

"We came here to make a plan." Denny interrupted, giving Billy a withering look.

Now it was Billy's face growing red and he closed his mouth.

Paul didn't miss the exchange, and his eyes went to the third empty glass on the table but said nothing. "I was home, just fell asleep when I got there. I'm going to borrow Joe's car and take Julie back to Malden. You guys head up to Denny's house, we'll figure this out in the morning. Crawford won't show up now, and he and his pals will all have big heads tomorrow." The two pairs headed out silently, lost in their own thoughts.

(72)

MOSSY ARRIVED back at Chandler's sometime after midnight. He had explained his plan to the boys and they had agreed to help him get what he needed. He just had to close the loop with the McCauley's and find his way in the tunnels. The boys had told him the lab entrance was still accessible, and from there he could find his way. He wasn't concerned about finding his way out. As he went over the plan in his head he began to drift off to sleep. Then his eyes snapped open and he sat up. He had felt no fear about executing his plan, but as another memory returned, so did the terror of what he was going to face.

Mossy rolled over and pulled the pillow over his head. But the knocking on the barracks door only got louder. He needed sleep; whoever was knocking would have to wait. His stomach clenched with cramps, the result of sleep deprivation and too much bad coffee. He'd been up for almost 48 hours straight going over the DNA sequences, but he could find no way to reverse the aggressive behavior of the creature. The blood lust. Two days ago, an assistant who entered the cave to take temperature and humidity readings never came out. His right hand still held the clipboard but that was the only part of him they found. If he could just sleep for a few hours, he was sure he could find the answer.

The door exploded inward and Mossy knew there would be no sleep. Something else had happened, he was sure of it. The two MP's had weapons drawn as they entered through the shattered remains

351

of the door. "What is it? What do you want?" Not for the first time since working on this project, Mossy was afraid.

"Get dressed and come with us. General's orders."

"What's happened?" Mossy croaked. Both men remained stoic, offering nothing. Mossy sighed deeply, a sense of dread and finality overtaking his initial fear. He knew what Gunlinger was capable of and how far he would go to protect his reputation. Whatever had happened for him to send his goons after Mossy had to be bad. He slowly got dressed, his mind spinning, looking for a way out. He had to find out what happened and let Gunlinger give him another chance. Another wave of nausea struck and he had an idea. As he bent to tie his boots, he jammed a finger down his throat. It was all his turbulent stomach needed and a spray of vile vomit shot from his mouth as he turned to the soldiers. "Oh God," he moaned and ran for the bathroom, sure the soldiers wouldn't immediately follow. He flipped on the faucet in the sink and continued to make gagging noise as he slid open the window as quietly as he could. The bathroom door had no lock but Mossy grabbed the curtain rod from the shower and jimmied it between the door and the wall. It wouldn't do much but it might give him a few extra seconds. He made one final gagging sound, then leaped out the window and ran into the night.

He'd only made a few steps when he heard the soldiers knocking on the bathroom door and asking if he was alright. He sprinted between the buildings and paused—should he try to talk to Gunlinger or get to the creature and end it? If Gunlinger had sent for him, it wasn't to plan the next steps, it was to tie up a loose end. He headed for the entrance to the underground lab.

He stayed in the shadows, sticking close to buildings and vehicles for cover. He immediately noticed the lack of activity on the base. No, not a lack of activity, an absence of it. Gunlinger must have ordered lockdown. It was worse than Mossy thought. Sacrificing cover for speed, he ran as fast as his legs would carry him. He arrived at the entrance to the lab ready to try to overpower the guard, but there was none. He cranked open the trap door and scrambled down the ladder into the tunnel. As he approached the cave that held the natural holding tank for the creature, he paused. There was something wrong. The air smelled of copper and gunpowder. Shooting and death. Steeling himself for the worst, he stepped into the cave.

There were bodies everywhere. Not bodies, body parts. It was a massacre. The air was still heavy with smoke. Whatever had happened had been recent. An orange glow at the back of the cave caught Mossy's eye and he turned quickly, tensed for a fight.

"I knew you'd show up here. I sent my best men to get you but I knew you'd get away. It's over Moses. The end. An abject failure."

"General, what happened?" Mossy felt the bile rise in his throat. If he hadn't already emptied his gut, he would have then.

Gunlinger inhaled deeply on a cigarette as Mossy moved closer. He saw a large weapon in Gunlinger's other hand and knew that he had in fact been waiting for him. "Man can't control creation, Moses. Even his own creation."

"Sir, I just need a little more time to figure out the flaw in the sequencing…"

"There is no flaw, Blaakman. The creature is doing exactly what we wanted. Killing. But it will kill our own as efficiently and coldly as it would kill the enemy."

"I can fix it…"

"No! We've gone too far. I've gone too far. This can't be fixed. But it can be stopped."

Mossy stared at him. His utter calm was unnerving with the carnage that surrounded him. Mossy knew now that what he had feared was true. Gunlinger was quite insane. "I know how to kill it."

Gunlinger uttered something that might have been a laugh. "It's gone beyond that, Moses. We learned something very interesting this evening. The water you are looking at connects under the surface to the lake outside."

"How…" It hit him like a hammer. "Oh my God. How many?"

"How many is too many, Moses? The damage has been contained. My men have handled it, but I can't let it happen again."

Moses stepped toward him. "How many, damn it?" He shook with a mixture of rage and disgust.

Gunlinger raised the pistol and Mossy stopped. "It killed a young couple out on the lake. It was sheer coincidence that one of our patrols saw it happen just before dark. A couple of young lovers looking for a quiet spot to make love, perhaps just out to escape the heat. Their lives ended before they began. I can abide by sacrificing men who signed up for it, but not civilians." He flicked his cigarette into the water and it hissed out. "My men gathered the remains and left the capsized boat and lifejackets floating. By all accounts it will look like they went for a swim and drowned. But I know better, Moses. Now we know better."

Mossy could only stare, speechless. The look in Gunlinger's eyes spoke volumes. Unless he acted quickly, he was not getting out of this cave alive. He had to keep Gunlinger talking until he found a way to get the gun. "General, are you sure it was the creature?"

Gunlinger glanced up with dead eyes and nodded once.

"And are you sure it was just the two that it got?" He hated the way it sounded, as if two were not bad enough.

"I guess we really can't be sure, can we?"

"What happened here? Did you already kill it?"

Gunlinger uttered another barking laugh. "No Moses, I don't believe we did."

"I can kill it..." Suddenly the water swirled and the creature erupted. It stood on the shore, tentacles waving menacingly around it. Mossy stared at his creation. He looked into its eyes and shivered at the emotionless intelligence they held. Gunlinger stood and the creature turned toward him. It bared its rows of razor-sharp teeth and Mossy saw its body slowly crouch. He knew what was coming next. He screamed for Gunlinger to run and jumped in front of the creature just as it pounced. They collided in mid-air with a devastating impact that sent them sprawling to the floor of the cave in a tangle of human and reptilian body parts. Mossy heard gunshots ring out in the cave as he struggled with the creature. Its strength was incredible and Mossy was no match. As the shots echoed behind him, he was dragged into the water.

He began trembling uncontrollably and for the first time in a while, really wanted a drink. "Why am I still alive?" He spoke it out loud, but he had no answer; that part of the memory did not come. He knew it would eventually, he just hoped it would be in time.

{73}

CHRIS MCCAULEY opened the door and entered the gloom of the Witch's Hat. He carried a small duffel bag that held an expensive camera, a high-powered flash, and several rolls of film. Drawing in a deep breath, he scanned the bar, hoping not to find what he was looking for, knowing he would. Sure enough, Jake sat slouched in a stool at the end of the bar, staring at his glass.

Earlier that afternoon, Mossy had stopped by looking for Jake, saying he'd already been to Jake's apartment. They both pretended not to know where Jake was while Mossy explained a little more detail about his plan. He was going to get what he needed to make the poison canister, he wouldn't say how, and wanted to get in the tunnels within the next day or two if all went well. He gave Chris the camera to give to Jake. Deep down, Chris knew he would be the one using it when the time came.

He slid onto the stool next to Jake and signaled the bartender to bring him a beer. He had no idea what to say to Jake. After all, he hadn't seen what Jake saw. If it was half as bad as Jake described, Chris knew he might be trying to drown the memory too. He nodded his thanks when the bartender placed a beer in front of him, then took a long drink, struggling for the right words. Jake put him out of his misery.

"I'm sorry Chris. I thought I could do it, but I'm too scared." His speech was slurred, he'd been there a while. "I was home when

Mossy came by with the camera. That's when I knew. I stayed quiet until he left, then I came here. That thing…I'm so sorry Chris…"

Chris reached out and put a hand on his younger brother's shoulder. "Jake, it's okay. If I had seen that thing, maybe I couldn't go through with it either."

Jake smiled, a heartbreakingly sad smile filled with anguish and regret. "Sure you could, Chris. And so could Dad. I'm the weak one…too weak to face it and too weak to kill myself…"

"Stop it, Jake." He grabbed his brother's chin and forced him to look at him. "Enough of the bullshit drama. You're just as strong as Dad and I, it's this shit…" He picked up Jake's empty glass and slammed it down on the bar, drawing an annoyed look from the bartender. "It's the booze that keeps you down, Jake. I saw you the other night in here with Mossy, I saw the old Jake that didn't know how to quit. The Jake that hated to lose and rooted for the underdog and always tried to make things right. Seeing what you saw…I don't know…there's no way to know how to deal with it. But it doesn't change who you are, Jake. You're a good person who was dealt a shitty hand. Instead of playing it as best you could, you folded. But now you have a chance to get back in the game. Put it all behind you and start over. It has nothing to do with you being a part of killing this thing. It has to do with moving on. Now you know the truth about that day. If you had tried to save Willie, you'd be dead. Now there's no more excuses. You can get your shit together, or you can keep killing yourself one drink at a time. It's your choice."

He placed the duffel bag on the bar in front of Jake, then turned and left, not waiting for a reply, not waiting to see if Jake would follow.

(74)

THE SOUND of their footsteps was deafening, echoing endlessly through the empty corridors. They kept their flashlights off for the moment. The halls were lit with low-wattage "emergency" lights that kicked on after dark much like streetlights. Their shadows danced playfully as they approached and passed each of the lights. Denny turned again to glance over his shoulder, not really knowing what he expected to see but unable to stop himself from doing it. Next he stole a glance at his partner in crime—literally. The look on the old man's face frightened him. The combination of determination and fear was a mask covering a lifetime of sadness. In bright sunlight it would have been enough to make him turn away. Here in the gloom of the deserted school, it was all Denny could do not to turn and run.

They had "broken in" through a first floor cafeteria window. Denny had jammed the window's lock before leaving school that day. The irony of breaking into a school didn't escape Denny, as he spent most of his hours in class wanting nothing more than to get *out* of the school. "Turn here, we have to go upstairs," he whispered, startled at the sound of his own voice. Moses pushed open the metal door to the stairwell, which responded with a squeal Denny was sure could be heard as far away as the police station. Moses closed the door as quietly as he could and they started up the stairs. When they reached the second floor, they went through a similar and equally loud door. Denny went through these doors a dozen times a day and couldn't ever remember hearing them.

They reached the door to the science lab and a conflict of emotions raged in Denny's head when the knob wouldn't turn. Half of him was relieved, now they could get out before they were caught. The other half was aggravated, knowing any complication to their plan increased the danger to all of them. Both halves were scared. Moses nudged him aside and pulled something from his pocket. For a horrible moment Denny thought he was going to simply smash the glass of the door.

"Shine your light here, Denny." He fumbled with his light and finally found the switch. The light seemed too bright, like a beacon alerting the police. Denny was relieved to see Moses was holding a small screwdriver-like tool instead of a hammer. He bent over and jiggled the tool around the lock while Denny tried to keep the light still. Within a minute he heard a *click* and Moses was swinging the door open. "You learn a lot of valuable lessons on the street," he said with a wink.

They entered the room, Moses switching his light on as well. There were no emergency lights in the room; they needed to risk using their flashlights. Denny showed Moses where the chemicals were stored. From that point, his job was to hold the light steady and carefully place the various bottles Moses handed him into his backpack. It seemed like an eternity, but finally Moses signaled he was done. They made their way quickly and quietly out of the lab, and closed the door behind them. Neither noticed the headlights as a car pulled into the school's drive.

They retraced their steps down the stairs and into the first floor hallway. They turned to go into the cafeteria and Denny felt his bladder almost let go. They both stepped back behind the cafeteria doorway. Outside the window, silhouetted in a flashing blue light, stood what could only be a police officer. He was shining a flashlight of his own, a much larger one by the way, around the window that Denny and Moses had entered. *And foolishly left open.* The window was partially hidden by a small row of hedges. Denny and Moses had agreed that leaving it open would be safe enough—who would notice? Denny's mind was reeling, but it suddenly became obvious. The science lab was on the Center Street side of the building. A passing car, or maybe even a cruiser, had spotted the flashlight beams moving around. The cop did a quick check on the doors, and then began checking the windows. The next sound they heard was two heavy feet landing on the tiled floor of the cafeteria. He was inside the school with them!

Mossy grabbed his arm lightly, and Denny barely suppressed a scream. Moses pulled him backwards, further away from the cafeteria entrance. They backed slowly down the hall, keeping their eyes on the cafeteria doorway. The movement of the flashlight swept across the doorway several times. To Denny it meant the cop was probably searching the cafeteria for signs of vandalism or whatever. When the beam focused out the door, it was time to worry. Moses and Denny reached an intersection and turned. When they were around the corner, they began walking faster to distance themselves from trouble. They reached another turn, and when they were around this corner, Moses stopped and bent down to face Denny. "We have two choices—try to wait it out by hiding, or make a run for it. I'm for the latter." Denny swallowed hard, then peeked around the corner half expecting to be face-to-face with Haven's finest, but there was nobody, and no sign of a flashlight.

"If he calls for back-up they might decide to search the whole school. We can't hide. Let's make a run for it. If we go all the way to the back of the school it's as far away from the cafeteria as we can go. We can get out through the locker room door. If we can get across the football field and into the woods, we should be okay." Moses nodded and gestured for Denny to lead the way. As they made their way through a maze of halls, Denny heard the sound first: sirens. Back-up was on the way. They ran; getting out was now far more important than staying quiet. They cut through the gym and into the locker room. There were no windows in the locker room, or on the exit door. If the other police car decided to check this side of the school first, they were dead. Denny took a deep breath and pushed the door open. The coast was clear. Moses jammed a rock under the door so it wouldn't slam shut, and they were on their way. An unlikely pair, if ever there was one, to be sprinting across a football field.

They reached the edge of the woods without incident. Taking cover in a stand of pines, they bent to catch their breath and look for pursuers. They could see occasional flashlight beams cutting through the darkness, but no indication that they were headed toward them. Moses seemed to be having trouble catching his breath, but he was first to motion for them to keep going. Denny made his way through the trees until he came across a small path. He turned onto the path leading away from the school just as the lights came on. The exterior lights in the parking lots were first, then the loud pops indicating the field lights were being turned on. Denny glanced at Moses as the football lights began warming up, and he didn't like what he saw. Moses was laboring, his face etched with the look of fear. Not fear of being caught, but a deeper, more instinctive fear. The fear of death. He had his right hand up to his left shoulder, and he was staring at his left hand as he clenched and unclenched his fist. When he saw Denny staring at him, he shook his head and thrust his chin forward, meaning to keep going. Denny nodded, but veered off the path again, through some thin brush and a small row of hedges. He had to get Moses safe, but couldn't risk the trip back home just yet. He had an idea. He shrugged the backpack off his shoulders and placed it down carefully under a small hedge. "You stay here. Wait ten minutes, then keep going straight through there," Denny pointed through the bushes. "You'll come out on Briarwood Road. Wait in the bushes there until you see a car flash its lights, that'll be us."

Moses looked mildly dazed. He was still having trouble breathing. He nodded and sat down next to the backpack. "Ten minutes. Through the trees, flashing lights," he panted.

Denny frowned, unsure if leaving him behind was the right thing to do or not. He made up his mind, unable to come up with a better choice. He turned to go but before he could take a step a hand clamped down on his ankle. Moses was looking up at him with an expression Denny couldn't quite read. "Tell your mom I loved her.

362

Even though I did such terrible things. I left her to think I was dead." He paused to wipe a tear from his face, still sounding like he was trying to breathe through a thick blanket. "Tell her, Denny, please?"

Denny felt his own eyes filling up, but shook his head. There was too much left to do. And he couldn't do it without Moses. "Tell her yourself." And he turned and ran into the darkness.

(75)

JAKE MCCAULEY sat staring at nothing. Seated in his ratty old recliner in his dingy apartment, there wasn't much to look at anyway. He brought a can of beer to his lips, realized it was empty, and let it drop to the floor next to the chair. It wasn't his first, evidenced by the clang it made against the other dead soldiers on the floor, but he knew it was his last.

In his other hand was the camera Chris had left on the bar. He raised it up to examine it again, but in reality he was examining his inner thoughts. Chris was right, Chris was always right; now that he knew the truth about what he saw, he could no longer play the help-less trauma victim. It was time to move on. Fish or cut bait. Shit or get off the pot. He smiled, a tight-lipped expression that most would have taken for pain. They would have been right.

He got to his feet unsteadily and placed the camera on the end table. Rays of bright sunlight filtered through the blinds, highlighting the dances of the dust motes. From the apartment below, the bass of hard rock music vibrated the floor under his feet.

It was Deep Purple's "Smoke on the Water." Christ, was that the only album he had? With a final look of longing at the camera, he stepped onto the shaky stool and slipped the noose around his neck. He'd known since Chris stalked angrily out of the Hat that this was how it had to be. There was no way he could face that thing again. There was no way he could drink away the shame of being unable to face it. This was the only way.

His heart raced in his chest and a dagger of despair ripped through his gut when he realized that he was too much of a coward to go through with it. Sobbing with the regret of a child who missed going to the circus because he hadn't cleaned his room, he reached up miserably to undo the noose. And that small movement combined with the countless beers was enough to throw off his already tenuous balance. He felt himself reeling, then overcompensated by shifting his weight too quickly. He was terrified and relieved when he felt the stool kick out from under his feet.

He struggled, clawing at the rope, his instinctual will to live momentarily winning over his desire to die. Very quickly, his oxygen-starved brain shut down those struggles.

He wasn't sure if the song was still playing or it was only echoing in his head, but he knew time was, indeed, running out.

As he spun slowly in a circle of impending death he found himself facing the small table with the camera on it. His last thought was that the lens looked like the eye of that beast and it was mocking him, even now.

{76}

DENNY CRASHED through the woods blindly. Stray roots grabbed at his ankles while branches tore at his clothes and skin. Still, he ran. He broke through a set of bushes and literally tumbled onto Briarwood Road. He scanned the street quickly as he got to his feet, making sure nobody saw his grand exit from the woods. Of course the street was silent. Many of the houses were in complete darkness. Bluish light flickered from a few windows where late-nighters or insomniacs used the television to keep them awake or to help them sleep. Denny got his bearings and set off at a run.

At Father McCarthy's house, Denny noticed a light still on as he hurried up the front steps. He could see McCarthy through the bug-covered screen door, fast asleep with a book open on his chest. Smiling to himself, he knocked loudly enough to disturb whatever peace McCarthy had found, scattering scores of mosquitoes, beetles and moths in every direction. When he saw McCarthy stir, he knocked again, this time more softly.

"Denny?" whispered McCarthy. "Come in, is something wrong? What time is it?"

Denny pulled open the door and slid in quickly so the bugs wouldn't follow. "I need your help, its important. I need you to drive me to pick up my...a friend, then I'll explain everything. Will you do it?"

McCarthy gave Denny an up-and-down glance, taking in the torn clothes and scratches on his face and arms. But without hesitation the old priest grabbed his keys off the end table and shooed Denny out the door. Once in the car, Denny told McCarthy where they were going and no more. It was too hard to explain in such a short time and wouldn't make sense. Without a word between them, they arrived at the spot Denny had told Moses to meet him. "Father, I need you to flick your headlights on and off, that was the signal."

McCarthy turned to him with a frown "Denny, this all seems a bit dramatic…"

"Father, please? It's to help Paul…" Once the name was out of Denny's mouth McCarthy grabbed the switch and pulled it in and out rapidly. Denny peered out the window, expecting Moses to come out holding the backpack right away. After a minute or two McCarthy repeated the signal but there was no movement from the woods.

"Denny, if this is some kind of joke…"

Denny was already reaching for the door handle. Two thoughts were swimming in his head. *Without Moses we can't kill it…*followed by…*My grandfather might be dead.* And he was ashamed at the order they came in. "It's no joke, wait here," and he ran into the darkness.

As quickly as he could he retraced his steps through the brush, almost tripping over Mossy's prone figure on the ground. Denny's breath caught in his chest and he felt lightheaded. *No, it can't be…* He reached down, placing a shaky hand on Mossy's forehead. It felt cool and clammy. He slid his hand down to Mossy's chest and exhaled loudly when he felt a heartbeat. *At least he's not dead.* He bent closer and could hear Mossy's breathing. It didn't sound great to Denny, but at least he could hear it. He began lightly slapping Mossy's cheeks—it was what they always did in the movies. "Mossy, can you hear me, Mossy, are you okay?" No response. He got to his feet, looking around, now what? He could go get McCarthy but what good would that do? McCarthy wasn't strong enough to help carry Mossy out. Denny felt paralyzed with indecision until he heard a rustling sound below him. Mossy's foot was moving and he was blinking his eyes. He bent down quickly. "Mossy, are you okay?"

Mossy looked confused, like he was having trouble focusing on Denny—*like my mother looks*—and he tried to sit up. Denny put an arm under his shoulders and tried to help, finally wrestling him into a sitting position. "Denny?" His voice was gritty, like he had just gargled with sand.

"Mossy, are you okay, what happened?"

Moses swallowed hard. "I'm not sure, I was waiting for you, counting out ten minutes in my head. I sat down...I think I fell asleep!"

Denny's eyes widened in surprise. "I thought..." Then he started laughing. For a minute Mossy stared blankly at him, then realizing what Denny meant, he joined him in the laughter.

"It'll take more than a close scrape with the police to put me out of commission," he said with a smile. "Now help me up and let's get out of here. The bugs are eating me alive. Ha, get it, alive?" And he began to laugh again as Denny helped him to his feet. Denny grabbed the backpack and they headed out.

As they made their way through the dense brush Denny began to fill Mossy in on Father McCarthy. Denny stopped short and Mossy almost bowled him over in the darkness. "Denny, what..."

"Shh. I think I heard something." Denny whispered. From all around them the soundtrack of night seemed to grow louder. Crickets, peepers and mosquitoes harmonized while a wispy rustling of leaves from the warm breeze provided background. Then the crack of a nearby branch silenced the crickets and sent Denny's heart to his mouth. He stood rooted to the spot as another twig snapped even closer. *Run or fight?* Running wasn't an option with Mossy to think about. He knew it wasn't the police—they'd have flashlights at least. The other possibilities ranged from Crawford and his thugs to whatever the contents of the backpack were meant to kill. As the branches directly in front of him began to part, he aimed his flashlight to where he thought was eye-level and as soon as a shape moved from the branches he flicked it on. He hoped to temporarily blind the person (*thing*), shove him (*it*) to the ground and make a run for the car. The first part of his plan worked great—Father McCarthy couldn't see a thing once the light hit him. "Father, what the hell are you doing? You scared the shit out of me." From behind him he heard a snort of laughter out of Mossy.

"Denny, is that any way to talk to a man of God?" Mossy snickered.

McCarthy blinked and tried to shield the light with his outstretched hands. "Denny, turn that thing away. I thought the Lord himself had come to get me. And your friend is right, what kind of language is that for a young man?"

Denny pointed the light toward the ground and waited until his heart rate came down to a safe level. "Sorry, Father. I thought it was…" *No point in getting into* that *right now in the middle of the woods*, the Great and Powerful Oz chuckled. "Sorry. Let's get out of here." Denny saw McCarthy glance at Mossy with a frown and a look of…recognition? Then he turned and headed back to the car.

Nobody spoke as they made their way back to the relative safety of the street and into McCarthy's car. But that was as long a reprieve as Denny would get. "Okay, Denny, it's time you fill me in on whatever is going on. And…Mr. Rodman is it…what are you doing with this young boy?"

Denny opened his mouth, still unsure of what was going to come out, but was interrupted. "Perhaps I can help explain. My name isn't Frank Rodman, it's Moses Blaakman. I'm Denny's grandfather." Mossy got the reaction he was going for as McCarthy's eyes shot to the rear view mirror to get a better look at the man. "I came back to Haven to finish what I started 35 years ago. Denny was just showing me around the old neighborhood."

McCarthy said nothing as they drove through the empty streets but his eyes kept flickering to the mirror, as if he thought this man claiming to be Denny's grandfather might disappear as quickly as he had shown up. When they pulled into McCarthy's driveway, he finally spoke. "Let's go in the house, I'll make some tea, and we'll all figure this out together."

"Sounds lovely," Moses said a bit too gleefully. He sounded to Denny like he'd just been asked to attend a dinner party more than to explain why he was hiding in the woods in the middle of the night with a twelve-year-old boy he claimed was his grandson.

(77)

FATHER MCCARTHY sat staring at the unlikely group in his living room. The old man, Moses, had been talking for a long time, pausing only to sip his tea. And the story he told…it was incredible. More than once McCarthy glanced at the bookshelf that held his books on Bigfoot, Loch Ness and UFO's. This tale put those to shame.

"So, Father, that's how I ended up back here in Haven. I'm sorry I had to lie to you that day at the cemetery, but I hope you understand, I didn't want to involve anyone unnecessarily."

"But you were willing to involve a couple of children." McCarthy snapped.

Mossy's faced reddened and he cast his eyes toward the floor. For a minute, McCarthy didn't think he was going to answer. "Yes, I know it was wrong, but I had to get what I needed to make the poison. And I still need them to help me get to the caves. Then they're out, and I go in alone to…do what I have to do."

McCarthy felt bad for sounding hostile. This man had been through so much, and lived with so much…it was an inconceivable burden. And to return here at his age to finally face this thing— and McCarthy believed that there was in fact a "thing" to face—it was very courageous. "I'm sorry Moses, I do understand, I just don't want any more harm to come to Haven's children."

The three talked on, Mossy outlining his plan. He would go home and make the poison; tomorrow the boys would take him through the woods to the entrance, then go home and stay away from the lake until they heard from him. Then they would deal with matters closer to home, *family* matters. He made it sound no more difficult them stopping at the store for a loaf of bread.

Denny knew better. "What if...something goes wrong...you don't kill it..."

"Then God help us. If I'm not back by dark, you and Billy get Paul and come here. Call the State Police, call the newspapers, keep Crawford out of it. But find someone to believe you. And stay clear of the woods and the lake."

Denny nodded, a tear slowly sliding down his cheek. He had his own plan that didn't quite go along with his grandfather's. Mossy gave Denny a hug, and slipped off into the night like a ghost.

(78)

IT SEEMED to Chris that the light would never turn green. He tapped anxiously on the steering wheel, changed the station on the radio, glanced impatiently in the rear view mirror. Surely the light must be green by now. But when he looked up, the red light stared back. He caught sight of a young woman leaving the bank wearing a tight skirt, and watched her as she walked, how the skirt clung to her ass and how tan her long legs were. She had a mane of blonde hair falling wildly down her back. She reminded him of Lori, of things never to be. The honk of a horn behind him brought him back to the present and he gunned the car forward.

What a jerk, he thought, laying the ultimatum on Jake the way he did. Is that how you help your kid brother? He had been kicking himself since he walked out of the bar last night. He had almost gone back, but in his anger the thought that maybe this time he'd gotten through to Jake sounded logical. Instead, he'd gone to Chandler's looking for Mossy. Betty told him the old man was out and about, but did he want to stay for a slice of pie. He'd almost declined, wanting to go drag Jake out of the Hat and bring him home to sleep it off, but it *was* fresh blueberry, Betty teased. Now, in the bright morning sun after a long restless night, he needed to make things right with Jake.

Finally arriving at Jake's shitty apartment, the feeling eating at his stomach felt like something worse than guilt; it felt like fear. He pulled over to the curb and ran up the stairs to the third floor. Music was blasting from somewhere and the smell of pot wafted through the stairwell. Now that he was so close, his thoughts were running wild, getting the better of him. What if his little sermon had worked, and Jake had gone off half-cocked (literally) to the lake to find the thing himself? As he pounded on Jake's door calling his name, he was suddenly sure that's exactly what had happened and that he would never see Jake again. When he turned the knob and pushed the door open, he wished he were right.

He uttered an unintelligible cry when he saw Jake's body. His brother's face was a horrible shade of bluish-purple, like a giant bruise, and his tongue lolled from his black lips. Chris leaped across the room and grabbed Jake's legs, trying to lift him and take the weight off the rope. It was only when he felt the impossible coldness of Jake's legs that he realized his futility. He fell to his knees, holding his head in his hands as tears of guilt and sadness rolled down his face.

Sometime later, it could have been five minutes but just as easily could have been an hour, Chris got up to call the police. His gaze fell upon the camera and the burden of his guilt became even heavier. The beast had claimed another victim, and this time Chris had been an accomplice. He would not let this go unavenged. As he snatched the camera up and slipped it into his pocket, he saw that there was a note under it. Shit. On the paper, scrawled by his brother's drunken hand were just two words: *I'm sorry.*

Chris crumpled up the note and shoved it in his pocket with the camera, then found the phone and called the police.

DALE CRAWFORD took a long drink from his beer before speaking, his eyes never leaving Buddy and Tony. He knew he had to play this just right if he was going to enlist their help, and he couldn't take Greymore down alone. But another part of him, the part that was getting harder and harder to ignore, wanted to bash their skulls together. He was sitting on the same rock that Chris McCauley and his girl had been diving off so many years ago. He brought them here to show he wasn't afraid of anything in the lake.

"This is not just some personal vendetta I have with Greymore, this is about the safety of this town and the children that live here. It's also about the sanity of my father." The look that passed between Costa and Dentner did not escape him. It was a look that said *"Is this the same guy who was smashing cars with a tire iron and almost raped an underage girl?"* Dale went on, sounding more like his father with every word that left his lips. *Feeling* more like his father. The still-sane sliver of his mind knew this wasn't a good thing. He spoke with the calmness and reason of an English professor, the conviction of a fire-and-brimstone minister and the sincerity of a seasoned politician or court-appointed defense attorney. "This guy is killing kids, just like he did before, until my dad caught him. My dad knows it but there's no evidence this time. My dad's hands are tied and it's killing him. I came home the other night and found him...he was..." Crawford choked back a sob and took another long

375

pull on his beer. "I found him staring down the barrel of his gun. He was about to eat it."

He had Costa, Christ the kid was a pathetic sheep, but he needed Buddy. He flipped the empty beer can over his shoulder and heard the satisfying splash. He was daring whatever people thought was in the lake to come get him. And he knew the two clowns in front of him were buying what he was selling. Now, he went in for the kill. "My dad can't do anything legally, but I can't let another kid die because it would kill my father. Shit, Buddy, you have a kid sister, what if that freak..." He stopped and grabbed another beer out of the cooler. He wondered what Buddy would think if he knew Dale had once paid a visit to the same kid sister he was so concerned about and ripped her shirt off to feel up her nice young titties. And he would have done more if Mrs. Dentner hadn't come home. "I'm going to do this with or without you guys, I have to. But we've been through some shit together and it would mean a lot to have you with me."

When the inevitable agreement came from both Costa and Dentner, Crawford outlined his plan as they emptied the cooler.

(80)

THE LOUD knock on the door startled Mossy out of a light doze. He'd worked late into the night and had gotten up early to finish making the poison. He wasn't sure how long he'd been out. He stumbled to the door, wiping his eyes. He expected Denny and Billy but when he opened the door, Chris McCauley burst in. He looked like he'd aged a decade since the day when Mossy had first met him at the gas station. The haggard look and the fact that Chris was holding the bag of camera equipment filled Mossy with a dreadful idea. Hopefully it only meant his brother was back on the bottle...

"He's dead, Mossy. He hung himself. I'm going in with you."

Mossy sat down on the edge of his bed and put his face in his hands. How many lives...no, deaths, would he be responsible for? He looked up at Chris and nodded. "This ends tonight for me. I kill that fucking thing or die trying. I can't ask you to come in with me, but I guess I can't stop you either. I've got so much goddamned blood on my hands..."

Chris stepped closer and put a hand on his shoulder. "I don't blame you for any of this, but you're right, you can't stop me. I have to do it for Joe, and for my dad."

Mossy nodded. "I finished the poison earlier today. I need to rest before I go in, and there's still a couple of things I have to do...to get my affairs in order I guess. You know there's a good chance we both might die in there, Chris. I'm sure the poison will work, but that thing is so damn fast and strong, it might kill us first."

"I know. But I won't sit back and let you try alone. I can't. My father wouldn't have. In a way this thing is responsible for everything I've lost in my life. I know what I'm getting into, Mossy."

"Alright then, pick me up here at six o'clock. Don't breathe a word to anyone."

Chris nodded and left without another word. Mossy knew there would be no more rest this day. With a heavy sigh, he sat down at the desk in his room and began to write. He needed to get everything down on paper for Denny to give to his mother. Dear Jan. The words poured out of him onto the paper as tears poured out of his eyes. He included everything he remembered, the experiments at the base, the creature, his life on the streets, and finally his return to Haven. He thought he might be strong enough to face Janice and tell her everything but he knew the odds that he would get that chance were not good. When it was done, he folded the papers and put them in an envelope, sealed it, and wrote Janice's name on it.

He was drained; he felt like the tears had left him barren, nothing but a husk of flesh and bones. He glanced at the backpack that held the canister of poison, then at the clock. He would be long gone before Chris came to pick him up. He closed his eyes and did something he hadn't done in...forever; he said a prayer. When he opened them, the clock had crept closer to his destiny.

(81)

CHERYL PEROIT'S eyes flickered open and she thought she must still be dreaming. A familiar face was leaning toward her from the bedside chair. She closed her eyes but when she opened them he was still there, now a slight smile playing on his lips. As if reading her mind, he spoke.

"It's not a dream, Cheryl. I heard what happened, the stories...I had to see you."

Seeing him brought it all back and she started crying. He put a hand softly to the side of her face and she didn't shake it off. Her stay at the hospital had been a lesson on loneliness. None of her old friends came, her parents showed up randomly, usually wasted, and she pretended she was asleep until they left. Mostly, she just *thought*. She'd had two surgeries to repair the damage to her ankle and she'd be laid up for a while.

"The stories are true, Charlie. I'm sorry."

Chuck Brantley smiled sadly. She'd never called him Chuck, always Charlie. "Please, tell me..."

Cheryl was silent for a long time, to the point Chuck thought she was drifting back to the safety of sleep. Finally, she spoke. "When I realized I was pregnant, I didn't know what to do. I didn't want you involved, it sounds so unfair now, but at the time I thought it was best. I broke it off so I could figure things out and you wouldn't have to know. Time passed and it was too late to have...to do anything. I decided I could keep it a secret from everyone. I read books about childbirth, I knew how to do it. When it came, Charlie, it looked like you..." She covered her face in her hands and couldn't continue for a while.

"I'd been so good during the pregnancy, hardly drinking and no coke. But then, it was just too much. I started doing coke again and just kept doing it. I got an idea that since nobody knew about the baby, I could get rid of it and nobody would *ever* know."

"But you would know." The look on his face was unreadable: hatred maybe, or pity, or just plain sadness.

She nodded. "I went to the lake with him and I was pretty messed up. I was going to take him into the water and...I had rope and weights..." She broke down again and this time the look on Chuck's face wasn't hard to read at all. But he said nothing. "When I got there, I couldn't do it. I swear Charlie. It all came to me, so clearly. I could get help raising him and finish school, I would name him Carl after my grandfather...but then it came and took him. It was the Angel of Death. This is my punishment, Charlie. God is punishing me for what I've done and the thoughts I had.

"Cheryl, did you kill our baby? There is no Angel of Death, there's just death."

"I know how it sounds Charlie. But I saw it..."

"You were full of coke, Cheryl, you don't know what you saw."

She looked at him, her eyes clear and bright. "I do know, Charlie. It rose out of the water and took our baby. It looked at me...it could have taken me...but it didn't. It passed judgment and knew it would be worse for me to live than die. And it was right, Charlie." She closed her eyes and drifted back to sleep.

Brantley stayed while Cheryl slept, trying to make sense of what she said. It was too much and he began to doze fitfully in the chair next to her. Of all the things he had given up by getting involved with Crawford, nothing was more precious than Cheryl. As if on cue, the door flew open and in stepped Dale Crawford, Buddy Dentner and Tony Costa. Brantley recognized immediately they were drunk.

"Chuckie! Your mom said you'd be here! Get your shit together, man. We're going hunting."

"I'm not going anywhere with you Dale. You went too far with the O'Brien kid. And everyone knows you were the one that had Cummings' dad beat up. I'm out."

Dale stepped forward and leaned in close to Brantley. "That fucking freak killed your baby. Are you that much of a pussy that you will let that go?"

Brantley stared at Crawford, then looked over to Cheryl. Her eyes were shut tightly, her breathing shallow, like she was having a nightmare. Christ, why wouldn't she be. Finally he stood. "Whatever you're up to Crawford, I'm not part of it. Now get out of here and leave us alone."

Crawford's face went red and he looked like he was going to erupt. He stepped closer until they were almost nose to nose. Brantley didn't back down. Crawford frowned, like he'd seen something in those eyes he didn't understand. Suddenly he smiled. "It's okay Chuckie. Me and the boys will take care of this. We don't need some chickenshit getting in the way. You can thank us later for getting rid of Greymore." He turned and left, his faithful followers behind him.

Brantley stared after them after the door closed and then felt a hand on his arm. He turned to see Cheryl with a look of terror in her eyes. "Charlie, that man Greymore they were talking about, he didn't kill Carl. Something came out of that lake and took our baby, and it wasn't human. Please, don't let them make this worse."

He nodded, then went out the door to find Crawford.

(82)

DENNY LAY awake in his bed, fingers laced behind his head, staring out the window as the sun finally rose. The combination of Billy thrashing around on the cot next to Denny's bed all night, the oppressive heat, and the fear of what was in store for them today did not add up to a good night's sleep. Denny had slept fitfully, tossing and turning, finally giving up and waiting for the sun. Now that the room had begun to take in some of the dawn's light, he got up and went to his desk and pulled out his journal. He began writing and didn't stop until he heard Billy stir.

"Working on a new sonnet, Shakespeare?"

Denny grunted but felt his face redden. He could never let anyone read his writing, it would be like opening the most secret part of himself. He couldn't bear the thought of it. "No, just working on a story about a kid who throws his best friend out the window the morning after a sleepover." He closed the journal and tucked it away in his desk drawer. An icy chill made him actually shiver as a terrifying thought jumped into his head: *What if that is the last entry I make?* He shook it off and turned to face Billy. "I slept like shit. I'm kind of tired to go monster hunting." Joking was the only weapon he had against his fear.

"Tell me about it. That cot is like sleeping on a set of monkey bars. And you might want to mention to management that the air conditioner isn't working."

"Are we really going to do this?" Denny's voice was barely a whisper. Visions of bones and dark tunnels and Bear's name tag flashed in his head.

"I guess we are. That's really why I didn't sleep. Weird dreams."

Denny nodded. "I thought about it a lot. Half of me thinks we're both crazy and so is Mossy, my grandfather. But the other half knows it's true. We have to do this for Paul and Mossy and your dad."

"I know, Denny. But I'm scared shitless."

"Me too. That...thing killed so many...killed my dog."

"Yeah, I know. We'll get Mossy to the caves and tell him how to follow our markers. Then we get the hell out of there and away from the lake."

Denny nodded again slowly. "Yeah, let's go get some breakfast." He had a different plan altogether.

Denny's mom was up when they went downstairs and offered to cook them bacon and eggs. The boys inhaled the first batch so quickly, she mixed up another pan of scrambled eggs and fried up more bacon. She did all of this without saying a word, a few times stopping in the middle of a task for so long that Denny had to look away. As they polished off their second helpings, another morbid thought found its way into Denny's head: *What if this is your last meal?* He finished off the last of his orange juice, feeling like his throat was closing.

After they helped clean up, Billy went home to get dressed. When the breakfast dishes were dried and put away, Denny turned to go get dressed and found his mother staring at him from the kitchen doorway. The look on her face was so strange, a cross between awe and something else, embarrassment maybe, that he could only stare back. "Denny, I had the strangest dream last night. It was the night of the explosion at the army base. It was so real. But instead of a neighbor coming to tell us what happened..." She laughed, the sound so alien she covered her mouth with her hand as if it surprised her too. "It sounds silly, but my father...your grandfather...came home and told us. But instead of being burned or smoky, he was wet. I hugged him and he was soaking wet...I wanted to ask him why, but I woke up. I tried to fall back asleep, thinking I could fall right back into that dream and find out..."

Denny felt like an Arctic wind had just blown through the house. He felt his entire body go gooseflesh and he was actually trembling. He was unable to speak. He went to her silently and paused with his arms half-raised to her. *Will she be soaking wet when I hug her?* He pushed the bizarre thought away and threw his arms around the broken woman that was once his mother.

"Will Billy be staying for dinner?"

Denny realized the moment was over. He dropped his arms from her. With all of the unbelievable things going on in Haven, now his mother was having...what...premonitions? At the same time, he realized that she had been back, briefly yes, but back. She had laughed, for Christ's sake, when was the last time he'd heard that? *Not since before You Know What,* the Great Oz replied.

He was suddenly sure that his mother seeing Mossy would fix her. *If she doesn't drop dead from a heart attack*, the other voice commented. He was more anxious than ever to get Mossy to the caves and get this over with. He began planning quickly. *She doesn't know about Joe,* Denny thought. "Ah, yeah, I asked you last night if it was okay." He hated himself for lying to her and taking advantage of her memory lapses. "We're going to bike into town, we'll be home for dinner."

The mention of something that his mother didn't remember seemed to push her fully back into her mental hiding place. Denny felt worse when he saw the lines on her forehead crease into a frown and her eyes begin to get distant. He waited for a reply but it didn't come so he bolted upstairs. After he got dressed he checked in with her again, but she was back in her emotional fortress, drawbridge raised. Denny swallowed hard and started down the hill to Billy's.

>> <<

By the time they arrived at Chandler's it was close to noon and the temperature was in the mid-nineties and the humidity at least that high. The sun was hiding behind a mask of haze and the people of Haven were hiding indoors. They parked their bikes on the front walkway and made their way up the steps of the front porch. Before they could ring the bell, Betty Chandler was at the screen door.

"Good morning, boys. Can I help you? My goodness, look at the state of you two, you're melting! Come in and have some cold water."

Denny looked at Billy and realized what she was seeing. The ride had left them both red-faced and covered in sweat. "Yes, ma'am, a drink would be nice. And if you could tell Mo...Mr. Rodman we're here. I'm Denny O'Brien and this is Billy Cummings."

She paused as she was opening the screen door to let them past, her face clouding for a moment. "Denny and Billy, of course. Denny, is your mom well? And Billy, how is your dad? Terrible thing to happen in our town."

"My dad is getting better, he should be out of the hospital soon," Billy answered.

Denny piped in, following them into the house, "And my mom is okay, I'll tell her you were asking for her."

"Yes, yes of course. Billy, do the police know who assaulted your father?"

They were now in the large kitchen and Betty was in full hostess-mode gliding around from cabinet to freezer to sink filling up two large orders of ice-water.

"No ma'am, they don't seem to know what happened." Billy glanced at Denny and rolled his eyes while Betty's back was still turned. Even they knew that all town gossip went through Betty Chandler, and some of it originated with her.

Handing the glasses of ice-water to the boys, Betty eyed them both. "Now, what would you boys want with Mr. Rodman?"

She knows, Denny thought, *she knows who he really is.* The boys exchanged a nervous glance. "Uh...we are...interviewing him. For a school project." Denny stuttered. He felt his face flush; lying was not his strength. He felt Betty's eyes piercing through his soul, seeing through the weak story. But she didn't question him, just nodded curtly.

386

"Let me go fetch him, you boys drink up all of that water and take more if you need it. Hot as blazes again out there." Then she was gone.

Denny gulped the rest of his water, then went to the sink and filled it up again. "She knows we're lying," Denny whispered.

Billy laughed. "Probably. My dad says she knows everything about everyone in Haven before they know it themselves. Says she's the Official Witch of Haven, like the ones they have in Salem."

Denny gaped at him wide-eyed. "Shhh, what if she hears you?"

Billy refilled his own water glass at the sink, glancing out the window at the sky. "What's she going to do if she does?"

"Just be quiet, okay? I want to get out of here and get this over with. Shit."

"Yeah, me too. This whole thing is nuts."

"Hello, boys."

Mossy/Rodman walked in and Denny gasped. He looked ancient. He shuffled into the kitchen, slightly stooped over. There were huge bags under his eyes and he was so pale his skin almost looked transparent.

"Hi, Mr. Rodman. Ready for Denny and I to interview you for our school project?" Billy asked, a bit too cheerfully.

Mossy picked it right up. "Yes, sir, looking forward to it." He slung the backpack he was holding over his shoulder. "Let's take a walk while we talk, shall we?"

Betty, seeing her chance to eavesdrop disappearing, jumped in front of him. "Walk? Why Frank, it's almost a hundred degrees out there. Why don't you all have a seat on the front porch in the shade and I'll fix a pitcher of lemonade?"

"That's kind of you Betty, but an old man needs his exercise. Perhaps we'll take you up on your offer when we get back."

The three left Betty huffing in the kitchen and made their way outside. They buckled Mossy's backpack to Denny's handlebars. Billy's backpack was at his house loaded with flashlights and spare batteries. They knew Mossy's held the poison canisters that they hoped would put an end to the killing in Haven. They pushed their bikes down Chandler's walkway and onto the sidewalk, not having to turn around to know Betty was watching. When they got around the corner, Mossy stopped them. "I feel like we're running out of time. Walking won't cut it. Can you boys ride double?"

The few Haven residents who noticed could only wonder why the old man was riding a kid's bike through town.

(83)

JULIE PEERED out nervously from behind a display of stuffed animals in the gift shop of Haven Memorial Hospital. She had ducked in the gift shop when she spotted Dale and his stupid gang getting off the elevator. Not that they were hard to spot; she could tell from their raucous behavior that they were probably drunk. Once they went past and burst out the lobby doors, Julie headed for the elevator. Then she stopped, her knees feeling like rubber. *What if they were here to finish off Dad?* She suddenly gulped a hitching breath, not realizing she had forgotten to breathe when the thought hit her. She ran for the elevator and began pounding on the button, ignoring the annoyed stare of an elderly woman holding a ridiculous stuffed giraffe.

After an eternity, the doors slid open and Julie ran straight into the chest of Chuck (Charlie to Cheryl) Brantley. Her heart skipped; she thought she'd avoided Crawford's gang and ended up literally running into one of them. *I have to get to Dad*, she thought, and began pushing Chuck. The old woman *harrumphed* in disgust and stepped past them.

"Julie, calm down. What's wrong?"

"Let me go! What have you done to my dad?" Now she was crying and Chuck was staring at her with a look of horror.

"Julie, I was here to see Cheryl. Please, calm down."

Then it hit her: Chuck had fallen from grace with Crawford. He had "pussied out" of some foolishness that Crawford wanted

389

him to take part in and was persona non grata in the elite circle of Dale Crawford.

"Chuck. I just saw Dale and his gang leave, I think they were here to hurt my dad."

Chuck nodded slowly, putting the pieces together. "I don't think that's what they came for, but I'll go up with you so you can check, then I'll tell you what they wanted." He glanced at the older woman, still waiting impatiently for them to move so the elevator doors could close. Her impatience had turned to curiosity; she was clearly waiting for this little drama to play out. When she noticed Chuck staring she tightened her grip on the silly giraffe and turned to face the row of buttons. Julie pushed the button for Joe's floor and she moved to the back of the car with Chuck. Neither spoke until the woman exited one floor up.

"How is Cheryl? I wanted to see her...but...I've heard weird stories..."

Chuck made a noise that could have been a laugh or a grunt. "I'm not sure how she is, she's talking crazy. Anything you've heard will pale in comparison to her stories."

Julie actually had to suppress a grin despite the situation. She'd forgotten what a smart kid Chuck was and how he spoke like a forty-year old man before he'd been indoctrinated into the punk-speak Crawford used. Before she could ask another question, the elevator *dinged* and came to a stop on Joe's floor. Julie slid through the doors the second they had opened wide enough and started running down the hall. A nurse was just coming out and she greeted Julie with a smile.

"Your dad is sleeping, dear, but you can go in and sit with him if you like."

Julie nodded as Chuck joined her. "Are you sure he's alright? Did anyone try to get in his room today?" Julie had driven up from Malden with her mom but had been dropped off downtown to meet a friend and have lunch.

The nurse frowned and Julie realized how odd the question sounded. "He's absolutely fine, dear. We had a nice visit this morning while I was taking his blood pressure. He said he hadn't slept well, mentioned some bad dreams, and said he was going to take a nap. And that's what he's doing. Your mom was in earlier but said she was going back to your aunt's house to pack. Your dad will be going home today." Her smile was beaming; she had been Joe's primary nurse during his stay and, like most people, liked him a lot. Julie could see the woman was truly happy that Dad was okay. "Go ahead in, but please let him rest."

Julie felt a hand on her shoulder. "No, I just needed to make sure, I'll let him sleep. I was just worried about him. I'll come back later." The nurse nodded and headed to the next room. When she was out of earshot Julie turned to Chuck. "What's going on with Cheryl? And why *was* Dale here?"

As they made their way back to the elevator, Chuck began telling her Cheryl's story. Julie listened, not saying a word. They were in the lobby now but Julie felt trapped, claustrophobic. She took Chuck's hand and stepped out into the welcomed *openness* and blazing heat. Finally, she spoke. "Chuck, what do you think? I mean, it sounds so crazy, but I know Paul Greymore is not a child-killer."

Chuck looked torn. "I don't know, Julie. I want to believe her... but part of me is afraid that she did kill the baby and this is her mind's way of coping." Suddenly his look turned to fear. "Oh my God...Julie, Crawford is planning on doing something to Greymore. That's why they were here, they wanted me to help. Whatever did happen at the lake, Cheryl is positive it wasn't Greymore."

Julie felt the dizziness of déjà vu overtake her. She had been in time the night of the carnival, but could she get to Greymore fast enough to warn him again? "Ch...Charlie, we need to warn Paul!"

"I can take you. I...uh...borrowed my mom's car." He grabbed Julie's hand and pulled her toward the parking lot.

(84)

DENNY AND Billy pushed their bikes up Hillview Street while Mossy walked the edge of the woods bordering the road. The ride through town had been uneventful, though Denny and Billy had a few laughs watching Mossy getting the hang of Denny's bike. They weren't laughing now as the enormity of what they were about to do settled on them. Denny flashed back to a blurry memory of a dream about being pressed with rocks. The heat and fear were combining to sap not only Denny's strength, but his will to make the trek to the caves. He would give anything to sit in front of his fan reading a book. It hit him how much he took things like that for granted.

Both boys had glanced involuntarily at Billy's house as they went by. Neither spoke but they both knew what they were about to do was in part for Joe Cummings. When they reached Paul's house, they stuck closer to Mossy on the far side of the road. As much as Denny knew they couldn't let Greymore see them and risk him wanting to go in with them, it was exactly what he *wanted* to happen. Somehow he knew Paul would make the odds a lot better. He's battled it once before and won. *Did he really win?* the Bad Voice countered. As they passed the house it looked as empty as Billy's.

They crossed the road after Paul's house was behind them and didn't offer a glance at Lovell's, although they couldn't help but notice a couple of cats wandering around. When they were passing the woods that separated Denny's house from Cat-woman's, they stopped and looked nervously at each other.

Finally Mossy spoke. "Okay, boys. Make it quick so we can get this done." He shook his head and tried to laugh but it came out sounding like something much worse. "All these years and suddenly I'm in a big hurry. Go on, Denny. Tell your mom you're going for a little hike. Grab some food if you can." His voice broke when he added, "God I miss her."

Denny nodded. "Cut through these woods but keep the house in sight. There's a path that starts just behind the back fence. We'll meet you there in a few minutes."

The old man looked longingly at Denny's house for a moment, then turned and walked into the trees. "Okay, Billy, let's go." He started to cut across the front yard then stopped. He turned and saw the same wide-eyed terror on Billy's face that he knew was on his own. "I'm so scared, Billy." He felt near tears.

"Me too, Denny," was all Billy said.

He turned and walked toward the house trying to compose himself. Most likely his mom would be off in Never-Never Land and he would get in and out without as much as a word. Then a thought hit him, a thought so perfect he smiled to himself: if this really worked and Mossy came back with them, he might get his real mother back. That thought pushed the fear aside and he almost felt giddy. *It'll be a two-for-the-price-of-one bonus like they do at Maddie's Ice Cream Shop before they close for the winter. I'll get my mother and my grandfather! No extra charge!* He chuckled out loud and turned to see a bewildered look on Billy's face. "Just thought of something funny," he muttered and went into the house.

His mother was in the kitchen, staring out the window over the sink. Denny's heart fluttered—that window looked out over the backyard. *What if she saw him?* "Mom?"

She turned slowly, and Denny took a step back. The look on her face was...he thought back to a vocabulary word he had learned at some point...*serene.*

"I'm going to make spaghetti for dinner, even though I can't stand the thought of lighting the stove on a day like this." She stopped and her face brightened as if she'd just had a great idea. "Remember how your father hated eating spaghetti in the hot weather?"

Denny stared wide-eyed at his mother. She *never* brought up memories of his dad. Ever. "Yeah, he used to call it winter food." His mother smiled and nodded. Denny felt dizzy; he turned and looked at Billy. He knew they had to go meet Mossy, but he felt like this might be some sort of breakthrough. His mother remained at the sink, with that strange look on her face. Kind of dreamy with a hint of a smile.

"Do you think he can see us, Denny?" Her voice was small and shaky, like a little girl.

He moved closer, wanting to put his arm around her but afraid to. "I'm sure he can," Denny's own voice was cracking badly, "and he's probably telling Jimmy how crazy it is that you're going to cook spaghetti in the middle of a heat wave." He felt his eyes filling up, smiling at the same time. He stepped closer to his mother and put his arm around her waist. His smile disappeared when he felt her whole body tense at his touch. "It'll be alright, Mom. I miss them every day, but it'll be alright."

"Denny, we should get that hike in before it gets too dark."

Billy's voice broke the spell and focused Denny. "Yeah, Mom, Billy and I are going to hike in the woods for a while." His mother was gone again, so he turned to leave. He and Billy had reached the hallway when she spoke.

"Denny?"

"Yes, Mom?"

"Stay away from the army base, okay? That place...just stay away from it."

Denny felt the temperature drop just like it did when his mother mentioned her dream earlier that day. "Sure, Mom, we'll stay away, we're mostly just trying to stay out of the sun."

She stared at him. Really *saw* him. He could feel her trying to read him. Finally she nodded, satisfied, and turned back to look out the window again.

Denny and Billy left and walked around the back of the house. When they reached the end of the yard, Billy grabbed his arm. "Denny, is she okay? I know she acts weird sometimes, but what was that all about?"

Denny smiled a faraway smile, "I think my mother is coming back, Billy. Let's go kill this fucking thing." Billy looked dumbstruck but Denny said no more. Before he bent down to climb through the broken fence he glanced back. His mother was still there in the window, watching. He half-raised his hand to wave, then let it drop, and turned to the woods without another look back at the window.

(85)

JULIE'S MIND was spinning. *What the hell was going on?* The drive through town seemed endless. Charlie...that's what he liked to be called before becoming a Dale Crawford disciple...drove cautiously. And why wouldn't he, he didn't have a driver's license. Julie watched him as he drove, she could see the focus in his eyes, and admired his bravery. He had basically stolen his mother's car to go visit the girl he loved, faced down the gang of bullies he used to run with, and was now helping her try to save Paul. She knew it was all for Cheryl and she thought it was romantic. An image of Denny popped into her head. *Take your filthy hands off her, Crawford, she's as sick and tired of your shit as I am.* If Charlie had taken his eyes off the road at that moment, he would wondered why there was a slight smile on Julie's face.

When they reached Hillview Julie was relieved to see no Mustang parked on the road or in Greymore's driveway. She jumped out of the car, then leaned back in and instinctively kissed Charlie softly on the cheek. "Thank you. You may have saved a man's life. Please, tell my dad what's going on when you get back to the hospital, he'll know what to do. Then be with Cheryl, she needs you." Without waiting for an answer, she slammed the door and ran up the walkway.

She banged on the door, at the same time looking around helplessly for any sign of Dale. She felt like time was running out. She raised her hand to knock again and Paul was suddenly there.

"Julie, what's wrong? Is it Joe?"

"You have to get out, Paul. They're coming again."

Paul smiled. "Haven't we done this before?"

Julie opened the screen door and grabbed his arm. "Yes, and we're doing it again, please. We'll take the canoe again. We can dock at Cat-woman's house and I can see if Denny and Billy are at Denny's house. Something bad is happening, Paul. Can't you feel it?"

Paul stepped out the door and Julie could only think of one word to describe the look on his face: haunted. "As a matter of fact, I can. Let's go."

Each of the properties on the lake was built on a cove. There was a natural barrier of rocks and trees jutting out into the lake that gave each residence privacy from their neighbors. Paul began to row out into the lake to get around the small peninsula.

"Cheryl said something came out of the lake and just took her baby. She called it 'The Angel of Death' but described it as having tentacles."

Julie watched Paul's face as she spoke. It had been unreadable until that moment, then she saw him flinch. They were around the peninsula and heading in toward the Cat-woman's small dock.

"What is it, Paul? Does that mean something?"

The moment stretched as she waited for Paul to say something. Something that would make sense out of all the craziness that had taken place over the last few weeks. As they approached the dock, Julie squinted to see if Cat-woman was out there or if it would be just the cats to deal with. She could only make out a couple of shapes on the dock that looked like sleeping cats.

"What the..." Paul had stopped rowing and had pulled one of the oars out of the oarlock. He was fishing at something in the water. "Oh, shit."

Julie leaned over to see what Paul had found, and the canoe tipped precariously to that side. Paul shifted to compensate the weight change and when he leaned back, Julie saw the bloated body of a cat drift by the canoe. Julie's first thought was that it had drowned but then he saw the fish swirling around the half-submerged body, nibbling at the entrails that were hanging from a gaping wound in the cat's belly. It looked like it didn't have all of its paws, either. Julie groaned and swallowed bile, willing herself not to hurl all over the place.

"What the hell did that?"

"Let's get to the dock." Paul began paddling faster. Julie jumped onto the dock and felt her world shift. There were no sleeping cats on the dock but instead there were mangled cat parts strewn about. A head of one of the old tiger cats lolled near Julie's feet, its unseeing eyes cast upward to Julie, or the sky. The deck was slippery with blood and viscera. Julie almost lost her footing; fear of landing on the gore prevented her from falling more than her sense of balance did. She staggered off the dock and onto the firm sand, bending down to the water, checking first for any dead cats before reaching in to splash her face.

"Paul, what the hell is going on?" Paul had tied the canoe up and joined her. Julie figured he had seen a lot worse things in prison than a few dead cats.

"Let's go, Julie. We don't want to be around here when the police come." They made their way up the Cat-woman's backyard, avoiding the mangled pieces of her cats along the way. Paul stopped abruptly, causing Julie to almost collide into his back, and then he was off, running across the grass toward the house. Julie broke into a run behind him. When he stopped he was standing over another body. This time it wasn't a cat. It was the Cat-woman.

Paul bent down to roll her over. Another light breeze caused her to shiver, this time it carried the sickly-sweet smell of blood. When Paul got the Cat-woman onto her back, Julie turned and gagged again. She was mutilated. Most of her insides were hanging out of her wide-open stomach. There was nothing left of her neck or face; the white of her cheekbones was blinding in the hot sun. Her pale legs jutted awkwardly from beneath her tattered housecoat. "Let's go," Paul said again, staring at the Cat-woman's body.

Julie couldn't speak. Her mind was trying to process what she had just witnessed. She grabbed Paul's arm, pulling him around to look him in the eye. She tried to speak, to yell, but nothing would come. Paul bent down to Julie's height and that's when Julie knew. In Paul's eyes she could see the knowledge, the recognition. This wasn't the first time Paul had been so close to death. He had held the dying girl in his arms in 1961, trying to save her. Or was he?

"Julie, you've got to hold yourself together." Paul grasped Julie's shoulders. "Julie, do you understand?"

Greymore's eyes had turned to a blue like nothing Julie had ever seen before, so deep, bottomless. She felt her head nodding. Finally she was able to speak. "Paul, what happened here? You know. I can see it in your eyes."

"There's no time to explain, we've got to get out of here before Crawford gets here." As if to emphasize his point, the roar of a muscle car cut through the heavy silence. Neither doubted it was a Mustang.

Julie nodded. "We'll go to Denny's house. Come on, we'll cut through the woods, there's a trail."

CRAWFORD SLAMMED the cruiser into park and threw the door open. The humid air slapped him as he strode purposefully toward the other officers on the scene. "What the hell have we got?" he grumbled. Things were starting to get to him. In '61 he had been the hero, arresting Greymore and ending the summer-long killing spree. Nothing less was expected of him now. Sweat began to run down his face, his shirt already soaked through.

Officer Ortiz stepped up and gave him the report. "Doris Lovell is dead, apparently from loss of blood. She was mutilated. There are dozens of dead cats around here, ripped to pieces, some flayed right down to the bone."

"Cats? Jesus Christ, what next?" Crawford wiped his face with a sweat-stained handkerchief and started moving. He walked around to the back of the house and quickly took in the sight. Ortiz wasn't exaggerating; there were a lot of cats' bodies. What a mess. Why would Greymore do this? It must have taken quite a while to do this kind of damage; he must have completely snapped. "Ortiz, I want every available officer looking for Greymore, enlist civilians if you have to."

"Chief, we've already had one lynch mob. I think..."

"I don't give a rat's ass what you think, Ortiz. I want Greymore tonight, dead or alive." Crawford continued around to where Doris Lovell's body was being bagged by the coroner. "Hold on a minute, let me see her." Crawford leaned over to get a good look at the body. He wanted to see the work of this madman, to feel personally the horror he had inflicted. Mutilated? Christ she was gutted, he almost said aloud. Just before he stood he noticed her legs. He saw what Greymore had seen just a short time before him: a straight line of large red welts running across her thigh. Like a symmetrical row of bee stings. Crawford stood unsteadily. He had seen those before and he knew exactly where and when. Greymore and the Larsen girl had both had the same markings when Crawford found them. The information was never leaked to the press and existed only in the police reports. And in Crawford's memory.

"I want a full autopsy," he snapped at the medical examiner. "I want to know what made those marks." He walked down to the edge of the lake where there was a small dock with a canoe tied to it. In the water he could see more dead cats floating around. "What the hell is going on around here?" he whispered.

As he stared out over the lake he went back to the night he found Greymore with the girl.

It had been pouring rain, the first rain in weeks. Before that it had been hot as Hell. Someone had called in reporting a boater out on the lake. Not a good idea the way the lightning was touching down. He had been pissed that he had to go out and check it out. He had stopped at the Barrows' place and seen the canoe himself through the blinding rain. He saw it heading for the next house up the street. He got back into his car, thinking that whoever it was would be okay once they hit shore. They could call from the house, or maybe they even lived there. Lightning flashed, followed instantly by a sharp crack of thunder. Shit, how would it look on a report if he didn't follow up? He drove up the hill to the next driveway and pulled in. Having to struggle to push open his door in the howling wind, he was met by a pelting of cold rain. Goddammit, why me? Hunched over against the wind, he went around back, furious at whoever was making him be out in this. I hope they've been drink-ing, he thought, I'll haul them in for sure. He moved toward the back, the lake now coming into his view. It looked more like the ocean, the wind causing whitecaps to pound the shore. He saw the canoe, drifting a few feet off-shore. Shit! If I have to go in and drag somebody out of the lake...

His thought was cut short when he saw the heap half-way between the lake and the house. As he got closer he could see it was two bodies, an adult and a child. Maybe they'd been hit by lightning he thought. He kneeled down to check it out. The little girl was in bad shape, blood everywhere on her clothes. The guy was a mess in a different way. His face was scarred badly, disfigured to the point of horrible ugliness. He felt for a pulse on the guy and found it weak and irregular. The girl's was the same. Suddenly her eyes snapped open. They locked on Crawford but he knew instantly they weren't seeing him. She looked crazed, like a rabid animal, her eyes open wide in spite of the rain that was pelting them. "The monster, keep it away. Please." She said it so calmly, like she was asking for a piece of pie after dinner. Then her eyes had slowly shut. Crawford checked her pulse but this time found none. He quickly started CPR, thunder and lightning crashing around him, rain beating him. But it was no use. He couldn't bring her back. A touch of sadness came over him. Not for the girl but for the lost opportunity. He would have been a hero, saving a little girl's life in these conditions. He looked at her face, serene in death, the wildness of a few moments ago gone. An idea jolted him as though he'd been struck by the lightning that danced all around him. He looked again at the wounds, the blood, and suddenly he knew. The Butcher. "The monster," she had said. He turned to look at the body of the man beside her. His face was gruesome, monstrous to a little girl. He slapped his cuffs on the unconscious man and hurried back to the car to radio for help. A blessing in disguise, he thought to himself, well worth getting a little wet over.

Crawford started as someone tapped him on the shoulder. "You all set here, Chief? We're getting some people in to start cleaning up the animals. Wish we could find Bugsy, he'd be the guy for this."

Crawford stared at the man for a moment, returning to the present. "Sure, get whoever you need. No police, though, I want everyone looking for Greymore." As the officer walked away Crawford felt a familiar feeling creeping over him. It was a feeling he was used to. Doubt. He had felt it first when he had seen the same marks on Greymore's body as those on the girl. The medical examiners were unable to identify them. That was why they couldn't be included in the report to the press. Crawford had personally seen to that. Now here they were again, seventeen years later on another dead person, just a few hundred feet from where he had found Greymore and the Larsen girl. What could have made those marks? He went back to his car and slumped heavily into the driver's seat. Making sure nobody was around, he reached over and opened his glove compartment. He would push aside the doubt the same way he had been for all these years. The way he had to when he woke up sweating, heart pounding, knowing something was missing but not wanting to know. He unscrewed the cap and drank deeply from the bottle.

(87)

ORTIZ SLAMMED the door to the empty police station and collapsed in his desk chair. He felt trapped. Choices. Right and wrong. Guilt and innocence. He had already violated police protocol once by calling a warning to Greymore. What next? Crawford wanted him to call out an APB, deputize volunteers and perform a blanket search for Greymore. Crawford was clearly losing it, but to disobey a direct order would likely spell the end of his career. To follow orders would go against a cop's best friend: his gut. Ortiz relied heavily on his instincts and was rarely misled. Right now, his gut was telling him Greymore was not killing people and that there was a lot more going on in Haven than even Crawford knew about. He thought of his career, the risks of what he was contemplating, an innocent man's life, the safety of his town. He glanced at the clock. Crawford would expect action. Decision time. He stood slowly and walked toward the radio desk. He stopped to fill himself a cup of water from the cooler, taking a sip as he reached the radio. With no further hesitation, he poured the cup of water onto the back of the radio. There were no sparks, just a faint crackle before the box went silent.

Ortiz felt surprisingly calm as he pulled the fuse from the cruiser that powered the car radio. With his penknife, he broke the filament and replaced the fuse. Radio silence. Through no fault of his own, or so he could claim, he was unable to call in the APB and organize the search. Plausible deniability. His alternatives were to try to

405

find Crawford or begin the search himself. Perfectly justifiable to consider driving around Haven looking for Crawford as a waste of time. Plausible deniability. His flimsy alibi in place, he set out to find Greymore himself.

On his way through town, Ortiz's attention was drawn to the gathering clouds. The heat was still unbearable and they had watched these cloud formations come and go with no rain before. The trees were deathly still, as was the town. Everyone was either over at the fairgrounds or hunkering indoors waiting for rain, or simply afraid to venture out. He pulled into the hospital lot, and with a final dubious glance at the sky, headed in to see Joe Cummings. The elevator ride was endless; more waiting. With a nod he breezed past the desk and stepped quietly into Cummings' room. Christ, what a mess. The parts of his face not bandaged were a dark rainbow of bruises. His swollen eyes fluttered open as Ortiz moved toward his bedside. "Sorry to bother you, Mr. Cummings, I was hoping I could ask you a few questions?"

What might have once been a smile, now a disturbing grimace, crossed Joe's face. "Not a problem, Officer Ortiz, my afternoon is open."

Ortiz hesitated. He had to play this right. "Please call me Robert. I'm here on my own time, not on official police business." He removed his hat, as if that would confirm it.

Cummings eyed him for a moment, nodding. "Alright, Robert, what can I do for you?"

"I'm looking for Greymore…"

"That sure sounds like official police business to me, unless you were planning on catching a movie together?"

Ortiz quickly realized Cummings was not one to be played. His friendship with Greymore was too important. Once again following his gut, Ortiz plunged ahead. "Right now, Chief Crawford is at Doris Lovell's house. She's dead, Joe. Her, and a bunch of her cats. Mutilated. Crawford sent me to get Greymore. Dead or alive. But it doesn't feel right. I need your help..." Cummings closed his eyes. After a few minutes Ortiz thought he had fallen asleep, probably still sedated. He turned to leave.

"Paul is innocent. I can't prove it, but I know it. If we don't start with that as a fact, this conversation is over."

"That's why I'm here, Joe."

"This is going to sound crazy, but it's something about the lake. Paul thought there was something in there, and he had these marks all over..."

"Wait. What marks? There was nothing in the report."

Joe sighed, shaking his head. "Who wrote the report? Anyway, the marks looked like bee stings, only bigger, and lots of them in a straight line. Paul was out of his head after he was caught, but he kept saying 'Stay away from the lake, it might still be alive.' There's something in there, isn't there? Find Paul, make sure he's safe."

Ortiz could see the agony in Joe's eyes, even through the mask of bruises on his face. "I'll find him, Joe. That's a promise. After that, I don't know what happens, but I'll find him."

>> <<

Back in the cruiser Ortiz hesitated. Now what? He'd basically cut himself off from any official resources by disobeying orders. He was on his own. It's something about the lake. Ortiz closed his eyes, calling up the incidents since Greymore returned. Tony DeMarcy last seen in a canoe floating around on the lake. Bugsy's gun found on the shore. The Sheehan kid and his dog ripped apart. The Peroit girl's baby taken by what she called a monster. Jenkins. Now the Lovell woman. All six tied to the lake.

The thing that made Ortiz a good cop was his mind. He had an innate sixth sense that allowed him to take seemingly unrelated or insignificant events and find the connection. To him, it was like one of those old maze puzzles where you slid the pieces up and down and across until you got them in the right place. Jumbled, they made no sense but laid out properly, they formed a picture. Another piece slid into the right place when Ortiz remembered the papers in Bugsy's truck. All of the data pointed to less roadkill around the lake, this year and back in '61. Unless Greymore had an appetite for killing squirrels and possum, there was something in the lake killing them. And sometimes bigger prey. Ortiz started the car and pulled out of the hospital parking lot. He needed to talk to Greymore, to see what he remembered about the marks on his body the night he was arrested. But first he had another hunch to follow up on. He had to be sure. He headed back to the station to break a few more rules.

CHRIS MCCAULEY glanced at the clock for the millionth time. Not a single minute had ticked by since the last time he looked. After visiting Mossy he'd worked a half day at the station. After the usual morning rush, the place was dead so he closed up early. He'd gone home and cleaned up, then tried to take a nap but sleep would not come to his overactive mind. He'd taken a ride to the lake but couldn't make himself even get out of the car. Something in there had scared his brother so profoundly that he'd taken his own life to avoid seeing it again. He'd paced around his small house mindlessly. There was no way he would make it until six o'clock at this rate. He'd decided to walk over to the Witch's Hat. It was Jake's favorite place, it seemed right to be there. Now, still nursing his first beer and glancing obsessively at the clock, he began to feel a sense of calmness. Maybe his brother's spirit was here.

He turned from the bar to take in the place his brother had spent so much time in. It wasn't much, but maybe for Jake it eased his tortured memories. A few years later Chris would be watching *Cheers*, a Boston-based sitcom about the regulars in a bar and would think of Jake with tears in his eyes when the patrons cheerfully yelled "Norm!" when one of the characters walked in. Now, he saw a lonely bunch of people searching for something in the bottom of a glass and he only felt sadness.

His mind turned to the task that lay ahead. It was all so improbable, a man-made monster that lived in the lake of their small town.

It was the plot to so many bad horror movies, yet Chris believed it. He had to, the alternative was madness, mass-hysteria and he could not think in those terms. He noticed a small group of older men at a table looking at him, and he raised his glass before turning back to the bar and looking at the clock again. He drained his beer, dropped a five on the bar, and headed out. He would walk back home, get his car, and pick up Mossy early. The wait was over, it was time to act.

(89)

ORTIZ PULLED into the parking lot and walked briskly into the station. It was still empty with no signs of anyone being there since he'd disabled the radio. He began looking through the filing cabinets for the old case reports and was shocked to find them gone. Had Crawford snapped and destroyed them in case there was something that hinted at Greymore's innocence? He shook his head, immediately knowing the files were all in the Chief's office where Crawford had been obsessing over them since Greymore's release. He hurried to the office and found the door locked. He knew he didn't have a lot of time. Either the Chief himself or one of the other officers would be back to the station soon. Without a second thought he stepped back and kicked the door just below the knob. He was mildly surprised when the cracking sound he heard was the door jamb and not his foot, and the door swung open. He grabbed the files from Crawford's desk, fully aware of the consequences. He was risking everything he had worked his entire life for.

Robert Ortiz had known at a young age the difference between right and wrong and the deep valley of gray between. He was left alone on the streets of Miami at the age of 15 to fend for himself when his parents were killed in a drive-by shooting. It could have been gang-related or it could have been a random act of violence common to the poverty-stricken neighborhoods of big cities. Whatever the case the result was the same: Ortiz had no parents and no place to call home. The easy route for him would have been the gangs, dealing drugs, small-time robberies, and eventual jail time. But his parents had taught him well. He managed to finish high school while living on the streets and picking up odd jobs wherever possible. His senior essay about the homeless subculture in Miami won him a scholarship to Boston University. With no car and no money, he hitched from Florida to Massachusetts following graduation. He had survived the thieves and perverts that travel the interstates and fulfilled his parents' dreams by finishing college with a degree in criminal justice. The police academy was the next logical step. He had always thought everything he had, everything he had been through, was represented by the badge and gun he carried and the uniform he wore.

As all of these thoughts filled his mind, he picked up one of the folders and quickly scanned the notes for the location of the disappearance. Then the next and the next. It was too clear, too obvious. All of the disappearances or the last-seen-locations of the victims were in the direct vicinity of the lake. Not Greymore's house, but the lake itself. There was no way Crawford could have missed this. He unbuckled his Sam Browne belt and laid it on Crawford's desk. He did the same with his badge. They didn't represent him, they didn't symbolize his life. If they did then it would have to be true for Crawford too. And he was not like Crawford at all. Crawford had wanted to make a collar and make a name, Ortiz wanted justice. Without a look back he headed out of the police station, maybe for the last time.

(90)

ORTIZ STEPPED into the dimly lit bar and quickly assessed the situation. The place was more than half-filled early on a Saturday afternoon. The Haven Day event was in full swing over at the fairgrounds. The carnival always ended on Haven Day, celebrating the town's founding. Various events took place, including the strong man competition that Teddy Stavros always won, and ending with a fireworks show. That meant he was looking at a room full of what he considered "professional drinkers." Those with nothing to go home to, or something at home they were trying to avoid. He knew from experience it would be a tough crowd, one that kept to itself. He slowly made his way to the bar, feeling the suspicious eyes follow him.

He had been driving slowly through town thinking about what Joe Cummings had said. Alone in his own vehicle, no gun or badge, doubt had crept into his mind. Had he just thrown everything he worked for since he was fifteen down the sewer? His cop's instinct, alive and well with or without a gun and badge, screamed "NO!" Ortiz began applying logic to the situation, rearranging the data over and over in his mind, knowing he would hit the right combination eventually and a pattern would show itself.

He didn't know the whereabouts of Greymore. Ditto on Father McCarthy. Bugsy was probably dead. Crawford was unapproachable. He needed a link, something connecting these people to each other or the lake. He replayed the conversation with Joe Cummings in his head and there he found the next step he was looking for: the Witch's Hat. From what Joe said, his assault was premeditated and probably involved someone at the bar to turn off the lights in the parking lot when Joe left. Now, here he was.

The bartender stared him down with a look somewhere between wariness and contempt. These guys had an instinct too; they knew a cop when they saw one. "Can I help you, Officer?" The words were clipped, not your friendly, neighborhood bartender type.

Ortiz smiled knowingly; this wasn't going to be easy. "Just a beer, and a few answers." He pulled out his wallet and laid two twenties on the bar, never taking his eyes from the bartender's. The burly man raised his eyebrows, then turned to pour the beer. He placed the glass on the bar in front of Ortiz, the cash still lying there. His eyes swept the bar. Ortiz did the same. Most of the regulars had gone back to their own conversations, apparently satisfied by the beer that this was not cop business.

"Some answers aren't for sale, I think you know that. First beer is on the house, the rest depends on the questions."

Ortiz nodded. "Fair enough. Some friends of mine have run into trouble. One is missing, probably dead, the other is in the hospital beat up pretty bad. His son is missing too. For the record, I don't give a shit how many people sitting here were part of the little party in the parking lot that was arranged for Joe Cummings. I'm here to help my friends. I turned in my gun and badge today, there are no repercussions."

The bartender nodded and scooped up the cash. "Okay, fire away. But I reserve the right not to answer any questions I don't like, and to throw your skinny ass out of here if I *really* don't like them."

Ortiz grinned. Even though the bartender seemed shady and probably participated in all sorts of illegal activity, Ortiz liked him. "You're the boss. All I want to know is if you've heard about anything strange happening around the lake."

"Besides kids getting dead?"

Ortiz took a long pull on his beer. "Yeah, besides that."

The bartender nodded slowly, taking Ortiz's glass and topping it off. "Bugsy Cronin has been coming in talking to his crew about the lake. From what I gather he thinks something is killing some of the wildlife around there. His pals think he's gone over the deep end, razzing him about it. He also said he met that Butcher guy and that he thinks he's innocent. That didn't go over well. Come to think of it, haven't seen him around lately."

"I don't think you will. He disappeared out by the lake. I found his empty truck up on Hospital Hill." He let that sink in, seeing by the look on the bartender's face that this wasn't new news. "Is there anything else? You probably hear a lot of shit, drunk talk and nonsense, but is there anything else you can think of?"

The bartender looked thoughtful for a moment, Ortiz's plea seemed to break through the man's suspicious and protective posture. Suddenly his eyes went wide. "Wait a minute, this might be something. A few nights ago, maybe a week now, the McCauleys were in here with a guy I'd never seen before. Old guy, looked like a veteran drinker but he was only having soda. By the end of the night, Jake McCauley was only ordering ginger ale too."

He said this last part with such awe, and Ortiz knew why. He'd dragged Jake McCauley into the drunk tank himself on a number of occasions. Then his brain went into overdrive cop mode, referencing everything he knew about Jake McCauley. And there was the link he's been searching for: McCauley was at the lake when one of the killings took place in 1961, he'd seen it in Crawford's files. "This is important: what were they talking about?"

"They were talking about the lake! At one point I almost threw them out; Jake smashed a glass on the table and cut himself. Later, they all looked like they were crying. They kept it down for the most part, but they were definitely talking about the lake."

Ortiz downed the rest of his beer and put two more twenties on the bar. "What did this other guy look like?"

The bartender reached for the money, but pushed it back toward Ortiz. "He was older, probably seventy, gray hair. Had the look of someone who didn't have it easy: I know that look, I see it a lot. Check Betty's, I think I heard he's staying there. Oh, and Chris was in earlier. Had a beer and left, never said a word."

Ortiz reached across the bar and shook the man's hand. "I appreciate everything, you may have saved some lives." He turned and left the bar, leaving the cash behind.

(91)

GREYMORE KNOCKED loudly on the screen door, waited a few seconds and knocked again louder. He glanced at Julie and could only imagine the terror and confusion he saw on her face mirrored on his own. *But yours will be a train wreck of scars and look so much worse.* Before he could push the thought from his head, the door opened and he was staring into the empty eyes of Janice O'Brien. For a moment he didn't think she was going to acknowledge him, but then her eyes seemed to focus.

"Hello, Julie. And you must be Mr. Greymore? I'm Janice O'Brien, so nice to meet you." She held her hand out.

Paul grasped it gently, unable to take his eyes from hers. *Did I imagine the look I just saw? The one that I see in the mirror most days?* "My pleasure, Mrs. O'Brien. We are looking for Denny and Billy, are they here?" Her eyes changed again and her face slackened and Paul knew he hadn't imagined anything. This was a woman barely able to keep it together. He glanced at Julie and she just shrugged.

"They aren't here, they went for a hike. Trying to stay out of the heat."

Paul's stomach flipped and his legs went loose on him. Then he heard the roar of an engine and the screech of rubber. The engine cut out. They were either at Cummings' or Greymore's, time to move. He took a deep breath, looking again into the eyes of Janice O'Brien, not the ghost of her. "How long ago did they leave?" He was barely able to keep his voice from shaking.

"I think...I don't know. I sometimes lose track of time..." Her voice trailed off and Paul could see the confusion in her eyes. Then the eyes grew wide and alert again. "I told them to stay away from the old army base. They said they would but I think that's where they went. Why would they go there? I told them it's dangerous. My own father..."

He reached out and put a hand on her shoulder. "Julie and I will go get them and bring them home. I promise."

She looked at him for a moment as if she had never seen him before. Then she looked at Julie. "The trail starts right behind the yard, you know it Julie?"

"Yes, Mrs. O'Brien. We'll be back soon, okay?"

She only stared, her focus gone. Paul heard the 351 engine explode to life and mag wheels spinning on the dirt road. He looked at Julie, urging her with a look that it was time to go. Then there was a firm hand on his arm.

"Wait, just one minute?" Then Janice was gone, the screen door slamming.

Paul glanced nervously down the hill, expecting the Mustang to come screaming into view. Then the screen door squealed open and Janice was handing him a flashlight.

"If they did go to that godforsaken place, you'll need this." Her eyes now shone with conviction. "Bring them home safely. Please."

Paul nodded, then grabbed Julie by the arm and ran around the house to the yard. Behind them, the Mustang's engine grew louder.

92

ORTIZ SPED through the silent town, and his thoughts moved along faster than his vehicle. He knew Chris McCauley would have already closed up his station, so he would question Betty Chandler first before going to Chris's home. Who was this mysterious stranger? What did he have to do with what was going on? He pulled to the curb in front of Chandler's and bounded up the steps to the front door. As he reached up to knock, the door flew open and Betty stood in front of him clutching a notebook. She uttered a surprised gasp, almost bumping into Ortiz.

"Mrs. Chandler, I'm Officer Ortiz." A harmless lie, more of a timing issue than a lie, he thought grimly. "You look like you're in a hurry, but if I could have just a moment..."

Betty Chandler studied him with a still-surprised look before answering. "I was actually on my way to the Police Station. I tried calling but I couldn't get through."

"Well, I'll only take a few minutes of your time. I need to know if you have a guest, an older gentleman, gray hair?"

"Oh my gosh, that's why I was calling the police. Mr. Rodman... but he's not really Mr. Rodman, he's Moses Blaakman!"

Ortiz's instincts were in high gear; he could almost hear the final pieces of the puzzle clicking into place. "Please, let's sit for a moment, perhaps this will save you a trip to the station, Mrs. Chandler." He motioned toward the porch swing with all the hopefulness of a boy trying to get his date to sit there for a little making out before the porch light flipped on.

"Please, call me Betty. I don't really know where to begin Officer Ortiz…"

"Calm down, Betty, we'll get through this just fine. And call me Robert. When did this Mr. Rodman or Blaakman show up?"

"Chris McCauley brought him a few weeks ago after the bus dropped him off. The three of us had dinner that first night. He paid for a month in cash, up front, and I've hardly seen him since. He comes and goes a lot, sometimes at strange hours. But then Chris showed up and I…heard them talking, here, on the porch. That's when he told Chris his real name. He told this awful story. It was crazy." She paused, looking as scared and confused as Ortiz had ever seen anyone look. "But he got Chris to agree to let him talk to his brother. I didn't know what to do…but today I went into his room and found this." She held out the notebook. "Officer…Robert…it's horrible, it can't be true. I think the man is crazy. I'm afraid he is the one killing kids and he made up this awful fairy tale and somehow Chris believed it…" She broke down, her body heaving with sobs and shaking with fear at the same time. "My Lord, he went out somewhere with Dennis O'Brien and Billy Cummings! Robert, he was in my *h-house*!"

Ortiz nodded slowly, more pieces falling into place. He placed a gentle arm around her shoulders. "I'm sure those boys are fine. I know it's difficult Betty, but I need to know everything. Lives could depend on it."

She handed him the notebook. "It's all in here." she said flatly.

"Betty, I think I am running out of time, please, just tell me what you heard?"

She wiped her eyes with a lace handkerchief that seemed to appear from nowhere, quickly regaining composure, and began talking. "He was in the military, on the old base back in the forties. He claims the base wasn't an ammunition storage plant. He says they did experiments there and they…they created some kind of monster. He thought it was dead when the base blew up, but now he thinks it's still alive. He thinks it killed all those kids in 1961, that Greymore was innocent, and that it's back again. There are some tunnels or caves out where the old base was, he thinks it lives there."

Ortiz got up to leave, taking the notebook with him. He would try to find Chris then head into the woods to find the tunnels. "Thank you, Betty, you may have just saved a lot of lives."

Betty also stood and grabbed his arm. "There's one more thing... Moses Blaakman is Janice O'Brien's father."

And with an almost-audible click, the last piece of the puzzle was in place. He nodded, "Thank you again, Betty. Please don't tell anyone else about this until you hear from me. And if Mr. Blaakman shows up, call the station if you want, but I don't think you have anything to fear from him."

"Does that mean...you think...this is all true?" She sounded more scared than when she thought a mass murderer was renting a room from her.

"I'm afraid so. I don't know how there are such gaps in the killings, but I believe there is something in that lake responsible. I think Greymore is as innocent now as he was back in 1961."

Betty's face paled even more, the gravity of what that meant hitting her full on. She sat down heavily on the swing, looking shocked. "Make it right, Robert... for Haven..."

"I'll try." He jumped into his car and headed off to find Chris McCauley.

PART IIII

(93)

THE THREE figures crouched in the deepening shadows of the lantern light. The trees looked black against a deep blue sky. A lazy breeze was trying to gather strength, inspiring a slow dance from the lantern's flame. Crickets offered the soundtrack to the night, until a thrashing in the bushes silenced them, causing three heads to snap in the direction of the sound. "Just a fox, boys," Mossy rasped.

Denny looked around, saw Billy looking at him. "Let's get going before I chicken out."

Mossy shook his head. "I wish you would chicken out and let me do this alone, but I know I can't stop you if you follow."

Denny and Billy had done what the old man wanted—helped him find the entrance. It was then Denny revealed his real plan to go into the caves with him. It came as no surprise to Billy and he quickly agreed. "Like Denny said, let's do it. We've talked enough." Billy's voice had a hardened edge: an adult-like tone that sounded a lot like Joe.

The three silently shouldered their packs and with Mossy in the lead and Billy going last, they descended. Once below ground, away from the sounds of the woods, everything sounded louder. Mossy was out of breath climbing down the ladder. Billy's backpack buckle clanged against the rungs. The globe of Denny's lantern was loose, rattling in its seating. To Denny, it all sounded like a lunch bell calling the beast.

They took a moment at the landing to catch their breath.

"Boys, I know my way from here. Please, go back up the ladder and forget you ever saw this place." His voice trembled. He knew it was unlikely he would get out alive and he felt the weight of two more deaths on his conscience if the boys went with him.

Both boys shook their heads in unison.

Mossy sighed. "Okay, let's get this done and get home, I have a daughter to introduce myself to."

Denny and Billy took the lead, carrying the lantern and watching for the red markings they had left last time. They trudged along in silence. The darkness around them felt like it was getting darker, stronger, weighing down on them. Slowing them from getting to their destination...but that would mean it was on their side. The thought felt irrational, almost nonsensical, until a stray song lyric found its way into his head. *He would make the darkness his friend.* Somehow, it made sense to think of it that way. Now Denny's mind turned completely inward, a chaotic assault of random thoughts and memories. Had Mossy or Billy been speaking, he would not have heard.

In his mind's eye he saw his dad, casually throwing a baseball to him. When it bounced off his glove and dropped to the ground, his dad smiled and shouted some words of encouragement. Off to the side, Jimmy shook his head, and then joined in with his dad. "Next one, Denny, next one for sure!" His father's tan, smiling face was suddenly white, almost gray, looking up at him from a hospital bed. Bruises surrounded his closed eyes, and tubes were in his nose and mouth. Next he was at Revere Beach building a sandcastle. Sweat and saltwater and sand and sunblock covered him from head to toe. He glanced up at his mom to see why she had stopped helping and found her staring down at him. She looked like an angel, the halo of the August sun glowing around her head. She watched Denny with a look so filled with love...

Suddenly he was roasting in a different sun, uncomfortably warm. He was wearing a suit: it was his father's burial. His mother stood beside him, stoic. She was not crying, just staring.

426

Denny snapped back to the present with a pair of hands gripping his shoulders and tears streaming down his face. "Denny, what is it?" He was so disoriented it took him a minute of blinking into the lantern light looking wildly around before he realized where he was. He had no idea how much time had passed while he took his roller-coaster ride down memory lane. He felt like the time he had a molar pulled at the dentist. One minute he was counting backwards from one hundred with a mask over his face, the next he was bawling like a girl with no idea where he was, a gaping hole in his mouth where his tooth had been. "Denny? Are you okay?"

"Fine. Let's go." He wiped the tears with his sleeve, nodded at the bewildered faces of Mossy and Billy, and without another word, began walking again.

(94)

FATHER MCCARTHY sat rigid in the passenger seat of Crawford's cruiser, hoping to God he'd made the right decision. When he was unable to find Paul or the boys, he'd gone to see Joe Cummings. Joe had another visitor, a young man McCarthy recognized from the day at the gas station. *The day this all started*, he thought. The boy was telling Joe that he'd given Julie a ride to Greymore's to warn him that Dale Crawford and the rest of the gang were going after him. The boy said he thought he'd seen Dale's car heading that way as he was on his way back to the hospital. Joe was frantic but McCarthy had been able to calm him down. Joe also mentioned an ally in Robert Ortiz. Unable to track down anyone else, he'd gone to the police station in hopes of finding Ortiz.

What he found instead was an enraged Crawford. Sensing time was running out and that Paul and the boys were in danger, he'd confronted Crawford, telling him enough to convince him to get him to head back to the lake with him.

Now, he felt like he'd made the proverbial deal with the Devil and would have been better off going it alone. Crawford looked like he was about to explode. His face was bright red, littered with broken blood vessels. He was mumbling incoherently to himself as he sped toward the lake, periodically sipping from a flask he held between his legs while driving. McCarthy wasn't sure they would even get to the lake at this rate, and was less sure of what might happen if they did find Greymore and the boys.

"Chief, maybe you should slow down with whatever is in the flask and concentrate on the task at hand."

Crawford ignored him; McCarthy realized he probably hadn't even heard him. He screeched onto Hillview Street and pulled into Cummings' driveway and was out of the car before it had stopped bouncing on its shocks. He pounded loudly on the door, yelling for anyone to open up (*it's the police goddammit!*). He finally gave up, and with a final scowl at the dark house, tore up the street, repeating the process at Greymore's. This time he didn't give up when nobody answered, he thrust his meaty shoulder into the door until it swung open from the splintered frame. McCarthy watched him disappear into the house, knowing Greymore was not to be found. Crawford burst back outside and lumbered through the yard to the back of the house. Finally, he returned, looking at McCarthy as if he'd forgotten he was there. "Canoe's gone." He thought for a moment. "Son of a bitch, that was his canoe tied to Lovell's dock. Now her and most of her fucking cats are gutted—what do you think of your friend now, Preacher?" He drank deeply from the flask, his face turning a deeper, somehow more dangerous shade of red.

"Chief, they're heading for the caves. Or tunnels, whatever they are. Under the old army base. A boat would be faster but we can get there through the woods."

Crawford's face took on a sudden calmness, a resignation. "Then let's go for a little hike, shall we?"

His gaze was maniacal. McCarthy said a silent prayer, crossed himself, and got out of the car. God only knew what they would find or how this would end. With the enemy at his side, he walked resolutely through the now-abandoned massacre at Lovells and into the woods.

(95)

ROBERT ORTIZ didn't have to look far to track down Chris McCauley; as soon as he pulled out of Betty's driveway he saw the man walking purposefully toward the house. He pulled up to the curb beside him. "Chris, hop in, we need to talk."

Chris leaned in the open window. "Sorry Officer, I'm in a bit of a hurry."

Ortiz saw the pain in the man's eyes. Christ, he found his own brother dead, who *wouldn't* be hurting? Ortiz had spent a good deal of time talking with him at Jake's apartment. But this looked worse somehow. "He's already gone, Chris. Rodman, or Moses, whatever you want to call him. I know most of what's going on but I need your help with the rest. Please, get in."

Chris's expression went from haunted to savage in an instant. "What do you mean 'gone'?"

"I just spoke with Betty, he left a while ago. The O'Brien boy and Billy Cummings were with him. Told some story about interviewing him for a school project. Let's go, Chris, I feel like we're running short on time."

Chris looked once toward Betty's, then got in the passenger seat. "I know where they're going. Christ, I wish I didn't. We need to get to the lake, to the old army base." He was thrown back in his seat as Ortiz peeled away from the curb. "There's some caves or tunnels there. Something lives there, something Blaakman *made*." He looked at Ortiz, anger slipping toward fear. "He's going there to kill it, Robert. He says it's responsible for the killings. Now and in 1961. I believe him, as crazy as it sounds, I believe him. My brother saw it, he killed himself because he was too afraid to see it again. In his mind or in the flesh."

Ortiz sped through the darkening town toward Hillview Street, praying he would be in time.

(96)

DALE CRAWFORD pounded on the screen door, standing in exactly the same spot Paul Greymore had stood moments before. Behind him, the Mustang growled while its riders sat warily. If Crawford could read minds, he would likely kill both Buddy and Costa for doubts they had. It was fear, not loyalty, that kept them from fleeing. The door finally opened and Crawford did his best to seem sane. "Hello, Mrs. O'Brien. Is Denny home?" He used his best Eddie Haskell voice. The smell of spaghetti sauce wafted by Janice O'Brien and Dale noticed her tense at his question.

"No, he went...out with his friend Billy. Maybe they're at his house?"

Dale ground his teeth trying to maintain the fake smile that was torturing his face. "No, ma'am, we just checked there. I'm pretty sure he came here."

"I'm sure they'll be home for dinner soon. Maybe they rode their bikes to town."

The woman was lying. Dale's rage-o-meter went into the red. The smile twisted into a sneer. "That would be difficult, since both of their snotty little bikes are RIGHT THERE!" Before the woman could react, Crawford was on her. He threw the door open and shoved her roughly to the ground. He straddled her, his knees on her shoulders and slapped her face, forehand then backhand, forehand then backhand. "WHERE. ARE. THEY." If she was going to answer, she couldn't as he continued to slap her, her face jerking violently from side to side with each blow. It was fatigue that made him stop, not the blood flowing from her mouth and nose. He cocked his head to one side as if hearing something, then nodded and pulled his knife. The blade opened with a satisfying snap and Dale leaned in holding the blade below the soft flesh of Janice's eye. "Tell me where he is and you can keep your eye. I'm not going to hurt him, just that freak Greymore."

She stared, tried to speak, and choked on her own blood. Dale slid the blade closer and watched with fascination as the tip slid under the skin below her eye. A quick flick of the wrist and he could pop the eyeball right out. It suddenly seemed like the best thing in the world he could do. Her gurgling voice interrupted his train of thought.

"The woods...hiking...please...don't...hurt him..."

Satisfied but disappointed he wouldn't get to hold her throbbing eyeball in his hand, he got off her and went outside. "Kill the engine, grab the flashlight out of the glove box and let's go, they're in the woods."

He glared at them through the dirty windshield, willing them not to move fast enough so he could carve someone. Sensing the danger, they came quickly. The three sprinted through the yard and hopped the fence, following the path to the base. They moved quickly into the shadowy woods. Much quicker than their quarry.

(97)

PAUL AND Julie scrambled through yet another tunnel, unsure of where it led or how they would get back. Greymore was not afraid of a bunch of liquored-up punks, but the knowledge that they had a least one gun between them was enough to keep him moving, if only to keep Julie safe from harm. They had just found the bloody sock that marked the cave opening when they first heard their pursuers. Crawford had bellowed in triumph from the top of the hill and fired a careless shot in their direction. It was more than enough to get Paul and Julie moving in a higher gear.

No matter what happened tonight, Greymore would deal with Crawford soon enough. They ran as fast as the conditions allowed. The unsteady beam of the flashlight and uneven cave floor and walls were a treacherous combination if they weren't careful. They stopped at the next fork to catch their breath and gauge what kind of lead they had on Crawford. Above the sound of their own gasping breaths, Paul could hear the sound of running and yelling. "They're still behind us, we have to keep moving," he whispered.

Julie was clearly more winded but what Paul saw in her eyes was a fear and determination that would keep her going. She nodded and gestured for Paul to pick which branch of the tunnel to take. Paul hesitated: bearing right would take them deeper based on the slope, left might lead to another way out as it sloped upward slightly. Fearing the potential exit might be blocked, he took Julie's hand and started down the right fork. They were forced to slow their pace as this part of the tunnel twisted and turned more frequently, and the ceiling was becoming lower as they progressed. Paul hoped Crawford would bear left, thinking he and Julie would be looking for an exit. Then he heard a cry of pain behind him. The acoustics were tough to decipher, but Greymore thought they sounded closer than before. One of the gang must have fallen; hopefully it would give them time to make up more ground.

They continued on through the tunnel, moving as fast as the conditions allowed. They came to no more forks or side tunnels and Paul began to fear they might end up at a dead end. Then they would have to stand and fight. Paul began picking up the pace, dragging Julie with him. He sacrificed safety for speed, desperately trying to give them a lead over their pursuers. Julie was tiring quickly, gasping for air and stumbling but refusing to quit. Paul put his arm around her waist and half carried, half dragged her along. They rounded yet another sharp curve in the rock just as Julie stumbled. Paul felt her legs give out and lost his grip on her. She sprawled headlong into the wall of the tunnel, barely getting her arms up to protect herself. She hit the wall hard, and with a moan, slid to the ground.

Paul ran to her side quickly and shined the light on her face. She was bleeding from a cut in her forehead and a nasty goose-egg was already forming. When her eyes opened Paul saw nothing but pain and exhaustion. He turned the light forward and nearly cried out in surprise. The cave opened into a cavern, too large for the light to penetrate to the far side. It must be the one Denny told him about. Shining the light along the floor, he saw the strange white powder and chunks of bone.

"Mr. Greymore…"

"Julie, can you walk?" She didn't reply, only uttered a weak moan. Paul began helping her up when another sound came out of the darkness. The gang was back on the move, their voices approaching quickly from behind. "Hurry, let me help you," he whispered. He got an arm around her waist and dragged her into the cavern. The sound his steps made was making him ill knowing what was crunching beneath his feet. He felt along the cave wall with one hand and the weak flashlight beam, dragging the semi-conscious Julie with the other. He got her into a recess in the cave wall just as twin beams of light stabbed through the darkness from the tunnel. Greymore snapped his own light off and crouched against the wall. There was no chance of sneaking up on Crawford with the noisy flooring. *I should have waited by the entrance and taken them as they came in,* he thought. No time for that, he would just have to wait and see if he would get another opportunity, or maybe the gang would keep going without searching the cavern.

"They definitely came this way...holy shit!" The first beam swept the cave, bouncing off walls and then disappearing into the inky darkness. "Dale, this fucking place is huge!"

The second beam entered the cavern. "Hey numbnuts, shut your sperm-trap before the freak gets you."

Paul waited for the third voice, trying to control his rising anger. The events of the day, hell, the events of his whole life were building like a flammable gas. That word was the spark, threatening to send Paul into an explosion of temper and violence. He closed his eyes and slowed his breathing. The third voice never came and Paul wondered if the cry of pain he heard earlier was enough to leave one of the gang behind and even the odds a bit. And in the dark of the cavern, the only sound the run-off from the lake, the final memory came to Paul.

He hacked blindly at the weeds or vines or stray piece of rope that had wrapped around his calf. When the blade made contact he began sawing frantically, and despite the numbing sensation he felt the vine slide free of his leg. Even in his panicked state he knew something was wrong. Because the vine hadn't just slipped loose, it had slithered. As his mind tried unsuccessfully to grasp this, he began to feel something else. Despite the raging storm and the roiling lake waters, despite the injured girl and her probably-dead mother, Paul was beginning to feel calm. Serene. And this frightened him more than anything else. He quickly flopped onto the bottom of the row-boat and thought, oddly enough, this might be a nice place to rest and wait the storm out. The thought made no sense but it suddenly seemed like a great idea. The storm had taken on an almost surreal appearance and to Paul was beautiful.

"No!" His rational mind, what was left of it, was aware of the illogical feelings he was having. Before this diminishing saneness could think twice, Paul raised his Buck knife and drove it straight through his shoe into the top of his foot. Even in its numbed state, the pain registered. Like an eight-point-five on the Richter scale of pain. With that pain, clarity returned. And with the clarity came the fear. He yanked the knife from his foot, feeling nauseous and wondering vaguely how it got there. He must have done it freeing himself from the vine. He looked down for the first time at the calf that had been tangled. And what he saw changed everything: the same rows of welts that the girl had were there, burning red rings with a pus-filled white centers. Before he could begin listing the possibilities of what could make marks like that, he had his answer.

The beast surfaced without as much as a ripple about five feet from the rowboat. Even in the height of the storm, Paul could see this was no creation of nature ever recorded by man. Its head was large with froglike features. Bulbous eyes with translucent lids that blinked slowly regarded him with an intelligence that nearly loosened Paul's bladder. Its long, wide mouth opened, revealing multiple rows of deadly-looking teeth. Then it slithered toward him. The water swirled around the beast and suddenly there was movement flashing at him from all sides. They were tentacles, but unlike anything Paul had ever seen. Instead of the suction-cups on an octopus, these had rows of what looked like stingers.

One of the tentacles lashed at his leg but fell short. Paul realized with a bizarre feeling of pride that it fell short only because he had hacked the end of it off when it first grabbed his ankle. Another one shot at him and he tried to block it but it was too strong. The massive tentacle pinned Paul's arm to his body at an angle that snapped his wrist bone cleanly in half. Sickening pain shot up his arm as the tentacle moved to wrap itself tighter around his back. From the corner of his eye he saw another one of the beast's weapons sliding toward his leg. Knowing he couldn't fight this thing off *alone, not without some heavy artillery, he lunged forward, Buck knife extended.*

Either God or luck was on his side and the knife found the creature's eye. Paul felt a slight resistance then felt the knife slide home. He wasn't sure if he actually heard a pop, or just imagined that's what it would sound like. The beast released him, its tentacles flailing madly at the knife. Paul let go of it and scrambled toward the canoe. With his one good arm and a lot of adrenaline, he pushed the canoe free and dove into it. The vessel rocked wildly for a moment, threatening to dump Paul and the girl back into the lake. Back into the clutches of whatever beast Paul had just battled. When it stabilized, Paul got himself into the middle seat. He grabbed a coil of rope from under the seat and used it to lash his useless arm to the paddle. Grabbing the other oar with his good hand, he began rowing, using his entire body to pull the left oar as his dying arm screamed in agony with every movement. He ignored the pain, rowing like the Devil himself was chasing him. Just maybe it was.

Paul's mind tried to reject this memory. A wave of terror like nothing he had ever experienced during his panic attacks engulfed him. The dread wrapped itself around him, paralyzing him.

"What the fuck..." Dale muttered.

Paul's eyes snapped open to see both beams pointing to the opposite end of the cavern where a flickering yellow glow was brightening. One beam clicked off. "Kill the light." Dale ordered, and the second light blinked out. Paul watched as the glow brightened and his eyes adjusted to where he could make out the shape of another entrance at the far side of the cave.

And before Paul could plan his next move, everything changed.

(98)

PAUL WATCHED in silent dread as the glow resolved itself into a lantern, and that lantern was followed into the cave by Denny. He stood in the entrance for a long moment and Paul began to think he had ventured here alone. Then he turned and said something before stepping deeper into the cavern. Two figures followed him, and though Paul could only see silhouettes, he knew one was Billy and figured the other to be Father McCarthy. They spoke in hushed whispers made indistinguishable by the distance and the strange acoustics caused by the walls. Paul ran through a series of ways this scene could play out, and none of them ended well. The three figures were huddled together and Paul saw the spark of a match. Suddenly the three figures were illuminated by the light of a more powerful lantern and as Paul's eyes adjusted, he realized the third person was *not* Father McCarthy.

"Well, well, well, look who's here!"

Denny, Billy and the old man (*who is that?*) stared in the darkness beyond the reach of the lantern. His mind flashed on that night back in Billy's house when there was a mysterious third glass on the table. Flashlights clicked and Dale and Buddy were grinning like a couple of demented jack-o-lanterns as they held their flashlights shining up on their faces. They stepped into the circle of the lantern's glow and snapped their flashlights back off.

The old man spoke, unaware of just how bad this shit was going to get. "Boys, you need to get out of here, it's not safe."

Dale turned to Buddy. "Did you hear that? It's not safe!" Buddy brayed like a jackass as Dale reached into his belt and pulled the gun. "You bet your wrinkly ass it's not safe, old man."

The old man took a step toward Crawford. "What the hell are you..."

He was cut off and stopped in his tracks as a gunshot cut the stillness. Dale had fired into the air. It was deafening as it echoed in the rock chamber and Paul made his move. He whispered to Julie to stay put, unsure if she was still conscious or not. He covered the ground quickly, hoping Dale's ears were still ringing. Either hearing Paul's footsteps crunching toward him or else alerted by the looks of surprise on Denny, Billy and the old man, Crawford turned as Greymore launched at him. The gun exploded a split second before Greymore hit Crawford. He hit him high, ramming his shoulder square into Dale's sternum. The blow sent Dale's arms and head flailing as the two flew through the air. The gun crunched to the cave floor in a small cloud of bone dust as Paul came down hard on top of Crawford. Paul leaped to his feet to retrieve the weapon, but Denny had already pounced on it. Dale moaned and gasped, trying to get precious air into his lungs. Buddy was staring warily at the scene, unable to make a move without orders from his fallen leader. Denny was wildly swinging the gun back and forth between Dale and Buddy while Billy and the old man stood silently, waiting for whatever came next.

Paul had hurt his shoulder in the collision with Dale and tried to move his arm to loosen it up. He went to rub it with his left hand and was confused when he felt the warm, wetness on his shirt. Realizing Crawford's bullet hadn't gone astray, he wiped his hand on his pants and took charge, sensing the good guys were in control of the situation. He would deal with his own problem later. "Billy, your sister is over against the cave wall. She's hurt but she'll be okay. Take this shit's light"—he jerked his chin at Buddy—"and go get her. Denny, keep the gun on Crawford while...I'm sorry, who are you?" He was looking at the old man.

Mossy stepped forward. "I'm Moses Blaakman, Denny's grandfather. Call me Mossy."

Paul shook the man's hand, wincing as he did. The old man was looking at Paul's shoulder with an eyebrow arched. Paul gave a barely discernible shake of his head and the man nodded in understanding. "Paul Greymore, pleased to meet you. Give me a hand with this piece of garbage, if you don't mind." The two men forced Buddy to the ground in a sitting position, and with rope from Mossy's backpack, tied his hands behind his back.

"Dale! Where are you!" The voice echoed insanely through the cavern.

Paul knew immediately it was the third punk that had been left behind when he hurt himself. Before he could react, Buddy yelled. "We're in here..." Paul silenced him with an elbow to the head.

"Come on, Mossy, more trash to pick up. Denny, are you okay with him?"

Denny only nodded and Paul looked at him for a long moment before deciding he would be okay. Crawford was still not moving. Paul grabbed Mossy's sleeve and led him back in the direction he and Julie had entered from, knowing that's where the voice came from.

(99)

FATHER MCCARTHY glanced nervously at Cody Crawford. It had crossed his mind more than once as they stumbled through the dark woods that Crawford might just be crazy enough to kill him. The man had ranted about Greymore, pausing only for occasional gulps from his flask. Finally he had raised the flask to his lips and nothing came. He looked at it with a mixture of confusion and anger before grunting and throwing it into the darkness. That had plunged him into a morose silence interrupted by random mumblings that McCarthy could not decipher, yet which chilled him more than the earlier outbursts. One thing was sure, however: they were lost.

"Do you really believe in God, preacher-man? I mean *really* believe?"

The question and the weird tone with which it was asked put McCarthy on high alert. "Of course I do, Chief, don't you?" McCarthy waited, thinking Crawford wasn't going to answer. Finally he did, then McCarthy wished he hadn't.

"I believe in death. And I believe in evil. But God? No, no god would let things happen the way they do." He reached for his flask but came up empty. "You also believe Greymore is innocent, so where was your god while he was rotting away up in Braxton? Where was he when I was tossing my dead wife's body down a well?"

McCarthy knew the story of Crawford's wife up and leaving him with Dale still a baby. But was this...this *confession*...real? "So you believe in death and evil. Do you believe in good? And do you think the same end comes to a good man as an evil one when they die?"

Crawford answered without hesitation this time. "I believe there are good people, sure. And I think they go to a different place when they die than the bad ones. Just because there isn't a God doesn't mean there isn't a Heaven or Hell. Or something like them. I know where I'm going when my time comes, I'm just not sure about Greymore..."

His voice trailed off and McCarthy was suddenly thankful for the darkness; he had no desire to see Crawford's eyes. "Chief, I don't have to be in a confessional to hear sins."

Crawford grunted. "I don't need your forgiveness. I'd do everything I've done over again. I just want this over. Once and for all." He stopped walking, pointing the flashlight back and forth. "Goddamn, here's the trail I was looking for. Not sure how I missed it." He started walking faster and McCarthy struggled to keep up. He stopped abruptly and stepped close to McCarthy, holding the light pointing up so they could see each other. "Do you believe in evil, Father? Because we're about to see it, whether you believe or not. It might have the face of Greymore, or something else. But we are sure as shit about to see evil. What else would kill all those kids?" With that, he turned and began walking again.

(100)

DENNY TRIED not to let his hands shake as he held the gun aimed at Dale. He couldn't believe what was happening. He had never even held a gun in his life, and here he was ready to shoot one at another human being if Dale were to actually try something. But could he really do that? Could he really pull the trigger and put a bullet in Dale, wounding, if not killing him? He was about to find out: Dale was stirring. He risked a quick look around, partly to assess the situation, partly to look for help with Dale. Billy had disappeared into the shadows in the back of the cave to help Julie. His grandfather and Paul had gone off to get the third member of Crawford's trio, probably Tony. He was definitely on his own to deal with Dale.

He stared at Crawford, thinking of the years of torment he had caused Denny. Dale moaned and opened his eyes. Denny tried to swallow but his throat was as dry as the bone dust he was standing on. All of the moisture in his body seemed to be seeping out of his palms, loosening his grip on the gun. *Wait, not all*: he felt like his bladder was about to let go. His fear began to consume him. His whole life was spent afraid and now in his one redeeming moment he was going to piss his pants. *No, no way that is going to happen.* He knew if he melted down now it wouldn't just be embarrassing or cost him a beating, it could kill him. Things were so far out of hand that Dale might just be crazy or desperate enough to kill him. He took one hand off the gun and wiped the sweat on his pants. Dale was starting to lean up on his elbows; he still looked dazed but his eyes were clearing. Denny took the gun in his dry right hand and wiped the left on his pants. Dale was fully conscious and staring down Denny with a look that confirmed his earlier fears: Dale would kill him given the chance. Denny slowly brought his left hand back up to the weapon and adjusted his grip. "Don't even think it, Crawford. I will put a bullet in you with no remorse. It won't just be for me, it will be for every Denny O'Brien you fucked with during your miserable life. And I'll smile while I do it." Denny felt his lips curl into a smile. Not a smile he'd want captured for his school picture. This was a cruel smile, victorious and hateful. Dale's eyes widened, his face twitching with rage. Denny was nodding, beginning to hope Dale *would* make a move. He felt oddly calm, in control. Dale's eyes narrowed, the look of hate now fading to confusion. Denny only held his smile and kept nodding.

A loud splashing sound caught both their attentions. Dale's head snapped in the direction of the lake, Denny remained focused on Dale. Only when he saw Dale's gaze fixed on the lake did he steal a glance. The water was roiling, a violent whirlpool forming a few feet off the shore. Then the lake erupted sending cold water in all directions. The source of the eruption made Denny forget all about Dale. The thing that came out of the water had to be from Hell, or a Creature Double Feature. It was huge, at least six feet above the water, and who knew how far below. Two more feet? Three? Its head was dinosaur-like...yet almost insect-like at the same time. Like a cross between a praying mantis and a T-rex was all Denny could think of. Its jaws opened slowly, revealing multiple rows of teeth, before snapping shut with a horrific noise that sounded like a bear trap closing. Its body was a scaly green, reptilian, with tentacles swirling around it—*four of them,* Denny thought, but it was hard to tell. Two thick arms ended in horrific talon-like claws. The worst was its eyes: black and bottomless, dead eyes that tried to hide intelligence behind hate and death and destruction. Eyes that held Denny's gaze, even as the creature began walking toward him. Its legs were powerful and as it stepped into shallow water, Denny could see webbed feet. Despite its slow, almost hypnotic approach, Denny sensed a speed and strength in the beast, like a coiled spring.

"Shoot it! Shoot the fucking thing!" Buddy screamed, his voice one pitch away from insanity.

It was Buddy, oddly enough, who probably saved Denny's life. At least for the moment. His panicked scream caused the creature to turn its attention from Denny, and when it did Denny reacted. He turned his body, and the gun, to face the creature, tightened his grip on the pistol, and began pulling the trigger. The first shot was deafening; the rest went almost unnoticed when the screaming began. The beast howled when the bullet struck. Then Denny saw just how quick it could move.

In a blur of flashing scales and swirling tentacles, it was on Buddy, even as Denny emptied the gun into its hideous body. Buddy's struggles were as short as they were futile, and as the hammer clicked on empty chambers, the creature dragged Buddy's limp body back toward deeper water. Denny let the gun drop from his hands as he watched in horror. Just before the creature took him under, Denny saw Buddy's eyes, open and aware, but somehow already dead. It wasn't until the beast was gone that Denny realized he was screaming too. When he managed to stop, it was a much worse sound that Denny heard. It started like the distant rumble of a train on faraway tracks, but quickly became thunderous. Denny's feet started vibrating and then the rocks began to fall: his shots had started a cave-in.

Greymore appeared, dragging Denny back from the water toward the back of the cave. Denny had no idea where anyone else was, including Dale or his own grandfather, but he was powerless against Greymore's strength guiding him to safety from the crumbling cave. They made it out the way Denny had entered, just as a shower of boulders crashed behind them: the cave was sealed. Denny immediately turned and began trying to dig through the rubble but again Greymore got hold of him and pulled him further away.

"Denny, we have to wait until it stabilizes. We aren't going to help anybody if we get crushed!"

Denny slumped into Greymore's arms and all of the fear and stress began pouring out in his tears. "Billy...my best friend...my grandfather..."

"I know, Denny. I promise we'll find a way back in, but not yet." Denny felt Greymore's body stiffen. "Denny, that thing, it's what killed the girl back in '61...it must have killed them all."

Denny wiped his eyes, tried to see Paul but it was sheer darkness. "And it killed my dog...he helped make it...my grandfather...and he knows how to kill it." And suddenly the freight-train roar started and the rocks began falling again.

(101)

ROBERT ORTIZ and Chris McCauley had no trouble finding the entrance to the tunnel left open by Mossy and the boys. Once they descended, they had trouble finding *anything*. Ortiz had a keen sense of direction but had no idea what he was looking for and had them zigzagging back and forth, all the while trying to stick to downward slopes that he knew would take them toward the lake. Ortiz was armed with a powerful flashlight and an equally powerful gun, this one his own, not police issued. McCauley was armed with nothing but the camera Mossy had bought for his brother. Perhaps, he thought, it was always meant for him. Bittersweet memories of his brother came, and with them came fear. *Something scared him bad enough to take his own life after spending 17 years trying to drown the memory of it, and I'm in its lair.*

Time was irrelevant down here; it could have been ten minutes or two hours since they had climbed down the ladder. They had already drained the small canteen that Chris had hooked to his belt. Now the only thing that mattered was walking behind the beam cast by Ortiz's four-D-cell flashlight and trying not to turn and run the other way. That and the unbearable quiet broken only by their own shuffling footsteps and heavy breathing. As they moved deeper, McCauley began to pick up another sound. Ortiz had figured it out before he could.

"Sounds like water. We're heading in the direction of the lake, there must be some run-off…"

The rest of his theory was cut off by another sound, and this one McCauley could identify even with the strange echoey acoustics; it was a gunshot.

"That came from up ahead!" Ortiz was already moving that way, fast.

They made their way as quickly as they could through the labyrinth of tunnels, and time played its tricks again. Finally, McCauley heard shouting, much closer than the gunshot: they were heading in the right direction. After a few steps, more shots rang out followed by screaming like he'd never heard before. But it wasn't that sound that stopped him, it was the next. A distant rumbling growing louder, then the tunnel began to shake violently and rocks began to fall around him. "Robert!" Ortiz hadn't stopped at the sound and had turned a corner out of sight, leaving Chris without light in the thickening dust and crashing rocks. This is how it's going to end, he thought. With only thoughts of his father and brother, he pinned himself as close to the side of the tunnel as he could and continued forward.

(102)

MOSSY TURNED when he heard the panicked screams of Dale Crawford and found himself reliving a nightmare. The beast reared out of the water and the gunshots began. It moved with inhuman speed but Mossy's eyes followed it. He bent slowly and shifted the backpack from his shoulder. He felt for the buckle, not wanting to take his eyes off the beast even for a split-second. Then the cave-in started and the gloomy, flickering darkness was obscured by thick dust. The sound was like nothing Mossy had ever heard...deafening and terrifying. He rose to his feet, the canister in the backpack forgotten. Where was the beast? He was struck from behind with enough force to send him sprawling headlong. He struggled to catch his breath while trying to turn and get to his feet. He got a hold of an arm and a throat and suddenly realized he was not battling the beast; just a boy.

"Denny?"

"No, it's me. Billy. What the hell is going on?"

Mossy wasn't sure if he was talking about the beast or the cave-in. "No time, let's find a safe place before this whole place comes down on us." He kept his grip on Billy's arm and started to move, but Billy didn't budge.

"My sister...Denny..."

"We'll find them, I promise, but we can't if we're dead. Let's move!" He dragged Billy toward the back of the cave, in the general direction of where Julie was. And more important, away from the beast. They found their way to the cave wall as rocks and dust continued to fly. The train-like rumble began to subside as they huddled under an overhang in the rear of the cave. Finally, it stopped, and with the exception of a few random rocks and pebbles falling, all was quiet. Mossy sensed Billy starting to get up. "Hold tight, Billy. Let's just make sure it's really over."

Billy uttered a frustrated sigh that turned into a dust-provoked coughing fit. A light clicked on and illuminated the dust-filled air into a swirling craze of shadows. "Reminds me of the moors from an old werewolf movie," Billy croaked.

"Indeed. It might not settle for a while but the shaking seems to be done. Let's find who's...let's find the rest of them and get out of here."

Billy handed him the light and together they began to tentatively explore their surroundings. They began moving in the direction they agreed Julie was, but were met immediately by a wall of rock. It went as high as they could reach. They began following it by feel in the direction of the water, and were stopped again by solid rock on that side. Fear crept into Mossy's heart; coldness spread from his chest to his limbs. Were they entombed? Left to starve or suffocate? He didn't realize Billy had left his side until he heard the voice through the dust.

"This way, Mossy."

The voice seemed to come from everywhere...and nowhere. He moved toward Billy, not because he could follow the voice through the strange acoustics of the cave, but because it was the only direction he could move. They picked their way through the cave blindly until they once again hit a wall of rock. Mossy closed his eyes; certain this time that they would have to dig for their lives, then felt a tug on his leg.

"Bend down; I think there's a way through."

Billy had found a tunnel down at ground level. Mossy bent down and followed Billy through on hands and knees. As they crawled through the tunnel the dust began to dissipate. Mossy's light caught a flash of something on the tunnel floor and for a moment he thought it was a trick of his mind. "There are markings on the ground, Billy! Someone has been here."

Mossy heard a hitching sob before Billy answered. "I know, it was me and Denny. We can get out this way, and get back to the underground lake the other way."

Mossy uttered a non-committal grunt and kept crawling. If they got out, he didn't know how to tell Billy that going back in wasn't a good idea. In his heart, he knew they were the only two getting out. Other than the God-forsaken creature that had drawn them there in the first place.

(103)

DENNY AND Greymore ran through the tunnel as fast as the light from Greymore's flashlight would allow. If the noise wasn't bad enough, the thickening dust was making breathing difficult. They rounded a sharp bend and came to a dead end. They doubled-checked the markers they left, knowing before they did that the way out was blocked. The cave-in subsided; faint rumblings continued but they were more like a hungry belly than a freight train.

"This way." Paul grabbed Denny's arm and pulled him down a smaller side-tunnel. It ended in a small cave that seemed intact. "We'll wait it out here for a bit, rest, make a plan. And you can tell me about your grandfather's theory on killing that thing."

Denny and Paul sat down against the cave wall and Paul switched off the light. "Gotta conserve the batteries."

Denny nodded, not realizing Paul couldn't see him. Then he began telling the story of Mossy. Paul interjected a couple times with questions, but for the most part Denny rambled on, barely stopping to take a breath, until he had brought Paul completely up to speed.

"And you think what's in those canisters will kill that thing?"

Denny thought about it. "Well, he believes it. So I guess, yeah, I do too."

"Good enough for me. We'll rest here a few minutes, find a way back into the main cave, and we'll fuck that thing up good."

Denny couldn't help but laugh at the absurdity of the situation, and Paul joined in.

After a few minutes, Denny began to feel drowsy, then he jolted, returning to a full wide-awake state from that mystical place between consciousness and sleep. He was half dreaming about being in his basement, but here he was, huddled against the damp wall of the cave. In the impenetrable darkness, his sense of hearing seemed heightened. The sound of his and Greymore's breathing was like twin steam engines chugging up a hill. *I think I can. I think I can.* Denny didn't know whether to start screaming or start laughing. He wasn't sure which would be a sign of insanity. The only other sound was water. There was water running somewhere nearby, and water dripping all around. It was maddening.

The sudden light made Denny gasp, then squint against the brightness. Greymore had flicked on his small flashlight and pointed it down, so a small halo of light illuminated both of them instead of shining on one and leaving the other in darkness. He noticed Greymore was looking at him, his expression hard to read. Partly because of the strange combination of light and shadow, partly because of Greymore's disfigurement. Mostly because his expression was one Denny could not evaluate. Denny swallowed hard, trying to think of something to say to fill the void. *I think I can, I think I can.* "What should we do?"

Greymore continued to stare at him, a hint of a smile playing on his face now. "Not much we can do, we'll wait here for a bit. Rest. Then we'll find our way out." His smile faded into a grimace as he changed position.

Denny's gaze fell on Greymore's shoulder and the widening dark stain. "Paul...you're hurt..."

Paul nodded, not even dignifying his wound with a glance. "It's fine. The bullet went all the way through, I felt the exit wound on the back of my shoulder. Muscle damage and some pain, but the bleeding isn't as bad as it looks."

Denny shook his head slowly. Paul had been shot and he was talking about it like he got a splinter. His admiration for the man swelled. It was an alien feeling but one that wasn't new, just dormant. He realized he hadn't really felt that way about anyone since his father was killed. As much as a wounded Greymore should have made Denny worry about their chances, Paul's strength filled him with renewed confidence that they would eventually get out of this.

The thought of waiting it out was only slightly more inviting than just trying to get out. He was scared. As much as he fully believed Greymore was not the Butcher, did not kill kids seventeen years ago, and did not kill anybody since getting out, it was all easier to believe the opposite sitting in a dark cave alone with him.

"Did you ever kill anyone, Paul?" The question came from nowhere. It never really entered Denny's mind to ask, but there it was, popping out of his mouth. And surprisingly clear, no quivering or shaking or stuttering. Like he was asking for the time.

Greymore's eyes shifted. Not his gaze or direction, but...his eyes. His slightly bemused expression was now gone, replaced by something else. Not something scary, but more wistful, remorseful. "Yes, Denny, I have. But not who you might think."

Denny felt a ripple of fear, but for some reason he wasn't that scared. He felt a connection to Greymore, maybe it had been there all along, but now it was about to be out in the open. Denny waited, not really wanting to hear about death and killing, but knowing it would help Paul to talk about it. Knowing it would help change his eyes back from wherever they were looking now.

"I didn't kill any of those kids, Denny..."

"I know, but..."

"It's okay, let me tell the story. I didn't kill any of them. I had never killed anything when they...when he put me away. I used to fish but I'd always throw them back. Never hunted. I just couldn't conceive of taking a life, animal or man. Hell, I used to catch moths and let them out the window when I was a kid.

"When I got to Braxton...I had never been away from home before. Never been to camp or on sleepovers. Now I was away from everything that felt safe. In a place where everyone else around me had done bad things. Really bad things. But they thought I was worse than them. They thought I killed kids.

"It started out slow. A lot of looks, a lot of whispering. And not just the inmates, the guards, too. Then more little things. Shit in my bunk when I came back from the yard. Smaller portions than everyone else at every meal. Stupid things. They were testing me, seeing how much I would take. And I took it all. Working out was the only thing that kept me sane. I punished myself every day, getting bigger and stronger. And angrier.

"Things had started escalating pretty quickly. Name-calling became shoving matches. Pretty soon fights in the yard, then beatings. Again, guards and inmates, they were all the same, all enemies united against the child-killer. The *freak*. It all made me work out harder. The workouts were, I don't know, a pressure valve for the anger I felt. Then they came for me one night. In the showers…"

"Paul, you don't have to…."

"There were a lot of them. Mostly prisoners, a couple guards. They held me down. Held me while one of them…hurt me. At the same time, others carved up my arms. At first I was afraid I was going to die, and then I wished I *would* die. I was losing my mind. Right then and there. I could feel everything human shutting down, like a turbine engine…shutting down, losing power. Then the yelling and calling I had been blocking out got through. 'Who's next, boys? Who wants sloppy seconds?'

"Then I wasn't shutting down. I wanted to live and I wanted to make these people pay. For what they were doing to me. For what they wanted to do. For putting me in that awful place. And I snapped. Everything that had built up inside me found an outlet. My hands and feet became weapons. Bodies were flying everywhere until I found the one who had raped me. I got him by the throat and I didn't let go. I heard things breaking in his neck. I looked into his eyes and watched the life drain out of them.

"I don't know how long I kept squeezing. The guards had been beating me the whole time. It wasn't until I was sure he was really dead that I would let myself feel their blows, acknowledge the pain. I woke up two days later in solitary. I had a concussion, broken ribs, bruises everywhere. They had stitched me up before throwing me in the hole. After that, I knew I would get out. It's not like I had a vision or found God or anything. I just knew. People left me alone, they were afraid. The 'incident' as they called it, was swept under the rug. What could they do? The guards were there helping, so my sentence wasn't impacted.

"After that I was a model prisoner, and the others let me be. I kept up my workouts. I still worked out hard, harder than anyone, but it was different. Before, it was like I had to, like I was preparing for that night…Anyway, it wasn't long after that when Father McCarthy started coming around. It started as a group thing, and then eventually it was one on one. He saved me. Father McCarthy, not the capital 'H' he. Or maybe they both did."

Denny swallowed hard. Of all the things he had expected Paul to tell him, this wasn't one. It made his own problems dealing with bullies in school seem laughable. Then again, it was really the same thing, wasn't it? Different degrees, certainly, but when all was said and done, it was the same. And Paul had overcome it all to return to Haven. To what end? To be trapped in a stinking cave with a scared kid? Denny shook his head, there had to be more. If there was anything he took away from his days in church, it was that God had some grand plan for everything. As the cliché goes "He works in mysterious ways." Denny had always thought this to be the great Catholic cop-out to explain away things that couldn't be explained with logic. What kind of plan could put these two unlikely allies in a wet cave, hunting—or being hunted by—some man-made predator?

"We should move."

Denny jumped at the sound of Greymore's voice. The shine from the flashlight was fading to a yellowish glow, the batteries draining away. "I'm scared, Paul. Scared to sit here hiding, scared to move."

Paul managed a weak smile. "Me too, Denny. Here's how I see it. We can't sit here forever. That means we move at some point. The longer we sit, the hungrier and more tired we get, the weaker we get. Our best chance is now, and we still have some strength and light left to work with."

It wasn't much, but it was enough for Denny. He stretched as he stood hunched in the low-ceilinged cave. He removed his backpack and pulled an extra flashlight, clicking it on briefly to make sure it worked. "You're right, let's go." He had wanted to sound brave, or at least not scared shitless, but it didn't work. His voice came out as a shaky squeak.

(104)

MOSSY AND Billy followed the markers, careful not to move too quickly. It would be too easy to miss a marker hidden by dust or fallen rock and make a wrong turn that could be deadly. They stopped at every fork or intersecting tunnel until they found the marker. At one point, had they veered off-course and gone left instead of straight as the marker told them, they would have met a very lost Robert Ortiz.

"Mossy, I think we should go back, this is taking too long." Billy recognized the whine in his voice but he was running on pure adrenaline and emotion at this point and had little control over what he sounded like.

Mossy stopped and bent to face Billy. "Listen, we know the others entered from the other side of the cavern. They must have gone in through the opening you found by the lake. We'll go out the way we came, go through the woods, and try getting back in from that side."

"And if it's blocked…"

Mossy grabbed him by the shoulders and cut him off. "If it's blocked, we'll blow up that bridge when we come to it." He said it with a confidence he didn't feel. "Let's keep moving, okay?"

Billy nodded and Mossy nodded back, his heart aching knowing Denny might be back there crushed under fallen rocks, or worse, killed by the monster he had created. Either way, how could he face his daughter? He stood and turned, focusing only on finding the next marker.

They arrived at the ladder exhausted and covered with dust from the cave-in. Mossy was barely able to climb the ladder and it was only visions of Janice and Denny that kept his body moving. He could see the events were wearing on Billy as well, mentally more than physically. His sister and best friend were in there, oh, and not to mention he'd just seen something that only exists in horror movies kill a kid he knew. He had not spoken of the creature since they left the cave-in, only of finding Denny and Julie.

"Billy…can you get us…to the other entrance?" Mossy gasped.

"Sure, but first can we take a break? Just a few minutes?"

Mossy looked at the young boy with a new sense of admiration. He had no doubt the break was for him, not Billy. The boy could run back the way they came, grab the backpack…Mossy's heart stopped for a full beat when he realized what he'd done. Now everything that happened this night had truly been for nothing. His heart restarted causing him to gasp. *I will find a way*, he thought. "No time to rest, lead the way, young man."

Mossy began to feel better in the fresh night air. It didn't hurt that they were moving downhill and not having to stop every few minutes to crouch down and move rocks looking for a marker. He didn't know how far a walk it was to the entrance, but as much as he wanted to get there quickly, he dreaded every step because of what it might lead to.

(105)

DENNY STEPPED into the cavern and flashed his light around. Clouds of dust still hung in the air but it had thinned enough for Denny to survey the damage. It was worse than he thought it would be. Giant mounds of rock obscured his view in every direction, except where the lake started. Part of the rear wall had collapsed completely, making the cavern seem much smaller than it had been. He felt deflated, exhausted. *There is no way anybody survived this.* He leaned against the wall and slid to the ground, unable to hold back the tears. His entire body shook from anger, sorrow and exhaustion. He felt a hand on his shoulder, and for some reason it calmed him enough to get his tears under control. He was still shaking as he stood and faced Paul. Shining his light up, he was shocked. Greymore looked like he'd aged ten years. His eyes were sunk in his head, surrounded by deep purple depressions. His face was pale and haggard, too pale. Denny moved the light down and saw his shirt was soaked completely through. The wound was worse than he'd let on. A lot worse.

Before he could speak, a sound came from somewhere in the cavern. It was a small sound, just a single moan generated out of sheer pain and terror, but to Denny it was hope. "That's Julie! Paul, you stay here, rest, I'll find her." Paul nodded weakly, his eyes starting to go glassy, and sat down against the cave wall. Denny pulled off his own shirt and wrapped it under Paul's armpit and tied it as tightly as he could on top of his shoulder. It would have to do.

Without thinking about what else might lie behind the rocks, he headed in the direction he thought would take him to Julie. "Julie! Can you hear me?" He listened carefully, and was rewarded with another faint moan. "Julie, I'm coming! If you can't speak, try to pick up a rock and bang it against another one!" He was moving from one mountain of rock to the next, searching for a way through. By the time he heard the clacking of two rocks, he knew what he would have to do to get to her. Swallowing a mouthful of rock dust and some of his fear, he headed toward the lake.

The cave-in extended partway into the water but not all the way to the far wall. As he took a first tentative step into the black water, he remembered the roiling whirlpool and the unearthly speed of the thing that came out of it and took Buddy. Still, he took a second step and a third, now up to his knees, feeling his way with his hands, praying for a break in the rocks before he had to go much deeper. The click-clack of the rocks, of *Julie's* rocks, kept him moving.

Four steps, now five. *Click-clack. Click-clack.* Up to his thighs. Six. Seven. He gasped as the icy water went to his waist. Eight. Now he had to hold the light higher to keep it dry. A couple more steps and he would have to swim. He inched his foot forward and his hand slid on top of the rocks. Carefully, he pushed his hand deeper and met with no resistance. He reached across with his other hand and placed the flashlight on the ledge. *Click-clack.* Fainter now even though he knew he was closer. "Almost there, Julie." He whispered, not sure if it was true or not.

He climbed carefully out of the water, the slippery rocks underfoot threatening to send him headlong into the beast's pool. But he was careful, and he was driven. Too much depended on this for failure. *Click-clack.* He was now kneeling on the small ledge and he could see a way to get down the other side. Where Julie was from there he didn't know. *Click-clack.* But he knew he was closer.

He climbed down into the shallow water on the far side of the rock ledge and scampered to shore. He made his way slowly toward the rear of the cavern where he thought Julie was, climbing over piles of fallen rock when he could, finding a way around them when he couldn't. He could see the far wall less than twenty feet away. *Where is she?* It had been a few minutes since he'd heard the rocks banging together.

"Julie! Can you hear me?" He listened intently, not breathing. Finally a sound, barely a sound, the rocks scraping together more than banging, reached his ears. It was from behind a pile of boulders just a few feet to his left, and to him the sound was beautiful. *Like the girl making it*, he thought with a grin, and started jogging toward it. Two steps later he landed flat on his face. In his haste he had foolishly tripped over a rock. Frustrated by his own carelessness, he kicked angrily at the rock and was shocked when it moved. More shocked by the clanging noise it made. He shone his beam and cried out in surprise. The backpack! He crawled over, and unbuckled it. Both canisters were there and they were both full. His elation of a moment ago turned to agony. *Mossy didn't make it.* Shining the light around the area of the backpack only confirmed it: huge piles of boulders were littering this section of the cavern. Fighting back tears, he stood and made his way carefully to where he now knew Julie to be.

She was there behind the last pile of rocks, more *under* it than behind it. Both of her legs and her left arm were pinned under the rocks. Somehow she had gotten hold of a rock small enough to lift and had been banging it against the very pile that held her captive. Without letting himself think of just how hurt she might be, he began moving the rocks that held her. She was unconscious, probably a good thing, as Denny struggled with some of the rocks and was probably hurting her more. But he had to get her out. He thought of calling for Paul's help but quickly dismissed it. Even if he could make it over, he was too weak to be of much help. It was up to him alone to save her.

He worked feverishly, moving rocks bigger than he had any right to. He had her arm free and her legs uncovered to her knees, but a huge boulder sat on both her ankles. Denny cringed thinking of what it had done to her bones. He grabbed it, and using his legs and back, tried to stand it up. When it barely moved, he felt panic begin to rise. *Now what?* Breathing hard, he closed his eyes to think. A soft moan caused his eyes to fly open and he flashed the light on Julie. She wore a mask of bruises and had several cuts that looked ugly but not dangerous. Her eyes widened when they focused on Denny, and amazingly, she smiled.

"I knew you'd come."

Denny swallowed hard. Her eyes had a strange look. *She's in shock*, the Great Oz told him. He *had* to get her out. "Julie, can you move your arms?"

She looked at him, her eyes not focusing, filled with confusion and fear. Then they closed. *You're on your own, kid, but you can do this.* It was his own thought but he chose to believe it sounded like his dad, or maybe Jimmy. He turned his back to the rock that was now his nemesis and bent low. He found handholds and gripped tightly with both hands. He took a couple of deep breaths and focused all his energy on his legs. With a strangled cry, he pushed upward with everything he had. He felt like his body was trying to tear itself apart from the inside, but he kept going. The rock moved, fueling Denny. With one last, great burst, he shot upward and the rock lifted on end. It threatened to tip back onto Julie's legs so he did the only thing he could think of and threw himself backwards into it.

For a horrifying second, he knew it was going to fall back the way it came, crushing him *and* Julie. Then he felt it overbalance and went tumbling on top of it as it rolled off of her. He let out another cry as the skin peeled off his bare back during his ride down the rock, and came to rest next to Julie. He turned his head and could see she was free, but now what? How could he get her over the ledge and to safety? He needed Paul. He scrambled to his feet and made his way back to the ledge. "Paul? Can you hear me?" He waited, thinking Paul might have slipped into unconsciousness.

"I'm here, Denny. Should I come over?"

Denny was shocked. His voice sounded stronger and like it was coming from just over the ledge. Maybe he had been at it for longer than he thought. "No, I think I can get her to the ledge if you can pull her over from there."

"Okay, give it a shot."

Denny scrambled back to Julie and gently patted her face, reminding Denny of when Mossy fell asleep in the woods by the high school. "Julie, can you hear me?" She stirred a bit but didn't come around. He went to the lake's edge and dipped his hands in, hurried back to her and once again slapped her face gently with his wet hands. This time her eyes opened. "Julie, can you hear me? Are you awake?"

She blinked, tried to speak but ended up just nodding.

He grabbed her hand and lifted it so she could see what he was doing. "Can you squeeze my hand?" Even in this situation, he felt himself blushing furiously. He felt her squeeze his hand and quickly hopped to the other side. "This hand now, Julie, can you squeeze again?" Weaker this time, but he definitely felt it. "Julie, I have to get you to the other side of the cave. I have to drag you. It's going to hurt your legs, I think." Incredibly, she raised her right hand and made a circle with her thumb and forefinger.

He got behind her and managed to get his hands under her armpits and lift her enough to hook his elbow under her, blushing again when his hands brushed the sides of her breasts. She made no sound but Denny knew he was hurting her. He began to drag her toward the ledge. "I'm sorry Julie, I know it hurts but we have to get you out of here." He was near tears, partly from exhaustion, partly from sympathy. When her hand reached up and grabbed his arm, he was rejuvenated, dragging her to the ledge and propping her in a sitting position.

"Paul, are you there?"

"Right here, pal. What should I do?"

"I'm going to try to lift her and have her arms up. If you can reach over and get a hold of them and pull, I can help push from this side."

"Okay, I'm ready whenever you are."

Paul's voice had lost some of the strength Denny had heard just a few minutes ago. This frightened Denny to the core. Paul was hurt bad, maybe bleeding to death. Denny was physically exhausted and emotionally numb. *How are we ever going to get Julie over the ledge, never mind out of the caves and back to his house?* Before the Great Oz or anyone else could offer an answer, Denny's eyes were drawn toward the water. For a split second he was able to tell himself it was just his imagination, but when he flashed his light over he could see the swirling and he suddenly understood the expression "deer in the headlights." He couldn't move. The swirling grew faster and spread into ever-widening circles and Denny stood mesmerized, waiting for the beast to appear.

{106}

ROBERT ORTIZ awoke from his rock-induced nap with his lungs full of dust and hands slapping his face. He had no idea how long he'd been out but he did remember what had put him out. When the cave-in started, he'd kept moving thinking Chris was right behind him. When he called back to him without turning and gotten no response, he stopped and turned. The damage behind him was frightening; the passage looked completely blocked, although the rising dust and still-falling rock made it hard to be sure. He couldn't leave Chris, so he tried to make his way back. He'd made it exactly one step when a rock fell from above, ricocheted off the wall in front of him, and caught him just above the ear.

"Chris, you're okay."

Chris reached toward him and Ortiz was terrified to see his hand disappear into a gray blur to his right. A second later pain erupted on the right side of his head and he felt everything start to slip sideways.

"Robert, stay with me." Chris sounded a step away from panic.

Ortiz struggled to hold on to his slippery grip on consciousness. A scary moment passed when blurry black spots formed and started to grow larger, blotting out everything. He closed his eyes and when he opened them, they had gone. There was still a gray cloud floating on the right side of his vision, but the feeling he was going to pass out had gone for now. "I'm okay, Chris. Help me up."

"Robert, are you sure? I think you should sit tight, you've got a nasty goose-egg and I didn't think you were going to come around." Maybe only half a step away from panic.

"I'll take it slow, come on, pull me up."

When he got to his feet, the black spots made an encore appearance. Gasping to get air and still dizzy, he clenched his fists and willed himself to stay conscious. *Concussion, and a bad one*, he thought. He heard Chris talking but it sounded miles away. He felt his knees buckling and leaned against the wall of the tunnel. "I'll be okay in a minute."

"Okay, Robert, take all the time you need. Seems like it's over, for now at least. Stay here, I think I see your flashlight beam on the ground."

Ortiz felt his head clear a bit and his stomach had settled. A moment later, Chris came back with the flashlight.

"It was almost buried, luckily it was still on and I saw the beam shining. It's a little banged up but still works."

Ortiz nodded, and only small black dots winked at him, a good sign. "I think we should keep going forward, toward the sound of shots that started the cave-in. There must be another way out in that direction, probably close to the lake."

Chris looked like that was the last thing he wanted to hear. "Okay, whenever you're ready."

"Let's do this. Take it slow, okay?"

With Ortiz leaning heavily on Chris, behind a flickering flashlight beam, they went on.

{107}

IT WAS Paul's voice that brought Denny back.

"Denny, get her over the ledge. Quick!"

He snapped out of it and went to work. With strength he didn't know he had—hell, a few minutes ago he *didn't* have—he reached down and hauled Julie up in a bear hug. This time he didn't blush when he felt the soft swell of her breasts against his bare chest. Holding her in a standing position, he grabbed her left hand and threw it up toward the top of the ledge. Without his light he couldn't see what was happening in the water. He didn't have to: he could hear it. "Paul, can you grab her hand?" He had to shout above the raging torrent in the lake.

He felt Julie's arm tug and knew Paul had her. He slid his grip down so he was hugging her legs and lifted, knowing Paul was pulling from the other side. He winced when he felt Julie's lower legs slide by as Paul finished hauling her over the ledge. It seemed like her ankles were made of sand instead of bone and her feet flopped around like nothing was holding them on but her skin. He pushed the thought away.

"I've got her Denny, you next, put your hands up as high as you can."

Denny grabbed his light and pointed it toward the water. What was illuminated there almost stopped his heart.

The creature was there, standing in the water beyond the ledge, thirty feet away if not closer. Its tentacles were in constant motion, swirling around it in an almost hypnotic way. Its eyes locked on Denny's. *It can't see Paul on the other side of the ledge*, Denny realized. "Paul, get Julie back to the tunnel on your side. I'll climb back over in a minute." He tried keeping his voice calm, somehow knowing the creature would pick up on fear or panic. He was amazed at how normal he sounded.

Paul's reply was soft, tired. "Okay, Denny."

He heard the sounds of Paul moving Julie, never taking his eyes off the creature. The creature glanced in that direction but made no move. Satisfied it was not going after Paul, Denny began to slowly move backwards toward the rear of the cave where he'd found Julie. The creature again fixed its murderous gaze on Denny. The tentacles all seemed to reach in his direction. Denny knew it would come for him. As if it had read his thoughts, it took a slow step toward him. Denny knew how quickly it could move and that outrunning it was not an option. If he could keep it moving slow he had a chance. With his bladder threatening to let go, he forced himself to take another shaky step backwards, then another. The creature's steps matched his own, almost tauntingly.

Finally he felt his foot hit the prize he was searching for and was rewarded with the sound of the canisters clanging together in the backpack. The creature was now out of the water and standing next to the ledge. Denny kept his eyes and his flashlight beam on it while he crouched and started unlatching the backpack's buckles. After some fumbling, he got them opened and grabbed one of the canisters. The creature had not moved, just watched. Denny had paid close attention when Mossy had demonstrated how to release the poison. It wasn't meant to be a lesson, but for some reason, for *this* reason, Denny had taken it as one.

Denny rose to his feet, the flashlight in one hand still trained on the creature, the canister in his other hand. The cave was silent except for the constant trickling of water and Denny's own breathing. The creature made no sound at all and Denny heard no movement from the other side of the ledge. Denny knew what had to happen next. The hand holding the light on the creature began to twitch, then shake. Denny's entire body was trembling and the creature cocked its head, confused when Denny took the first step forward. Barely able to take a breath, he forced a second step, then a third. The creature's tentacles began to swirl and it crouched slightly. Denny wondered if it was a defensive posture or if it was about to spring. If it was the latter, he knew he would not have time to release the contents of the canister. He stopped walking, now just fifteen feet from the monster and close enough to realize what a nightmare it truly was.

It stood at least eight feet tall. Its green and black body was protected by heavy scales, its arms and legs solid muscle. Its hands were clawed, almost talon-like, and the tentacles were decorated on the undersides with rows of suction-cup-looking things. Some of them seemed to have a sharp hook in the center, others didn't. They all pulsated, opening and closing as if searching for prey. One of them was shorter than the rest, ending in a stump, *an old injury of some sort*, Denny thought. But its head was the worst. Denny couldn't figure what DNA combination could have resulted in the horror he was looking at. Its jaw was elongated and Denny could see rows of teeth, no doubt razor-sharp. The closest Denny's mind could come was part dinosaur, part insect and part reptile. But it was the eyes that filled Denny with dread more than anything. Up close, they were pure cunning and evil. That's when he noticed they were not the same. One looked deformed...no...damaged. It was closed slightly and surrounded by scar tissue.

The moment had come and he slowly, very slowly, brought his hands together. The creature tensed more. It's intelligent, Denny knew this, and perceptive. Somehow it sensed Denny was a threat despite his slow movements. He thought he heard a voice (voices?) from the other side of the ledge. He had to hurry before Paul tried to climb over. Denny turned the lid of the canister until it clicked. Now he was just one pull away, similar to pulling the pin on a grenade, from releasing the poison. *What if it doesn't work?* He tried to swallow but his throat was a desert and caked with dust from the cave-in. He slowly began to pull the pin. Suddenly, the creature's head snapped to the left. It was tall enough to see over the ledge.

Denny saw his opportunity, yanked the pin and tossed the canister at the creature's feet. In a blur the beast was gone, over the rock ledge. As the poisonous gas formed a cloud where the creature stood just seconds ago, the screaming began.

(108)

GREYMORE MOVED as quickly as he could in his condition (which wasn't quick at all), dragging Julie's limp body to the tunnel entrance. He wasn't sure they could even get out that way and that they might end up lugging her right back over the ledge at some point. As weak as he felt now, he didn't know how that would be possible. And where the hell was Denny? He said he'd climb over himself but there was no sign of him. He was about to call him when something—instinct maybe—told him to keep silent. It was then he heard the shuffling sounds coming from the tunnel. He knew it could be Mossy or Billy, but it could just as easily be Crawford and his thugs. Thug, he corrected himself, the beast had evened the odds a bit.

There was no time to move Julie, who was propped up against the wall next to the tunnel. Instead, he grabbed a rock the size of a softball and crouched in the dark near the entrance. After a long few moments, he saw the beam of a flashlight reaching for the entrance and heard the sound of footsteps. He tensed, ready to leap at Crawford and rearrange his skull with the rock. He blinked in surprise when two adults stepped into the cave. He recognized one as the deputy that drove him home after his night in jail, but the other was a stranger. Another police officer perhaps. His mind could come up with no reason they would end up here. He spoke quietly, partly to not scare the shit out of them, but mostly due to the same instinct that kept him from calling out to Denny. "Robert, fancy meeting you here."

Ortiz wheeled around and a gun appeared in his hand from the folds of his shirt. Greymore blinked as the flashlight beam found his face and was relieved Ortiz wasn't jumpy enough to shoot blindly at his voice.

"Mr. Greymore." Ortiz said amiably, putting his gun away. "Paul, I thought I'd find you here."

Paul said nothing, only glanced back and forth between Ortiz and the other man, obviously confused.

Ortiz picked up on it. "This is Chris McCauley. He's here...unofficially, like I am. Whatever the hell you came down here to kill is responsible for his brother's death."

Greymore was stunned. *How can he know?* Then he noticed something off about Ortiz. He looked unsteady and seemed to be having trouble focusing on Paul. "Robert, you're hurt. What..."

The movement was so fast, so *eerily* fast, that Greymore knew it could have killed them all. The creature had bounded over the rock ledge and was standing just twenty feet from them. It was hideous, more disturbing than anything his memory or even his imagination could have come up with. It stared at the group, motionless except for its tentacles which waved slowly up and down. Its jaw slowly opened, dripping saliva and revealing murderous teeth before snapping shut. Its eyes then shifted, from one man to the next until they landed on Greymore. Something changed, something imperceptible, perhaps to everyone but Paul. *It remembers me.* The thought amazed him and terrified him. Its eyes stayed locked on Paul's, seeming to focus. The tentacles continued their slow dance around the creature's scaled body.

Paul glared back at the monstrosity, comparing it to the vague memories he had. He immediately noticed the one tentacle that ended so abruptly and the disfigured eye, both his handiwork. Chris McCauley was screaming, as was Julie who had come to at some point. Paul could only stare as the creature began moving toward him.

(109)

DENNY RECOGNIZED one of the screaming voices immediately—Julie! Without thinking, he grabbed the backpack and scrambled to the ledge. He felt like he sometimes did in nightmares, like he was moving in slow motion, like something didn't want him to get to the other side. When he finally reached the top, what he saw in the flickering light could only be a nightmare. Julie lay awkwardly against the cave wall, trying to slide deeper into the cave, dragging her shattered legs. Two men Denny didn't recognize were standing in the cave entrance behind Greymore. Paul was motionless, facing down the beast like a gunfighter in an old western. The creature was creeping toward Greymore, deliberately, tentacles swirling hypnotically around it. Denny knew as soon as it was in range, those tentacles would reach for him. Without thinking, Denny grabbed the second canister and jumped from the ledge.

He landed with a splash in the shallow water of the lake and slogged toward the creature while turning the top of the canister until it clicked. He looked up to see the creature had turned its attention from Greymore and was now focused on him. *It's marking me*, Denny thought, not even knowing what it meant. Then the cave was filled with a blinding flash of light followed by an unearthly roar from the creature. By the time Denny's eyes had adjusted following the flash—*what was that?*—the creature was gone leaving nothing but swirling water behind him. Then Denny realized Greymore was gone too.

"Paul!" He began sloshing deeper into the water until he was hauled back by his shirt. He struggled momentarily then stopped, unable to control the tears that came. He let himself be led back to the tunnel entrance where Robert Ortiz and Julie waited in stunned silence.

"Denny..." Ortiz had nothing he could say.

It was Julie that got through to him. "Denny, you saved my life."

He looked down, still dazed from actually seeing the creature and more from seeing Greymore being taken. Julie was looking up at him, smiling. It was a sad smile, hiding her own pain, but beautiful nonetheless.

The man who had dragged Denny back from the lake spoke next. "This is my fault, I took its picture. The camera flash...I don't know...scared it or hurt it and that's when it moved. If I had waited Robert could have shot it..."

Ortiz stopped him. "You did what you came here to do, Chris. I'm the one that failed; I didn't pull the gun fast enough, I hesitated..."

None of it mattered to Denny, Paul was gone, just like his dad. Julie was hurt badly and Mossy and Billy were probably dead. It was that sad smile that gave him any reason to keep going. That, and the thought of his mother, alone, and what would happen to her if he didn't come home. "It doesn't matter, let's get out of here. That thing will come back eventually. I'll set off the poison and...that's it." His voice trailed off miserably.

Ortiz took charge. "Denny's right. Chris, you'll have to carry Julie as long as you can, after that Denny and I can help. We'll set off the poison and be right behind you. Let's go."

Chris bent down and picked up Julie as gently as he could but Denny saw her face tighten and knew she was in a lot of pain. He realized too that Ortiz was hurt but didn't ask about it. He walked toward the water's edge and turned to Ortiz. "I'll set it here and activate it..." The water behind him erupted. Denny turned and saw the creature burst from the lake, standing waist-deep in the churning water and jerking its head from side to side.

This time Ortiz was not too slow. From behind him Denny heard the explosion of gunfire, much louder, from a bigger gun than the one Denny had fired at it. The beast threw back its head and roared, but still it came. Denny pulled the pin, made sure the poison was released, then stood and backed slowly away from it. The beast was moving forward, jolted by each gunshot, but Denny could see its scaly armor was protecting it from most of them. He remembered the damaged eye just as the gunshots ended.

"Robert! The eyes, aim for the eyes!" His scream sounded alien to him. Blinding flashes of light, Chris taking more pictures, illuminated the scene in dizzying snapshots. The creature moved forward relentlessly as the cloud of poison mushroomed in the cave. Denny continued his slow retreat as more gunshots echoed maddeningly. Then even those were drowned out as the freight-train rumble of another cave-in began. Denny saw the creature's already-damaged eye explode from one of Ortiz's bullet that found its mark just before he turned and ran. The beast's howl of pain and rage muted even the sound of the cave-in, then Denny was pushing Ortiz into the tunnel following Chris and Julie.

With every step he took Denny expected a slippery tentacle to wrap around him and drag him back (to Paul) to the lake. The ground was literally shaking under their feet as rocks rained down. Denny gripped the back of Ortiz's shirt like a drowning man clinging to a life preserver and followed him blindly through the tunnels. They moved as quickly as they could through the thickening dust, slowing only to climb over or around piles of rock left by the cave-ins. Only when the rumbling subsided did they stop to regroup.

They must have been some distance from the worst of the cave-in, since the dust wasn't as thick. The four huddled together in the small tunnel and Denny realized just how much of a failure their plan had been. Julie was unconscious in Chris's arms and Denny could see the unnatural angle her feet hung at. Chris looked like he was in shock, his face a portrait of fear and exhaustion. Ortiz was the worst of the lot. His face was swollen on one side to the point his eye was almost completely shut. He wavered as he stood and finally leaned heavily against the tunnel wall for support. His breathing was labored and even in the dim light from their remaining flashlights, Denny could see his entire body was trembling. How could they hope to get out of here?

The tunnel ahead looked clear, but was it a way out or was it leading them deeper into the labyrinth? "Rest here a minute and let me take a look around, maybe I can find something that looks familiar."

"Don't stray too far." Ortiz warned, his voice sounding shaky and tired.

Denny nodded and moved ahead, his flickering light reminding him of the scene back in the cavern. He came to a fork and hesitated, suddenly knowing he would become lost in the tunnels. His instinct to turn and go back to the group was overwhelming but to what end? He thought of the battered group and knew they couldn't survive taking wrong turns and backtracking. He had to get them out of here in one shot. Taking a deep breath, he quickly gathered a few small rocks and formed a crude arrow pointing back to the others. He went left for no other reason than he had to pick one of the two branches to start with. With every step his fear grew, the feeling that he would get too far away and not be able to find his way back. Stop it, he told himself, you're walking in a straight fucking line. *Yes but what about the next fork, and the one after that?* The bad voice; where was Oz or one of the smart voices when he needed them?

He wouldn't need any voice to tell him what to do next: the tunnel ended. Denny couldn't tell whether it was from the recent cave-in or had been blocked for a while. His chest tightened when the bad voice spoke again. *What if the other fork ends the same way?* Choking back a sob of fear, he turned back the way he came, praying the other tunnel wasn't blocked.

(110)

DALE CRAWFORD wandered blindly through the tunnels, feeling his way along the walls with his hands. His light had given out a while ago and he could not see his own hand in front of his face. He knew this because he had tried. "Dumb expression," he giggled and slid his left hand forward. His right hand held the gun that Denny had dropped after shooting that thing. Dale had reloaded it, and deep down he knew he might only need one bullet: for himself if he couldn't find a way out.

"I'll get out. I will kill that fucking freak when I do. And I will kill Denny O'Brien. I just have to decide what order. Maybe I'll do eeny-meeny." This brought hysterical laughter that turned into a hacking cough from all of the dust in his throat.

His mind was unable to accept everything he'd seen. That thing that took Buddy, dragged him in the water while O'Brien shot it point-blank with no effect. When the cave in started he'd grabbed the gun and crawled away from the direction Denny and that freak had gone. He'd made it into the tunnels where he'd found Costa... well his body anyway. Costa's head was crushed under a huge boulder and a pool of blood and brain-juice was still spreading when Crawford found him. He knew he'd been going the right way after finding Costa. The second cave-in sounded far enough away to give him hope he was still going in the right direction. But after his light gave out he knew he could be going in circles. That was when his mind finally snapped. "Kill my piece of shit father, too. Kill them all..."

A weak breeze carried the unmistakable scent of rain. "Shit, I think I left the Mustang's windows open." He slid his hand on the wall and stopped suddenly. In the darkness a cruel smile formed on his face. "I guess I'll get to use more than one bullet after all." This time he kept laughing as he slid his hand along the wall, following the smell of rain.

{111}

DENNY REACHED the fork he'd marked with an arrow made of rocks. Before trying the right tunnel, he'd formed an "x" out of more rocks at the entrance to the left tunnel. He called out to the others that he was okay and trying another direction and was shocked at how weak both Chris and Robert sounded in response. It was the lack of response from Julie that kept him moving. That, and the voice. *You're running out of time, kid, and out of tunnels*, the voice mocked. He shook it off and started off in the only direction he had left. Choices are easy when you only have one, he thought, and trudged ahead.

There was one heart-stopping moment where he thought this tunnel ended in a cave-in too when all he could see was the flat cave wall up ahead. When he moved closer, however, he saw it was only a trick of the light and a very sharp turn in the direction of the tunnel. And on the floor of the tunnel was a spray-painted arrow. Denny gasped, afraid to believe it for a second, then cried out to the others. "I found it! Come on, we're going the right way!" For another long second he had the sensation that he was in the tunnel alone and the others had just been some crazy hallucination.

When Denny was little, maybe seven or eight, he'd ended up with a bad ear infection and a dangerously high fever. Before the fever broke, in the loneliest part of the night, he'd seen a small group of soldiers come into his room. They each carried a metal folding chair which they set up in unison around his bed and sat. Then they each pulled out a pipe and, again in perfect synchronization, lit them and started smoking. The room quickly filled with the sweet smell of tobacco and became so thick that he could barely see the soldiers. The temperature had risen and Denny was sweating profusely, trying to get out from under the prison of his blankets. He must have screamed because his parents and Jimmy were suddenly there, the soldiers and their smoke gone. He fell back asleep, exhausted. When he finally woke up, fever gone, he asked his parents who the soldiers were and what kind of medicine was in their pipes. It had been real to him, so real.

He thought of all this, could almost smell the sickening sweet tobacco, in just the second it took for Chris and Robert to call out a response. Denny waited, keeping the light aimed back the way he had come as a beacon for them to follow. He was suddenly terrified. Knowing they were going the right way had somehow put the thought in his head that it was all just a tease. That they would *almost* get out and find the way blocked, and have to head back in to the tunnels to search for another way out. After an eternity, the others caught up. They looked worse and somehow this calmed Denny, put him back in a role that left him with no time to panic. Silently, he turned from them and led the way.

From there it was almost easy. Denny found the markers while Robert and Chris took turns carrying Julie. She would slip in and out of consciousness, occasionally muttering a few unintelligible words then slip away again. The memory of her smile kept Denny moving. He focused on each step, fighting back thoughts of Billy and Mossy trapped or already dead, thoughts of Paul taken, and worst of all, thoughts that the thing was still alive. Behind him, Chris and Robert grunted as they passed Julie from one to the other. Then they were out. The crisp night air washed over them like a cool drink. The temperature had dropped and it actually felt like it might rain. Denny helped them maneuver Julie through the opening and prop her gently against the rocks. Chris and Robert collapsed next to her. As if on cue, Denny felt the first spitting drops of rain.

Denny noticed the small canteen hanging on McCauley's belt.

Instinctively he reached down and unhooked it. "We're close to the lake. I'll go fill this up, we can use the water to clean up the cuts as best we can, and then we head back." The others just looked at him, too exhausted and hurt to speak. Denny took their silence as assent and turned toward the lake. He moved quickly through the dark. There were no crickets chirping, no owls hooting, no bats screeching. The rain had started in earnest and the drops smacking the leaves were the only sounds. Then another sound broke the quiet. Voices! Denny stopped, frozen in place, moving just one finger to click off his flashlight. A moment later, another light bobbed toward him, floating like a ghost through the trees. Friend or foe? Denny glanced back and saw only darkness. Robert must have heard the voices too and shut off their light. Denny nearly called out but something kept him silent. Denny could only make out two silhouetted shapes as the light moved slowly through the trees thirty or forty yards closer to the lake. *Exactly where I would be if I hadn't heard them*, he thought.

The light stopped moving and Denny heard muffled voices. When the gunshot broke the unearthly silence, Denny sprang to action. Keeping his own light off, he moved toward the lantern-light. Behind him, he heard Chris and Robert also moving. In front of him, the sounds of a scuffle erupted and a voice he finally recognized called out in anger and fear. "Crawford! No!" Another gunshot rang out and Denny sprinted toward Father McCarthy.

What he saw in the small circle of light thrown by the lantern in the old priest's hand froze him for a second. Chief Crawford was straddling another man, strangling the life out of him. When the impossible fact that the other man was Paul Greymore finally registered, Denny moved without thinking. He ripped the lantern from McCarthy's hand and swung it in a sweeping arc, connecting with Crawford's head in a blinding explosion. Crawford's screams shattered the night and he rolled off of Greymore. His head and torso were completely engulfed in flames! Still screaming, he turned and ran, a human torch heading for the lake.

Denny and McCarthy went to Paul. He was alive, breathing, but his skin was icy to the touch. Denny finally remembered his own light and snapped it on. Crawford's screams echoed in the distance as McCarthy opened Paul's eyes one at a time and shined the light in them "His pupils are reacting, that's good." Denny held the light while McCarthy quickly looked for signs of injury. When he lifted Greymore's shirt they both saw the damage. Amid the scars stood an angry row of red welts in a line across Greymore's chest. The mark of the beast.

Denny heard the others behind him and was once again stunned into silence. Robert was standing there holding Julie in his arms, Chris next to him. But coming behind them were Billy and Mossy. Denny broke his paralysis and ran to them, leaping into an embrace of relief and love. The three stood clinging to each other for a long moment. Then Denny grabbed Mossy by the hand and led him to Paul, shining his light on the line of red marks. He locked eyes with Mossy and incredibly, Mossy was grinning.

"It's like a sedative, it isn't fatal. He might be out for a while but he'll be fine."

Denny felt too many emotions at once to react. Then he frowned. "But it took him, that thing in the caves took him in the water…" Mossy's grin stretched wider.

"I think I can explain that too…"

Another scream exploded, barely human. At first Denny thought it was the weird acoustics that made Crawford's scream sound like it was behind them and not down by the lake. Then the sound of running steps crashing through the brush behind them made them all turn. It was Dale Crawford running at them holding something…The gunshots came quickly as Crawford ran straight for them screaming. Bodies flew, and Denny didn't know if they were hit or just diving for cover. But he stood his ground and by the time Crawford was close enough to see the insanity in his eyes, the gun was clicking on empty chambers. He stopped in front of Denny and dropped the gun. The rain poured down as the two faced each other. Crawford reached into his pocket and pulled his knife, the blade snapping to life with the touch of a finger. "Let's dance," and he giggled crazily.

Denny heard the sounds of the others getting up. *At least they're not all dead*, Denny thought without emotion. His world consisted only of Crawford and that knife. That goddamned knife that had started all of this. Crawford made his move, advancing quickly and raising the knife to strike. Denny watched it all in slow motion as the blade arced toward him. With agility he never knew he possessed, Denny dodged the blade. Before Crawford could recover and take another shot, Denny hammered him with a punch, landing it squarely on Crawford's nose. Crawford stumbled back a step, then touched the stream of blood dripping from his nose. He giggled again and started toward Denny.

Denny made no move, he stood ready, somehow not afraid and sure he could dodge Crawford's knife all night and land every punch as he had his first. He felt invincible. When Crawford's face morphed from the insane smile to an expression of abject terror, Denny thought for a split second that Crawford had sensed Denny's inner strength and was actually afraid of him.

Then Denny realized Dale's focus was beyond him, toward the lake. Crawford's eyes grew wider. Looking into them was like looking into the very soul of madness. Then he turned and ran into the woods without uttering a sound. Denny wheeled around and saw Dale's father, or what was left of him, staggering toward him. His shirt had burned off and his upper body was scorched, screaming red and oozing blood and pus. Crawford's face and hands were a hideous sight, charred black with chunks of skin sliding off. His hair, ears, lips and nose were gone, his eyes were two melted lumps of wax. But still he came.

Ortiz stepped in front of him and put a hand on his chest to stop him. Layers of skin slipped away leaving a red handprint. "Crawford, it's Robert Ortiz. It's over."

Crawford's exposed teeth yawned open and a garbled sound came out. Then he collapsed to the ground. Ortiz took the cuffs from Crawford's belt, rolled him over roughly and snapped them on his wrists.

The others gathered around silently as the rain fell around them. A moan from the bushes broke the odd reverie and Denny realized that Father McCarthy was not among them. They found him lying in the brush, blood flowing from a wound just below his ribcage. Crawford's bullets hadn't all missed their mark. Ortiz tore off his shirt and placed it against the wound in a futile attempt to staunch the dark flow of blood. Paul pushed his way groggily through the others and knelt beside McCarthy.

"Father, can you hear me?"

McCarthy's eyes opened and immediately found Paul's. "Paul, you're okay?"

"We all made it." Tears mixed with the rain running down his face. He gripped McCarthy's hand in his own.

"Did you kill it?"

Paul looked up at Denny, sadness and panic in his eyes. Denny nodded as his own tears began to flow.

"Yeah, we killed it," Paul replied.

McCarthy closed his eyes in relief and Denny didn't think he was going to open them again. "You did good, Paul. The story has a happy ending after all."

Paul spoke softly. "You saved my life, Father. And...I can't save yours..."

McCarthy's face was serene. "It's my time, that's all."

Denny watched Greymore carefully, knowing exactly how he felt, remembering his own losses.

"I'll never forget you, Father."

McCarthy smiled, his grip on Paul's hand tightened, then he was gone. Paul sat there for a few minutes, holding the old priest's hand while all around them the cleansing rain continued to fall.

(112)

THE UNLIKELY band of hikers arrived at the picket fence behind Denny's house several hours later. Each of them were hurt, physically, emotionally or mentally, and exhausted beyond words. The trip had been mostly silent, hindered by the now torrential rain and the injuries. Paul had insisted on carrying Father McCarthy the entire way despite only having one working arm. His mind kept flashing back to a different rainy night, carrying another body. Chris carried Julie most of the way himself except for a short stint when Billy and Denny tried to carry her. Ortiz half-dragged, half-pushed Crawford while Mossy struggled to keep up without any burden other than age. There was no sign of Dale Crawford.

It was almost comedic getting everyone over the fence or through the opening in the pickets but finally they all trudged across the muddy backyard and around to the front door. Denny glanced with revulsion and a deep sense of foreboding at the Mustang in the driveway. "I'll go in and let her know what's going on before we all just barge in and scare the shit out of her." He was too tired to notice the looks he got for his swear and far too out of it to see the look of fear on Mossy's face.

Dripping rain and mud, he stepped into the house and called softly for his mother. He had no idea what time it was. He slipped out of his muddy sneakers and sloshed down the hall to the living room where he could see a light was on. He stepped in and realized this

491

night of horrors was still not over. *Will it ever be over?* His mother was sitting rigid in one of the chairs staring at nothing through a swollen blood-caked face. "Mom!" It came out of him in a strangled scream more than a word. He was at her side in two strides, his hands lightly touching her face, his eyes searching hers for something. Remembering the Mustang, Denny knew Crawford had done this and silently vowed vengeance.

Her eyes moved to focus on his. "Denny, thank God." And her arms were around him, pulling him tightly to her. It was the dream moment he'd waited for. She was crying hysterically and clinging to him like a second skin. "I thought you were gone, too," she finally managed.

He'd been hugging her tightly but now he pulled away and looked at her again. Her face was a mess but her eyes...they were *her* eyes. "I'm fine, Mom. But Paul and...some others are hurt. They're outside. I'm going to bring them in and call for help, okay?" He was terrified she was going to blank out again, but she nodded, her eyes staying focused. He slowly pulled away and went to fetch the others.

Ortiz had put Crawford in the Mustang and handcuffed him to the steering wheel. Greymore had laid McCarthy carefully in the back seat. The rest of them piled into Denny's house. Denny's mom had moved to the kitchen and put on the tea pot. Chris gently deposited Julie on the couch while Mossy huddled in the shadows of the hall near the front door. His expression hurt Denny to look at. He looked like he might just run out the door and keep running. Denny went to him and took his hand. Without a word, he turned and pulled Mossy. There was a moment of resistance, then they were moving toward the kitchen. His mother had her back turned. She pulled cups out of the cabinet for tea or coffee. When she finally turned, it was the embodiment of a cliché the way her eyes widened and the cups slipped from her hands to shatter on the floor. The kettle was boiling, starting to whistle. Denny heard a moan from Mossy, then they were both at his mother's side.

Denny helped Mossy get her into one of the kitchen chairs, then shut off the kettle and made a cup of tea for his mother, not knowing what else to do. Ortiz and Chris had come running when the cups broke, but Denny had waved them away. Denny placed the tea on the table, then ran a washcloth under cold water and laid it on his mother's forehead. Her eyes snapped open, staring at Mossy who knelt by her side holding her hand.

"It can't be..." Mossy broke at the sound of her voice,

"Oh, honey, I'm so sorry..." He collapsed against her, shaking.

Denny watched his mother carefully, still unsure which way this was going to go. His mother's eyes met his, and he realized with near-giddiness that they *were* his mother's eyes, not that zombie that took her most of the time. She smiled then, a sight that despite her wrecked face, was beautiful. Then she wrapped her arms around her father and cried with him. Denny walked over, put his arms around them both and cried right along. Sometime later the rain stopped and the sun rose majestically over Haven. It was Father's Day, 1978.

EPILOGUE

THE LATE-SUMMER sunshine painted the trees and flowers with brightness, illuminating their color to a surreal tone. The humidity that had hung over the town like a cloak was gone; it was picture-perfect weather for the day ahead.

Denny arrived at Paul's at the same time Billy did from the other side. They slapped palms grinning, and went to get Paul. The three were headed to Boston to see the Red Sox play, using the tickets that Paul have given to Billy on that impossibly long-ago birthday. Paul came out to greet them, his arm finally out of the sling, his gunshot wound healing.

"I wish we had another ticket for your mom," Paul said wistfully.

Denny smiled. Summer vacation had come and gone in a blur, as summers do when you're twelve years old. Paul had been spending a lot of time with his mom and Mossy. A collection of broken souls trying to help each other heal. His mom's cuts and bruises had healed without a trace, and although she still drifted away sometimes, it happened less and less and the trips were brief. She had put on a little weight and actually looked younger than she had since Dad and Jimmy died. Paul sometimes looked at her funny, and Denny wasn't sure how he felt about that. They jumped into Paul's car, an old Cutlass he picked up to get around town. There was still a sadness about him that Denny didn't think would ever go away. He missed Father McCarthy deeply but had already befriended the new priest in Haven, and he had Joe and his family, and now also had Denny and his mom. Paul gunned the engine and pulled out of the driveway, rolling slowly past Billy's house. Denny could see a figure on a lounge chair in Billy's backyard facing the lake. As they went by, Julie's hand went up and waved without turning around in her chair. Denny grinned, thinking she was probably in a bikini and felt his face flush. Billy punched his arm, reading his mind, and Paul honked and started laughing. Julie had undergone multiple surgeries on her shattered legs, and while she was still unable to walk, doctors expected a complete recovery. She never spoke about the time in the caves, but Denny felt a new bond with her, something they shared that would never go away.

Driving through town to the highway took them past the police station. Robert Ortiz was acting Police Chief until a permanent one was appointed. All signs pointed to Ortiz remaining in the position. Crawford was recovering at the Shriner's Burn Institute in Boston and was still in bad shape after numerous attempts at skin grafts. If he recovered, he would likely end up under investigation for his various crimes over the years. Once Crawford was out of commission, throngs of townspeople came forward to report his wrongdoings. Stories of bribery and corruption were rampant, and many of the gang at Russell's barber shop were first in line to tell them. There was even suspicion by many that Crawford was the Butcher all along.

They passed the gas station and turned up the on-ramp to the highway. Chris McCauley had written a breathtaking piece about the events of the summer, interwoven with excerpts from Mossy's letter. Despite the general skepticism and in some cases, outright disbelief of his story, he'd been asked to write for the *Haven News* full-time. Denny didn't know who ran the gas station now.

The story was unbelievable. Denny read it over several times and even though he lived it, it still didn't seem possible. The pictures had come out grainy and dark and blurry and were generally thought to be fake. Nevertheless, the story was out and there are always some that want to believe in the unbelievable. The lake had gained a reputation as being the next Loch Ness. Tourists flocked there to get a glimpse of the monster and Betty Chandler had more people to gossip with than ever before.

Authorities had decided the caves were unsafe and had hired demolition experts to seal the entrances permanently. Denny sometimes wondered if it was because they were too afraid to find proof of the creature. Secretly, he and Billy and the rest knew they didn't seal all of the entrances. Paul's appearance at the lake after being taken by the creature *inside* the caves was explained by Mossy. The same thing had happened to him on the night he escaped from the base. There was another cave, accessible only from beneath the surface, that the creature took its victims to after injecting them with the venom that paralyzed them. It left them there to die before bringing them back to the main cave to eat. Who knew why? Paul, like Mossy, must have developed some sort of immunity to the venom after his first dose of it. In both cases, they had done the only thing they could: dove in the water and swam for their lives, both coming out on the lake side of the underwater cave. If they ever wanted to, and God knew none of them did, they could get back in that way. Denny shuddered, getting looks from both Paul and Billy. They just looked away. They knew.

>> <<

Denny sat at his desk, exhausted and exhilarated at the same time. The day at Fenway had been magic, despite the results. Somehow the three had turned a devastating Red Sox loss into a memory that would last forever. Denny closed his eyes and pictured the emerald green grass and the looming of the "Monster" over left field.

Guidry had pitched a two-hit shutout for the Yankees on the way to a 7-0 rout. The Red Sox lead in the division, once double-digits, was down to one game. Denny felt the familiar dread of a Red Sox fan; it was going to be another year without a pennant.

It had taken a long time for Denny to get his thoughts straight enough to put down in his journal. Finally, the words had come and he was satisfied with the entry, closing the book and placing it back in his drawer. It was late and a half-moon hung heavily over the lake outside Denny's window. He flashed his light at Billy's window and waited. No response. Billy was either asleep or in the living room with his family. This thought no longer made Denny sad or jealous, instead bringing a smile to his face. He loved Billy's family.

From downstairs, the sound of his mother's laughter mingled with Paul's and Mossy's was like a dream. His mom had asked Paul in for tea after they got home from the game. That was hours ago. Still smiling, he jumped in bed and closed his eyes. They snapped open when the sound of a branch breaking disturbed the quiet. It wasn't the creature Denny feared, it was Dale Crawford. Since running off after seeing his burned father stagger up from the lake, Dale had not been seen. Many thought he wandered back into the caves and was sealed in there after being lost. Others thought he wandered out of the woods and just kept going, starting over somehow in another town. Denny sometimes thought he was still out there in the woods, biding time, waiting. More laughter from below and the sound of the deer crashing through the woods eased his fear.

While they were all in agreement the creature could not have survived—the bullets, the poison and the cave-in all too much for anything to live through—it still seemed possible at times like this, alone in the dark, that it had. He sleepily wondered where he would be in seventeen years—if the thing had somehow survived and was hibernating again, that's when it would awaken—and somehow he knew he would be here in Haven watching the papers for stories of missing children or murders or maybe driving the roads by the lake in the spring looking for roadkill. For now, time stretched out in front of him in an endless road to great adventures and he lay awake in bed as crickets played background music to the laughter from downstairs.

ACKNOWLEDGEMENTS:

WRITING A book is hard. For a lot of the time, it's lonely hours spent squeezing words out of an exhausted brain, long after everyone else is asleep. It's agonizing self-doubt and crippling fear of failure. Finally, it's time to show the world what you've done...and it's terrifying. I dedicated *Haven* to my daughters because, in a way, this book is like their sibling. I started writing it when they were small children, and finished it when they were both in college. There were years when the book went untouched, overshadowed by life, but *Haven* was always there. Waiting. Whispering in my ear. Growing.

As solitary as writing a book can be, it is by no means a one-person accomplishment. Without the help of countless people, *Haven* might never have seen the light of day.

First and foremost, my heartfelt thanks to Brian Freeman and Richard Chizmar for taking a chance on an unpublished writer. I had long been a fan and customer of Cemetery Dance before submitting a manuscript. It is an icon in the horror genre and I am humbled to be a part of it. It took a lot of hand-holding to get me through the process, for that, Brian and Richard have my undying gratitude.

Without the help of the next person on my list, *Haven* might never have gotten to the point I was brave enough to send it to Cemetery Dance. Stewart O'Nan. Stewart was kind enough to read my extremely rough draft, and not only did he provide extensive notes, corrections, and the hard-to-hear criticism that I needed to hear, he gave me a blurb that I believe is what caught the eye of the publisher.

Over the years I have come to realize that the horror genre is filled with amazing, generous people like Brian, Richard, and Stewart, who are willing to help out an aspiring writer. Among them are some of today's biggest names: Christopher Golden, John McIlveen, Rio Youers, Bracken MacLeod, Sloane Kady and Jonathan Maberry—thank you all for your kindness and patience.

Of course, at the heart of it all is family and friends. There are so many friends over the years that played some part in the completion of Haven, too many to name. But you know who you are—thank you all. Family...I would be remiss not to mention my wife, Sheila. She gives me endless support and encouragement, and believes in me even when I don't believe in myself. My brother, Mike, one of the first victims of the rough draft, provided invaluable notes and critique. And my daughters, Shannon and Alyssa, it always comes back to them, for everything.

61805540R00302

Made in the USA
Lexington, KY
25 March 2017